T0367854

One Gone

One Gone

A Biographical Novel

Jasper S. Lee

ARCHWAY
PUBLISHING

Archway Publishing books may be ordered through booksellers or by contacting:

Archway Publishing
1663 Liberty Drive
Bloomington, IN 47403
www.archwaypublishing.com
1 (888) 242-5904

ISBN: 978-1-4808-6762-8 (sc)
ISBN: 978-1-4808-6760-4 (hc)
ISBN: 978-1-4808-6761-1 (e)

Library of Congress Control Number: 2018912687

Print information available on the last page.

Archway Publishing rev. date: 10/31/2018

Contents

Introduction   vii

Acknowledgments   ix

Dedication   xiii

Prologue   xv

1   Growing Family   1

2   Digging Roots   15

3   Searching for Direction   35

4   Running to the House   45

5   Gaining a Life Partner   59

6   Facing Tragedy   77

7   Healing   101

8   Living a New Way   123

9   Adjusting and Loving   157

10   Working Left Only   187

11   Paying the Preacher   207

12   Loafing Stores   235

13   Dealing with Faith and Phantoms   249

14   Being Human   267

15   Keeping a Right Mind   277

16   Speaking Defensively   303

17   Living in a Female Majority   325

18   Mellowing in Life   345

19   Facing Frailties   359

Epilogue   379

Introduction

Tragedy and trauma often create human hardship. Such was the case with Jasper Henry Lee.

In this fact-based biographical novel, a young farmer was involved in a major farm accident that forever changed his life. The setting is a Southern plantation in a farm-oriented community in 1943. The story begins three decades before and extends four decades after the tragedy.

Strong commitment to family and farm was a tradition that had served generations. Life had been shaped by ancestors and the agricultural situations of the previous one hundred years. Of course, the U.S. Civil War was a major factor in precipitating change; evidences of the war were all about. In the best of times, life was not easy; and in the worst of times, life was hard. Changes had created a chasm between city and rural dwellers. How Henry's city-dwelling sisters' lives compared with his life on a farm in the rural South was envy-creating.

Scrapping together a living required hard work and good use of resources. Just as people were getting over the Great Depression of the 1930s, the Second World War was requiring major sacrifices by citizens. Win-the-war initiatives reached ordinary people in towns and rural areas alike across America. The effort needed in 1943 to provide for a family required long hours of hard work. Even the best and most notable intentions sometimes resulted in personal disaster.

Living and coping with a major body loss was not easy then and would not be today. Adjusting to doing everything with one arm was a huge challenge that affected almost all aspects of life. Just getting dressed and going about life routines required concerted thought about how something was done. But, Henry tried as best he could to overcome the physical, social, psychological, and spiritual challenges perpetrated on life by the loss. Certainly, emotions and self-concept as well as phantom pains were factors in life that had to be dealt with.

Everything that was doable now had to be done differently. Yes, one arm was gone. Henry Lee adapted as best he could.

Note: The author may be reached at: jasperslee2014@gmail.com.

Acknowledgments

The author is grateful for the help of many people. A few are named here.

Certainly, ancestors of the main character in this book and of the author made major contributions. Old family records as well as online sources were used. Genealogy study and DNA analysis helped assure accuracy in family details and relationships. Anne Vanderleest, genealogy consultant, provided information that promoted proper unfolding of the story.

Manuscript readers provided many useful suggestions. These individuals were:

- Ann Tipton, a registered nurse and Florida attorney now living in Georgia, provided useful suggestions on the medical procedures, with emphasis on 1943. She also shared materials related to the win-the-war initiatives of World War II.
- Kelly Everett Hemphill, a Georgia physician's assistant, is acknowledged for her emphasis on the trauma and hospital areas, as well as useful suggestions throughout the manuscript.
- Tom Knecht, an agricultural communicator with rich experience that included leadership at the University of Illinois, North Carolina State University, and Mississippi

State University, is acknowledged for his manuscript review and suggestions about authoring
- Jacque Frost Tisdale, a Mississippi native with firsthand knowledge of Henry and Son while in high school and as he was a professor in agriculture; she also has a wealth of experience in agricultural areas at Mississippi State University.

Craig Ingliss, a teacher of German at the adult EAGLE Program of Sautee, Georgia, is acknowledged for help with German language and areas related to German traditions.

Two individuals made line art contributions. Jessica Webb, an art teacher in the Lumpkin County, Georgia, schools, is acknowledged for creating the cover design images, upper arm prosthesis, and the human torso drawing. Megan Hatfield, a graduate student at Piedmont College, Demorest, Georgia, is acknowledged for the line art of a tractor belted to a hammer mill. Her experiences with antique tractors were valuable in art preparation. Richard Thomas Hayes, Photographic Artist of Cleveland, Georgia, is acknowledged for the image of the author used on the back cover.

Also acknowledged are Charles Auslander, Laura Carter, the Mississippi Agriculture and Forestry Museum, the Mississippi Humanities Council, American Association of Retired Persons, American Congress of Rehabilitation Medicine, the Lillian E. Smith Center of Piedmont College, and the Mississippi Department of Archives and History.

Ronald L. McDaniel, of Danville, Illinois, is acknowledged for copyediting the manuscript and preparing it for publishing. He offered numerous helpful authoring suggestions. This wonderful editor has fine-tuned many books for the author. Thank you!

The encouragement of family members and friends is gratefully acknowledged. Ellen Miller Gabardi, of Madison, Mississippi, is acknowledged for her support of family study and DNA analysis. Ed

Ratliff and Bill Quisenberry, school classmates for twelve years in Clinton, are acknowledged for providing inspiration for the author to undertake this book.

This acknowledgement would be incomplete without naming Bob Prim. As pastor of Nacoochee Presbyterian Church (USA), he has offered so much encouragement with his weekly sermons, individual conversations, and role model. Sometimes he can tell you exactly what is needed, such as "don't whine." His overarching message is "God is love." Peace.

A special thank-you goes to the author's wife, Delene Willis Lee. Thank you, Delene!

Dedication

This book is dedicated to Jasper Henry Lee's grandson, Stephen. Oh, the things that the two of them did together! The bond of love between grandfather and grandson was special. From a very young age, Stephen would be in the pickup with his grandfather going anyplace, but likely to the farm, a store, or a produce stand. One arm gone was never an issue with Stephen!

In his grandfather's final years, Stephen helped make it possible for Henry and Doris to remain in their home longer. Some days, he would drive from the college he was attending and take them to the grocery store, a medical appointment, or wherever needed. The sporty red Toyota Celica he drove was a high school graduation gift from his grandparents.

It is most fitting that this book be dedicated to Stephen Jasper Lee.

Prologue

"Look, Mama, one gone, one arm gone," announced four-year-old Billy, as he pointed to a man with one arm at Baker's Store in the cotton-ginning hamlet of Pocahontas. Mama replied, "Shh, he might hear you. Yes, I see. Sad. I wonder what happened. Unfortunate. We'll talk more when we get home." Yes, the man (whose name was Henry) did hear. It wasn't nearly the first time he had overheard comments about him having only one arm. Though not easy, he had learned to ignore such comments. There was no way he could go back to the time before the day of the horrible accident and have two functional human arms again.

Overhearing such statements served to remind him of his life and tragedy. Maybe they caused him to feel inferior or seek sympathy or to feel that he could have achieved more. Anyway, coping with the loss of an arm was not easy. He pushed forward in life to achieve what he could and be as independent as possible. He tried to be a good husband and father, though he sometimes felt he was limited in doing so. Life as a farmer was filled with the frustrations associated with the loss of his right arm at the shoulder in an era of major farm change.

For this story about Henry to unfold, it needs to go back more than 30 years prior to the loss of an arm in a farm tragedy.

1

Growing Family

Living in a rural community in the early 1900s offered challenges and opportunities (don't forget the hardships). Put subsistence farming in the mix, and a lot of learning took place. Day after day in the field "bustin' clods" (plowing behind a mule) kept a boy out of trouble and gave him something to think about.

"Mr. Lee, you are the father of a boy!" Naomi, the midwife, exclaimed to the new father. "Isn't that what you wanted?" Those were sweet words to a cotton farmer.

"Hallelujah, Jesus!" was the loud outburst from Ira, the father. Right or wrong, boys were generally thought to be more productive than girls as workers in the fields of the South in the early 1900s. Nevertheless, this father, who wanted a boy, enjoyed his precious daughters and thought they were wonderful.

Jasper Henry Lee, who would be known as Henry, was born on August 20, 1910, in a farmhouse in Tinnin, Mississippi. He was the fourth child of Ira and Carrie Hendrick Lee and would grow up in the small farming community located five miles from Clinton and sixteen miles from Jackson, the state capital.

Jasper Henry Lee, 1911.

Though the Civil War had been over more than forty years, the farm was still struggling to cope in its aftermath. The loss of a system based on cotton as a cash crop resulted in more subsistence farming than anything else. Fields were much the same, meaning they were rather small patches divided by turn rows and creeks adapted to mule-power farming. Wagon trails went from one patch to the next. Some change had been made to create larger fields, but more was needed. Old barns, sheds, and fences were somewhat deplorable in condition; resources to build anything new were hard to come by. Only a few new ways of farming had been adopted; more were certainly needed. Mule-pulled mechanical planters, plows, and cultivators were used to make work more efficient and faster than by hand. Maybe the newborn boy would grow up to be a source of uplifting on the old Shepard farm, where Henry's paternal grandmother, Ellen Loretta Shepard Lee, had grown up. Maybe he would help create an impressive Lee-Shepard farm!

How Ira and Carrie divided responsibilities on the farm and in the home was fairly traditional. Ira looked after the farm, and Carrie, in her own way, looked after the household. Regardless, Carrie always provided say-so in the operation of things; she would quite willingly express her thoughts but would not so willingly go about doing much that required effort. Ira was quiet and reserved but firm when he needed to be; he really didn't care much about getting involved in running the household. Carrie's efforts in doing so were meager; she got Ira's mother, Ellen, to help her as much as she could. Gardening was somewhat shared, with farm hands often involved in plowing, planting, weeding, and harvesting vegetables.

Maybe Carrie thought her role was to have babies; she didn't waste much time in that regard. She often used that as an excuse for not doing other things. The family now consisted of Carrie and Ira, four children, and Grandmother Ellen, who was usually called Mama Ellen. The three babies before Henry were girls, and there would be three more girls afterward to live to adulthood. One reason Ira particularly wanted boys was to assure that the Lee family surname would continue another generation. Thankfully, Ellen was present to bring a certain degree of calmness. All of this influenced the family atmosphere in the home.

Ira wanted boys badly. It was reported that after the second girl was born, he secretly visited a voodoo queen on Farish Street in Jackson, Mississippi, seeking help in how to father boys. Whatever the queen suggested didn't work, as the next baby was a girl, though a boy (Henry) followed in a couple of years. Ira thought that it most likely took a while for the voodoo strategies to go into effect. (No Lee ever knew what exactly these were.)

Another, more compelling reason for boy babies was that Ira felt boys would grow into a better position to inherit the farm property and carry on the farming enterprise that had been in the family since the time of the Choctaw cessation in the 1840s. Ira knew that laws fairly well limited property ownership by females and the roles they could take in society. He was well aware that his mother had faced major challenges and fraud (downright theft) in settling his father's estate. This was some four decades earlier under the laws and district judges of the state of Texas. Fortunately, some talk of needed social and legal change toward women was in the news coming out of Washington.

The farm was located in the hill-and-creek bottomland near the town of Clinton in central Mississippi some thirty miles east of the Mississippi River. The soil had hills of loess (windblown material from the far western United States) and marine deposit from the ancient Gulf of Mexico. Strips of fertile water-deposited soil were along creeks.

The site was on an almost direct route between Jackson and Vicksburg. It was used by both Confederate and Union forces during the Civil War. Property destruction sometimes occurred when the troops would pass through and camp in the area. People were killed and injured during skirmishes of the troops. And, unfortunately, soldiers sometimes tried to take advantage of the farm women. It didn't matter if the women were of the landed aristocracy or laborer families.

Despite reconstruction efforts by the federal government, recovery was long and hard. Old-timers who had lived through the war often talked about their experiences. Years during and after the war were not good. Money for reconstruction sometimes failed to go for its intended purpose; often it was thought to have been stolen or wasted or to have gone into the pockets of influential people who typically were wealthy anyway (more about that later).

As the first boy after three girls in his family, Henry was given farm responsibilities at an early age. His grandmother Ellen's teaching gave him good insight into why and how things were done. His father taught him to use the simple mule-pulled farm equipment of the day. In his younger years, he began developing good dexterity and had learned to do basic skills, such as driving nails, using a square, and sawing and measuring boards. He could harness draft animals to implements and go about using them. With good arm strength, he could hold plow handles in position as the mule pulled the plow along. He could hold and manipulate the plow lines to direct a mule down a row or across a field. He could competently do about anything requiring simple manual skills by the time he was twelve years of age. This was beneficial as he gained more years.

Henry knew about cotton and other farm crops; he knew about farm animals and draft animal power. That helped him become a valuable young man in many ways around the farm.

Cotton had been king on the farm and in the surrounding area. It had been so since the farm was established in the 1840s and continued through the Civil War. Major adjustments to crop production had to be made following the war and emancipation of the slaves. The arrival of the cotton boll weevil in the early 1900s created an impediment to larger, more profitable yields. People initially tried several ways of controlling the boll weevil but had limited success. Attention was turned to other crops, including corn, sweet potatoes (often called "taters"), and pinder. These were of limited use in generating cash as was the case with cotton, which was commonly referred to as white gold.

You may be wondering: What is pinder? It is a part of the subculture of the Gullah communities in the southern United States and means "peanut." It was an especially important crop with farm hands, who, as slaves, introduced it in the southern states from West Africa. Pinder continued to be a major on-farm food crop for many years even though all the farm hands on the Lee-Shepard farm were born in the United States. None were brought here as slaves.

Farms often produced pinder for use as food by the workers and the family; little was sold for cash. Its popularity grew with plantation owners and others of non-African ancestry. Pinder was eaten raw, boiled, roasted, and in various ground or pulverized forms. Fortunately, pinder was an excellent source of nutrients in the human diet. As is widely known, George Washington Carver, of Tuskegee Institute, did far-reaching research and development on the many uses of pinder. Of course, other crops brought from Africa were widely grown in the South. Slaves from rice-growing areas of Africa were particularly desired in areas of Georgia and South Carolina where rice was produced.

Okra is a garden vegetable crop that was also brought by slaves from Africa. Since okra is botanically kin to cotton, it grew well in the South wherever cotton grew. Farmers soon learned to leave some space between where okra and cotton were planted, as the crops might interbreed, resulting in cotton bolls without fiber and other unacceptable plant traits.

Only a few foods for the family were not produced on the farm. Seasonal vegetables were grown in the garden and in small patches near the cotton fields. The Irish potato was a daily staple. A sort of handed-down stewed potato recipe was used day after day. (Some family members said that Carrie brought the recipe when she married Ira.) Anyone in the house had to accept eating this potato concoction with skillet corn bread. Chickens, pigs, calves, and a few other animals were occasionally butchered on the farm. Turkeys and ducks were infrequently raised and slaughtered. In some cases, farm families would trade or barter foods with their neighbors. Mackerel and sardines were sometimes gotten in small barrels preserved in fish oil at a mercantile store. Salt, sugar, coffee, tea, wheat flour, seasonings, and herbs and spices were a little more frequently bought. As needed, home-remedy medicines and coal oil, aka kerosene, was bought.

Occasionally game animals were used as food. Squirrels, rabbits, and doves were most common. Rarely, a wild goose, opossum, or raccoon might be taken and "readied" for use as food. Ira used a double-barrel gun left to him by his grandfather Shepard. A used 12-gauge was bought from a pawn shop on Farish Street in Jackson for Henry, who hunted a little and occasionally harvested game for the family.

On one occasion, a wild goose, for some reason, came onto the farm. It must have traveled quite a ways to get there; maybe it was from somewhere a thousand or more miles away, such as Minnesota, Michigan, or Maine. One of the farm-hand women incorrectly thought it had been injured or was sick. Anyway, it was shot and taken down as it passed low over the hogpen (scared the squeal out of the hogs!). The dead bird was prepared for cooking, but it was realized it was an old bird and much more cooking time would be needed. In cleaning it, the crop was cut open. Surprisingly, it contained a few plum seeds; no one knows where the plums grew. The seeds were planted in the edge of the yard. A couple seedlings came up and over a few years became bushes that produced plums. For years, the plum bushes grew near the yard fence and were referred to as "wild goose plums."

Raccoons and opossums for food? Yes, they were sometimes used as food, particularly by sharecroppers on the farm. Carrie didn't have many rules about food preparation except with 'coon or 'possum. Her rules covered the practices from harvesting to serving at the table. (Even after following her procedures, she might not eat any of it!)

For Carrie, preparation would begin with capturing the critter in some sort of night hunting. A man might place a carbide light on his cap to shine ahead so that both hands would be free. A carbide light involved using acetylene gas and fire; the gas was made right on the cap with the reaction of calcium carbide and water. In the fall, after dark, and under or in a persimmon tree would be a good place to look, because critters liked ripe persimmons. If a raccoon or opossum was spotted, one approach was to shake it out of the tree and quickly throw a croaker sack over it. The animal would be caught under or in the sack on the ground. A person would grab the sack holding the top together to entrap and restrain the animal. Sometimes a dog might catch a raccoon or opossum, or a gun might be used to shoot the animal (shooting resulted in a less-than-desirable carcass and an animal that was dead).

Carrie insisted on beginning with a live animal so that it could go through a time and process of purging. Why purging? In the wild, raccoons and opossums sometimes ate a range of foods that humans did not appreciate, including dead rodents, remains from home waste disposal, or manure from hogpens. Purging involved keeping the animal alive in a cage for several days and feeding it grain or vegetables and giving it good water. Its digestive system would clean itself out. Once that was accomplished, the body was said to be "purged" (clean) and ready for slaughter and cooking. The animal would be killed, gutted (always removing internal organs before skinning), skinned, and cut into desired pieces.

An additional benefit of the raccoon was that the pelt had value and could be sold. Such a pelt needed to be in one piece. Having a whole pelt involved a procedure known as casing. With casing, the pelt was pulled off in one big piece and stretched on a frame to dry the fur. It took practice to learn how to case an animal.

Just as she demanded purging, Carrie insisted on casing followed by thorough washing of the carcass. Everyone around the home knew that Carrie did not lift a hand to pan-ready a 'coon or 'possum; this preparation was always another person's job! Ira rarely did the readying; nor did Henry, his sisters, or Ellen. Sharecroppers on the place or people who lived in the community often did it.

Carrie's favorite recipes with opossum were 'possum and taters (sweet potatoes), 'possum pot pie, and 'possum stew. Similar recipes were followed with raccoon. Of course, some family members avoided such game, but they might not have had much to eat at the rare meals when 'coon and 'possum were served (maybe stewed potatoes). The two meats were not mixed. And, just for any preachers who might be reading, 'coon and 'possum were never served at meals when a man of the cloth might be there with a Sunday-after-preaching appetite. Again, one of Carries rules!

With only small creeks and no ponds on the place, fish had minimal impact on family meals. Catfish were sometimes caught in Bogue Chitto Creek, but they were mudcats (bottom feeders) and not particularly good. Bream and bass might also be caught but not with any degree of abundance.

Carrie and Ira had ideas about other aspects of their family. One of these was education of children. Going to school did not receive high attention for the only boy in the Lee family (though his sisters were expected to be more diligent about attendance). His mother was content with whatever his father said. Neither, unfortunately, cared much for schooling. Henry was needed to do farm work. Before quitting, he went through the eighth grade and into the ninth. Maybe he tired of taking a biscuit with molasses for lunch each day!

The Tinnin School was in session only a few months each year, so there wasn't a lot of time for teaching and learning. Henry was good in arithmetic and geography; he could name every state in the United States by its shape (forty-eight at the time, with Arizona the last to join). He knew that Mississippi was the twentieth state to join the Union, about a hundred years before his study of it in school.

Of course, he knew a little about Mississippi leaving the Union to be a part of the Confederate States of America. His father had told him that his great-grandfather had voted against it, but that was the extent of what was taught; the old South was still trying to get over being defeated by the Union.

Henry needed glasses to correct his vision for reading and other schoolwork. Only a few children wore glasses. Henry was fortunate to have the ones he had, though they were not very well suited to his vision needs. His eyes were not examined so that prescriptive lenses could be obtained. Children who wore glasses were sometimes ridiculed both in and out of school by other students. Behavior toward them was sometimes ugly and frightening. Just a loud statement like "Look at four-eyes" was degrading.

Most of the older and larger boys in school were nice to Henry, but one was a bully. An example of bullying is the day fifth-grade Henry, by chance, met up with Earl Clampton as they walked the cow path through the pasture to the Tinnin schoolhouse. Earl lived in a little shack of a house and was always jealous of Henry for living in a big house. On this day he was more expressive of bully behavior. He teased Henry about his glasses and called him a baby-faced sissy. He pushed Henry down and pulled him by one leg through a freshly dropped cow pile (danged cow). Earl laughed and taunted and then hurried on his way to school to get away from his horrible behavior. Henry got up, rubbed in the grass to clean off as best he could, and continued to school.

When he arrived, the teacher scolded Henry for coming to school dirty and smelly. Henry tried to tell the teacher what happened. His explanation didn't matter; he was made to sit in the corner away from other pupils until school was out that day. When he got home that afternoon, he tried to explain to his mother what had happened. None of his sisters saw the incident; they couldn't vouch for him. His mother was not sympathetic; she rarely was toward him. And, this was a time when some motherly love would have been so good for this developing boy.

Nothing about life on the farm bustin' clods was ever easy. The work was hard, and the days were long. Children learned to do work and assume a share of responsibility at young ages. Farming was the way of life—no one in the family escaped. Everyone had to contribute to getting work done and surviving as a family. Work duties varied with the size, age, and gender of family members. Workdays sometimes began before daylight and ran until dark (there were no electric lights).

Life was meager, even with long days and hard work. The family didn't have excesses of anything. Children often had hand-me-down clothing from older siblings and from neighbor children who had outgrown the clothing. Occasionally, clothing from a child who had died would be available. Sometimes a child might even brag about wearing clothing previously worn by another, especially by a child who might have lived in a fine house in Boston or Chicago (if the donation could be identified as being from there).

Clothing might also come from charitable sources in the North, particularly New England. Some New England churches would have annual clothing drives to collect used things to ship south to what the congregations thought were "barefoot and starving children in impoverished communities." An example was the small (by Baptist standards) National Association of Congregational Churches. Boxes packed with pants, dresses, shirts, shoes, and the like would be sent as freight on a train or through the U.S. Post Office from one of their congregations to a local school or church for distribution in the fall. Some of these things were put to good use, particularly any shoes that might have been sent. Children would go barefooted all summer, but the winter months would be cold enough for them to need shoes. Their feet would develop tough skin on the bottom to protect from thorns, sharp stones, and insect bites. Whether the Northern children lived that much better is not certain, but the Southern children and families certainly liked to get the boxes! It has been said that some people would get the boxes and sell the contents to have a little money. Selling donated items didn't happen very often.

New clothing was typically handmade at home, though some might be bought ready-made from mercantile stores in Pocahontas or Clinton or from merchants along Jackson's Farish Street. Occasionally, there would be something that gave hope and inspired youngsters to live and grow.

In 1911, each child got a portrait made by a photographer in Jackson. Only four living children had been born at that time. It was a special treat for the family to go to Jackson and have some time there. The pictures were talked about, displayed, and enjoyed by friends and family. Some of those pictures have lasted more than a century and are still looked at today. They have helped great-grandchildren learn a little about the personal features of ancestors of more than a hundred years ago.

Some children have the benefit of having a strong adult in their lives. Henry was fortunate to develop as a small child with his grandmother Ellen Loretta Shepard Lee living in the home. She was born in 1847, became an adult during the Civil War, and was away from her parents for nearly twenty years after getting married. She died in 1918 when Henry was eight years of age. Those few years together were very important in his development. She was a wise, thoughtful, moral, and compassionate person. Henry reminded her of her own son and only child—Henry's father, Ira. Her receptivity to change and acceptance of new developments had a major impact on the life of developing Henry.

Henry grew into adulthood with the physical ability to do about anything on the farm. His sometimes sickly father relied on him in many ways. He could operate the draft-animal-powered Southern farm implements of the day. He could repair harnesses and implements and skillfully perform other maintenance work. As he advanced through teenage years, he assumed more duties with responsibilities. He could plan and do farm construction and repairs. Fence building and mending and other work that required good manual dexterity of a skilled adult were routine for Henry.

When Ellen died, things changed. The love Henry had experienced disappeared. His own mother often failed in this regard. After all, she had eight other babies over about a quarter century (two died as infants). This was way more than the family could afford. (Chapter 2 provides more detail on the interaction of Henry with his grandmother Ellen about family and farm.)

Newfangled ways of bustin' clods were on the way. Some Lee family members were accepting the idea of using powered equipment in farming. Before they could use it, however, they had a lot to learn about how to do so productively and safely and how to maintain it.

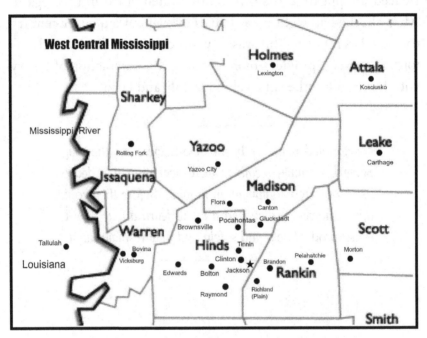

Relevant Locations in West Central Mississippi.

2

Digging Roots

"Mama Ellen, tell me about you," seven-year-old Henry said. "And, how'd you get here? Were you born here? Who was your papa? Your mama?" Answers would take Ellen a while. For some reason, Henry wanted to hear about things related to his heritage and the farm. She was happy to tell him.

"Really? I will try, but I won't be able to tell you everything," Ellen said. "There is a lot to say. You know some already. It'll take a long time to tell you much of the story. I'll tell you things over several days, one story at a time. I'm getting some years on me and may not be around much longer.

"You know, Henry, I was born here on this plantation. It was in a different house. Times were different. Pull my rocking chair over near the porch swing. I'll sit in the chair, and you in the swing. Let's begin when my father was a very young man in the state of Indiana. Okay?"

"Yes, Mama Ellen, that'll be okay," Henry said. "And I want to hear the details. It is a nice day to be on the porch with you. I want to hear what you will say. Everybody around here thinks you are a great person."

So, Ellen began.

"It's important for you to learn about your family and the farm. You are the only boy in this generation, and, likely, you will inherit the farm. When you do, the right thing for you to do is to pay your mother rent for using the land and, after she dies, pay each of your sisters a fair amount for their portion of the land. You need to know about this place and how things are done. I've always been told that history helps us understand why things are done the way they are. The plantation has been a part of our family for many years. We want to keep it that way. If I say something you don't understand, tell me; I'll go over it again. Sometimes I may use words you don't know. Ask me, and I will explain."

"Oh, Mama Ellen, this sounds good to me," Henry said, "and you know I kind of like history at school."

"I'll start with a young man by the name of George Washington Shepard," Ellen said, "and since he was my father, I'll call him Pa George. He was born in Kentucky on July 16, 1814, as the first child of John and Rachel Shepard. The family moved to Washington (Davies County), Indiana, shortly after he was born. In the following years, twelve children were born in his family.

"There were three girls and nine boys. He, as the oldest, was always expected to do things at a young age. The place where the family lived in Indiana was twenty miles from the Illinois state line. The land was good midwestern prairie soil; it was good for growing corn, oats, wheat, and other crops but not cotton. As a young man, George learned a lot about farming and farm life. He also became an accomplished well digger and cleaner. Doing well work was a way he could earn a little money beyond farming.

"George helped with the farm and did other jobs. He didn't think he could make very much money growing corn. When he worked other jobs, he made $2.50 a month! He felt he had to improve his lot in life. He had heard that a man could make more money working and farming in the South and, maybe, become wealthy. That was when white people in the South were thriving and before slavery and the stubborn notions of influential people about slavery brought the South down.

"Young George saw an article in a small newspaper about moving to Mississippi and getting Choctaw cession land for farming. Different from Indiana, he understood that he could also own slaves to do the farm work needed to grow cotton, but he wasn't sure he wanted to do that. He thought about his future; he talked to his Papa John. He didn't know anything about cotton but thought he could learn. Once he left home, he would likely never see his family again, but he went ahead with his decision. It was in the year 1841, and he was twenty-seven years old.

"You're probably wondering about Choctaw cession land. The Choctaws were natives here in these lands long before other people came. They didn't know about laws and traditions that were brought to the United States from Europe and other places. They didn't readily conform to some of the things the other people wanted them to do. Sometimes there were big disagreements and fights. Occasionally, a person might be killed.

"To promote peace, the United States made treaties with the Choctaws. Among other things, the treaties often took their land without paying them. Sounds bad, and it was! The land became cession land that was made available free or for a small charge to white settlers who wanted it for farming and settling. So, this farm was part of the land the Choctaw Indians had owned before they were sent to live out west or to a reservation in Mississippi. Many people feel that the Choctaws were treated very badly. And, I agree. Government treaties robbed them of their land and made them walk hundreds of miles to relocate. In the long walks, many became sick and died. Some people call these relocations the Trail of Tears. Yes, it was a time of sadness and the shedding of tears."

"Mama Ellen," Henry said, "this is interesting. Don't you think my sisters should hear it? Also, do you think you can tell me in fewer words?"

"Maybe." Ellen spoke: "We'll get your sisters another time. Let me continue with the life of young George Shepard.

"George was smart. He figured out how he would travel to the South. He rode on a wagon to the landing where boats stopped on the Ohio River. He was able to get a job working on one of the riverboats that traveled down the Ohio River to where it ran into the Mississippi River near Cairo, Illinois. At that place, he got a job on another boat that was heading south on the Mississippi River toward New Orleans.

"When the boat reached Vicksburg, Mississippi, he gave up his job and got off. He liked what he saw. After talking to a few people, he decided to catch the train eastward to a little cotton town known as Clinton. In Clinton and off the train, he had no place to stay. He found a house not far from the depot that offered room and board; he got a room there. He asked around and found a man who had a dug well that needed cleaning. He spent his first full day cleaning the well and was paid $2.50. He was told afterward that he could have gotten more, maybe as much as $5.00 for doing the work. It was surprising to him that wages were higher in Mississippi than in Indiana. That's not so anymore."

"Mama Ellen," Henry asked, "why Clinton? Why not Vicksburg? Was the land good for farming? Was the money better?"

"So, why Clinton?" Ellen repeated. "Interesting. The community had been known as Mt. Salus. The name was changed in 1828 to make it more acceptable as a possible capital for the state of Mississippi (Mississippi became a state in 1817). It was not chosen as the capital, though it was a good town. The publicity it received promoted considerable growth. During the 1830s, Clinton became the third largest town in the state, behind the river port cities of Natchez and Vicksburg. Jackson grew fast after becoming the capital city. This also helped small nearby places to grow such as Brandon, Richland, and Raymond.

"A railroad was opened through Clinton in 1831 that provided transportation west to Vicksburg and east to Jackson. A lot of baled cotton was shipped from Clinton to Vicksburg. In Vicksburg, it would be loaded on a boat or barge and sent down the river to New Orleans. From there, it would be sent across the ocean to places in Europe. Some 20,000 bales of cotton a year were shipped from Clinton in the 1830s.

"It made sense that George came to Clinton because of its size and businesses and the thriving economy the town had. There was also a land office in the town, and he could use it to try to get land for a plantation. The town had two learning institutes and was a leader in education in the state. Those institutes might later be useful to the family he thought he would have. He felt it was a safe place that valued education and Christian principles. One more thing: just because Clinton was the third largest town in the state did not mean it was big, but it did have thirty or so businesses.

"Being raised in the Midwest, George had some different values and approaches to life. He knew how to work hard and get a job done. He valued education and being honest and fair in life. He had to learn about southern climate, soils, crops, and the like. Overall, he felt very good about his move. As I have said, before he could get land he worked digging wells so farmers and residents could have water. He also did other jobs around Clinton to make a little money. Some of his work was in a farming community known as Tinnin.

"He liked the Tinnin area; it was only five miles from Clinton. The land was excellent, as there were hills and creeks, wildlife and water. The area also offered a peaceful place to live. A dirt wagon road connected the community with Clinton. That road made it easy to get to the train depot and go to Jackson or Vicksburg. Tinnin had a country store, a small school, a couple of churches, and three cemeteries. Of course, back then, the bodies of dead people were sometimes buried in the woods or backyards of houses.

"Tinnin turned out to be a good place for George. He met the love of his life, Sarah Elizabeth Ratliff. Her parents were Zachariah and Susan Elizabeth Tinnin Ratliff. It is interesting that the Tinnin community was named for Susan's father. George and Sarah were married July 16, 1845. I was born September 15, 1847. They were wonderful parents to me and the other seven children. As the oldest, I often helped with the younger children."

"I am wondering," Henry remarked, "how is Zachariah spelled? It is different from most other names I know."

"Good question." Ellen spelled the name, "Z-a-c-h-a-r-i-a-h."

Henry repeated the spelling, and Ellen continued.

"Using the land office in Clinton (Mt. Salus) and buying from owners, your great-grandfather George at the peak had 1,200 acres of land. At first, a few small houses, along with a horse stable, corn crib, and barn, were built. There was also a small shed that had tools for working on plows, harnesses, wagons, and the like. It had a forge for heating iron and steel to make plows and for sharpening plow points as needed.

"The property had creeks, hills, and bottom land that made good places for crops. Some of the land was in trees and had to be cleared for planting. Work on the farm was done by slaves, family members, and a few hired hands. George did not like owning slaves, but he did so because that was the way farming was done. It took a lot of money to buy them. He treated his slaves better than other masters in Tinnin. As owner and master, he was responsible for providing food, clothing, and housing. Much was grown on the farm, but there were some things he had to buy.

"Pa George would occasionally go to Vicksburg when he needed to buy more than a few supplies (he could get a few things in Clinton). To do so, he would drive a horse-drawn wagon into Clinton and catch a train for the thirty or so miles to Vicksburg. There he could buy a wide range of materials at a couple of mercantile stores and catch the train back to his waiting horse and wagon.

"One of the stores in Vicksburg he went to for provisions was the Duff Green Mercantile Co. (successor to Wm. P. Swinney). It was located at the dock at the end of the railroad line near the Mississippi River and convenient to unloading cargo from large boats and barges that traveled from New Orleans and Natchez. For example, on March 9, 1854, Pa George went to Duff Green for supplies for the plantation and his developing family. On that trip, among other things, he bought a 60-pound sack of coffee, a 42-gallon barrel of molasses, and a half barrel of Dexter Whiskey. You may wonder why he bought the whiskey. He was not a person who drank except if he thought he needed a little medicine. It was for medicinal purposes that he bought it for members of the family, slaves, and farm hands who became ill.

"Another store he sometimes frequented was Shawver and Pollock, dealers in groceries and plantation supplies. The store was located very near the Mississippi River at the corner of Levee and Crawford Streets. When he went, he would buy large amounts of some provisions that were needed on the plantation. On one of the trips (October 20, 1856) he bought, among other things, a half barrel of fish (No.1 mackerel in fish oil), fifty pounds of sugar, and a barrel of salted pork meat.

"All the merchants charged what was known as a drayage fee. Drayage was the cost for hauling/delivering the food, tools, and cloth he bought back to Clinton on the train. He hauled the goods in his wagon from the depot to Tinnin. He took enough gold with him to pay the costs of merchandise, drayage, and his personal transportation. Costs might run a couple hundred dollars or so. Sometimes, Ma Sarah would go with him.

"Henry, you are probably wondering how I know all these details. You see, I have kept statements, letters, and the like in a trunk in the attic of this house. There are letters from the early 1850s in which Pa George heard from his parents in Indiana. Another letter written a little later in the 1850s was from one of his younger brothers who had gone to Texas to 'find his fortune.'

"Every now and then, I go to the attic, open the trunk, and look at those letters. Sometimes I get a little sad thinking about my father, mother, and family. Once in a while, I add something if I have a letter or paper that is meaningful. It is a way of keeping up with our family history. And, for your information, that trunk was there during the Civil War when troops came through here and took things with them. I hid the trunk so they couldn't find it. I hope you will keep the trunk after I am gone."

"Mama Ellen, did you say 'gone'?" Henry asked. "Where are you going? I don't want you to leave. I would be sad and lonely without you."

"Oh, I'm not going away, Henry." Ellen continued, "I will be 70 years old in another year. That is a long life for people around here. Anyway, I want to be buried in my father's family cemetery just up the hill a bit; I am staying here!"

"Okay," Henry said. "Please don't leave us. Stay. Now, tell me more about my family."

"I will." Ellen continued. "As the family got larger, George and Sarah needed more space. They were very cramped in the small farmhouse that sat on the hill near the old cedar tree. So, in 1857, Pa George had a new, much larger house built. He hired Mr. Bull and Mr. Horn, two carpenters from Pelahatchie, to build the house. I was about ten years old and remember them well.

"The house Pa George wanted had somewhat of an Indiana

prairie appearance about it and did not look like a fine house of the Old South. The builders brought heart-pine lumber and needed materials from Pelahatchie to Clinton on the train. Pa George helped move the materials from the depot to the house site with ox-drawn wagons. I remember seeing the long wagons with the beautiful lumber. You may wonder where Pelahatchie is located. To get there from here, you go to Clinton and catch the train through Jackson, go east to Brandon, and then go to the next depot stop, which is Pelahatchie. So, it is fifty or so miles from here. When the builders came, they stayed for a while to get the work done. They pitched a tent near where the house was built in the place where the henhouse stands today.

"Slaves on the plantation worked with the carpenters in doing the building. The foundation was made of limestone rock quarried in the highest wooded hills on the place. You know, Henry, many long years ago this place was in what is now the Gulf of Mexico. The limestone contained fossils, which are the skeletons, shells, and plant remains that lived in the seawater. Big rocks were moved to the house site by oxen pulling slides over the ground. This house has held up well; it was built sixty years ago and is still a very good house!

"Let me tell you about an accident that happened with the train bringing the materials from Pelahatchie. The train derailed; we don't know why. Some lumber was broken and damaged beyond use. Mr. Bull and Mr. Horn, as well as the train company, tried to salvage all they could. They had to buy a few new materials to replace lumber that could not be used. You wouldn't want to use bad materials. That delayed the construction for a few weeks.

"I always found it interesting to see how the lumber was put together in construction. Wooden pegs and handmade nails were used. Slaves used blacksmithing tools to shape small slender pieces of steel and then beat them into nails with a hammer on an anvil.

"Some main parts of the house frame were fastened together with wooden pegs. An auger was used to bore through lumber at just the right places for the pegs. The pegs were made of strong wood that would last, such as heart pine, and just about the same size or slightly larger than the holes bored in the lumber. The pegs needed to fit very tightly. Once the holes in the two pieces of wood were lined up, the pegs were driven in with a large hammer or maul. If the pegs were not tight, the construction would not be solid. Bricks were used in the hearth and chimneys. These were handmade on the farm. Some bricks to this very day have the fingerprints of the slaves who made them.

"During the U.S. Civil War, 1861 to 1865, both Union and Confederate troops came through the farm. They pillaged the house—this house—that had been built about five years earlier. They often took things they wanted. I know; I was there! We learned how to hide some of our animals, food, and other things so the soldiers couldn't find them. Away from their homes in the war, the soldiers were often hungry, sick, and poorly clothed. They missed their families. Sometimes we left things out just so they could easily find and take them, such as some meat in the smokehouse. It seemed to me that the Confederate soldiers suffered more hardship and had more need for clothing and food than the Union soldiers.

"The South didn't have much of a chance in the war. Southern soldiers fought for a cause they couldn't win. Anyway, I have never understood why they were motivated to go to war. Their violence killed and injured thousands of men and destroyed a lot of property. Some of the soldiers were rowdy and ugly, especially to women. I had to punch a soldier in the belly one time to defend myself; I'll tell you more about that sometime.

"Union troops once threatened to burn this house. Pa George, Ma Sarah, and all of us children begged them not to do so. Pa George told them that he had voted the Union ticket. At that point, the company commander asked if any Confederate troops lived here; none did. He said that they would not burn the house but, if a soldier ever lived here in this house, they would come back and burn it. To this day, no soldier has lived here. My family was mostly girls, and now your family is too; armies want men. Regardless, the Union troops were nicer than the Confederates.

"Now, I am going to tell you something that is very personal to me." Ellen said, "If you want to hear more, let's get your sisters to join us."

"Yes," Henry said. "I wanna hear all you'll tell me. I'll call my sisters."

———   ———   ———

When Henry's sisters arrived, Ellen began.

"It was during the war that I was becoming an adult. You know, young folks need to get out on their own and not stay home waiting for their parents to look after them. This meant that they got married and started families. Young women had to search for men; often men searched for women, but these were difficult times. Many men were away in battle, enduring hardships that often damaged their minds and bodily well-being. Others had been killed or very badly injured. I wanted a good man that Pa George and Ma Sarah would approve.

"I found a man whom I grew to love in Brandon in 1863. His name was Jasper Henry Lee. I didn't know much about him. He was several years older than I, but I did learn that he'd moved to Brandon from his childhood home near Columbia, South Carolina. He now had a job that paid a few dollars a week working for the railroad; a little money was good. He told me that he loved me, and I told him that I loved him. So, we decided to get married.

"I had him come to Tinnin several times and meet Pa George,

Ma Sarah, and my sisters. On one of the visits, we said we wanted to get married; that surprised Pa. He took Jasper aside for a walk to the garden for talking. I don't know what Pa asked him, but whatever it was turned Pa against him; he totally rejected Jasper as my future husband. Pa later said something to me about Jasper being too old for me and having had other women. I don't know about other marriages; Jasper never told me. I always wanted him to be open and honest with me.

"On March 1, 1864, we got a marriage license in Brandon, and the following day we were married in Clinton by the Reverend Joseph Autry at his house near the depot. Pa George did not like my new husband; he told us never to come to his house (which is this house). We didn't. We planned our lives based on moving West. So, we rode a train to Vicksburg, caught a ferry across the big Mississippi River, and rode another train across Louisiana into Texas. We got off the train in the little town of Athens, Texas. We began making our home in the farm area of Henderson County, Texas. That's a long way from here; we had no family around. We made our way as best we could; it wasn't easy having enough food and a place to stay. I missed Tinnin but realized I was starting a new life. Exciting!

"We found a farm that Jasper bought using a loan. You know, Henry, women couldn't own property; women had few rights, and to this day they don't have the same rights as men. Sad! I feel that women are just as good as men.

"Our lives changed again on February 3, 1868. A baby son was born. We named him Ira Jasper Lee. Of course, you know him as your father. He was a good baby; Jasper and I tried to be good parents. Jasper worked hard on the farm. He registered to vote in 1869 shortly after he bought the land. As a woman, I couldn't vote. I hear that Congress is considering a law that would allow women to vote; each state has to approve it. Somehow, I don't think Mississippi will vote to do so.

"A few months after buying the land, Jasper suddenly died. There I was, a single mother alone with an infant son far away from my parents and sisters. It wasn't easy, but I survived. I stayed in Texas, settling Jasper's estate and trying to find my way in life. There were many men who would take advantage of my being a widow; they would take the property that belonged to my husband. Yes, steal it! Finally, I returned to Tinnin in 1881 to live in this house with my Ma Sarah and Pa George and a few other family members. By then, Ira, was thirteen years of age and old enough to do work that was really needed on the farm.

"So, Henry, you and your sisters have my personal story. It isn't one that I talk about much. I get sad when I do. I had a lot of hardship when I was away in Texas. I am so glad that my family let me come back home and that I returned to Tinnin."

"Mama Ellen, you surely do know a lot," Henry said. He then asked, "What happened to the slaves who were here? Their families? How important were they to the farm? Tell me more."

"The slaves were good people and very important," Ellen said. "Your great-grandfather George tried to treat them well. After they knew they would get their freedom, they did not all immediately leave. They didn't have a better place to go so quickly. But, by 1865 all were gone or were farming on shares. Those who left moved to towns; some moved to big cities of the North to be near factories that had good jobs.

"Situations changed during the Civil War. Before the war, the South was often viewed as better for earning a living. But afterward, that changed, and the North was better, particularly for the former slaves. You need to remember this: Your great-grandfather was as good to slaves as any slave owner—in fact, better than most. He respected and cared for them, but this didn't mean that they lived in good conditions. He wanted them to stay. Remember, their leaving created hardship on the farm. Who was going to do the work? Some of my sisters pitched in and helped, but what they did wasn't nearly enough. Overall, by the end of the war, my family had lost a lot of what it had before the war. During and after the war, we had almost nothing. We weren't alone. Other plantation owners were much the same. Troops destroyed and pillaged much of what we had. All the money that your great-grandfather had spent buying slaves was gone and could not be gotten back. The war was bad on people.

"Reconstruction programs were set up by the federal government after the war. These programs were intended to help the South overcome the hardship and devastation caused by military activity. Sometimes the programs didn't turn out as intended. Aid for poor folks on farms often never reached them; rich and powerful people elsewhere tended to steal it or divert it to their personal use. Anyway, the plantation your great-grandfather George set up before the war lasted through it but was greatly changed. He rather successfully managed it until the war was over and tried to pick up the pieces. That plantation is the farm on which you now live.

"A crop lien program was used after the war to try to help farmers and their families live and produce crops. With a crop lien, a farmer would be allowed to get needed items during the year when there was no income and no money. A record would be kept of what was gotten. Once the crops (primarily cotton) were harvested and sold in the fall, the amount owed would be paid back. Sounds good, right? But it didn't always work out as intended. It seems that the merchants and store owners sometimes cheated the farmers. So, by 1886, the crop lien program was stopped. It wasn't stopped, however, before your great-grandfather was caught in the trap and lost a few hundred acres of land.

"An example of a crop lien on this farm is the Merchant's Deed of Trust dated July 28, 1883, between your great-grandfather George and the E&S Virden Company. Under the agreement, the merchant would provide a cash advance up to $150 and select farming supplies needed to complete the crop year. In this case, the money was to be paid back by November 1, 1883. Five cows, four yearling calves, an 11-year-old horse named Jim, a 9-year-old gray mule named Judah, and some land were put up to cover part of the repayment. A quantity of harvested cotton was also pledged to repay the loan. The agreement appeared one-sided in favor of the merchant.

"Times were hard; people had virtually no money and were desperate. Fortunately, Pa George was able to meet the deadline with the payment using harvested cotton as the major source of income. The deed was undersigned by S. Livingston, Clerk of the Circuit Court of Hinds County. So, in one way or another, local government officials had some sort of role in helping those who loaned money to take advantage of farmers and sometimes cheat them. On another occasion, Pa George wasn't so fortunate. He lost a few hundred acres of land in a faulty property lien. This embarrassed him. He never talked much about it, but I could tell he was ashamed. People were so poor; they didn't have many choices.

"Another practice intended to help farmers have labor after the slaves were gone was known as convict leasing. This involved plantations and factories using prisoners from jails to do work. The convicts were under the care of plantation owners and treated much like slaves but often worse, such as being shut up in a cage when not at work. When at work, they might be chained together forming 'chain gangs.' Guards with guns on horses looked after the chain gangs and forced them to work hard even when sick.

"Some farmers who knew people in higher-up county or state jobs took unfair advantage of convict leasing. Your grandfather George did not like this program and never used it. Convict leasing to farmers was phased out in the 1880s because of abuse of the convicts, but chain gangs continued, mostly working on roads and public property. The guards often rode horses and held loaded shotguns ready to shoot at a moment's notice.

"I've talked so much that I'm tired and hoarse. Let's take a break until Sunday afternoon. We'll talk then about how the farm survived. Okay?"

"Yes, Mama Ellen," Henry replied. "That'll be fine. You are smart and know so much."

Sunday afternoon at 2:30, Henry, his grandmother, and two of his sisters sat on the porch near the swing. The third sister, Ellen, said she couldn't join them that day because her sweetheart, Glen, was coming to the house and they were going for a ride in his carriage.

Before the talk began, Mama Ellen called Ellen to her side and spoke: "Now, Ellen, you are seeing Glen a lot these days. Be sure he is always a gentleman, and never let him take advantage of you. Have a nice ride today."

"I will," Ellen replied, "and I will see to it that Glen behaves. He will not do anything I don't want. Okay?"

Mama Ellen began her farm talk on the porch: "I think I will review just a little that was said last time. The Shepard plantation began in the 1840s and continued through the Civil War with George W. Shepard as the owner. Times after the war were hard. People barely had enough to survive. Some people got sick and died; two of my sisters died of yellow fever in 1878. Farm acreage was lost to crop liens (I mentioned crop liens earlier) and other bad money practices.

"After the war, work was done by family members, hired farm hands, and sharecroppers. The sharecroppers received a ration of food and sometimes a small amount of money during the year. They worked hard producing and harvesting crops. The farm owner provided small houses for them and their families. Typically, the houses were shacks, as you see by some of the abandoned houses on this plantation.

"The sharecroppers would farm on halves or thirds, meaning they got a half or a third of what they produced, depending on the agreement, and the farm owner kept the remainder. Costs of growing a cotton crop were subtracted from the income amount. The farmer kept records of a sharecropper's expense and subtracted it from his earnings. Pa George tried to be honest and fair; he did not cheat as we have heard other farmers did.

"As I said before, I returned to Tinnin in 1881. My son, Ira (your father), was with me. Sometime I'll tell you how we made the trip but not today.

"When I returned, all my sisters had left home. My brother, also named Ira and the youngest child, left home the very year I got back. Occasionally, a sister would come back for a while if she had family or health problems. Some in the family thought that brother Ira Shepard would take over the farm. He didn't; he went up into the Delta area of Sunflower County and struck out on his own to be a plantation owner and businessman. He was successful. So, who was going to take over the farm when Pa George died? That person was your father, Ira Jasper Lee.

"Pa George tried to train your father in the operation of this farm. Besides crop and animal production, Pa tried to teach him to be honest, fair, and considerate. Increasingly, careful management of money was needed; a farmer had to plan how money was to be made and not just how to grow food crops for home use. Your father became an adult on this farm. Henry, you will do the same. It is a good place to grow up and learn. This farm means so much to our family. It would be very sad if it ceased being a farm and being owned by our family.

"During the final fifteen years of Pa's life, he worked as he could to assure that the farm made it to the next generation. Your father became a man during that time and took over most of the farming work. Pa George gradually became frail and unable to do much on the farm. It was a sad day in 1895 when he died. Ma Sarah, his wife and my mother, died a few months later. Of course, my brother and sisters had an interest in the farmland. But, since your father and I lived here, they agreed to let your father work the land. They said he must do a good job and eventually pay a fair price to the sisters and brother, or their heirs, for their shares of the land. So, your father, Ira, began doing so. He worked hard, and things came along well. He paid annual rent to the family and saved what money he could to get enough to pay for the place.

"Now, that covers almost sixty years of the farm. I will tell you more sometime soon. Telling this gets long; I don't want to tire you out."

"Thank you, Mama Ellen," Henry said. "What you've told me and my sisters is important. It helps me have a good feeling about being the boy on the farm and growing up here in Tinnin. This farm and my family are so closely tied. I'll always carefully look after the place. Please tell me more sometime soon."

"Henry, I will," Ellen assured him. "I want you one day to operate this farm and be very successful. We want it to stay in our family. All of us have put too much effort into it for it to be lost. Once gone, it will be gone forever."

A week passed. Henry and Ellen hadn't talked about the farm or family. Henry thought it was time to do so again. "Mama Ellen, you haven't talked to me in a while about the farm," Henry said. "I hope you will tell me more soon. How about Saturday morning while Papa and Mama are gone to the store?"

"Okay, " Ellen said. "Yes, just after breakfast on Saturday."

Saturday morning arrived. Henry said, "Mama Ellen, I put your favorite rocking chair near the end of the porch in the direction of the chicken house, but it isn't so close to the edge that you'll fall off. Is that okay for our talk this morning about farm and family?"

"Yes, it'll do. Let's start now," Ellen said. So they went to the end of the porch and sat. Ellen was in the rocking chair, and Henry on the floor with his back against the wall.

Ellen began where she left off the last time. "Henry, today I'm gonna talk about your family and how it relates to the farm. Your father was well into running the farm at the turn of the century. At about the same time, he was certain that he had found a young woman whom he loved and who would be a good wife and partner in life.

"On August 7, 1901, he and Carrie Cheers Hendrick were married. He was thirty-three years of age, and she was nineteen. She had lived on farms and was well aware of the work that went on to live and be successful. The newlyweds lived in this Shepard house, which was becoming known as the Lee-Shepard house. It had plenty of room for them. I also lived in it, along with one of my sisters and her young daughter. My sister was here temporarily following a problem in her marriage.

"Ira and Carrie had plenty of room for children. Your oldest sister, Ellen, was born on August 20, 1902. About three years later, on May 20, 1905, another sister, Sudie, was born. Your third sister, Ivie, was born on March 1, 1907. These three girls grew and developed nicely. They welcomed you as their brother on August 20, 1910. You were named after my husband and your grandfather, Jasper Henry Lee. You remember he died in Texas some forty years before you were born. Your sister, Ethel, was born on April 28, 1913. You had a brother, Ira Nelson, born on April 4, 1915, but at age two he became ill and died. You remember his funeral about a month ago on June 2, 1917. As of now, your family has four girls and one boy, and you are the boy. As such, much is expected of you!"

Henry had heard something before like "As the only boy, much is expected of you." Frightening to a seven-year-old!

"Your father is teaching you how to farm. He wants you to have pride in farming and living on this land. That is why he takes you to the field and has you do such work as chopping and picking cotton. He gets you to pick and shell corn and pick beans and other vegetable crops. He has taught you a little about how to harness and use a mule to plow land for planting and to pull a mechanical planter and about how to drive a wagon. You are learning well. I have a feeling that you will be very successful as you grow and develop. You know how to use most tools and do a lot of farm work at your age of seven. You go to school a few months in the winter, where you are learning arithmetic, history, and geography.

"So, Henry, I have told you a lot about the farm and your family. You can be very proud of who you are and what you stand for. Ask me anytime you want to know more or have questions."

"Mama Ellen," Henry said, "thank you for all you have told us. I'll try to remember as much as I can. I want this farm to be successful and continue its long tradition. I will work hard to make it better. Mama Ellen, you mean so much to me."

Henry learned a lot about his family from his grandmother Ellen. Though she was aging, she could relate well to her only grandson but couldn't forecast the future. Henry's family would add two more sisters and a brother, who lived a couple of years; an unnamed brother was stillborn. Ellen didn't live long enough to tell the complete story (she died in 1918).

3

Searching for Direction

Farm income had been fairly good for a few years after
World War I; maybe it was time to indulge a bit. Some
folks said, "Not so fast; things seem to be going bad
again." What was a farmer to do? Hunker down and
survive with subsistence farming or try to plan a better
future? Being broke and without money wasn't much of
a life. A new direction was needed.

Engine-powered vehicles were beginning to come into use in the 1920s for
both farm and family transportation. Henry was inquisitive about
automobiles and other uses of gasoline engines. A good learning
opportunity occurred when his family bought a new 1923 Ford
touring car.

The Lee family first had a demonstration of a Ford car in 1917. It
was a time to learn about the major mechanical systems, including
fuel, power, steering, and braking. Buying was put off for another
six years. In the intervening years, Henry carefully observed the
few vehicles around. He would talk to their owners. He would give
suggestions to his father about how they needed an automobile. The
day to get an automobile finally arrived!

Car dealerships were beginning to open in both large and small towns of the South. Far away Detroit, Michigan, was known as the home of the automobile. Henry would occasionally visit a local dealership if his family went near one. He figured that he could drive a car if given the opportunity. He had his first chance as a teenager when his father finally made the decision to buy a Ford from a dealer in the tiny cotton-gin town of Flora, Mississippi.

The day to get a car arrived. Henry and two sisters accompanied his father. The trip to the dealership was some fifteen miles in a horse-drawn wagon, so they left quite early that morning. After the car had been paid for in cash (a total of $469), it was time to drive it and the wagon home to Tinnin. Most of the family rode in the car. Henry, to his dismay, was given the responsibility of getting the horse and wagon home. When Ira told him he was to drive the wagon home, Henry exclaimed, "Papa, I don't want to! I want to ride in the car. I want to drive the car. I am old enough!" After frowning for a short time, Henry did what his papa had told him to do. The frowns on Henry's face did not change his papa's mind.

Henry's sisters and father drove the Ford slowly along the dirt roadway (about the only kind of road there was at that time). They took turns driving and rarely went faster than Henry in the horse-drawn wagon. At one point, they stopped and allowed Henry to drive the Ford while his sister, Sudie, drove the horse and wagon. Glorious! Henry enjoyed it so much. But that didn't last long. Sudie soon stopped and got back into the Ford, and Henry drove the horse and wagon on home. Once home, everyone carefully looked at the Ford and admired it. They opened the front and checked on the engine; they looked at how to put in gasoline and use a crank to start the engine.

Both Carrie and Ira took turns trying to drive, as well as the four older children. Ira was not very good at it. In fact, Ira never learned to competently operate a motor vehicle. The accelerator, clutch, shift knob and lever, brakes, and steering all posed obstacles. Steering was a problem most of all; he could not see the direction the wheels were turned because of the fenders. He said he wanted to remove the front fenders so he could see the wheels and drive better, but he never did. Nobody appeared to be more skillful in driving than 13-year-old Henry.

Everyone in the family seemed to enjoy riding and driving the vehicle, even though only wagon trails and dusty farm roads were used. The family members were, as the old saying goes, "in high cotton." Those first years of the 1920s were good for the family. But, something kept telling the family that this couldn't last forever!

Ira and Carrie Lee standing beside 1923 Ford Touring Car.

A low period followed relatively good economic times during the early 1920s, and those times made it seem severe. By the late 1920s, industrial markets far away from the nation's farms were beginning to fall apart, and investors were losing money. (Because of this, Henry always said that buying stock was like rolling dice.) Factories were laying off workers and closing. People could not get money for food and clothing. People in towns and cities sometimes faced starvation. Times became very tight economically on farms, including the Lee farm. Many farms focused more on subsistence than on producing products for markets.

The Great Depression began arriving with the stock market crash of 1929. The crash, however, was not the only factor that created the Depression. Hard times fully arrived in the early 1930s. Henry was a young adult at this time.

Major national efforts led by President Franklin D. Roosevelt were put in place by the federal government to cope with the effects of the Depression. Thank goodness for the leadership of Roosevelt!

Henry assessed how well he thought the farming operation was going—that is, the degree to which it was making money, if any. He approached his father, Ira, in the late winter of 1933. Henry said, "I am worried about the farm. Are we going to be able to keep it going?"

Ira hesitantly responded, "You know I am, too. I am worried. I have stayed awake at night trying to figure out possibilities. We could plant a little more cotton acreage, but then there is the danged pesky boll weevil. What do you think?"

Henry thought and said, "I don't know. Maybe we could expand into growing more sugar cane; we now have only a few rows. Some farms are planting small patches. Maybe we could get a juicer mill and cook pan. We could make syrup; city folks call the kind of syrup we make molasses. It is good stuff made from Louisiana Ribbon Cane juice! The syrup could be placed in gallon cans and sold. You know a few hundred gallons could certainly help out when sold for the big price of a dollar a gallon."

In the late 1920s, a few rows of sugar cane were started on the farm. This cane was harvested for sale as chewing cane in the fall. Some people really liked the sweetness of juice inside the stalk. This cane growing gave a little experience in how to plant and harvest the crop; much of the production and harvesting fell to Henry. He was intrigued by sugar cane and felt it was like growing some kind of big grass. His interest continued.

Along with a few other potential producers in the community, Henry went to a meeting on sugar cane production held by the local county agricultural agent on a farm in nearby Madison County. The event was an early 1931 field day that covered planting, growing, harvesting, juicing, cooking, and canning. The county agent said he would follow up with on-farm visits to provide individual help for those who wanted it.

Henry learned the details of how to plant and grow sugar cane. He did follow up on the meeting and invited the county agent to come to the farm and help select the small fields to use. Planting was done in the spring by placing stalks or sections of stalks from last season flat in a furrow and plowing loose soil over them. In a couple of weeks, the nodes on the stalks would sprout, and grasslike plants would emerge. Over summer, the stalks would grow to 10 or more feet tall. Weeds were pulled by hand or cut from the field with a hoe. A few good showers were needed to promote growth. Some dryness late in the season promoted sugar formation.

Harvest was another important part of sugar cane farming that Henry learned. It took place in the fall after the stalks had matured and sugar was stored in the sap of the plant. Harvesting was done using a cane knife (machete), but this required great care to prevent personal injury. A cane knife was a couple feet long with a thin, sharp blade attached to a wooden handle. Some cane knives had small hooks on the end to use in picking up cut cane stalks. The knives were rapidly swung to slash cane stalks from their roots at ground level. They were then used to trim the bladelike leaves from the stalks.

Not only was the harvest knife hazardous, but the leaves on the stalks had sharp edges that could cut human skin and injure eyes. Long sleeves and heavy long pants, along with a hat and gloves, were worn when doing this work. Cut stalks were loaded onto a wagon and hauled to the place on the farm where juicing and cooking would be done.

Henry quickly learned about juicing stalks and cooking the cane juice. This was entirely new to him. He selected a site some 100 yards in front of the home for the juicing mill and cooking pan. He ordered a juicing mill and cooking pan through a general mercantile store in the nearby village of Pocahontas. He installed the mill on posts about four feet above the ground. The area around the mill had to provide a radius of twenty or so feet of free space. Juicing involved using a mill with three heavy iron rollers about eight inches in diameter and fifteen inches long. The rollers were mounted in an iron frame so that they almost touched each other. A long wooden pole was attached to the shaft at the top of the mill. Gears applied turning motion from the shaft to the rollers.

A mule, usually a gray one named Frank on the Lee farm, was hitched to the end of the pole and made to walk in a circle. This turned the rollers so that when stalks of cane were pushed endwise one after the other, the rollers would pull the stalks through. The turning, pressing rollers would squeeze juice out of the stalks. The juice would be channeled into a collection barrel and crushed stalks sent out the other side of the mill. As a dependable and strong mule, Frank had the physical traits to go round and round pulling the pole for hours at a time without stopping or having to be directed to pull and do the work.

The collected juice was strained to remove impurities and placed in a large, flat syrup-cooking pan. Henry was responsible for coming up with a plan and materials to build a fire pit under the 5-by-10-foot, 8-inch-deep pan about fifty feet from the mill. This involved using brick for the pit and building a pole shed over the cooking pan. The metal pan was designed to fit on the brick fire pit and use a wood fire built underneath to heat the twenty or so gallons of juice in the pan at any one time. Heat evaporated much of the water in the juice to create a thickened and sweet molasses. The molasses would be dipped out of the pan and placed in clay jugs or metal gallon cans. Cooked and canned molasses was used on the farm as well as sold by the gallon to individuals and stores in Jackson.

The first year of sugar cane and molasses production was good. Production was nearly 100 gallons. The extra hundred dollars from its sale was certainly helpful to a family living on very little in difficult economic times.

Henry thought that more was needed for the farm to survive and for the Lee family to be fed and clothed. He knew about some of the programs being established under the direction of President Roosevelt. He was happy he voted the Democratic ticket to help re-elect Roosevelt as President. One public relief effort established by the federal government in 1933 was the Civilian Conservation Corps (CCC). It was for unemployed and unmarried men from families that needed financial help. The men were provided shelter, clothing, and food, along with a small wage of $30 per month, of which $25 had to be sent home to their families. The men were unskilled workers who planted trees, created trails, constructed lodges in national parks, and did other useful work in some 800 parks nationwide. Henry thought about this a little, but his family didn't qualify for him to join. He had to figure out other opportunities.

Somewhat along the line of the CCC, the U.S. Congress created the Works Progress Administration (WPA) in 1935. Millions of unskilled men were hired to do public works projects, such as the construction of public buildings and roads. The goal was to create paying jobs and alleviate human suffering in helping end the Depression. Again, Henry, as result of living and working on a farm, did not readily qualify for a WPA job. He was rapidly getting beyond the age of participating in another program known as the National Youth Administration (NYA), which was for the youngest men. The NYA was also created in 1935 to aid young men in getting jobs, as the rate of unemployment nationwide was around 30 percent. (Note: The CCC, WPA, and NYA programs were discontinued in 1943. At that time, the World War II effort provided full employment.)

Henry didn't give up searching for a way he could supplement money coming to his needy family on the farm. By the mid-1930s, he still had three sisters living at home. He tried not to become discouraged. After all, farm life allowed a great deal of self-sufficiency. In fact, the family produced much of its food on the farm.

Henry heard that the local railroad office in Pocahontas was hiring a few young men to work in track construction and maintenance. He had many of the kinds of skills the railroad needed. He applied and got a job. His regular pay was a great benefit to the family. In addition, he qualified for Railroad Social Security. The unique R and 700 number designated him all the remaining years of his life as having Railroad Social Security before Social Security for all was in existence.

While working for the railroad, Henry worked part time on the farm. After all, he was the only adult man around to help Ira with the farm and supervise the sharecroppers. After a couple of years, Henry made the tough decision to leave the railroad work and return full time to the farm and its four sharecropper families. Of course, the railroad pay was beneficial to the family, but his father's failing health resulted in some work on the farm not getting done.

The ups and downs of the farm economy are sometimes tied to nonfarm ups and downs; others exist independently in the agricultural industry. Getting the first automobile was certainly a part of a major "up," but things soon began to fall apart. Before the downturn was over, things would go about as low as possible.

4

Running to the House

Times were changing. Farms were going away from mule power and to "running" things. Not everyone wanted change. Sometimes new things caused disagreements; other times changes were readily accepted. Regardless, the Lee family humbly tried a few of the new "runnings."

The beginning of the replacement of animal power with mechanical power was now underway. The farm tractors of the 1930s did not have a lot of power, but they were replacing mules and oxen on some farms. The tractors were cumbersome and mostly used to pull implements (not many attachments, such as planters and sprayers, were available). Henry talked to people who had tried a tractor; he gathered information and talked to his father about getting a tractor.

"Papa, you know I've seen a couple of tractors in operation," Henry said, "and I even drove one for a few minutes over on the Middleton farm. I think one would be useful to us. And, remember how long it took us to get that Ford? We have really enjoyed the car."

Ira replied, "I hear that tractors cost a lot of money. You know, we are poor folks; don't have no money. A big depression is going on. Crop prices are down." After a pause to let this soak in, he continued. "Henry, what do you really know about engines and how to keep them going? What if one breaks down or if a wheel loses a lug?"

After a couple of minutes, Henry replied, "I can handle most of those things with what I know. I am friends with a couple of men who work with tractors. They can teach me what I don't know. It is like this: I can do about anything with my hands and arms. My two hands have worked together well." Henry continued, "I consider myself good with mechanical kinds of things, like using tools, figuring out how something works and what is wrong when it doesn't, and hitching machinery. Let's get a dealer of Farmall or Avery tractors to demonstrate one here on the place." Ira reluctantly agreed. A demonstration wouldn't cost anything.

The next time Henry was in Jackson, he went by the Farmall dealer on Gallatin Street and talked with a salesman. Henry told a little about the farm and asked which tractor might be best. The salesman suggested a general-purpose tricycle type with steel front and rear wheels. He showed one to Henry and cranked the engine. He said he would be happy to bring a tractor for demonstration on the farm. So they set the following Thursday morning as the day for the first tractor ever to be brought onto the Lee farm. Henry told where the farm was located in the Tinnin community. The salesman said he would bring a disk harrow attached to the tractor. Now Henry knew there was one thing he had to get straight: What did the tractor cost? The salesman scratched his head a bit and said, "The tractor you are looking at costs about $535 without any extras you might get. The disc harrow is an additional $81." So they shook hands, and Henry left saying that he would look forward to next Thursday.

It was time for dinner when Henry got back to the Lee farm. Seated at the kitchen table were Ira, Carrie, and Henry, along with Henry's two youngest sisters, Edna and Lyda. Henry mentioned his day and how he had arranged for a Mr. Quimby of the McCormick-Deering Tractor Business in Jackson to come to the farm on Thursday and demonstrate a Farmall tractor. Henry said the man would haul it to the farm on an International Harvester bob truck, and he would unload it by backing up to the gully near the cane mill.

Now, this was the first time that Carrie had heard anything about a tractor for the Lee farm being discussed. As she was prone to do, she "flew off the handle," disrupting the meal.

"No!" she shouted. "No! Ain't no tractor gonna be on this place. Whose idea is it?" There was a moment of silence. Carrie spoke again: "Who can drive it? How will we pay for it? We ain't got no money." More silence, as people gave her some time to get over her temper fit. Over the years, everyone had become accustomed to such behavior.

Carrie continued in a loud and irritated tone of voice: "Tractors make a lot of noise, scare the mules and hens, and require gas. My hens may even stop laying the eggs that are so needed by the family. Those darn lugs on the steel wheels dig up the farm trails; they make little holes in the ground everywhere the tractor goes. Tractors shake the ground and may cause our pigs to break out of their pens!"

Henry had been silent long enough; he had seen her angry many times before. He thought about how to deal with Carrie's anger in this situation and began to speak. "Mama, be reasonable. Tractors are beginning to replace mules. We don't want to get behind other farms in how crops are done. A tractor can do way more work than a man with a mule-pulled plow. You don't have to feed them, though they do use gasoline. The mules and hens will quickly adjust to the noise."

Carrie interrupted, "Where did you come up with that silly bull dung? At the Ratliff Store I have seen dogs, chickens, and people run from a silly tractor. It just clunks along and always sounds like the engine is about to stop running. Anyway, who here can operate the darn thing and keep it running?" Edna and Lyda said nothing and slunk down in their chairs until the storm their mother had created was over. Ira mostly kept quiet but did say, "Now, Carrie, Henry has learned some things about tractors, and he knows a couple of men who are good with them. I think Henry can both drive and maintain a tractor. We also have at least one sharecropper I feel can drive a tractor." Carrie snorted a big "Ha!" in referring to Henry's skills. Just like always, she disparaged Henry's abilities.

Ira did not like Carrie's degrading their adult son's mechanical skills. He spoke: "Carrie, Henry has got a lot of farm ability. He can do many things. His hands and arms work well in doing things. Henry, hold out your two hands. Now, Mama Carrie, those hands are very capable of doing about anything. Some days I think you should be put where your daddy was when we got married. You know what I am talking about. Remember, he got out of the insane asylum just for the day of the wedding and then he went right back."

"What about that awful danger?" Carrie asked. "I hear that a tractor can turn over and kill the driver. I hear that some of the things hooked to tractors can injure or kill people. You know, those newfangled devices are dangerous. I heard that there was a man near Pocahontas got his leg cut off when a wheel ran over him. Over toward Clinton, a tractor ran over a nice pig and killed it; couldn't be used for anything because it was so smashed and torn up. We do not need such a thing around here. The more I think about it, the closer I am to cussing. You know, when I start cussing, I can really get it done. Damn!"

Everyone at the table stayed quiet and tried to finish the meal. The family members gradually got up and left to sit on the porch or do other things; anyway, they drifted away from the table and the presence of Carrie. The two girls went to wash the dishes. Carrie went to sit in her chair in the bedroom in her usual sulking way. Ira and Henry went outside to sit on the porch and talk some more. Henry reviewed how Mr. Quimby was bringing the tractor with one implement—a disk harrow. A small land area would be needed for the demonstration. He repeated that the tractor would cost about $535 without implements. Since it was early March, having a tractor would certainly be good in preparing cropland for planting. Less time would be needed than if it were prepared using mules and plows.

Thursday morning came; Carrie was still pouting. Folks knew her pouting would pass just as it always had. A truck appeared on the farm road driven by Mr. Quimby. It had a tractor and disk harrow on it. The tractor wasn't much bigger or heavier than a good-sized mule, and much of its weight was in the rear wheels. Mr. Quimby cranked it, unloaded it, and proceeded to go over how to check the engine oil, add fuel, start the engine (using a hand crank at the front under the radiator), and make it move forward and backward. He let Henry drive it around a bit; Ira wouldn't try. The lugs on the steel wheels made it kind of clunky. Ira said the clunkiness hurt his insides.

Then Mr. Quimby hooked it to the disk harrow in the edge of a pea patch to show how it would aid in preparing the soil for planting; no mule was needed. During all this, Carrie peered off the porch at what was taking place a couple hundred yards away. She fumed, stomped her feet, and muttered. She probably said some of the cuss words she had promised, but no one was there to hear.

One of the features Mr. Quimby reviewed was the belt pulley on the right side of the tractor about halfway between the engine and the rear wheels. He told how a belt could be placed around the pulley and extended around the pulley of another piece of machinery. When the engine on the tractor ran and the gear of the belt pulley was engaged, the belt would rotate, turning the pulley and the shaft on the implement. Mr. Quimby told how some farmers were finding this a very useful feature in grinding corn.

Tractor similar to the one demonstrated on the Lee farm in the 1930s. (Note the prominent belting pulley on the side in front of the rear wheel.)

Mr. Quimby also mentioned safety. He cautioned against driving the tractor where the ground was wet and told how the steel wheels could spin slightly, causing the tractor to bog down. He said a fence post or other heavy wood piece could be placed next to a lug and the tractor would lift itself up from the muddy bog. (It was never mentioned that the wheels might spin the wood piece around so that it hit the driver; severe injury could result.)

The demonstration was over. Mr. Quimby asked if he should leave the tractor and disk harrow with them. Henry was ready for it; Ira wasn't. Mr. Quimby loaded the tractor and disk harrow on the truck and started the drive back to the Farmall dealership. Getting a tractor was an important decision. The family might have to sacrifice a few things.

As Mr. Quimby drove the truck loaded with the tractor and disk harrow up the hill and onto the main road, Carrie came to life again with her opposition to a proposed tractor on the farm. She talked and shouted at anyone who was within her range. One of her big matters on this day was that she needed an icebox in the home. She didn't have one. She improvised a double-walled two-foot square wooden box with an inch of sawdust between the walls to serve as insulation. The box had a top hinged so that it could be opened to place a block of ice inside. She wanted a state-of-the-art, three-door oak icebox made by the American Company so that she could buy ice on Friday and Tuesday, when the ice truck came through the community.

Carrie cornered Ira as he came in for lunch. "I need an icebox more than the farm needs a ridiculous tractor," she said. "Everyone in the family can benefit from an icebox. Just think, we could have ice for sweet tea and other uses." Of course, the notion of iced sweet tea sounded good to Ira, particularly after work on a warm day in the field. Carrie continued, "Don't expect me to be making tea for you if you get the tractor before the icebox."

Henry sat down for his lunch. His mother jumped him with scorn about the possibility of a tractor. Her tactic (one she had used before) was to talk about safety and how tractors cause injury. She said, "A man in Bolton was driving a tractor with his small boy riding on it. The boy fell to the ground, and a big lugged steel wheel rolled over his leg." She continued, "It was very serious. The boy hasn't walked right in two years and likely never will. Aren't you afraid of driving a tractor?"

Henry thought a few moments and responded, "Mama, safety is important. The demonstration we had included safety. I am confident that I can operate the tractor and use its power so that no one is injured."

"Getting hurt is something you really need to think about

before buying a tractor." Carrie continued, "Mules are much safer; they don't have wheels." Of course, she didn't mention that mules could deliver serious kicks or make blood-producing bites. That would have compromised her story.

Henry didn't talk back, though he knew that mules could cause injury to people. He quickly finished lunch, got his mule at the stable, and went back to the field.

Carrie soon saw that the safety objection tactic, though very important, was not working. She then spoke about a daughter, Edna, getting ready for marriage and how the family needed extra money to help with this once-in-a-lifetime event. Weddings of previous daughters didn't rate a high allocation of resources, and this one would likely be no different. But, to Carrie, it sounded like a good excuse for not getting a tractor. Additionally, Carrie usually became highly emotional at the time of the marriages of her daughters, so saving money for a wedding didn't rate very highly among the Lee men as an objection to getting a tractor for the farm. Henry wondered whether his mother really cared about the marriages of her daughters.

Next, Carrie brought up the need to get running water into the house. She remembered something about a plan discussed a few times over the years to use gravity flow in a three-quarter-inch pipe to move water from a spring high up in the woods to the house. The distance was nearly 2,000 feet. There was no electricity in the area and wouldn't be to most places in the Tinnin community for another fifteen years. She said, "That is wonderful spring water. Remember that we talked about this over the years." She continued by saying, "Henry, don't you remember the idea? Tell me what you think about it."

Henry heard her and did remember some of the details. With a little stammering to collect his thoughts, Henry responded by reviewing what had been planned but not done a couple of years earlier. Henry said, "The way I figure is that we could capture water in a barrel or tank as it comes from the ground at the spring. The bottom of the barrel would have a pipe in it so that the water flowed out and into the pipe." Henry continued, "The water would flow by gravity through the long pipe sections down the hillsides along the spring branch and to the house, where it would run into a large barrel or tank. The barrel could be on posts about eight or more feet high. This would create just enough pressure for the water to flow out of the tank. A faucet could be placed into one side of the barrel at the bottom for getting water. Or, maybe, a pipe could be run to a faucet in the kitchen of the house."

"You have a good memory," Carrie said, "and that is what I want." She continued by asking, "How much will it cost? How will we get it put in? Do you know anything about using pipe?"

"Well, if you are really interested," Henry replied, "I will check on supplies and costs the next time I go into Jackson."

"Yes, I am interested." Carrie said. "Do it soon."

Henry indicated that he would. He figured that his mother could more likely tolerate a tractor if she got the water she wanted. One thing the men didn't need was for Carrie to be continually griping and complaining to them about wasting money on a tractor once it was bought.

A few days passed. Henry told Carrie that he was going into Jackson to check on pipe and fittings for the water system. While there, he did some other things: he investigated tractors some more by visiting an Avery dealer. The tractors were similar to Farmalls but cost a bit less. One reason for lower cost was that instead of two wheels in front, the Avery had one right in the middle under the radiator frame. The one wheel was slightly larger and sat straight rather than angled toward the middle, as with a Farmall. Ira and Henry were invited to a demonstration of the Avery at a nearby farm. They went and reached a decision without involving Carrie; they knew what she would probably do.

- 53 -

A general-purpose, gasoline-powered Avery row-crop tractor was bought in 1938. This slow-moving, steel-wheeled tractor could pull wagons and plow land with a one-furrow moldboard plow, a single-gang disc harrow, or a sectional spike-tooth harrow. The rear steel wheels had lugs for gripping the ground and producing forward movement. The front steel wheel was smooth and round to direct tractor movement. A selling point given by the dealership was that the steel wheels could be replaced with rubber-tired wheels at some future time when they became available, but Ira and Henry did not think they would do so. A tractor left a lot of work still to be done with animal power, primarily mules. Single-row planters, fertilizer distributors, and cultivators used mules for power. A man with strength and stamina could walk behind and guide an implement and direct the mule. The mule-pulled cultivator could be maneuvered to take out weeds and leave the crop plants.

Most farm tractors of the day, such as Farmall, Case, Avery, and Fordson, had a large belt pulley on the side between the engine and the transmission. The Avery the Lees bought was no exception. Gears and a shaft connected the pulley with the drive train of the parked tractor. A large belt could be used around the pulley to transfer rotating power from the belt pulley to another pulley on equipment a few feet away. One of the implements that could be operated with belt-pulley power was the hammer mill.

The tractor was purchased with a loan from the Bank of Clinton. The promissory note was to be paid off when the cotton was harvested that fall. The shiny new tractor was delivered, and Carrie saw it arrive. She flew into a frenzy. Most of all, she harped on wasting money on a tractor without having running water in the house. She screamed and hollered incoherently. It never occurred to her that she didn't fix any supper for the family, so each person ate leftover cold greens with old corn bread intended as dog food soaked with lard from frying pork sausage. Finally, Ira and Henry promised they would get water running to the house next year after the fall harvest. She needed to calm down; she did a bit. She wound up going to bed exhausted from her tirade.

Careful measurement was made of the distance from the spring to the house using a surveyor's chain. Steps were taken to minimize the amount of pipe needed. So, on July 21, 1939, 1,860 feet of three-quarter inch galvanized iron pipe, along with coupling fittings to connect the pipe joints, were purchased from the National Hide and Fur Company in Jackson for a total of $123.30, which included sales tax and $1.50 to make delivery to the Lee farm. Following delivery, Henry, Ira, and farm workers proceeded to install the pipeline and tanks on each end.

Finally, installation of the water pipe was finished, and the water was flowing. The system worked, but its long-term operation would require more maintenance than anticipated to clean out sand, remove debris from the barrels, and, in cold weather, repair pipes that burst from freezing. Carrie was as satisfied with the water system outcome as she ever was with anything. But, it was no more than a pipe that brought water from the spring to the yard at the house. No fixtures were initially installed in the house. Water was gotten in a cedarwood bucket from a faucet at the bottom of the tank in the yard.

The tractor had been providing power for plowing and other farm work for more than a year. Everyone (except Carrie) seemed pleased. There had been no breakdowns and no injuries caused by the tractor. When not in use, the tractor was kept in a shed. Henry serviced the engine and provided clean fuel. The tractor was always operated safely. Of course, it moved slowly and kind of just clunked along. Folks on the Lee farm thought about more ways the tractor could help, such as pulling a mechanical seed planter, pulling a tractor-mounted cultivator, and having mowing machines and rakes attached for use in hay harvest.

As thoughts began to turn to other ways the tractor could be useful, one was with a hammer mill. Hammer mills were becoming more popular for grinding corn and other grains and fodder. The mill design of the late 1930s was a base made of heavy iron and a top hopper made of thin sheet metal. A belt pulley on the sturdy base received rotating power via the belt connected to the tractor's power pulley. The strong belt was about four inches wide. The belt would move at a fairly high rate of speed. Screens or sieves in the mill could be changed to vary the size of the finished ground product. For example, a fine screen was used to grind cornmeal for human food, and a coarser screen was used to grind corn chops for feeding chickens. A lot of power was transferred in a rotating motion from the tractor's engine to the flailing hammers of the mill that reduced larger particles of grain to smaller particles of feed or food materials. To some folks, this machinery sounded downright scary. However, water-powered stone mills would no longer be needed.

The danger with a hammer mill was not so much from the high speed of the enclosed flailing hammers as it was from the belt that transferred power from the tractor engine to the rotating hammers. Some belts had guards that kept them out of normal human finger, hand, and arm range; others didn't. Not a lot of emphasis was placed on safety with a hammer mill, for it didn't have wheels and move about; it stayed in place. Just as with most things, Ira and Henry did not rush out to get one. They knew that the Ratliff Store in Tinnin had one with a Farmall tractor belted pulley-to-pulley that was sometimes made available for use by other people. So, they would try to "borrow" access to a hammer mill for the next year or so. And, that worked pretty well, with a small rental payment made for its use—often a portion of the meal or chops that were ground.

Family and farm problems and opportunities were addressed with "running." And that was running water for the house and a running tractor for the field. The water system wasn't complete but did result in spring water being available at the house. The tractor was started with a crank and, with its steel wheels, could go from house to field and back. Things should get better.

5

Gaining a Life Partner

"You are now joined together as Man and Wife in the holy state of wedlock," spoke the Reverend B. M. Hunt as he finished the exchange of marriage vows with the couple. He continued, "You are now Mr. and Mrs. Lee. The groom and bride may kiss."

Doris Elaine Sloan, age 25, and Jasper Henry Lee, age 30, were about to be brought together in marriage. Henry knew he should get Doris a diamond ring and a wedding band. The couple had talked a little about rings, but money was tight. Fortunately, Henry had a helpful brother-in-law who ran a jewelry store on Capitol Street in Jackson, Mississippi, very near the major train depot. The store was well known for its work and integrity. In fact, it was so good that it was designated as the official railroad watch repair business in the city. The brother-in-law knew how to assess ring and diamond quality and establish a fair price.

A ring was chosen, and Henry paid cash for it. A few weeks before the wedding, he gave Doris the diamond ring to commemorate their engagement. It was a very nice secondhand ring that had been on the finger of a previous bride. In the back of his mind, Henry wondered about the earlier wearer—what she was like and what happened to her marriage. He told himself that when times were better, he would get Doris a new diamond ring.

Jasper Henry Lee and Doris Elaine Sloan, 1939.
(A year before their marriage.)

At the same time Henry purchased the engagement ring, he also bought Doris a wedding band for the ceremony. The couple agreed that she would not get a wedding band for him, as he felt he would only lose it somewhere around the farm. Besides they needed money to move ahead in their lives, such as to set up housekeeping.

On August 3, 1940, in the home of the Reverend Hunt (he was pastor of the Capitol Street Methodist Episcopal Church in Jackson), the marriage was solemnized in the presence of several family members and friends. The attendants were Edna Earle

Lee Huddleston (sister of the groom) and her husband, Brunner M. Huddleston. The newlyweds had obtained their marriage license only the day before from Hinds County Circuit Clerk Bubba Ashford. The ceremony was simple and demonstrated love and commitment between two individuals who formed a handsome couple. A newspaper account of the wedding indicated that it was a single-ring exchange of wedding vows.

Doris was very happy with the first diamond ring and wore it for about fifteen years. Then, Henry went to the same brother-in-law's jewelry store and bought her a new one with a somewhat larger diamond. Now, there would be no more wondering about the previous wearer and why the ring had become available fifteen years ago.

Doris grew up in Rankin County, Mississippi, and was fortunate to go to high school and college. She attended Central High School in Jackson, though she lived a distance away in Rankin County. She rode into Central each day with a person who worked in the state Capitol, which was quite near the school. The high school served the white citizens of Jackson; another high school served minorities, who were not allowed to attend Central High School because of unfortunate racial segregation. Outlying county areas did not have much in the way of secondary education. After high school, Doris attended Belhaven College in Jackson and graduated with a major in French (no one could ever explain why it was French!) in 1936. She then taught school. Two years of her teaching were at the Tinnin School, where she lived in the teacher's home and became somewhat acquainted with the community. She met Henry while living in Tinnin.

Henry had a home for the new couple to begin their lives together. It was in the house where he grew up, now shared with his parents, a sister, and one of his mother's sisters, Susie Hendrick Heckle. Henry and Doris had two rooms: a bedroom that doubled as a living room and a kitchen with eating area. There was no bathroom. Occasionally another relative would temporarily live in the house while dealing with some sort of personal problem, such as a wayward husband.

The house, which was plenty large enough, was built as a cotton plantation home in 1857 by Henry's great-grandfather George W. Shepard. It had virtually no conveniences, such as electricity, a plumbing system, and adequate heat. The small wood heaters and a couple of fireplaces for the large rooms with high ceilings were inadequate to warm the place. Screen wire and paned window glass had been placed over the large window openings so that the shutters no longer had to be closed at night, in bad weather, or to keep out flying pests. A two-holer outhouse was behind the house, and a little more distant in another direction were a smokehouse and several barn structures, along with a shed for the car. Beyond that was an animal lot where horses, mules, and other animals were temporarily kept. With regard to hogs, some would be put into a small pasture, and others in a pen if they were being fattened for slaughter.

The house still had what Carrie had long advocated: spring water running to it through a conglomeration of long pipes that ended at a barrel sitting up on poles outside the back porch. For his new bride, Henry ran one pipe from the barrel across the yard and through the wall into the room used as a kitchen. A faucet was put on the end of the pipe located over a small enamel-clad sink. A drainpipe went from the bottom of the sink through the floor and across the yard, where it discharged at the edge of the cow pasture. The couple viewed themselves as fortunate to have this limited running water and a sink in their home.

Doris had a higher expectation for her home than had been the standard in the Lee-Shepard home. Maybe it was because she was a college graduate or because she could earn some of the money needed to buy what she wanted and not simply depend on a man to earn it for her. She wanted to have "store-bought" furniture and make her home neat, reasonably classy, and presentable. Before marriage, she and Henry bought a bedroom suite with double bed, dresser and mirror, and bench to go with the dresser. Doris would use the dresser. They got a chest of drawers that Henry would use. This wasn't an extravagant investment in furniture, but Doris wanted something that would last. She took good care of it, too. It looked as good as possible in a nearly 100-year-old room with high ceilings and few finishing touches. There were no closets in their bedroom. A couple of corners had strong twine stretched diagonally across from a nail on one wall to a nail on another wall. Clothes were hung on the twine. Later, Doris put a curtain on a rod to shield the hanging clothes from view.

Doris had temporarily lived with electricity, though she grew up without it. Her first introduction to electricity was while she was a student at Belhaven College. She thought it was kind of nice but with little use except for lighting and a few other things. Uses still needed to be developed and manufactured. President Franklin D. Roosevelt and Congress created the Rural Electric Administration (REA) in 1935 to take electricity to the rural areas of the country, including central Mississippi.

In the early 1940s, no electric lines had been extended to Tinnin. Rural electric cooperatives were just forming in much of rural Mississippi. The one created to serve the area where the Tinnin community was located was the Capital Electric Power Association of Clinton. Doris would have to get along without electricity in her home for a few years.

Light at night dark for the young Lee family was provided by a couple of coal oil lamps. With flat wicks, the lamps worked to provide light by absorbing and bringing the kerosene fuel to a small flame enclosed by a clear, open-top glass globe. The lamps were lighted each evening and blown out at bedtime. Early morning, they would be lighted again if still dark when Doris and Henry began their day. The lamps would be carried from one room to the other, as needed, such as from the bedroom to the kitchen and back.

Every now and then, Henry and someone (often one of his brothers-in-law) would get into a discussion over the difference between coal oil and kerosene. In use, there was little difference, though they were distinctly different substances. Coal oil was first introduced in the United States in the early 1800s and was made from particular kinds of coal; kerosene was made from petroleum oil. The first kerosene was made in Canada in the 1850s and given the proper name of Kerosene. This soon led to large-scale refining of kerosene from petroleum, and by the 1860s, about all so-called coal oil was actually kerosene. The name "coal oil" was no longer applicable, though it was used for many years. Kerosene was the product used in the 1940s.

Carrie and Doris had separate kitchens in their areas of the house. Neither was modern at all. Until Doris and Henry's marriage, most families in the house got by on kitchen items from the era when the house was constructed. Doris wanted more, however, and Henry wanted her to have it. Henry had farmed for years and was able to put back a little money. Doris had taught school, and though the salary was low, she had lived in the teacher's home and saved some of her money. Carrie did not agree that Doris should have these modern things; she wanted Doris to go about food preparation just like it was done at the turn of the twentieth century or before in the house. Carrie ranted about Doris wasting money on buying newfangled household things. Of course, Doris and Henry were frugal; they bought from a store on Farish Street in Jackson where prices were lower than at stores on "highfalutin" Capitol Street.

Henry and Doris agreed on four items and bought them for

their kitchen. They bought a kerosene-fueled cookstove with four burners and an oven. What an innovation over the old cast-iron wood-burning stoves of the previous generations! Neighbor families came over to the Lee-Shepard house to see a kind of stove they had not seen before. The stove had a large clear glass globe that held kerosene; typically, a filled globe would last maybe a week for Doris. The globe was placed upside down in a bracket on the "cool" end of the stove and would release just the right amount of kerosene. Its location was above the burners so that the kerosene flowed to each burner by gravity through small pipes or tubes. With this stove, there was no more waiting for the wood to start burning and warm the heavy iron of the stove. Only a match was needed to start a burner or the oven. Safety was always important.

Another kitchen item the newly married Lees bought was an icebox with a compartment for a fifty-pound block of ice and two other compartments that were kept cool by the presence of the ice. Occasionally a truck would pass through the Tinnin community selling ice. Otherwise, someone would drive to an icehouse in Clinton and buy a block of ice. At the icehouse, they would carefully wrap the ice with a couple of burlap sacks and put it in a tub in the back of the car. At home, the ice would be placed in the proper compartment of the icebox. Pieces would be chipped off with an ice pick and used for cooling sweet tea or for making homemade ice cream. Over time, a part of the ice block would melt, and the water would collect in a pan at the bottom of the icebox. Every now and then the pan had to be emptied. Filling of the pan was an indication that it was time to buy more ice. Rather than tossing the water out, it was used around plants or, sometimes, to add to the dog-watering pan. Occasionally a five-gallon can to buy kerosene for the stove would be taken on the same day as the trip to the icehouse.

After a year with the icebox, Doris and Henry bought a secondhand kerosene-operated refrigerator because it sounded like a good thing to have. After a short while, they learned why it was available secondhand: it didn't work satisfactorily. It was taken out of the house and abandoned in a big gully used for waste disposal. They went back to using the icebox.

Doris and Henry also bought a small dinette set. The table was just right for their kitchen. It was made with a metal tabletop and wooden legs. The metal top had a coating of heavy enamel to resist wear and maintain an attractive appearance. Four matching chairs came with the table as part of the set. Also, for the kitchen, they bought a cupboard. In this case, it was a stand-alone piece of kitchen furniture with shelves and doors. Dishes, food items, and other kitchen devices could be stored in it. There was an old food safe that they acquired from Carrie when she no longer wanted the "deplorable thing." (That is how she described it to Doris, as she appeared not to want Doris to have anything decent.) So, the couple's kitchen was fairly well appointed for the big old house without the conveniences of running water, a plumbing system, and electricity.

As soon as they got a little money, Doris and Henry bought a few more pieces of furniture for their meager home. All furniture was of the same approximate style, color, etc. The new things included a wardrobe (chifforobe) with two doors. Drawers were at the bottom on one side. The wardrobe was put in their bedroom. It was purchased so that the clothing hanging on twine stretched across the corner of the room behind curtains could be hung elsewhere. They also bought a dining table with chairs, a buffet, and a china cabinet that was placed in one end of the long, wide hall just outside their two rooms.

Doris set about getting something labeled "fine china" and, about the same time, sterling silver tableware. Certainly, in the old Lee-Shepard home, she wasn't going to be doing much entertaining, but it was just an element of trying to raise social status of young folks who had grown up during the Great Depression. Doris gained

personal satisfaction from owning household furnishings that neither her family nor the Lee-Shepard family had ever had. Most of
the previous furnishings in the home had been rustic, homemade
belongings. They had at least some usefulness, although they might
be thought of as borderline junk. Just this little progress with their
home provided Doris and Henry much hope for their lives together.

The next furniture was a sofa (that could be made into a bed)
with an end table and a couple of side chairs. One of the small
items Doris bought that was coordinated with the furniture was
a magazine rack. This was important to her. She liked magazines.
Look, Life, and *The Saturday Evening Post* were among the ti-
tles she subscribed to and always looked forward to arriving in
the mail. She was not that interested in news magazines, as the
battery-powered radio would give enough of the political and war
stories. Interestingly, many years later when she had to dispose of
her household belongings because of poor health and inability to
live independently, she kept the magazine rack. It went wherever
she had to go for her needed life care.

Henry was highly confident of his ability to move forward with
his newly forming family and earn income for a good standard of
rural country living. He felt he could do just about anything!

At the time of his and Doris's marriage, Henry was well into
farming and running the Lee-Shepard farm in partnership with his
father. Unfortunately, his father was experiencing declining health.
More responsibility for the farm had to be taken on by Henry to
support his new family as well as his parents. Doris, now that she
was married, could not hold a teaching job in a public school.
State law in Mississippi prohibited married women from teaching
in the public schools. This was too bad; she was an excellent and
well-prepared teacher who had to quit and become a full-time
homemaker and, maybe, a mother.

Doris was not much into farming, though she did help some

with the garden in planting, cultivating, and harvesting produce. She had the responsibility for running the couple's two-room living quarters in the big house, not easy with her mother-in-law so close by. Carrie did not like some of the things Doris talked about doing to make things better. Ira really did not care about organization of the house. He just wanted folks to get along with each other. With Carrie involved, getting along always took extra patience. Sometimes it seemed she preferred disagreement over harmony.

October arrived. Fall harvest was well underway on the farm. Doris thought she was pregnant, or, as they might say in the local area, "with child." With a college education, Doris knew about the importance of proper care by a qualified physician who could assure that she and her baby were thriving. At first, she used a general physician in Clinton but later changed to a more highly qualified physician in Jackson near the Jackson Infirmary, where she planned to deliver the baby. It was a somewhat old and rundown medical place near the Governor's Mansion in downtown Jackson but the best available. She made regular visits for care. Henry would always drive her (though she was quite capable of driving herself). Being involved was a sign that he was quite happy to become a father.

On some days that October, Ira was not able to help with harvest or other activities on the farm. On the warmer days, he would sit in a rocking chair on the big front porch and gaze off into the distance. On cooler days he would sit inside in front of the fireplace and gaze into the fire. He would occasionally get water or coffee to drink; sometimes he would slowly pace on the porch or around an inside room, or he would venture down the steps into the yard. Some folks were concerned about his walking and going up and down the steps. They thought he might fall or wander off. Some days his mind seemed not to be aware of where he was, the day of the week, or the time of day. Fortunately, he never fell or wandered far away. Doris tried to keep an eye on him. Carrie didn't pay much attention to anything he might do. Nevertheless, Ira's health was gradually deteriorating.

Thanksgiving came and went. Christmas was at hand. Plans were being made for a family holiday time. Henry's sisters Ellen and Ethel and their husbands were planning to drive from Montgomery, Alabama, to spend a few days at their homeplace. Sisters who lived locally would drive out for special days, meals, or gift giving. Only one sister, Lyda, still lived at home. Everyone sensed that Ira was not doing well, but he made it through the holidays.

On the morning of New Year's Day 1941, Ira was not well at all. He was barely breathing. He was struggling through asthma issues of the past as well as other problems. Henry drove into Clinton to summon a doctor (there were no telephones), and in a matter of minutes Dr. Ashford was seen driving his 1939 Buick down the long gravel driveway to the house. A well-respected family physician, he immediately examined Ira and said there wasn't much hope; it would be just a matter of a few hours, and he would be gone ("gone" was a Southern word for "dead"). The doctor gave him some paregoric to ease the end of his life. Henry left to go to Pocahontas to alert Brother Murrow (pastor of the Pocahontas Methodist Episcopal Church) and ask him if he would come to the home to comfort the family and assist with the funeral that would be in a couple of days.

The family wanted to bury Ira near his mother, Ellen Loretta Shepard Lee, in the Zachariah Ratliff Family Cemetery in Tinnin, which was about a mile from the home. Burying him near his father, Jasper Henry Lee, was about impossible, as his grave was in the Smith Cemetery in Henderson County, Texas. Making Ira's final resting place near his father might have been more fitting, as the marker for Jasper Henry Lee's grave stated that he was the father of Ira Jasper Lee. (There was no mention of his wife, Ellen Loretta, though she loved him very much.) The last few days before Ira's death were quite rainy, and the ground was soft and boggy.

With family input, it was decided to bury Ira in the cemetery at the Pocahontas Methodist Episcopal Church, where Brother Murrow was the preacher. Everyone went along, particularly the funeral director, who would have had great difficulty in getting to the Zachariah Ratliff Family Cemetery. The route to Pocahontas had some gravel roads for travel. Choosing Pocahontas also allowed the use of a church house for the memorial service as well as for the body to lie in state. Space would be allowed next to Ira for the burial of Carrie. The Pocahontas cemetery was a good choice. Over the years, it has been well maintained, whereas the Zachariah Ratliff Family Cemetery has fallen into disarray, has grown up with trees and thistles, and is not accessible.

The funeral was held, and wintertime activities around the farm returned to routine. The family gathered and, with a few fairly firm opinions, decided that Henry would be fully in charge of the farm and would pay Carrie $600 a year rent to farm the land and use buildings on the farm property. This was about all the income she would have, as there was no Social Security, welfare, or retirement benefits for people of her age. The truth be told, Carrie really didn't care much about what went on as long as she got her rent money from Henry, received some produce from the garden, and had a place to live. Life was simple; there were no utility bills or anything else to pay. Of course, Carrie was quite capable of voicing her opinion about some of the goings-on at the farm.

Doris had been told that the time of delivery of the baby she was carrying would be at the end of May. She and the baby appeared to be coming along well. Sure enough, as the end of May neared, Doris felt she was going into labor. She told Henry; word spread around the house. With all of the Shepard and Lee babies born there in the house over the years, folks didn't get very anxious until now; this birth was going to be in a hospital.

Henry got out the car and parked it near the porch steps. Doris, with what she was taking for the hospital stay, got into it. Though the trip was only about 16 or so miles, it would take a while on the dirt and gravel roads to get to the paved streets in Jackson. Carrie came out of the house walking briskly toward the car. Everyone thought that maybe she was going to offer her best wishes, but no, not Carrie. She was throwing a big hissy fit because Doris did not have the baby at home with the help of one of the sharecropper women who had midwife skills. Henry quickly drove away in the car for the trip to the Jackson Infirmary, where an 8-pound 8-ounce baby boy was born the next day, May 29, 1941, at 3:15 p.m. Dr. L. Q. Hall delivered the baby.

Based on family tradition in naming babies in the Lee and Shepard families, the boy was named for his father and included his mother's surname. They agreed to call him Son. Doris and baby stayed at the hospital for four and a half days. Her sister Dolly spent the night in the room with her. When Henry checked her and baby Lee out of the hospital on June 2, they had a whopping bill of $34.20. Itemized, the bill included $5.25 a day for a hospital room, $5.00 for the delivery room, $1.00 a day for care of the baby, and a few other minor charges. Because they paid cash, they received a 12 percent discount!

Before their baby was born (they didn't know if it would be a boy or a girl), Doris and Henry made preparations for it in their bedroom. The Lee cradle that was used when Henry and siblings were born was used with Son. Doris was calm and well-prepared. She took extra care to give the baby what was needed; Henry was quite busy with the farm, but in the early morning, at noon, and late in the afternoon, he had time to hold and adore his son. Financial success had not yet arrived in the young Lee family, though they had a livable income by subsistence farm standards of the day.

The crops grew and were harvested in the fall. This year, with Henry fully in charge, seemed to go well. Of course, self-sufficiency continued, such as gardening and home meat production. Meat was mostly pork. A few pigs were raised and fattened for slaughter on the farm. In late November, as the weather cooled, a couple of the best pigs were killed, scalded in a tilted half-barrel of hot water (heated by a wood-burning fire around it), and scraped to remove hair from the skin. The carcass was worked up into desired products. Hams and sides were placed in the smokehouse. Some meat was ground into sausage with a small hand grinder. A favorite pork meat was fresh, fried tenderloin. All parts of a pig were used: liver, feet, tail, head meat, brains; everything had a use. Cooking sometimes relied on old family recipes. Hog brains, for example, were mixed and scrambled with chicken eggs. Everybody wanted a little of the brain-and-egg dish, accompanied by biscuits and molasses, with cow's milk to drink.

Economical salted meat was also prepared. This involved using low-value pork belly parts or sides (not stomachs). While fresh, the sides were cut into slab pieces with an inch-or-so-thick layer of fat attached opposite the skin. The sides often had a few streaks of lean meat in the fat. These large pieces would be placed for several weeks or a couple of months in a container that allowed covering with salt. The process allowed salt to penetrate through the belly side, providing seasoning as well as preserving the meat. The salt would draw water out of the meat and dry it. The resulting product was sometimes known as dried salted pork meat or just salt pork. The meat would keep with minimal spoilage throughout the late fall, winter, and early spring. Warmer weather of late spring and summer sometimes turned the salt meat rancid. After a time of salting, meat was sliced and fried or put in beans or other vegetables and cooked as seasoning. The liquid fat gained from frying was used as seasoning or in cooking, similar to lard. The fat would also be used in cooking dog bread; canines needed to have food, too! A lot of fat made the bread more like meat.

Henry had also begun using the hammer mill at the Ratliff Store for making cornmeal and grits for the family, as well as chopped corn for farm animal feed. To grind these products for the Lee family and farm, the shuck (husk) had to be removed from the corn ear and the kernels shelled from the cob. A hand-crank-powered corn sheller with a heavy flywheel was bought for use in shelling corn. Once the person turning the crank got the heavy flywheel rotating, centrifugal force would tend to keep it turning. Henry would sometimes help the owners and other people with their grinding needs. Of course, the owners were paid in cash or barter for allowing the use of the hammer mill. Henry was known as a good, responsible equipment operator.

Farm life and work moved ahead. Henry expanded the production of truck crops, including vegetables such as squash, okra, beans, peas, and roasting-ear corn. In season, the routine involved early morning harvest (occasionally late afternoon) and delivery to grocery stores in the Jackson, Mississippi, area. One of the selling points Henry used to get the stores to buy and stock his produce was that it was "picked in the morning dew before a ray of sun touched the field." Most store managers liked the notion of such freshly picked produce. Each day he gained a few dollars and cents. Henry believed in frugal living and saving as best he could. He always wanted to avoid debt and pay cash. Selling vegetables supplemented the income from cotton.

In the spring of 1942, as their son was nearing one year of age, Henry and Doris decided they needed a passbook savings account for him that was more than placing coins in a piggy bank on the dresser. Setting this up would be in conjunction with his birthday. On May 20, just a few days before their son's birthday, Henry made his morning trip into Jackson with squash, snap beans, and a few heads of cabbage on his old pickup truck. He soon delivered and sold all he had to the Jitney Jungle and A&P grocery stores on West

Capitol Street. On his way back to Tinnin, he went by the Bank of Clinton and spoke with its president, a Mr. Godbold. (He always wore a suit with a white shirt and tie; impressive!)

Of the twelve dollars and a half that he got for his produce that day, he used ten dollars to open a savings account in the full and complete name of Son. Surely, interest would accumulate and help grow the account. No more deposits were made in 1942. On December 31, 1942, seven cents of interest was credited to the account. Wow! That young boy would soon be wealthy! Ha! In the next few years, even when the family was facing adversity, additional small deposits were made. How they thought the money might be used was not very clear at that time. Maybe Son would go to Mississippi A&M College (somehow, the habit of using that name continued even though the name was changed to Mississippi State College in 1932), buy cattle, or pay for marriage to a smart, energetic, and good-looking young woman. Anyway, a savings account was underway, and additions had to be made so that it could help fund worthy goals. Growing the principal would be slow; they didn't have much money to add to it.

That December, Henry and Doris enjoyed being Santa Claus for their year-and-a-half-old son. Henry cut a small cedar tree from the fence row near the sweet potato field. He brought it to the house, and Doris nailed a board onto the cut end of the tree to hold it up. She decorated the tree with a string of red holly berries on a thread and a similar string of popcorn. By the way Son looked at it, you could tell he liked it. Santa came on Christmas Eve and brought a few things, including a small stuffed dog that was really a hit. Little Son carried it with him when he toddled around and slept with it in his cradle (he was about to outgrow the cradle). Christmas Day brought a big crowd of family members to the Lee-Shepard home. Most of Henry's sisters and their husbands and children came to see Carrie and bring her gifts. A few of the sisters brought small gifts for Son.

Henry, Doris, and Son did not stay the day, as they drove their ragged, undependable car to Doris's home in Plain (Richland). Mom Amelia and Paw Paw Sloan were always nice to Son. On this day, they had a present under the tree for him and one for each of his two girl cousins. He was their oldest grandchild and only grandson. There were two granddaughters within a year of Son's age, and he loved to visit when they were there (though he always felt intimidated around girls).

What might the future have in store? Henry and Doris talked late one night after Son was asleep in his cradle. They were afraid of how the war was going to influence their future lives and hoped the war would end soon. (The attack on Pearl Harbor greatly expanded the war threat to the United States.) Together, they developed goals for themselves and how they would support Son. Henry expressed that he wanted to get income from the farm increased to a level that would make for a good living. He already had plans in place for the next crop year and thought these plans would boost income. He would begin by talking with a banker near the end of January.

Doris said that she wanted to run their household in a thrifty manner and conserve as best she could. She also said that she wanted to be a good mother to their son. Henry indicated that he would like for her to have a maid to help her with running the house (Doris really didn't think she needed one). They also talked about one day building a house in the town of Clinton. This would be a house that was built with new materials and had electricity and running water, as well as an indoor bathroom and toilet. This house would be warm in the winter and located on a paved street. It would be near where Son and his possible future brothers and/ or sisters would go to school. They also wanted to get a new car that was dependable and comfortable. Henry wanted a new pickup truck for the farm and a new tractor; the new tractor would be one with rubber tires. Of course, Doris frequently thought in the back of her mind that she might be able to get a teaching job to help with family income.

"What about goals for Son?" Henry asked. "Shouldn't we expect him to go to college? After all, Doris, you went to college. Maybe he can get one of those degrees in agriculture and become a teacher, county agent, or agricultural writer."

Doris said, "I agree. If we don't have goals for him, who will?"

Henry and Doris felt good about their lives and budding family. Henry, in particular, was feeling euphoric about his life that lay ahead. He knew he could do anything to be successful on the farm. He could cope with the restrictions the war had placed on farming and life. He felt the war would end sometime in the next months or few years and he would be able to move forward by leaps and bounds. In addition to hard work, he knew that a little good luck would be needed. Henry quietly closed his eyes and said a brief prayer asking for God's guidance and help in the years ahead. Oh, the confidence he had!

Doris and Henry wanted many things in life. They wanted to achieve! Some of what they wanted involved their toddler son who had little idea about the world that lay ahead. He knew nothing of the goals that would be ascribed to him by his parents. Could he achieve these goals?

6

Facing Tragedy

Wednesday, January 20, 1943, began much as other days in the small Lee household. Henry and Doris would have coffee and breakfast, hold and play with Son, listen to the news on station WJDX. Farm news followed local and national news at 6:00 a.m. each day. No one knew it, but this day's routine would be severely shattered before night fall!

With World War II well underway, there would always be news on the radio about the war and related political events. President Franklin D. Roosevelt's activities were often cited in his role as Commander-in-Chief of the United States military. War news that morning dealt with a report on American and Australian forces combining to take back part of New Guinea and action by the USS Silversides (a submarine) in the Pacific Theater against Japanese ships near the Solomon Islands. These were such faraway places; a person living in Tinnin could only imagine what it would be like there. On the other hand, several young men from Tinnin had been drafted into military service and sent to these faraway places. Two didn't return.

The war effort had impacted so much of the daily life of Henry and his family. Certain farm supplies and implements were very limited. Some were not available. Many implements had to be patched or repaired repeatedly to continue using them. Almost everything in farm life was used very sparingly.

Household operation and food preparation were challenging. Such food items as coffee and sugar were quite limited. Unless you lived on a farm with a cow or two, milk was scarce. Evaporated milk (often called Pet Milk because of the brand label) was promoted as a good source of family nutrition, but fresh milk was often not readily available for U.S. citizens. Special wartime-ration books for preparing delicious and nutritious win-the-war meals were published. Recipes included egg patties, bean loaf, and sweetbread casseroles. Because of the shortage of chocolate, a recipe for a molasses milk drink was touted as an alternative to chocolate milk. That simple recipe was to mix a cup of evaporated milk and a cup of water, adding a tablespoon or so of molasses. Bean sausage, beef tongue rolls, kidney creole, and pork brains with scrambled eggs were also used to extend scarce food supplies and provide adequate human nutrition. Some of these made their way into Tinnin diets.

After opening and emptying tin cans with food, the cans were smashed down flat for recycling. Of course, in the summer, Doris canned much of the family's food (tomatoes, beans, peas, etc.) in glass jars, using a pressure cooker. Even the tinfoil in packs of chewing gum and ready-rolled cigarettes was saved. Savings stamps bought/collected from the government and added to books could be used to buy U.S. savings bonds. Much was at stake in the war. Henry feared living under the flag of Japan. Maybe that fear was promoted by government reports that described wartime atrocities to get citizens to make sacrifices in their lives. Of course, level-headed people often wondered if the war was really needed or if it could have been averted if government leaders had negotiated on their differences.

Not much was said that morning on the newscast about President Roosevelt (often referred to as FDR). It did mention that he was at the Little White House in Warm Springs, Georgia. Aha! What was going on there of interest to him as a man? As President? Press releases of the past indicated that he would sometimes go there to huddle with his advisors on war strategy. But, was that why he was there on that day? To attempt to answer the question, let's go back a few years.

FDR married Anna Eleanor Roosevelt, of New York City, in 1905. Yes, the fact that his wife's maiden name was Roosevelt sometimes provoked condemnation. She was a niece of former President Theodore Roosevelt and a fifth cousin once removed to FDR. Such an "in the family marriage" of blood relatives was viewed as scandalous behavior by decent folks in the Tinnin community. Nevertheless, most Tinnin folks really liked him as President and many of the programs he proposed to lift the Nation out of the Great Depression.

The Roosevelts had seven children that they both apparently loved and appreciated. But, things in the marriage weren't always hunky-a-dory (a word used in Tinnin when things weren't quite right). FDR had affairs with other women over the years. Maybe it was partially because Eleanor had her own ideas and issues which she was passionate about.

The future President Roosevelt was stricken with polio in 1921 at age thirty-nine, about ten years before he became President. Polio was debilitating in his life. He engaged in the treatments that were available at the time. FDR had a lot to overcome, and he did well with the challenge. There were always a few people who thought he might have contracted the disease from one of his women; the medical community didn't think much of that notion. Most people have given him a lot of credit for his leadership as President of the United States during World War II.

Maybe he went to Warm Springs for the comfort of swimming and splashing in the naturally warm mineral water that was near the Little White House. He was in the process of planning a facility where others with polio could come for treatment and relaxation. The water was soothing to polio survivors. Since he no longer had much use of his legs, he was usually in a wheelchair. He might have swum or waded about, but other things also went on, and Henry and Doris had heard of some of that. They admired how he overcame the problems that polio gave him in life. Sometimes they wondered how they would have responded to such a life-changing tragedy. Henry thought what it would have been like if he had suffered a disability similar to that of FDR. He shuddered at the thought.

From time to time, FDR promised Eleanor that he was going to mend his ways and forego other women, but that promise never lasted. Other women were just too appealing to Roosevelt, and they liked him! Maybe it was his wealth and government status; maybe it was something else. A preferred mistress was said to be Lucy Mercer Rutherfurd. She was likely in Warm Springs that very day. In earlier times, she was the social secretary for Eleanor but tended to travel wherever FDR went. Eleanor first discovered love letters between FDR and Lucy in 1918, well before he became the President.

What FDR was up to was always a point of curiosity with Doris and Henry (and most other citizens), and this morning was no exception. His amorous behavior was often a hushed subject of conversation in the community among the women and a not-so-hushed one among the men. Polio apparently didn't slow that part of his life down very much. Despite Roosevelt's personal life, when time to vote came, FDR got a majority of the votes in the Tinnin box.

Eleanor compensated for her husband's lack of fidelity in marriage through public activism on social issues. After becoming first lady, Eleanor Roosevelt pursued a high profile as a well-known social activist for worthwhile causes, particularly racial matters.

FDR usually found a way to stay in fairly good graces with Eleanor by helping make some of her social welfare activities possible, and he did it again not long before he died. This time it was to intervene with the U.S. Postal Service to get delivery of a controversial and then forbidden book authored by Lillian Smith entitled *Strange Fruit*. Smith was a social justice advocate who wrote about an interracial love affair between a black boy and a white girl. The post office had banned sending the book through the mail. FDR helped postal authorities to see their errant ways and allow the book to be mailed. Smith did much of her writing and social justice work from a mountain-top farm/camp in Rabun County, Georgia. She even had interracial dinner parties that tended to bring out the wrath of local citizens. Of course, her actions would have been considered to be scandalous among residents in Tinnin if they had known about them.

Eleanor was held in high regard and later (after the death of FDR) was referred to by President Harry Truman as "First Lady of the World."

Earlier in World War II, Henry was almost drafted into military service. He went before the Selective Service Board in Jackson, Mississippi, and was granted a farm deferment for a year. The crops produced were in high demand in the war effort. The United States exported many food and fiber crop products to Great Britain and the European mainland. Without cotton, soldiers would have no uniforms to wear or bandages for their wounds. Both U.S. soldiers and those of allied armies depended on American agriculture. Without grain and other crops, soldiers would have no food. Without Henry, who was the sole person in charge of the Lee farm, the farm would close down. The farm needed him, and he and his family needed it. He had goals that would propel him and his family to success. He was continually thinking, planning, and striving toward meeting goals, particularly those that he and Doris agreed upon.

After morning routine in the house, Henry went to feed the pigs and milk the cow (Son needed cow's milk for proper growth, so Henry thought!). Afterward, he brought the milk to Doris in the kitchen. She would strain it through a clean cotton cloth and store it in a cool place next to an outside window (kind of cool in January), and that would keep the milk from spoiling until it was used. Doris would sometimes heat the milk in a large boiler until casein (a major constituent of milk protein) began to form on the surface; this was her way of pasteurizing it. As with most mornings, that morning Henry would hold Son in his hands and raise him high in his arms toward the ceiling a couple of times to get smiles and giggles out of him. Next, he would kiss Doris goodbye and say, "Honey, I love you. Take good care of my boy. You know I kind of like calling him Son."

"I love you, too," Doris replied. "Son is fine, and I will take good care of him. I hope he takes a nap so I can get some work done washing and ironing clothes. He gets irritable when he doesn't nap. Bye. Be safe."

Next, Henry prepared to go to the Ratliff Store to run the hammer mill that was kept in a side shed. He was to grind corn-meal that day. He and his farm hand, Otho, loaded croaker (bur-lap) sacks of shelled corn into the pickup truck; they took empty clean cotton-cloth sacks to receive the ground cornmeal. The fresh ground meal had to be kept clean. Then, off he and Otho went in the Lees' somewhat dilapidated pickup truck (at least it cranked that day).

They arrived at the store, and Henry briefly went inside to say hello and get any information on the day. Henry made sure it was okay for Otho to help him. He then went to the shed where the hammer mill was located. A 1940 steel-wheel Farmall tractor was already parked just outside the roof cover of the shed at what appeared to be the correct distance from the hammer mill, or about twelve feet pulley-to-pulley. The belt power pulley on the tractor seemed to be in line with the pulley on the hammer mill. It looked okay, but was it?

The tractor needed to be in position (parked and blocked) so that the belt would stay in the middle of both pulleys as it turned. You did not want the belt gradually to move to one side or the other of a pulley and, possibly, slip off as it was rotating to power the mill. Proper alignment was needed for safe operation. Things can happen quickly when the belt is moving at a high rate of speed. Again, everything looked okay. The proper screen was installed for grinding cornmeal. This screen replaced the one used the day before in grinding larger chop-size feed for chickens. Oil was applied to the shaft that rotated from the wheel through bearings to inside the body of the mill. This shaft would turn at high speed and needed to be well lubricated. A couple of fifty-pound croaker sacks of shelled corn were placed near the hopper on the mill.

Henry would take care of equipment operation; Otho would be responsible for adding corn to the hopper and other grinding work. They would share getting the newly ground meal into one of the cotton sacks by holding an open sack under the sacking spout at the bottom of the feed collector.

The engine on the tractor was started (with a hand crank). Final maneuvering of the tractor was made to make sure the two pulleys were lined up correctly for efficient and safe belt operation. The brakes on the tractor's wheels were set and checked to make sure they were in the locked position. The clutch on the tractor that transferred power from the power train of the tractor to the tractor's belt pulley was engaged. The tractor's pulley turned so that the belt began to slowly move, rotating the pulley on the mill. That pulley was attached to a shaft that went into the mill. This rotation caused the hammers inside the heavy metal chamber to flail and grind whatever was in it.

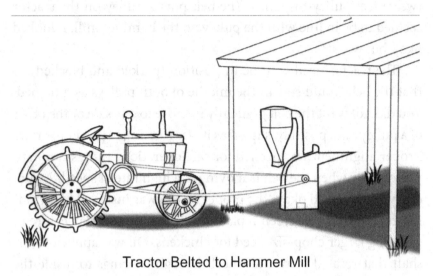

Tractor Belted to Hammer Mill

Belting a Tractor Pulley to the Pulley on a Hammer Mill
Transfers Rotating Power to Operate the Mill.

Once everything checked out okay in slow rotation, the speed (rpm) of the tractor's engine was increased so that the mill's hammers were turning at the proper speed for grinding. The belt appeared to be working properly. Some shelled corn was poured into the hopper to test how the grinding process would work (and to clean out any residual from the previous grinding). Everything seemed to be all right.

"Otho, does it look like it's running okay?" Henry called out in a voice loud enough to be heard over the noise of the tractor's engine, rotating pulleys, moving belt, and action of the hammers inside the mill. "Is it doing right?"

"Ya sir," Otho loudly responded. "It bees running des right. Should mo corn be added? I got some here in dis croaker sack."

"Yep," Henry shouted. "Put some in. It's time to go ahead and get this work done. I want to finish so I can go back and see Son."

Otho slowly (you just don't dump a whole sack in at once) poured more shelled corn into the hopper at the rate the hammer mill could handle without choking down. The mill labored a bit with the additional load. The meal bin was getting fresh, fluffy, newly ground white cornmeal in it. Henry noticed that the belt tended to move to one side of the mill's pulley when under operating load. (He used only a white dent kind of corn that was extra high in starch; it made the best meal.) He looked, and everything was still lined up properly. He picked up a short piece of 1-by-4-inch board to push against the outer edge of the fast-moving belt to get it back onto the middle of the pulley.

Suddenly things went wrong. The belt flew off the mill's pulley. Still around the tractor's power pulley, the looping belt was moving at high speed. The other end of the powerful belt loop ever so quickly wrapped around Henry's right arm, grabbing it near the shoulder. The moving belt flung Henry to the ground at the base of a pole that helped hold up the shed. In doing so, it substantially tore the arm from the shoulder. The bone was broken multiple times near the shoulder. Muscles and ligaments were separated but were sufficiently attached to hold the arm in place. Skin and other tissues were stretched to the tearing point, and the arm was severely mangled and partially severed from the body. Dangerously small amounts of skin, muscles, blood vessels, and ligaments just below the arm pit remained intact and kept the arm attached to the body.

Henry lay on the ground lifeless for a few moments. He soon began to regain consciousness. His right arm was no longer properly attached to his body; it was hanging from his body without control. He was bleeding from the arm injury. Fortunately, the extent of bleeding was not so great as what some medical people would have thought. Another small spot of blood was on the ground with three upper front teeth in it (knocked out by the slamming of his body against the pole). The extent of his injuries was unknown at the time but turned out to also include dislocated vertebrae, a concussion, and bruises elsewhere on the body. Otho saw that this was serious.

Otho quickly stopped the tractor engine and rushed to Henry's side. He called out to the people in the Ratliff Store. "Mr. Henry done been hurt bad! Get hep fast!" Otho kneeled over Henry and worked to untangle the heavy belt from Henry's arm and body. He spoke to Henry, saying, "I'm gonna hep you. Please, Mr. Henry, be all right." Henry at first made no sound; maybe he was breath-ing, but that wasn't known. After a couple of minutes, he began to groan. He then gasped for air to get over the heavy blow that knocked the breath out of him.

"Please come fast!" Otho shouted to people in the store. "Get a doctor!" One man looked out and saw some of what had happened. He came dashing to Henry. Another man followed.

When the two men arrived and saw the situation, one of them turned back and ran to bring his car close to the tractor shed. He re-alized that Henry would need to be quickly driven for medical care.

Henry was somewhat alert and struggled to get up from the ground and stand. Otho helped him. Henry was able to shakily stand. He held onto the shed pole with his left hand to keep from falling. He was dazed and knew nothing of what had happened to him. He stood a couple of minutes and took a short, stumbling step. Otho was by his side. He then took another short step. The tip of his right hand was almost touching the ground so that it would have been dragged along with his steps.

The tissues that kept the arm attached to the body were stretched by his standing. Otho saw the situation; he gripped the arm in a squeezing motion and lifted it. Some blood was being lost, but Otho's gripping the arm and the pull of the weight on the blood vessels tended to close them and hold back the loss of more blood.

One of the other men then gripped and lifted Henry's damaged right arm while Otho helped him walk.

With help, Henry struggled to the car and lay on the back seat. The man driving the car (a Mr. Echols) said he was going to take him to the emergency room at the Baptist Hospital in Jackson.

"Tell Doris about me," Henry mumbled, "and where you are taking me. Tell her to take care of Son. Tell her that I am going to make it." Henry then went silent. It appeared that he was saying a prayer. His lips quivered; his eyes closed. "Oh, God," Henry moaned, "please help me." The car sped away down the bumpy, curvy graveled road. Driving was smoother and better when the car reached the paved highway and the city streets of Jackson.

Luckily, a wall-mounted crank telephone had been installed a couple of years before in the Ratliff Store. A Mr. Mason, who was in the store at the time, called and alerted the Baptist Hospital that a man with a near-death injury was being driven to the emergency room in a private car. Nurses at the hospital began preparing for Henry's arrival. The head nurse notified a physician who often handled trauma cases about the situation.

A young man named Jack Lily came by the store and heard about what had happened. He agreed to go to the Lee-Shepard home and tell Doris. When he got there, she was gathering eggs in the henhouse; Son was napping. Telling her wasn't easy, but it had to be done. He chose the best possible way to do it. Mr. Lily offered to drive her in his personal car to the hospital to be with Henry. Doris took him up on being driven, woke Son, and grabbed a few things that she stuffed into a cloth flour sack. She carried Son and ran to get into the car. She knew it would not work well to talk with unpredictable Carrie or leave Son with her. She also knew that Henry would want to see Son as soon as he could. On the way to the car, she shouted to Carrie's sister, Susie, who was in the yard, about the situation and that they were going to the Baptist Hospital to check on Henry. Tears ran down her face.

She held Son tightly and kissed his cheek. "Mother loves you," she said, "and you will soon see your daddy." Doris was afraid. Thoughts ran through her mind. How badly was Henry hurt? What if he died? (Carrie would likely make her move out of the house if Henry failed to live.) So many things came to her mind. She was so afraid. She was shaking. She said a silent prayer asking for strength to deal with the situation. Jack Lily drove the sixteen-mile trip to the hospital in record time. On the way, he offered to help Doris in any way he could. He said he would get the pickup home from where it was parked at the Ratliff Store and put it in the usual place under the shed.

The car driven by Mr. Echols with injured Henry arrived at the Baptist Hospital a few minutes before Doris and Son. Fortunately, an old army veteran who everyone called Chapman was loafing at the store at the time of the accident. He rode in the car with Henry. Chapman had cared for injured soldiers on battle fields in Europe during World War I. He knew a little about how to deal with injuries until medical help could take charge. He tried to reduce bleeding on Henry's mangled arm and shoulder by applying pressure to exposed blood vessels. Regardless, Henry lost a lot of blood but not his life on the ride to the hospital.

A physician and two nurses had been called to duty when the telephone operator heard that Henry was on the way. An orthopedic specialist had been summoned, but the hospital did not know when or if he would arrive. A surgeon, Dr. Brock, was highly respected as a qualified physician who could handle trauma situations. He was a well-known, long-serving physician in the Jackson area. His age was beyond that of men being readily drafted for military service, so he often had extra medical duties with trauma cases. He had a baccalaureate degree from Mississippi A&M College and a degree in medicine from Emory University in Atlanta. Only well-trained and experienced nurses worked with Dr. Brock. By the time of arrival, Dr. Brock had changed from his suit into scrubs for ready service in the emergency room.

At the hospital, Henry was put on a gurney and quickly taken inside. He was rapidly moved to the emergency room. Dr. Brock and staff immediately began assessing the extent of the injuries. A nurse with some training in anesthesia had been called to administer medication to relieve the great pain Henry was likely to suffer. Of course, pain medicine could not be administered before head, neck, and other injuries were evaluated. Assessing those injuries required that Henry be able to respond to questioning. In addition to the severe arm trauma, the medical staff observed cervical disc herniation (some called it dislocated or slipped disc). This appeared to affect three of the seven vertebrae (cervical discs) in the neck. The discs could be dealt with later; need for attention to the arm was immediate. Henry would just have to bear the pain while that was under way, and hopefully it wouldn't take long.

Doris and Son were driven to the door of the hospital. It was nearing one p.m. Jack Lily told Doris that he would wait a while to see what the situation was. He said he would come inside and check in a few minutes.

"Where is Henry?" Doris asked when she went through the hospital door. "Henry Lee, my husband. I am so worried about him."

"He is in the emergency room being assessed and prepared for surgery," the receptionist said. "You cannot go in there. You must sit in the waiting area. We will give reports on the situation. The nurses and physician are now trying to stop the bleeding and assess what would be best to do next in terms of his right arm."

Being very concerned and one who could usually control her emotions, Doris was about overcome by the situation and pleaded, "Please tell me what is going on. I am very fearful. Is Henry alive? Dead? Will he be okay?" The receptionist offered no more information.

Doris walked in the direction of the emergency room. Just when she got close, the door was opened a few inches by a nurse who had to reach outside to get a special instrument a driver had picked up at Foster General Veterans Hospital for this surgery. As the door opened, Doris could glimpse inside. She got a fleeting view of the surgically lit operating table with Henry's body draped to prevent contamination. She saw his right shoulder area with protruding shiny handles of various clamps, hemostats, and locking forceps being used to stop bleeding and prepare for the next procedures. That was shocking to her. She wondered what the medical team was doing to him.

The receptionist again told Doris to go have a seat in the waiting area. She was told that if she didn't follow instructions, she would be asked to leave the hospital premises. Doris complied. She didn't want to get thrown out while her husband was undergoing serious medical procedures.

After a few minutes, Jack Lily came inside, and Doris told him what she had been told. They reached the conclusion that he should go back to Tinnin and tell the family the situation. She would stay there. A small cafeteria-type dining place was nearby. Jack Lily left and suggested that she could call the Ratliff Store and tell anything new that she had been told. The waiting area did have a public phone, and she used it to call Harper's Store in Plain, Mississippi. Since her parents and her sister Dolly lived only two miles from the store, she thought someone at the store could alert them to Henry's situation.

A nurse from the emergency room came to speak with Doris about Henry. She asked Doris to bring Son and come into a small examining room that wasn't being used. The nurse asked Doris to prepare to talk with Dr. Brock. Thoughts raced through Doris's head (many were the same as before): Was Henry dead? If alive, would he lose an arm? Would he be able to go about life in a normal way? The doctor came into the room and introduced himself as Dr. Brock. Doris, as tears rolled down her cheeks, expressed concern for Henry.

"How is Henry doing?" Doris asked. "Tell me about him. What can I do?"

Calming and reassuring, Dr. Brock appeared professional and capable. He explained that he and the nurses had been able to stop the bleeding and stabilize vital signs. He said he needed to talk quickly so he could get back to Henry's care. The nurses were preparing him for "arm surgery"; he did not use the word "amputation." Dr. Brock described other injuries that had been determined, such as bruises to his left arm, cervical disc herniation (neck vertebrae damage), head injury with a concussion, and the loss of three upper front teeth. These resulted from the hard crash against the shed pole that the belt caused in throwing Henry sideways to the ground.

The only thing that could be done with the arm, according to Dr. Brock, was to surgically separate it from the body (still no use of the word "amputation"). He quickly referred to a poster-size drawing, pinned to the wall, of the anatomy of the human arm. He pointed to the humerus bone, muscles, nerves, and blood vessels. He stated that the humerus is the only bone in the upper arm and that it extends from the scapula in the shoulder down to the elbow, where the radius and the ulna begin forming the lower arm. Dr. Brock further stated that the humerus of Henry's right arm had been pulled from the scapula and mostly sheared off just below its anatomical neck near the shoulder. He said that the humerus bone itself had been broken into several fragments by the accident and would not be salvageable. He indicated that he did not think any of the bone in the arm could be kept to form a stump. (Though unspoken, the notion of "amputation" was now settling in on Doris.)

Dr. Brock explained that some of the muscle tissues would be kept. Skin would be shaped (cut) and stretched to fit over the end of the retained muscle mass to form a nub. Henry would likely have very little control and ability for movement in the nub. Dr. Brock further indicated that Henry would have a near normal life in most regards, but adjustment to the loss of the arm would take time. He said that nubs sometimes have sensations that are hard to explain, and these may persist for years after the surgery. Doris appreciated the explanation but was quite concerned. She was filled with sorrow. Regardless, she wanted Henry's life to be saved; she loved him so. She did not understand some of the explanation, but she thought back to the health and human body class she had taken in college. Some of the terms in the explanation sounded like things she had heard before. She was relieved that Dr. Brock was a mature man who demonstrated good medical skills and patient-family-care abilities.

Dr. Brock assured Doris that, though Henry was badly hurt, the prognosis for his survival was good. He indicated that an immediate goal was to make him comfortable, relieve pain, and minimize risk of infection.

"I need to ask you," Dr. Brock said, "if I have your permission to perform the needed amputation and related care."

"Yes," Doris replied in a strained voice. "You have my permission. Please take good care of Henry. He doesn't deserve this tragedy. Thank you for your help."

"I will see you in about an hour or a little more," Dr. Brock said, "and give you details on how everything went in the procedure."

Dr. Brock left for the surgery. Doris and Son went back to the waiting area. Doris was so concerned and nervous. She recalled that just that morning Henry was fine and happy. And now his life had fallen apart. She realized that she had to help him put it back together again.

In a little over an hour, Dr. Brock came out of surgery to see

Doris, as he had said he would. Doris was so fearful that the surgery hadn't gone well and Henry had died. She didn't get any reports during surgery, and that heightened her fears. Dr. Brock said that the procedure had gone as well as could be expected. He talked about it a bit.

The upper end of the humerus was severely damaged, as explained by Dr. Brock. That end of the humerus has a nob that fits into the scapula (shoulder socket) like a ball in a glove. He said he made the remaining arm nub as long as he could, and it would likely wind up being about 3 inches. He indicated that the procedure involved tightly and securely placing the ends of muscle groups and ligament tissues into a mass. Blood vessels and nerve endings were salvaged as best they could be and shaped for the nub. Skin flaps were tapered and closed tautly over the mass. Sterile catgut was used to suture and hold tissues in place for healing. Special, newly developed needles were used to do this suturing. Dr. Brock said that the stitches would need to be removed after some healing.

A rigid dressing was used over the site of amputation (the nub) to keep down postoperative pain and edema. Dr. Brock explained that edema was the swelling caused by excess fluid trapped in tissues. He told how taut (tight) dressings helped prevent edema by pressing back on any fluid in the area. He did express some concern over nerve endings and properly treating nerve tissues, as these were always difficult to handle in surgery.

Within a half-hour of the call to Harper's Store and during the surgery, the phone in the hospital waiting area rang. Someone answered and said the call was for Doris Lee. It was Doris's youngest sister, Dolly, calling from Harper's Store to say that they had gotten the message about Henry being in an accident. She offered to get Paw Paw Sloan to bring her and Mom Amelia to the hospital (it would be in their 1937 Plymouth car). Doris asked them to come; she needed the comfort of knowing that a caring family was there.

They left immediately for the Baptist Hospital, which was a drive of about twenty miles.

Upon arrival at the hospital, Doris's family hugged and shared a few tears. Mom Amelia held Son in her arms and comforted him, though he didn't understand what was going on. She gave him a sugar cookie to chew on (he liked sweets). She had brought a half-dozen other cookies that she would soon likely need to keep him settled and not run about. (And, just think. She had used some of her limited food sugar ration to make the cookies before this came up, and now she was sharing with her grandson.)

A nurse brought word to Doris that Dr. Brock wanted to speak with her at the nurse's station. She quickly went. He said that Henry was asleep in the recovery area. He indicated that Henry appeared to have come through the surgery okay and that once the anesthesia wore off, they would have a better understanding. She could go see him but could not bring any family members. She went back to the waiting area to tell her family that she could now see Henry but that the doctor had asked that no family members go at that time. She quickly went to the recovery room. Doris was shocked to see Henry in such condition. Her eyes filled with tears. She leaned over and kissed him on the forehead. She whispered, "I love you" and "I am here for you." She quietly said a prayer asking for Henry to heal. The nurse told her that he would likely be very sedated for at least another hour and unable to talk. She said that he would then need some additional sedation to reduce the pain he might have.

After several minutes, Doris, realizing that Henry was nonresponsive and in a sad condition, returned to the waiting area. She wanted to see Dolly, Mom Amelia, and Paw Paw Sloan. She told them a little about what she saw but withheld the shock she witnessed. After a few minutes, Dolly said that she had come prepared to spend the night with Doris and help look after Son. The hospital likely had a room with a couple of cots they could use. In a bit, Paw

Paw and Mom Amelia left for their home. Paw Paw said he had butchered a 240-pound barrow (hog) that morning and it needed to be cut up. They said that they would be back the next day to check on Henry and determine what Dolly's plans might be. They said to call Harper's Store if anything major occurred (they were likely thinking if Henry died).

Just as they were leaving, the family physician from Clinton came into the area. Dr. J. A. Ashford was a longtime, highly respected medical practitioner. He was there to check on Henry and lend support to Doris. He said his office had received a call from the Ratliff Store about what had happened. Dr. Ashford went into the physician area and talked with Dr. Brock. He returned to see Doris and give her the assurance that Henry should come along okay, though it wouldn't be easy adjusting to such as catastrophic loss. He asked if Doris had any questions. She was too emotional to speak. Dr. Ashford said he would come back tomorrow, as he had two other patients in the hospital to also check on.

Doris left Son with Dolly in the tiny room with cots and went back to check on Henry. It appeared that he was beginning to awaken; a nurse was providing constant monitoring. He was lightly groaning and moving his legs a bit. The nurse knew that it would take a while for him to awaken from anesthesia and that he would be groggy for several hours. She suspected that he would need something for several hours or more to relieve pain. Doris stood close by his bed and talked to him in soothing, loving ways, sincerely showing the unconditional love she had for him. Then he opened one eye just a bit; this was a sign that he was continuing to overcome the effects of anesthesia. He did not know exactly what had been done to him at the hospital.

"Where is Son?" were the first audible words that Henry mumbled.

"He is with Dolly," Doris replied. "She and Mom Amelia and

Paw Paw Sloan came here, and Dolly is spending the night. The hospital let us have a small room with two cots for less than a dollar a day. The nurses have been really nice to me. You can see him in a little while. Is there anything I can do for you?"

Henry continued to recover from the anesthesia. In unclear speech he asked, "What happened to me? Where am I? Why am I here?"

"You were hurt while running the hammer mill," Doris said. "Otho helped untangle you from the belt and get you into the car. Mr. Echols at the Ratliff Store rushed you in his car here to the Baptist Hospital in Jackson. The doctors and nurses have been treating your injuries."

Sedation resulted in his drifting back asleep for a few moments. He awoke again and asked, "What has been done to me?"

"It isn't easy for me to talk," Doris said. "The answer is hard to give. Your right arm was so badly injured that the doctor had to remove it. You are going to be fine. Just rest easy, and you will heal."

Henry, appearing agitated, mumbled, "Right arm gone. How can I farm and provide for my wife and son?" He paused and then asked, "Why did this happen to me? Oh Lord, why did this happen to me?"

Deep in thought, Doris responded, "I will always love you. I will help you, and we will be fine together. You were at work to help us. It was an accident. We don't know why it happened. The belt between the tractor and the hammer mill suddenly flew off and grabbed your arm."

Henry was becoming more awake and aware of his surroundings. His thoughts focused on all that had gone on and was going on now around him.

"How long will I be here?" Henry asked. About that time the lead nurse appeared. Doris asked her to respond to the question.

"About a week or maybe more, but that decision is up to your physician and depends on how you come along." The nurse continued, "You know, Mr. Lee, you were seriously hurt. We are doing our best to help you recover and heal. In a few minutes, you will be taken to your room. You have awakened adequately, and your vital signs are acceptable for you to go to a room."

Henry mumbled, "Good, I am ready."

The anesthesia nurse made one more check before allowing him to be moved to his room and saw that his vital signs were satisfactory. Another nurse checked the bandage to see if it was as taut as it could safely be but not too tight. About that time, Dr. Brock walked in and introduced himself to Henry. He told Henry a little about his injury and the medical procedure used. He pointed out that recovery would take time. He indicated that he would be available to support him. He told Henry that the nurse would give him something for pain, as needed. Dr. Brock said he would be by to check on him both in the mornings and late afternoons for the next few days.

Doris was by his side as Henry was rolled down the hallway to his room. Once transferred to his bed, he needed comfort and sedation. He continued to drift in and out of wakefulness. Doris asked the nurse to get a cot for her so she could stay in the room with Henry that night. It was soon delivered, and Doris readied it for her stay. She wanted to be with Henry and comfort him as best she could. Henry dozed back asleep, and Doris went to the room where Dolly and Son were waiting. Doris told Dolly the situation and suggested that they prepare for the night. Son did not need to go in to see his father at this time. Dolly and Son went to the cafeteria for a light meal and brought back a sandwich for Doris, which they took to Henry's room. He was sound asleep. Son got a glimpse of his sleeping father.

Since it was nearing nine p.m. and the day had been a hard one, both Doris and Dolly with Son began to settle in for the night. Not a very comfortable arrangement, but it was good enough to get by. Doris used the cot in Henry's room and finally dozed off. About midnight she was awakened by sounds from Henry. He was awake and in pain. She got the nurse to give him something for the pain, and in a short while Henry went back to sleep. Doris could then try to get some rest.

As he said he would, Jack Lilly put Henry's truck back in its rightful place in the shed on the farm. He got Otho to help him drive it there late that afternoon. When he was there, young Mr. Lilly went to tell Carrie about the tragedy. He knocked at the front door, and she came to it and stepped out onto the porch. He said, "Hello, Mrs. Lee. I have something to tell you."

She greeted him back, "Hello, Jack."

Mr. Lilly continued, "It isn't good news, and I will make it as easy as possible. Henry was hurt in an accident at the Ratliff Store while using the Farmall tractor to power the hammer mill to grind cornmeal."

"What did that idiot fool do?" Carrie interrupted. "I warned him about tractors several years ago. I told him they could cause injury and death. I knew he didn't know what he was doing and how to do it."

Just as Carrie paused to catch her breath, Jack said, "I am sorry to tell you this news. I can't help it. I have offered to help Doris anyway I can. I am sure someone will be in touch tomorrow with an update. I wish the best for Henry. Now, I must go. Goodbye."

Carrie mumbled, "Goodbye," and went back into the house, slamming the front door hard as she did. Jack got into his car and headed the few miles toward his home, wondering what that woman was thinking.

What a life-changing day this had been! And, the big changes would bring big challenges. Coping with life routines would introduce new and unknown challenges! Both Henry and Doris were people who had the resolve to meet most life challenges when they arose.

7

Healing

Not easy! No, healing would not be easy. How hard it would be was unknown. Would healing ever be done? It would be tackled with the same energy as work and obstacles in life. Sometimes, reminders were needed about what is involved in healing.

Henry was waking up the first morning in his room at the Baptist Hospital when Dr. Brock came by about seven o'clock. He spoke with Henry, checked his vital signs, and looked at the bandage. He asked Henry how he was feeling, and Henry mumbled something. He told Henry to take it easy and try to pee and, a little later, eat something when food was brought. The nurse brought a hand-held male urinal, and Doris directed his attempt to "produce." The small amount of urine that was in the urinal afterward was a good sign to the hospital staff. This urine event was entered on Henry's medical chart. Maybe it was a sign of other good things that would happen that day.

In a dazed mind and under the influence of at least some pain-killer, Henry began to quietly think and assess what was ahead for him. Dr. Brock had left. Lying in the bed with a big bandage on his right arm nub and a body sore from all he had been through resulted in mental and physical challenges.

Henry felt lost without a right arm and hand. He wondered how he could ever learn to do anything. How could he farm? How could he dress and feed himself? His clothes mostly had buttons. Buttoning and unbuttoning was something he had never done with just his left hand. His pants had buttons and not zippers (zippers weren't used much in 1943 on clothing worn by farmers), and tying shoes with one hand would be difficult to learn. Maybe Dr. Brock could get him some help in doing these things.

At first, Henry didn't realize how fortunate he was to have Doris to help him with so many things. She had a lot of learning to do as well. Many of those things that her man had done so easily and readily would now be big challenges. She would have to help him. She would have to learn a lot of new things in the process, some of which would be more challenging than others.

About that time, a tray with breakfast food was brought into the room. Henry was encouraged to drink and eat what he could; he was told that nutrition would be critical in his recovery. He asked what was on the tray, and he was allowed to look. The nurse and Doris used the hand crank at the end of the bed to prop him to a sitting position so he could eat and swallow.

Henry had a lot to learn. He didn't know how to hold a glass or cup, spoon or fork, or much of anything else with his left hand. Doris lifted the small glass of tomato juice with a straw for him to take a sip. He tried and did get a tiny taste. He decided he wanted to try coffee, so Doris put cream and sugar in it and lifted the warm cup to his lips. She held a cloth underneath just in case some spilled.

Next, he tried a small bite-sized piece of biscuit with butter. Doris broke off the small bites with her hands and placed them in Henry's mouth. Neither biting nor chewing was easy. It was painful due to sore gums resulting from three teeth being knocked out in the accident. He got a little food chewed and swallowed. Next, he had a teaspoon of grits (not much chewing is needed with grits). Henry then wanted a sip of milk; Doris held the small glass to his lips, and he tried to drink a couple of small swallows. Henry then mumbled, "No more." And he continued, "It doesn't taste right. It hurts to eat."

Doris reassured him that a taste for food would return, and then she asked, "What would you like? I will try to get it for you."

Henry mumbled, "Corn bread and fried salted pork meat. Small pieces of both."

"I will see," Doris responded. "It might be at lunch."

As an active man, Henry was beginning to get restless; pain was returning. He wanted to see Son and get out of the bed. He wanted to walk around. He wanted to check on things at the farm—the pigs, cows, horses, and mules.

"I want to go to the Ratliff Store," Henry said. He added, "I want a can of Prince Albert tobacco and some cigarette paper. And a small box of matches." (He hadn't yet thought about how hard it would be to roll a cigarette or strike a match on the box with just a left hand!)

"I don't think you can go this morning," Doris said, adding, "You can go to the store when you are home and able to get about. You might see some of your friends." She didn't tell him that the hospital actually allowed patients to smoke in their rooms. (How could the hospital have done that?) Doris didn't want him insisting on doing it, though he might have had a craving for nicotine. Maybe it was time to quit smoking; Doris hoped it would be.

Dr. Ashford came into the room. He greeted everyone and said he was making his rounds, including seeing other patients who were in the hospital. Dr. Ashford always wore a dress suit. He was the longtime family physician and known as a straight shooter. He could be blunt and gruff; he could be gentle and comforting. He walked over to Henry's bed. Henry saw Dr. Ashford and tried to speak to him. But, Henry's speech was somewhat rambling and blurred (though better than the day before). While Dr. Ashford was there, Doris slipped away to tell Dolly to bring Son to Henry's room in a few minutes. Doris returned to Henry's room just as Dr. Ashford was leaving. She thanked him for coming and expressed appreciation for what he had done for the family.

Before he left, Dr. Ashford spoke to Doris. "Henry said he wanted some Prince Albert. Well, let me tell you something: don't let him have it or any other tobacco products. None of that Brown Mule chewing tobacco or Garret snuff (Henry didn't use snuff, so that wasn't a problem). Healing and overall health will be damaged if he uses tobacco."

Doris said, "Thank you. He won't get any as long as he is here in the hospital. And, how is his progress? When do you think he might be released to go home?"

"It will be a while," Dr. Ashford responded. "I spoke with Dr. Brock. He felt that in 10 days or so he would be recuperated enough. Henry has a great deal of progress to make. It will take a lot of adjustment for a man who had an active life. He may be hallucinating. I sense he needs something to relieve pain. I will ask a nurse to bring painkiller to him."

The "something to relieve pain" soon had an effect. Henry fell back asleep. About then, Dolly arrived at the room with Son, who viewed his father as a bandaged, sleeping, pitiful man. When a nurse came into the room, Doris left with Dolly and Son to talk about the days ahead. Doris told Dolly how much she appreciated her help and that she would be with Henry at least another week in the hospital. They chatted momentarily and decided that Dolly should go back to her home and take Son. (She needed to get back to attending her college classes at Belhaven College in Jackson.) She was going to call Harper's Store and ask that they relay the message to Mom Amelia and Paw Paw Sloan to come get them.

Paw Paw and Mom Amelia got the message and arrived at the Baptist Hospital around noon. Dolly and Son were in the cafeteria when they arrived. Eating away from home was quite an experience for Son; he was interested in all the foods on the cafeteria line. He wanted to stay there with Dolly. So, it worked well for Doris to briefly take Paw Paw and Mom Amelia to Henry's room; they saw him sleeping and looking like a very sick man. Doris told them that he had at least another week in the hospital. She wondered if Son could stay with them. They readily agreed. Doris hugged and kissed Son goodbye, and by 1:00 p.m. Mom Amelia, Paw Paw, and Dolly, along with Son, were on the way back to Plain (Richland).

In the meantime, a tray with a light lunch had arrived in Henry's room. It was mostly liquid kinds of things, though it did have what Henry had asked for: corn bread and fried salted pork meat. (Doris had relayed that request to the kitchen.) Henry was beginning to wake up from the last painkiller he had taken. Dr. Brock came by on an unexpected mid-day visit and spoke with a dazed Henry. He checked vital signs and examined the bandage on his nub. He told Henry that his lunch was here and to eat and drink all he could; he said that nutrition was very important to healing and getting to go home. Eating wasn't easy; it was painful. The hospital staff, including Dr. Brock, paid little attention to the gum with the missing teeth; they were more concerned about the life-threatening trauma from destruction of his arm. But, Doris had observed the missing teeth when she first saw Henry at the hospital. The nurse in the emergency room made the same observation and noted it in his medical records.

Eating wasn't easy for Henry. Doris helped him. She was able to get Henry to sip a little southern sweet tea by holding the glass for him. She got him to eat some strawberry gelatin dessert/salad by feeding it to him with a spoon. Next, she gave him small pieces of the corn bread. She used a knife and fork to cut the salt pork into small pieces and put some in his mouth. That didn't go well; he could not do the amount of chewing that was needed, but finally he was able to swallow a bit. The orderly came for his tray; he was promised more corn bread and salt pork at supper (the evening meal).

In mid-afternoon, Dr. Brock came by the room to check on Henry. As always, Doris was at Henry's side. Henry didn't talk much and hardly responded to Dr. Brock's questions. "You know, Henry," Dr. Brock said, "you need to get out of the bed and begin walking. I am going to have therapists visit you and develop a plan just for your needs. Therapists are in very short supply. Wounded soldiers coming back from war are getting most of the attention; civilians find it hard to get much medical care for serious traumatic injuries. But, I will get someone just for you and your therapy needs."

"Thank you. I sure need someone to help me," Henry mumbled. "Doris is doing a lot, but more would be good."

"A physical therapist will likely come by first to talk with you and Doris and have you do a few things," Dr. Brock said. "The person will develop a plan for you. Once you have a tentative plan, an occupational therapist will be by to work with you. Sometimes, a nurse with special skills in therapy may see you. The goal is to try to get you back on your feet again."

Doris thanked Dr. Brock (she was a big believer in thanking people; it was a part of building relationships). Henry was still in much of a daze and not able to think clearly and speak well. Doris said, "If the nurse will tell me what to do, I will try to help. I believe I can do a few things that will help him recover."

The physical therapist came by the room the next day. She introduced herself as Miss Jones; Doris said she was Henry's wife and was trying to help him. Miss Jones said she was a physical therapist and looked at Henry's chart and noted his failure to get out of bed. She assessed his situation and talked a bit. She concluded that

Henry needed to be up and active as much as possible. She said she would talk with Dr. Brock and Dr. Ashford and make a plan that would help him regain abilities.

Miss Jones said she would come back before the end of the day with a plan that included an occupational therapist. At that time, she would begin getting Henry out of the bed and gradually on the move one short step at a time. She explained that her role was to help remediate difficult things (impairments) resulting from the tragic accident, including the loss of his right arm. She explained that an occupational therapist named Miss Smith would help with daily living functions, such as dressing and eating. She also said some farm skills might be included. She talked about helping him have a good quality of life. In reality, Henry and Doris didn't care what kind of therapists Miss Jones and Miss Smith were as long as they could help.

After a couple of hours, Miss Jones returned. She had what Henry thought was a nurse with her, who was introduced to him as Miss Smith, occupational therapist. Miss Jones explained that she had talked with both doctors and had a plan that would help Henry in moving about and doing activities needed in daily life. She said it wouldn't always be easy. He would need to do certain exercises and practice doing things in new ways. He would learn how to better use his left arm and hand. Miss Jones said she spent most of her time at another hospital and Miss Smith would help carry out the plan that she developed.

Miss Jones explained that, first, they would focus on things for daily living and then on skills used in Henry's work of farming. At that point she asked Henry to lift and flex (bend) his left arm at the shoulder and elbow. The arm was sore and stiff, and it hurt just to bend the elbow. Also, she had him grasp and lift an empty small water glass a couple of inches. This was repeated several times. She talked about how this would help him later in getting better.

Miss Jones spoke to Henry directly: "Henry, I want you to stand beside your bed. Miss Smith and I will help you put your feet off the bed and on the floor. We will then help as you go about standing. We will be with you and make sure you don't fall."

Henry groaned at the thought of getting out of the bed. Miss Jones spoke again: "I know it won't be easy; it never is when recuperating from an injury. We need to get you going, or you will never be able to get out of the bed. You can do it. You are a strong man. It will take effort. I will help you. Let's get started."

Miss Jones used the crank at the end to lower the bed. She then helped Henry to move his feet slowly off the bed and toward the floor. He complained a bit about pain. No stopping now. As Miss Smith assisted, the two therapists now had him gradually slide off the bed but with his bottom still touching it. Then they helped him stand. Miss Jones asked him to place his left hand on the bed and move sideways along it. Maintaining balance might be an issue, so she stayed right beside him.

Henry was, of course, used to having two arms and hands, but now he had only one for keeping his balance and holding onto things, such as the side of the bed. Miss Jones explained that the arm loss would affect his balance when standing, walking, or getting up from a chair or bed and in other ways. After a few minutes, she and Miss Smith helped Henry back to his place at the side of the bed. They helped him onto the bed by having him sit on the side and use his left hand to rotate (pivot) on his bottom and then lift his legs and feet onto the bed. These movements were painful and doddering. Henry was not sure of himself. He was exhausted just from this. Miss Jones said he needed to do more to regain his strength.

Miss Jones said she had to go to another hospital but that Miss Smith would help carry out the plan. She said that Miss Smith was well qualified to help him and had just completed additional studies in providing therapy. Miss Jones said that she would be back

mid-morning the next day to check on him. She told Henry that between now and then, he should diligently do the things Miss Smith
requested. She said he would need to repeat activities several times.

Miss Smith began activities associated with eating and drinking. One of the activities was for Henry to lift and flex his left arm;
another was for him to grasp an empty water glass in his left hand
and lift it to his mouth. Sounds simple; it wasn't to Henry. The
purpose was to help him develop use of his left hand and arm.
Doris was listening to all the exercise instructions and watching the
activities. She thought she might be able to get Henry to do some
of what was recommended. She hoped he would be cooperative.

The next four days were routine as Henry continued to slowly
overcome the devastating loss he had suffered. His need for painkillers became a little less each day. Henry's intake of food and
drink increased a small amount each day. He did the exercises that
Miss Smith asked him to do. Every day she came by his room and
gradually expanded the number of exercises and the amount of
time devoted to them; occasionally the physical therapist came by.
Henry's ability to function without a right arm and hand made very
little progress. Maybe a better attitude was needed toward therapy.

Doris was right there to help him in drinking, eating, and body
waste elimination. She gave him limited sponge baths. Both Dr.
Brock and Dr. Ashford came by each day to check on him. They
and the nurses carefully assessed the big bandage and sutures. The
bandage was removed. The sutures were checked, and a new bandage was prepared. The sutures would likely be removed the next
time the bandage was replaced.

Preacher Murrow, of the Pocahontas Methodist Episcopal
Church, came by to visit and said a brief prayer but not much more.
He left a few minutes after arriving but said he would soon be back.

Henry's sisters Ivie and Edna visited him several times. Their
visits were usually encouraging and uplifting. His sister Lyda

brought their mother, Carrie, for a visit. Carrie said little; she appeared to realize that Henry was in serious shape. Doris asked Lyda if she would get pants, a shirt, and a few other items for Henry from the dresser in their bedroom and bring them the next time she came to the hospital.

Paw Paw and Mom Amelia Sloan and Dolly visited. Of course, they brought Son each time so that he could see his father and his father could see him. Doris was comforted by her parents and sister. They were always able to bring a little cheer into hospital-stay days.

With the help of a therapist and Doris, Henry walked a few steps out of the room after four days and sat in a chair during one of the therapy sessions. His balance wasn't good. When walking, he had to be held up to keep from falling. His body was still sore all over. Son stood by his chair. Henry asked Son to stand on his left (Son didn't know what he was talking about, but other people present helped get it straight) so he could put his arm around him. This was a precious, first-time moment for Henry since the accident. There would never again be a hug given with his right arm!

The Clarion-Ledger newspaper (a daily that served central Mississippi) had a short story on Henry and the accident. The article, dated January 22, 1943, two days after the accident, said that "...in some manner his arm was caught in the machinery and was torn from his shoulder." An article in The Jackson Daily News (an afternoon paper) published the same day as the article in The Clarion-Ledger indicated that "Jasper Henry Lee, Tinnin planter, was reported resting well following the amputation of his right arm at the Baptist Hospital Wednesday night. Mr. Lee's arm became entangled in the belting of a feed mill he was operating at a Tinnin store and [he] was immediately rushed to Jackson." The article went on to identify family members who had visited Henry in the hospital. People in Clinton, Tinnin, and elsewhere who knew Henry but had not heard of this tragedy now had the news.

On Sunday afternoon, January 24, Paw Paw and Mom Amelia Sloan and Dolly again came to see Henry. Henry was somewhat alert but still shocked the adults who had known him. He had become depressed. Dolly brought Son into the room, and Henry seemed to perk up; he did love that boy! He was now happier and more alert. Henry asked that Son sit on the bed at his left arm so he could touch him. He tried to talk to him. Son then lay down on the bed beside his father; that seemed to be so meaningful to Henry. After about 30 minutes, the Sloans left with Son and said they would be back on Tuesday afternoon. To Doris, the presence of Son, though it was for just a few minutes, seemed to give spirit and hope to Henry.

One week after the amputation, Henry was quite alert and more energetic but still weak. He was eating more food and drinking more fluids. In the process, he was mostly feeding himself.

Henry wanted to get dressed and go home. He couldn't walk alone, much less put on his clothes. Dr. Brock was asked about when Henry might go home. Henry said something like, "When can I go home? Doc, I really want to go. I have things to do."

"Continue practicing getting dressed and walking," Dr. Brock said. "Another few days may be needed in the hospital. Be patient, and remember you can't immediately do everything. Get your wife or another person to help you. When standing, have someone hold onto your left arm. You certainly don't want to fall. That would be bad, particularly if you landed on your right side."

"Doc, I have a farm to run," Henry said with some emotion. "I have animals to look after and fields to prepare. I need to get back on the farm. That place has been a farm in my family since the 1840s. It has withstood a lot, including military activity during the Civil War, and I have got to see that it continues."

"Yes, I know," Dr. Brock said, adding, "but take your time. You want to heal properly. You will need to gradually get back to doing things on the farm. Maybe you can go home in about three days, but you will still need to gain strength and learn how to go about life's routines. You can begin to practice here in the room with your wife and a nurse helping you."

"Yes, I will," Henry said impatiently. He continued, "I am so destroyed by this. How will I ever be able to get work done again?"

Touching Henry's left hand, Dr. Brock said, "Be patient. Begin doing things gradually. It is like this: The only limits you will have are those you set on yourself. Be positive. Have confidence. You can do it. Do not ever become discouraged."

On his way out of the room, Dr. Brock indicated to Doris that he wanted to speak with her in the hall. "Henry may be just now realizing that he has suffered a major loss," Dr. Brock began. "He will be challenged physically, emotionally, and spiritually. It is going to take some time for him to heal. He will need to take pain medicine for a while, but we don't want him to get addicted to it. I have a question: How would you feel about me calling Preacher Murrow and asking him to speak with Henry about some of the challenges he faces and how the church can be of help? It might be useful. Henry is in a fragile mental state and needs reassurance. Would that be okay?"

"Yes," Doris replied. "That would be okay with me. He came by the room for a couple of minutes a few days ago. He didn't stay long; maybe he will stay longer now. Henry has a lot of respect for Preacher Murrow. You should also know that Henry has his own thoughts about preachers. Go ahead and call him soon. Thank you."

The conversation in the hall with Dr. Brock was ended; Doris went back into the room. Henry was alert enough to ask, "What did Dr. Brock want to talk about?"

"About your care," Doris replied. "He thought it would be good for Preacher Murrow make a special visit and spend time with you talking about adjusting to life when you get home. I told him that I thought it would be a good idea."

"That will be fine," Henry said, "but I don't want to hear about hellfire and brimstone stuff. I need more than somebody praying for me and telling me to come to church and repent of my sins. Sins are not what I need help with. I need help with living and farming."

"I don't think he will talk about the fires of hell," Doris responded. "I feel that Preacher Murrow will focus on real-life issues. I have always thought he was a practical, human-focused person. You know, I went to Belhaven College—a Presbyterian school that tried to use a practical approach but was sometimes fundamentalist. Preacher Murrow will fit in with Belhaven's approach, though he is Methodist."

Preacher Murrow arrived the next morning. He greeted Henry, expressed concern for what had happened, and asked Henry if he was coming along okay. (He didn't want to begin with a prayer, and that suited Henry.)

"I think I am doing tolerably well," Henry replied, "but I don't know how I will be able to get by on the farm." A quiet pause was in the room.

"You will come along to the good," Preacher Murrow responded and then added, "You know, you were in an accident that would get most folks down. But, you are strong. You will discover how to do work and move ahead with your life in a godly way."

(Henry wondered, "What did he mean by the word "godly"? There was nothing godly about my accident.")

Henry nodded. Tears rolled down his cheeks. The room was very quiet. The preacher shuffled his feet, cleared his throat, and coughed. Yes, coughed, and a second time. Frankly, the preacher didn't know what to say in this situation.

"The only limits you will have are those you set on yourself," the preacher said, repeating what Henry had been told by Dr. Brock. "You will be able to do almost anything you want in a few days. Yes, some adjustment may be needed, but you can do it."

"Look at me," Henry sighed. "The big damn bandage and all are so damaging to my being. Do I look like I can do anything I want? I guess the Selective Service Board will not be interested in me now. Some of my friends in the war are winding up dead or in worse condition than I am. Sometimes I hear the news on the radio that war is bad. Here I am. I need help! I need to get my life going again. The therapist is helping me some." He thought to himself that this was a typical preacher with "pie in the sky" statements and goals without anything practical to back them up. Henry thought that maybe the preacher didn't know what to say and was using phrases he had heard at a church conference.

They chatted a little longer, and then Preacher Murrow said he had to go for now but would see him in a day or so. He said a brief prayer before he left. Just as he was leaving, the therapist came in to get Henry to do his daily exercises. Most of the time, Henry did not like to do the exercises because they were painful, but this day seemed different; maybe he felt better because the preacher he respected had been by and offered some confidence-building statements. (He had been given a painkiller a little earlier in the day.)

The therapy that day involved trying to walk and keep balance. The therapist explained, as Dr. Brock had earlier, that falling would be very bad, particularly if the shoulder with the amputated arm hit the floor. She suggested that he hold onto furniture, brace against the wall, or get someone to walk with him. The person should be strong enough to steady him and prevent falling.

Therapy that day included a range of activities: holding a fork with the left hand, buttoning a shirt (that was really hard to do), putting on socks, and brushing his hair. Doris had been dressing and feeding him. The therapist wanted him to do these things for himself so that he could develop more independence. She told him that she had to go but would be back in the morning. She said that he needed to practice doing the things they did today for himself.

The day to go home arrived. Doris had been told about it the day before but was asked not to tell Henry just in case it fell through. Dr. Brock came by to talk and check on him. "Good news today for you," he said. "Henry, you can go home today. I will send some pain medicine and have a fresh bandage put on your shoulder. Come to my office in three days for a checkup. Probably any remaining stitches will be removed, and a fresh bandage put on. Don't let the bandage get dirty. Keep it dry."

Henry said, "Okay. I am ready!"

Doris was listening and assured that Henry would make the appointment in three days. She didn't find it easy to manage Henry, but she thought she could this time.

Dr. Brock also said, "Henry, you should see a dentist and a prosthetic specialist. You need to get your teeth fixed and consider an artificial arm and hand. For pain, take the medicine I am sending. Do not take more than the prescribed amount. I do not want you to get addicted to drugs. Let me caution you: Don't overdo yourself; be patient, as things that were easy to do may not be so easy to do now. Watch your balance when trying to walk. Above all, do not injure your right shoulder."

Henry was especially happy when he was told he could go home. Doris went to the business office to take care of details and check him out. She then made a couple of calls before she went back to the room to help Henry get dressed. First, she called the Ratliff Store so someone there could notify the Lee family. She said to tell the family to have Otho come and get them at the Baptist Hospital shortly before noon today. (Otho was the farm worker helping Henry on the day of the accident.) She next called Harper's Store so the Sloan family could be notified. Henry and Doris wanted Son, who had been staying at his grandparents' house while Henry was in the hospital, to go home with them.

Doris returned to the room and helped Henry get dressed (he

couldn't do much for himself at this point, even after a few days of therapy). It was a learning experience. Putting on the shirt was first. The left sleeve of Henry's unbuttoned shirt was pulled onto the left arm and up and around the shoulder. The right side was draped over the right shoulder and bandage. Doris helped him put on his pants; he sat on the side of the bed, and Doris got both legs through the pants legs and pulled them up just above his feet. With his legs in the pants, he stood up so she could pull up his pants and button them at the waist and fly. She put his socks and shoes on him and tied the shoes comfortably for Henry to shuffle along with someone at his side.

Henry sat back on the bed and immediately stated that he needed to pee. Doris brought and held a male urinal; she unbuttoned his pants. Henry was able to use his left hand to be sure the pee went into the urinal. Afterward, she put the urinal down and buttoned his pants. (It was good he had that need over before getting in the car to head home.) The nurse arrived with a rolling chair, and Henry sat in it. He was too weak and feeble to walk all the way to the front door of the Baptist Hospital from his room. As he was leaving his room and being pushed along the hallway, Henry wanted to say goodbye to everyone who had helped him.

Otho drove the Lee family car to the front of the hospital to get Henry. He waited with the car at the entrance. A nurse pushed the rolling chair through the doorway and out to the car. Otho got out of the car and went to Henry. "Mornin'," Otho said. "Mr. Henry, how you doin'? We been missin' you. We all been prayin' for you. I come here to take you home. I will help you all I can." They shook left hands.

"I want to get home fast," Henry said. "I miss Tinnin so much. About all I think about is the work to be done. It is winter. Not much field work has been missed. The horses, mules, cows, and hogs need care."

Otho responded, "Don't you worry, Mr. Henry. We been takin' care of dem."

Otho was kind and gentle in helping Henry into and out of the car. This relieved both the nurse and Doris of some of the responsibility.

In the meantime, Mom Amelia, Paw Paw Sloan, and Dolly had driven from Richland to the Baptist Hospital. They brought Son, who was going to ride home with his mommy and daddy. Henry grinned big when he saw him (three missing teeth were quite obvious). Doris thanked them for taking care of Son while Henry was in the hospital. Son cried. He didn't want to leave his grandparents and aunt. They had been so good to him—even bought one-cent candy pieces at Harper's Store! Son was probably also somewhat uneasy about his father with the bandage, weak body, and uncertainty in walking.

Going home was frightening to Doris as well. She did not know if she could cope with all that Henry would need. Just dressing him, providing food, and taking care of elimination needs weighed heavily. She was determined to do what she needed to do. Her family background and German immigrant upbringing helped her to have the resolve to care for Henry. Sometimes, however, she did not know what he needed or the best way to do it. She also knew that they lived in the same house with Carrie, a mother-in-law who was not always friendly, understanding, and cordial. Carrie could not be counted on for any help.

Henry and Doris said goodbye to a couple of nurses who had helped them so much during the hospital stay. They rode away with Otho driving and Henry, Doris, and Son in the back seat. Son sat on the left side of his father next to his mother. Henry was on the right side of the car so he could put his left arm around Son. (Later, Henry would learn to always sit so that his left arm could conveniently operate a door.)

As they rode along, Henry watched Otho drive. He had driven for years, but now he saw driving in a new way. He observed steering, shifting, and other hand-operated car features. Of course, there weren't many automatic features because this was a 1938 or 1939 Ford (never quite sure of the year model, as they looked alike). Henry thought deeply about driving. He became emotional. Shifting gears normally involved using a right hand; steering called for both hands. The place for the ignition key was on the right side of the steering column. Starting the engine was with a floor-mounted starter pedal pushed with the right foot, so he could do that. He couldn't help but think about all the things he had done for years that would now be big challenges and, maybe, no longer possible. He figured that he would have to use his left hand to do everything. Shifting would require reaching across his body. Maybe he could brace the steering wheel with his left leg to keep it from turning while he was reaching across to shift.

It was a great sight to Henry as they neared the farm and headed down Shepard's Hill. A view of the Lee-Shepard farm driveway was in the distance. Otho soon turned the car into the driveway, drove a distance down the muddy, rutty road, and crossed the cattle gap. While crossing the cattle gap, Henry let out a loud shout, "Hallelujah!" He could see the big, pre–Civil War home where he had grown up and now lived. The car then went down the hill to the house. Otho parked near the yard gate rather than as usual under the car shed. This was so Henry could get out and have a shorter distance to walk to the house on the brick walkway. He said he would later put the car under the shed.

Henry looked around as much as he could, particularly toward the lot. He was soon reminded to focus on his walking to the house. He was weak and had some continuing balance issues associated with the loss of his right arm. Doris held onto his left arm to steady him. His body now had a new center of gravity, so to speak. Since an arm is about 6.5 percent of a person's the body weight, Henry had lost about 10 pounds from his body. In his mind, Henry thought the right arm was still there. He had to consciously think otherwise.

Keeping balance while walking required the continual focus of his brain on what he was doing. Doris and Son patiently walked with Henry; Doris and Otho helped him up the steps onto the front porch and across it into the house. Inside the house, Henry went to the bed in his and his wife's room, where he at first sat and then lay down. He said he was tired and would rest a bit before continuing to look around the farm. He said he needed to figure out which side of the bed was better for him with only a left arm to use in getting into and out of it.

Otho brought Henry's and Doris's belongings to the porch. He went back to the car and drove it under the shed. He came back to the front porch door and knocked to speak with Doris about anything else he could help with. "Yes, there is," Doris said. "Would you please build a fire in our wood-burning heater?"

Otho got about a dozen dry, stove-size pieces of split oak wood into the house and placed five in the stove and the remainder in the hamper on the floor. He used a couple of small pieces of pine lighter knot kindling to get the fire burning. Since no fire was in the stove while Henry was in the hospital, it was cold, and there were no warm embers to help get the fire started.

Doris then invited Otho to talk with Henry, who was not very alert and couldn't think of much of anything. Henry wanted to see the animals and fields. Getting to them was not very practical at this time. The paths and trails on the farm were not such that a car could go on them; most of the time, crops were checked by riding a horse, driving a mule-drawn wagon, or walking. Fortunately, it was late January, and no crops were in the fields. Otho said he would go to his house and return in the morning. He lived in a sharecropper house on the farm and had long been associated with the Lee family. He could walk to his house, which was only about a quarter mile away.

Neither keeping Henry comfortable nor getting him ready for bed was easy. Doris had Son to be very still on the bed beside him. She asked Henry what he wanted to eat, as it was near time for the evening meal. "Peas, pone, and pork," was Henry's response, and he added, "with a little sweet tea." (Ice wasn't usually kept in the winter, so the tea would be made with cool water.) Doris knew he meant dried peas, corn bread, and fried salted pork meat. This was a favorite comfort food for him.

Doris prepared the food in her meager kitchen on the kerosene stove they had bought when they got married. He ate a little; she and Son also ate. Peas, corn bread, and salted pork meat were long-term staples in the Lee family diet (regardless of nutritional value). Sometimes, the salt pork was referred to as "sow belly," which was a sort of very low cost food produced on the farm. This time it was from a hog harvested the Monday before Thanksgiving and preserved in salt in the smokehouse. The meat was popular with many rural folks in the South. At this time of year, the only peas available were dried and shelled black-eyed peas produced on the farm as food for the winter. (The jars of peas canned last summer were already gone; Doris knew that she needed to can more vegetables next summer.)

Henry was served a small plate of his food in bed along with a glass of cool sweet tea. There was no ice or refrigerator to make it cold and limited sugar because of rationing during the war. Doris had learned to use saccharin as a substitute for sugar to sweeten tea. With Doris helping to feed him, Henry ate a small amount. Son helped him eat but made a big mess of bread crumbs and peas in the bed; crumbs in a bed are uncomfortable and not good for sleeping! Doris brushed the crumbs off the bed and onto the floor and then swept the floor. She used a dustpan to pick up what been swept into a pile.

That evening she prepared a molasses milk drink (one of the

win-the-war food and beverage items mentioned in chapter 6). All she needed to do was add the right amount of molasses to a pint of fresh cow's milk and sprinkle a tiny amount of salt on top before stirring and serving cold or cool. If she had not had fresh milk, she could have used a cup of evaporated milk and a cup of water instead. The molasses took the place of sugar and added iron to the diet. Besides a few gallons of molasses were left from what had been produced on the farm last fall.

During Henry's homecoming, his mother, Carrie, was in the room across the hall in the house. She opened the door and stuck her head out only once to say welcome home and alert her daughter-in-law, Doris, to the fact that she was there in her room. She did not offer Henry, Doris, or Son any assistance and gave the impression that she would not want to be bothered. Doris did all she could to help Henry with patience and love.

Henry's youngest sister, Lyda, dropped in to see him. She had a perky influence that evening. She still lived in the house in another room toward the back while she was attending nearby Mississippi College in Clinton. She asked if there was anything she could do. "Our firewood in the house is about out. Otho brought in a dozen pieces but used about half of them," Doris said and added, "It would be very helpful if you could bring us a few sticks of nice split oak for the stove. It may get colder tonight, and we may need more heat." Lyda brought wood and said she would check in the morning to see if there was something more she could do. She went to her room for the night. Even around Carrie, Lyda was always calm and cool!

Tomorrow would be a new day. It would be the first time Henry would awaken on the Lee farm since the loss of his right arm. How would he respond? Doris was concerned that he might overdo himself and fail to recognize that he could not go about life and work as he had in the past. He needed to strive every day but never overdo himself as he went about recuperating.

The loss of an arm or leg typically involves a grieving process similar to what a person experiences at the death of a loved one. Would Henry manifest such grief? Would he express anger and stress? Would he express resignation to his situation? Would he face the challenges ahead as an integral part of his life? He would need to develop new skills and approaches to cope with the loss of his right arm. Maybe at first the focus should be on lesser things related to daily living, such as putting on clothing, holding a fork, and signing his name with his left hand.

No doubt, Henry had much to learn. Everyone hoped he would be patient and not hostile to the events that lay ahead in his life. Doris hoped she was up to the task of helping him learn to live with only a left arm. Having a good attitude would promote adjustment.

8

Living a New Way

Waking up his first day at home after his accident, Henry appeared anxious to get going but also reluctant to charge out into the new day. He knew that there were challenges ahead. He optimistically felt that he could handle whatever he faced!

Doris had gotten an early morning fire going in the soon-to-be-replaced wood-burning heater in their bedroom. It would take a while for a little heat to spread around the room; the heater never got the room warm but took away some of the chill. It was fairly cool this late January morning in central Mississippi—maybe a low of 38°F outside. There wasn't much of a rush to get the day going, but there was a compelling drive inside to do what needed to be done. This was Henry's first day home from the Baptist Hospital.

Henry lingered in bed. Doris prepared breakfast—a freshly scrambled chicken egg with cold corn pone from the night before—and brought it to Henry in bed. After eating, he sat on the side of the bed in what appeared to be deep contemplation. Days of the week tended to get confused when he was following a schedule that wasn't normal for him. Henry did not realize that this day was Saturday.

Saturdays were always favorite days. The pace of work and living was somewhat slower. The earliest part of a typical Saturday was filled with routine: tune the battery-powered radio to station WJDX to listen to the news (particularly about war in the South Pacific and Europe and a farm report by the Hinds County Agricultural Agent), have coffee, and eat a small breakfast. Of course, time for talk and play with Son was included.

Doris wanted to make this Saturday as much as possible like any other, but play with Son when he awoke would be limited. Henry wasn't sure Son would understand the situation, and he didn't. Son would be at least four years of age when he began to realize what it meant for his father to have one arm gone.

Getting dressed wasn't going to be easy. With only one room as bedroom plus a kitchen and a hall, Henry and Doris tried to be very quiet so that they would not awaken Son. Doris did not rush Henry. She tried to apply what the therapist had told her; she waited for him to say he was ready to get dressed. When he said so, she helped him remove his pajamas and put on clean underwear, pants, and shirt. She did the buttoning and the putting on of socks and shoes. She was very careful not to create pain with touching or other movements.

Though Henry said he had some pain, he put off taking pain medicine because he did not want to take more than he absolutely needed. Henry was aware that some people became addicted to painkillers. They would get them at the local drugstore and continue taking them beyond the need. Such painkillers were not currently well regulated by the U.S. Food and Drug Administration. Henry knew of returning soldiers with injuries who would sometimes become too reliant on painkillers. With only one room as bedroom, a kitchen, and a hall, Henry and Doris tried to be very quiet so that they would not awaken Son.

The morning sun was now beginning to warm the outside air

and brighten the day. The fire Doris had made in the wood-burning heater was beginning to take some of the chill from the room. Henry, with the help of Doris, got up and sat in a chair near the bed and not far from the heater. Warm rays of heat struck one side of his body. After some twenty minutes of sitting in the chair, he called to Doris, saying that he needed to go to the "two-holer." Doris knew this was a good sign, as body functions needed to be regular. Both he and Doris had to think about how to proceed. She placed a warm cap on his head and draped a jacket over his shoulders. She slipped some old work shoes on his feet. They went out of their room, down the hallway, and out the back door through the porch. He used his left hand on the handrail, and Doris assisted him to get down the steps. He slowly and carefully walked the short path to the two-holer, with Doris holding his left arm.

All went well as they walked; there was no stumbling or staggering. They arrived at the two-holer, and Doris opened the door. Henry was able to lift his right foot the couple of inches needed to get inside; then his left foot. Doris stepped inside with him and closed the door. She unbuttoned his pants and pulled them and his underwear down so he could sit, and then she went back outside.

There was a new catalog between the two seat holes, but Henry had not mastered tearing pages with only his left hand, so Doris responded and went back inside. She handed him torn-out pages, and soon all was finished. Henry stood up, and Doris pulled up his underwear and pants and buttoned the waist and fly of the pants.

They made it out of the two-holer and back to the steps at the back porch. They slowly went up the steps and down the hallway to their bedroom. Henry was exhausted and lay back on the bed for a nap but didn't doze off. By then, Son was waking up and wiggling around in his little bed. Henry noticed it and called for him to come over to his bed. Son toddled over and crawled in next to Henry, and that made Henry happy!

Once he was back in the house and rested a bit, Henry noticed that the weather was clear. He thought it was warm enough to go outside and look around the farm. He might be able to walk around the yard with help. He remembered an old oak-wood walking stick his father had used that was stored in the closet under the stairs in the hall. Doris went and looked for it. She brought it to Henry. He described how his father had used it to steady himself in his final years. Henry stood up and tried walking with the stick. Holding it in his left hand was not comfortable; his brain still wanted it held in his right hand. Doris suggested that he try a few steps walking with the cane. She would be at his side. Henry did try a few steps in the bedroom and was successful but cautious.

Next, Henry wanted to go onto the front porch so he could see from one end of it into the garden, which had only a few cool-season leaf and root vegetables and the relatively inactive beehives. On this cool southern winter morning, not much activity was going on anyplace except with the hens out and about in the yard around their house. Henry didn't see their rooster, so he asked about him. Doris had to explain that a fox tore into the chicken yard a couple of nights ago, captured the rooster, and carried him away. "Damn fox," Henry said. "We will get another rooster before Easter. We need fertile eggs when the hens start setting. Having biddies is important if we are going to eat fried chicken this summer. Maybe we need two roosters. Do you think thirty hens should have two roosters?"

Over the years, the Lees had occasionally had similar issues with foxes. They needed to be sure that the fence was in good condition and that the henhouse was closed each day at dusk and opened at dawn. From the porch, Henry could also see into the orchard in front of the house. He thought he could see a few buds beginning to swell on the half-dozen peach trees.

His time on the porch went pretty well, and then Henry decided he wanted to go down the front steps and out into the yard. He wanted to walk out of the yard to the sheds and animal lot. Just as he was preparing to go down the front steps, Otho came up. Yesterday, he said he would come in the morning and see if there was something he could do.

"Mornin', Mr. Henry," Otho spoke. "How you doin' dis mornin'?"

Both Doris and Henry replied, "Good morning, Otho."

"I am doing tolerably," Henry said. "I want to look around the farm some and see the animals and fields." Otho and Doris thought that it wouldn't be easy to do today. Then Otho proposed hitching a horse to the small wagon and using the wagon to ride around the farm. Now that sounded good to Henry.

"Yes," Henry said. "Do it. I want to go."

Otho went and got the horse and wagon and drove it up close alongside the porch. The two men came up with a plan for getting Henry onto the wagon. They would put a couple of wide boards across from the porch floor to the wagon bed, creating a ramp. Next, with Henry seated in a straight chair, they would tip the chair somewhat backward, and Otho would slide it on its two back legs along the boards onto the wagon.

After Henry was in the wagon, he wanted to stay seated in the chair for the wagon ride. Wagon movement made that seem unstable. Henry moved from the chair to sit on a low built-in plank bench in the wagon. He held on to the side frame of the wagon as best he could with his left hand as it began to move. Doris and Son went along (Son liked riding in a wagon). First, they rode to the lot and saw the mules, horses, hogs, a couple of milk cows, and three nanny goats and one billy. (Henry wanted to know if the animals were being fed and the cows were being milked.) Next, they rode by the stable, pigpen, and corncrib. They went out the gate and turned toward the sweet potato shed.

A few rough spots in the road made for a bumpy ride. This roughness caused pain. "Damn," Henry cried out. "I can't go any farther in this rough-riding thing. Take me back to the porch and help me off." So, Otho drove the wagon to the edge of the porch like before, used the same boards, and had Henry to sit in the chair that was tipped backward and slid across to the porch floor. He helped Henry out of the chair to stand on the porch. Henry slowly walked back inside the house and wanted to lie down to rest. Otho and Doris helped him to the bed.

Henry, with tears in his eyes, asked, "When am I going to get over this? When will I be able to do things?"

Doris tried to respond in a positive way. She said, "I think you are making good progress. You will need time and patience. Remember to do the exercises you learned at the Baptist Hospital."

Otho asked if there was anything else he could do. Doris and Henry didn't have anything, so Otho left to park the wagon and unhitch the horse. He said he would come back Sunday morning.

Eating was a challenge. Doris had mostly fed Henry until now. Using the left arm and hand required new ways. She fixed lunch for him and said he should try to go to the table to eat. He agreed. She helped him to the chair at the end of the table. Son was sitting in a highchair without its tray and pulled up close to the table. Doris sat on the side near Henry. It was a close unannounced contest between Son and Henry to see who dropped the most food on the floor. The left arm and hand didn't operate particularly well when the brain involuntarily kept thinking about using the right hand. A spoon was found to be best for eating at the present time; however, it was felt that Henry would soon be able to use a fork (but never a fork and knife together to cut food, as that takes two hands). Henry returned to bed to take a nap when lunch was finished.

About three o'clock that afternoon, a car came over the cattle gap near the top of the hill and down the long driveway to the house. Of course, no stranger could come to the house without being announced by a couple of barking dogs; despite their barking, they were said to be harmless. Doris heard the barking, looked out, and saw the car stop near the gate. Preacher Murrow got out. Doris went onto the front porch to reassure the dogs and invite Preacher Murrow inside to see Henry. Before he went inside, Doris gave him an update on Henry's progress.

"Henry continues to have some pain," Doris said. "He has some difficulty keeping his balance, holding and using a fork and spoon, and dressing himself. He can't go out and see the farm by himself. This frustrates him. I am afraid he is beginning to feel that he will never be able to run the farm. Any words of encouragement you can offer would certainly be welcomed. He needs uplifting."

Preacher Murrow went inside. Henry was lying on the bed, but he began to try to sit up as soon as he knew the preacher was there. Doris helped Henry sit on the side of the bed. The preacher extended his left hand to Henry to shake hands. Henry had so learned that the right hand was for shaking that he had to override his brain and get his left hand to function. Preacher Murrow tried to be very positive and upbeat.

Preacher Murrow offered a short greeting prayer that he, as a pastor, thought was appropriate for Henry. The preacher then asked Henry to talk about things, talk about anything he wanted. Because of weakness and continued use of some pain medication, Henry was not as alert as usual, but he mumbled a few things.

"How will I ever be able to provide for my wife and son? I love them so much," Henry stated with tears in his eyes. "And, the farm—when will I be able to go about work on the farm?" (The situation just about overcame Doris with emotion. She turned her back to them and faced away.)

Sensing the emotion present, Preacher Murrow paused and reflectively began to speak. "Henry, you are a strong man. You can overcome almost all the problems that come your way. You can continue to be a good husband, father, and farmer. I am, of course, interested in your relationship with God and Jesus Christ."

Henry was perturbed at this direction in Preacher Murrow's discussion. Henry said, "Preacher, I need help and not saving as you view saving. I was christened into the Methodist Episcopal Church some thirty years ago. Look at me now. I am in bad shape. Did christening help me? How will this saving stuff help me deal with life?"

Preacher Murrow contemplated Henry's statements. He searched for a response. As a preacher, in situations like this, he had been taught to use certain automatic responses, such as "Jesus loves you" and "Are you washed in the blood?" Neither of these fit the present situation. Preacher Murrow thought that if he said such, he would further agitate Henry. He needed to be more of a counselor and less of a preacher. He decided that this situation was beyond what he could handle on that day. He said he would soon need to go but would return in a day or two. He had to finish preparing his sermon for tomorrow. Henry was okay with that. Henry's feelings were that this preacher couldn't help him, so who could? He remembered that most preachers at Pocahontas were good at coming to dinner, giving funeral services, and passing collection plates.

On his way out, Preacher Murrow spoke to Doris on the front porch out of Henry's hearing range. He wanted to know how she was holding up. She replied that she was doing okay but that it wasn't easy. Henry was impatient about getting back out on the farm. She mentioned that Otho, a farm hand, had been very helpful in this regard. Doris also mentioned that one thing that really helped her was the presence in the home of a woman named Susie Heckle, who could help look after frisky Son. Doris explained to Preacher Murrow that Susie was Carrie's sister, who had come to stay with them after Carrie's husband, Ira, died. Preacher Murrow didn't see Susie because she was out gathering eggs for Carrie.

Susie had a pleasant disposition, and based on that, some folks wondered if she and Carrie were sisters! She was a single woman, who, once married, had no children. Her husband had died. Susie (also known as Susie Jane) lived mostly by staying in the homes of sick people and caring for them or by staying with relatives and helping them. Susie had a nice way with Son. He loved her and, even as a small boy, would do about anything she would ask. Her looking after Son at certain times provided some relief for Doris.

Not only was Doris concerned about the health of the husband she loved, but she was also concerned about income for the family and how she could afford to take care of Henry and Son if Henry were not able to return to farming. What would happen to the farm? There was no one else to run it. Preacher Murrow concluded; as best he could, he talked in understanding and sympathetic ways. He told Doris to let him know if he could help with anything. But, did he mean it? Was he capable as a counselor in this situation? Maybe Henry needed more than a preacher with limited theological training trying to help him deal with a major challenge in life.

The remainder of the afternoon was somewhat routine. Henry went to the table for a light dinner and afterward returned to his bed to rest. It was now Saturday night and time for Doris to turn on the radio and move its antenna wire a bit to better pick up the live broadcast of the Grand Ole Opry by station WSM in Nashville, Tennessee. Henry enjoyed listening to the music for a while and hearing advertisements about Martha White Flour, Watkins Products, and other items of the day that had appeal to rural farm listeners who liked country and bluegrass music. The comedy of Grandpa Jones and others was silly but interesting entertainment. Henry could almost sense that he was a member of the audience in Ryman Auditorium in Nashville when Roy Acuff took to the stage performing "Wabash Cannonball." And, to think, the Lee family did not have a radio of any kind until about 1930. Now, listening was a routine part of life.

The next morning was a little more relaxed; it was Sunday (not that the day of the week mattered much to incapacitated Henry). A couple of Henry's sisters were coming to see him. First, Sudie and her husband, James, would be there in the early afternoon. They would have their nine-year-old daughter, Jimmie Lee, with them. Not long ago, Sudie had delivered their second child. It was a son that they named Ira. James had been working as a mechanic at Capital Chevrolet in Jackson but had given notice that he was quitting that job. He was going to become a watchmaker/horologist at Huddleston Jewelers. Henry wanted the new job to go well. He appreciated how his brother-in-law at Huddleston Jewelers had helped him.

Sister Ivy was coming a little later with her husband, Milford, and five-year-old daughter, Suellen. When they came, they spent more time with their mother, Carrie, than with Henry and Doris. That was fine with Henry and Doris because they sometimes had ideas about things related to the farm property that could not be fulfilled. Besides, Henry wasn't feeling up to a lot of visiting.

Sunday passed. It was evening and about dark. It was time for another radio show. This time the radio set was tuned to 620 on the AM dial for a regular Sunday evening program named "Hawaii Calls." The show was broadcast directly from the courtyard of the Moana Hotel on Waikiki Beach in Honolulu. The radio waves were at first sent to the West Coast of the United States by shortwave radio and rebroadcast by AM radio stations. At its peak, some 750 stations around the globe carried the show. It had a large following because of the patriotic feeling among Americans following the attack by Japan on Pearl Harbor on December 7, 1941.

On that day, the "Hawaii Calls" show opened with the enthusiastic voice of announcer Webley Edwards introducing the show with "The sound of the waves on the beach at Waikiki…" accompanied by actual sounds of the surf. This broadcast was realistic and invigorating even to a young farm man in the South. It featured Hawaiian instrumental and vocal music as well as sounds of Pacific Ocean water movement on the beach. Some of the performers on the show, such as Hilo Hattie, became household names on the mainland.

With descriptions by Webley Edwards, listeners could almost see the hula dancers, such as Beverly Noa, performing on the beach. People in rural Mississippi could listen and gain some insight into the Polynesian culture of the Hawaiian Islands. They could envision being in the beautiful Pacific Island environment, watching hula dancing and enjoying music as palm trees swayed in a gentle ocean breeze. Of course, many people in the United States spoke during World War II about the "damn Japs bombing Pearl Harbor." That created a lot of unfortunate hatred toward the Japanese and boosted a love of Hawaii.

Sympathy for people in the Hawaii Territory was high. Patriotism in the United States zoomed. Most people in the U.S. had a lot of positive feelings for Hawaii, though few had been there unless as a soldier in war. Some people knew that the Hawaiian Islands became a territory of the United States in 1898. Since late 1941 the territory was under martial law and would be until 1944. Statehood for Hawaii would not be granted until 1959, when World War II had been over about 14 years.

Federal law granting statehood to Hawaii excluded the Midway Islands. These Islands were also known as the Midway Atoll because of the ring-shaped chain of coral surrounding them. These islands had been considered a part of the Hawaiian Islands, though their time zone was the same as that of Samoa. The well-known naval battle of Midway was fought in 1942, which was some six months before Henry lost his arm. People on the mainland were well aware of the Midway battle and the sacrifices of human life that occurred, including a few of Henry's acquaintances. But mainland people did not know that the battle was over such a small island area that was uninhabited and used as a wildlife preserve.

Once the "Hawaii Calls" radio show was over, the radio was turned off to conserve the battery so there would be power to listen in the morning to the news and farm program. Henry went to bed for the night. Listening to the radio program brought a certain peace to Henry's mind. He was steadily but slowly gaining strength and striving to overcome challenges created by the loss of his arm. He had an appointment with his physician the next day, which was Monday and twelve days after the horrific accident.

The next morning, Doris got Henry ready to go for his appointment. She still had to help in many ways: hold his arm when he walked, go with him to the two-holer, put on clothing, button shirt and pants, and assist him in getting up and down at the table for meals. On this day, Otho drove them to Dr. Brock's office in Jackson.

In the exam, Dr. Brock asked Henry how he was doing. Henry's response reflected depression about his condition; he used foul language to explain his feelings. "Not worth a damn," was the response by Henry, who added, "The son-of-a-bitch fox got our rooster. If I had my right arm, I would have filled his ass full of 16-gauge lead shots. Old fox would never have gotten another chicken. You know I am not big with guns, but I will certainly use one to defend my family and property."

Dr. Brock tried to figure out what Henry was trying to say and find a few things to cheer him up. First, he wanted the rooster situation clarified, and Henry explained. Since Dr. Brock had grown up on a farm, he knew the importance of a rooster to having fertile eggs that, when incubated by a hen, would hatch, grow, and provide fried chicken for Sunday dinner. Dr. Brock then had his nurse remove the bandage on the nub for observation and take out a few stitches. He examined the nub and had the nurse put on a clean and smaller bandage. Dr. Brock indicated that the wound was healing well and there was no infection.

Another part of the follow-up was to find out about pain. Dr. Brock asked Henry if he had pain and, if so, where it seemed to be.

Henry said, "Yes, I have pain. It is just plain old hurting and also other kinds of feelings in my right arm and hand. Sometimes it feels like a spider is crawling on my right arm; other times it itches or stings. This is a big bother. What can I do about it?"

"Your nerves are involved," Dr. Brock responded. "You have nerves throughout your body that send messages to your brain. Your "hurting" should be diminishing. Any movement, such as the nurse putting a new bandage on or a coat being put on over your nub, can cause pain."

Dr. Brock asked if Henry had questions. He had none. Dr. Brock continued, "And the pains you are having are also known by another name. They are called phantom pains. Phantom pains or limb sensations are feelings from your arm that you have lost. Injured soldiers often suffer phantom pains with missing arms and legs. As a doctor, there isn't much I can do about them now, but maybe someday new ways will come along. In your case, once your nub has healed more, some relief from these phantom feelings may be gained by massaging the end of it with your left hand when the sensations or pains strike. Thank goodness phantom sensations are usually only occasional occurrences and do not usually continue for long times. What do you think, Henry?"

"That 'phantom' sounds about like what I have," Henry said. "It is very hard to get the feeling to go away. I can't knock the crawling spider off my arm. When it finally stops, I get to rest at ease."

Dr. Brock added, "As I said, such sensations usually go away over time."

Next, Dr. Brock discussed how to care for the stump or, in Henry's case, the nub. "It should heal without infection or bruising.

Keep the bandage clean. Replace it at least every three days using sterile gauze and tape. Before bandaging the nub, apply some of this special new antiseptic cream (he handed Henry a small tube). Doris can do it now that healing is well underway. Avoid lying on or propping on the nub or doing anything that would cause an abrasion or restriction to it. You can get good gauze and tape at the drugstore in Clinton."

Dr. Brock said he wanted to talk some more. He asked Henry if he would like to see the therapy nurse for help with walking, eating, dressing, and bathing. Henry said, "No, I have Doris to help with that."

Dr. Brock said, "Your rehabilitation will require exercises to stretch and use muscles and teach balance. I know Doris can help, but you might find a specially trained person to be beneficial. Otherwise, you may lose the ability to perform certain job and personal living skills. With practice, you will be able to retain or regain some of these. Did you play a violin? If you did, you will not be able to do that again." Dr. Brock was probably smart to raise something that Henry didn't do, such as playing a violin. Of course, Dr. Brock made his point but could have named things that Henry had been used to doing, such as driving a nail or holding the plow lines of a mule pulling a plow; but he didn't, and that was good for Henry. This helped keep the conversation positive.

The next topic was dental care. Dr. Brock talked about Henry going to a dentist for help with teeth that were knocked out during the accident. Henry said he would go soon. Next, Dr. Brock talked to Henry about getting fitted with an upper-limb prosthesis or, as he described it, an artificial arm. He told Henry where to go and who to talk with. Henry said he would go; Doris was there and also said she would take him. Dr. Brock added, "You should wait a little while so that the nub heals and shrinks to its long-term size. You don't want to get fitted while the nub is swollen or enlarged." Dr.

Brock said that Henry appeared to be doing okay with healing and that he should come back in about three weeks or anytime he had a problem. He handed Doris a brochure with ideas about how she could help care for Henry.

The appointment was over. Henry and Doris checked out at the front desk and got another appointment in three weeks and one day. This would be near the end of February. Otho saw them coming out and drove the car close to the front door.

On the way home, Henry was more alert and talkative than he had been in recent days. Somehow the appointment with Dr. Brock had boosted his spirits. Maybe he was no longer taking as much painkiller medicine, and his mind was sharper. Henry began to talk about how he was going to use his left hand to do common things he had previously done with his right hand.

Henry expressed personal interest in himself by saying, "The hair on my head is getting shaggy."

Doris immediately promised, "I will give you a cut this afternoon. You know, I have those new hand clippers that work well. I want you to look like my handsome husband."

Henry said, "Okay. And, I want to look like somebody who is going to make it and is 'right' to live with you." Then there was quiet for a while as the car rode along.

As they approached Clinton, Henry said, "I want to go to Edwards to Dr. Calendar's dental office and set a time for getting my teeth checked. That office is on the brick street not far from the humpity railroad bridge near the water tank." Otho drove there. The small town of Edwards was about 10 miles from Clinton, with Dr. Calendar's office situated on the town square. He was an older dentist who had been in practice a number of years and had helped the Lee family in earlier years as the need for dental care arose. Doris got out and walked into the front office. She told the assistant why she was there and asked about a time to come back. An appointment was set at ten on Thursday morning, which was three days away. Doris thought that Henry would be strong enough and ready for dental work. And then, Dr. Calendar came out and said he wanted to see Henry. He walked to the car, and they briefly chitchatted. Dr. Calendar wound up by saying he would see Henry on Thursday.

After the dental office visit, Otho drove the Lees back to Clinton so that Doris could go to the drugstore to get needed gauze and tape. Mr. Epting, the druggist (aka pharmacist), met Doris at the front door. He asked about Henry and said he had heard about the accident. After helping Doris get the supplies, Doc Ept (as Mr. Epting was called) said he would run an account until Henry was better; he could pay the charges then. The druggist also wanted to go out to the car to speak to Henry. They shook left hands and chatted briefly. Henry had always regarded Doc Ept with high respect. Maybe it was past experiences of Doris and Henry at the soda fountain in the drugstore. Milk shakes were their rare favorites, but on this day discussion was about serious health matters.

Doc Ept sensed this and offered a few words of encouragement. He told of another customer who had lost a leg. "Henry," Doc Ept said, "losing a leg above the knee is quite devastating. A man can't walk without a crutch or artificial leg. You can walk. You can get about. You do not have that problem. You are much more fortunate." Henry smiled and nodded at Doc Ept. Their brief conversation had perked up his spirits. Doc Ept told Henry to talk to him at any time about any problems. He said he was always available. This sounded like good news to Henry.

Otho continued the drive from Clinton to the farm. Henry saw familiar places along the way and talked about some of them. One new thing was Russell's Store on Monroe Street at the north edge of town. It was run by a couple with two small children who had recently moved from Sunflower County in the Mississippi Delta.

Henry would soon get to know the Russells and become a friend who could use one of their loafing seats. He would find that conversations around those seats whirled with local news and gossip; sometimes the reputations of people were on the line. It was also a place frequented by local politicians, particularly during an election year. There were always a few people around.

Henry particularly enjoyed a politician named John Bell Williams. He had been awarded the Purple Heart for his service in WWII in Europe. Williams lost his right arm in conflict. He and Henry particularly identified with each other. Williams became a member of the U.S. House of Representatives from Mississippi and was later elected Governor of the state of Mississippi.

There were a few residences near Russell's Store and other sites for building. The area had electricity, running water, and city sewage. Telephone service was also in Russell's Store and some of the houses in the area. Henry thought one of those building sites might be good for him and his family. But, first he had to heal.

The car moved on north through the Sumner Hill community with its Black Cat Café and, in a bit, down Shepard's hill before it made the turn into the driveway to the house on the farm. It went past a couple of tenant houses. Henry called the names of the sharecroppers in those houses. When the car stopped in front of the Lee-Shepard house, Henry opened the door and got out on his own. He used a walking cane to help in moving from the car to the house. As he made his way along the brick walk, he mentioned that he wanted to go to the lot to see the animals and around the place to see what work was needed in the fields. He said it was about time to start trimming back the fence rows and ditch banks along creeks that ran through the small fields.

Henry arrived back at the house and, after handing the walking cane to Doris, used the handrail to go up the steps. Once on the porch, it seemed as if he was tiring. Doris thought he might be overdoing it a bit. She had him go inside and sit in his favorite chair at the eating table. Doris quickly fixed something for lunch for Henry, Son, and herself. During lunch, Henry mentioned how nice Doc Ept had been to him (this represented a kind of bonding between the two).

When lunch was over, Doris had Henry stand so she could move his chair away from the table. She told him to sit in it and she would cut his hair or, as she was prone to say, "I am going to lower your ears." Henry especially liked for her to comb and brush his hair; it felt good! It was a time of closeness. Henry put his arm around her waist and gently pulled her toward his left side and whispered something that could have been interpreted as a desire for romance. She said that she loved him and got the broom to sweep up the cut-off hair on the floor. She didn't know how this romance "thing" might work out. It was way too soon for anything in the next few days or weeks. Doris thought to herself that Henry had only enough blood to maintain life in his body.

There were basic things Doris needed to work on with Henry to get him to do for himself. Bathing, personal hygiene, management of clothing, and mobility were big areas where effort would be needed for Henry to function independently. Of course, without running water or a bathroom, bathing in late January was little more than a sponge bath where "particulars" (as they were called by Doris) would be wiped with a soapy cloth and then the soap wiped off. On mornings when the night temperature went below freezing, the pipe from the spring in the woods would freeze, and there would be no water. Doris would walk a hundred yards or so to the spring branch, crack the ice covering the water that was flowing underneath, and use a gourd dipper to put water into the cedarwood bucket kept for such occasions. A boiler or kettle of clean water might be warmed on the kerosene cookstove and poured into a wash pan for sponge bathing. More thorough bathing would wait until summer when water could be placed in a large tub and left sitting in the sun to warm during the day or when creek bathing might be possible.

Doris never liked creek bathing. She thought the water was nasty; snakes or human excrement might be in it. She thought that there was no way to get clean bathing in such water. Getting rid of waste water in an environmentally appropriate manner was never a high priority for the Lee family. They really didn't know what "environmentally appropriate" meant. Most of the time, used bath water was thrown out into the yard or over the fence into the pasture for disposal. Used dishwashing water was managed differently. It was put into a large bucket in the kitchen along with food scraps and fed to hogs as slop. The bucket was typically emptied once a day into a trough in the hogpen. Of course, in a few years, scientists determined that feeding slop with uncooked meat pieces could transmit diseases to hogs and other animals. This became an unacceptable practice in hog raising.

Henry had made some progress in dressing himself, but he still had a way to go. He could sit in a chair or on the side of the bed and pull up his pants to his thighs. Then he would stand propped against the edge of the bed and pull them to his waist. Taking them off involved reversing the procedure. Buttoning and unbuttoning pants presented a definite challenge. Henry learned how to lean against a bedpost or the wall to hold one side of his pants up and use his left hand to pull over the other side, push it over to align the button and buttonhole, and move the button into and through the buttonhole. It was easier not to fasten all the buttons. Some clothing had snaps; he fastened them the same way as buttons. It was hard to get the two sides of a snap fastener lined up for snapping. Zippers were a big advantage when years later they became widely used in men's clothing.

Putting on a shirt was different. No sweaters or pullover shirts were worn; only long-sleeve shirts with buttons, except in the warmest summer months. To put on a shirt, Henry would push his left arm through the left sleeve. He would hold the shirt in position with his mouth if needed. After the left hand was through the sleeve, he would drape the right shoulder and sleeve of the shirt over his right side and pull it to the middle. He would pull the left to the middle and, using between-finger gripping, pull the buttons and buttonholes together. He would then wiggle the buttons through the holes. It was helpful if the holes were a little oversized. He would tuck the right sleeve into the waist of his pants. He could not fasten the cuff button of the left sleeve after he had put the shirt on. Sometimes he would use his mouth to try, but that didn't work too well. Other times he would ask Doris to fasten it. He preferred shirts with larger cuffs that slipped on and off over his left hand without unbuttoning. Once buttoned, a left sleeve was not usually unbuttoned if the cuff was large enough to slip over his hand; he preferred leaving the sleeve buttoned.

Walking and moving about had become much easier for Henry. His ability to keep upright balance, particularly with a walking stick, was much better. His fear of falling had diminished. Most of his walking without someone at his side was in the house and the yard. If he tried to go to the farm lot, Doris usually went along with him. Henry was becoming more independent yet careful in his movements.

Henry got in his mind the notion of trying to drive the car, pickup, and tractor. He had driven engine-powered vehicles since his father got their first Ford car in 1923. Further, he really liked to drive. He walked to the car shed, looked at the old pickup, and went over and opened the car door on the driver's side.

He looked at what he had to operate in order to drive. The car had a starter powered by an electric motor. It was operated by pushing down on the starter pedal that was on the floorboard to the right of the accelerator. He could easily push down with his right foot to start the engine. He was glad that the car was not started by turning a hand crank in the engine at the front under the radiator. Steering with one hand would not always be easy, but he knew he could do it. Shifting the gears would be the most difficult thing. Gears were shifted with the left foot on the clutch pedal and a floor-mounted shift lever that was to the right of the starter pedal. Getting his left hand all the way across his body and moving the shift lever while steering was going to be the greatest challenge.

Sitting there in the parked car, he practiced quickly reaching across his body to the gearshift lever, changing gears, and then moving quickly back to the steering wheel. He got out of the car, uncapped the gasoline tank, and looked inside to see if there was fuel. Yes, it appeared the tank was about half full, enough for a short run.

He got in, sat in the driver's seat, and started the car's engine by pushing down on the starter pedal with his right foot. The engine was slow to start, so Henry reached across to the right of the steering column and pulled out the choke knob. The engine quickly cranked once the choke was pulled out; he immediately reached back across and pushed the choke knob in. He let the engine idle a few moments so it would be warm and ready to move the car when the clutch was engaged. He used his left foot to push in the clutch pedal, reached across his body, and moved the gear shift lever into the reverse position. He quickly returned his hand to the steering wheel. He gave the engine a little fuel and slowly let out on the clutch pedal. The car gradually moved backward out of the shed.

Henry turned the car so that it was pointed toward the main gravel road up the hill. About that time, Doris saw what was happening and came rushing to the car. "Henry!" she shouted. "What are you doing?"

Henry abruptly lifted his foot from the clutch pedal, the car jumped, and the engine went dead. This gave him a chance to talk without noise of the engine. "I am going to the Ratliff Store," he said. "Want to go with me?"

Doris said, "Yes, I will go. You can't go by yourself. I will drive."

"No," Henry replied. "I am driving today. This will be my first time to drive since the accident."

Doris got into the car on the passenger's side. Henry restarted the engine, put the gear in first (lowest gear), and slowly let out on the clutch pedal, giving the engine some gas by slowly depressing the accelerator at the same time with his right foot. The car moved forward. After a bit of speed, he pushed the clutch pedal down with his left foot and swiftly reached across with his left hand and moved the gear shift lever up and over to second gear. It stayed in this gear at a speed of about 10 miles per hour until he got to the gravel road. On the main gravel road, he put it into high gear (third) and went to the store at a top speed of 20 to 25 miles per hour. Once he turned into the store's driveway, he had to shift down to second gear. He did so successfully. After all, Henry had been a skilled driver before the accident.

Folks at the store saw Henry drive up and came to the front door. He parked the car, got out, and went to the store's porch to go inside, using his walking stick to keep his balance. Doris followed him inside. He sat near the drink box on an unopened nail keg used regularly by loafers.

The store folks welcomed him and shook his left hand as he sat; Henry was still learning how to be comfortable shaking with his left hand. Which hand to use didn't seem to matter to the store folks.

Henry checked to see if the store had Prince Albert tobacco, and it did. The price was now two cents more per can. The store also had the kind of roll-your-own paper he liked. He also checked to see if there was any Blood Hound Chewing Tobacco, and there was. He didn't buy any tobacco products, but he had a certain strong desire for some. He thought that this would be a good time to permanently quit, but he didn't make the commitment. He thought about how hard it would be to roll-his-own with just a left hand. It would require a flat place at least the size of the cigarette paper and a little more spit to hold the paper in place for putting the tobacco on it. Lighting would involve using a wooden-stem match that was struck after the rolled cigarette was in his mouth. He could suck on the cigarette—draw air through it—as he touched the flame of the lighted match to it. Dealing with his stress would likely result in his return to tobacco products in a few weeks.

Henry and Doris talked a bit with people in the store. When it was time to go, they went outside to put fifty cents worth of gasoline into the tank (gasoline was rationed because of the war but cost only about fourteen cents a gallon). After paying for the gasoline, they left for home with Henry driving. He parked the car under the car shed and walked to the house to go inside. He was feeling good about his reinvented driving skills.

When Thursday morning arrived, it was time for Henry's dental appointment. With some persuasion, Henry convinced Doris that he should drive. So, he did drive the five miles into Clinton without any problems other than continuing to learn new ways of shifting, steering, and the like. Doris drove the ten miles on to Dr. Calendar's office in Edwards.

Henry was welcomed to the office by Dr. Calendar. He asked Henry a little about his accident. Henry told about the three teeth that were knocked out. Dr. Calendar examined the tooth areas and said they looked to be healing okay. He discussed that all his losses were anterior teeth, or teeth in the front of the mouth. Henry mentioned that Dr. Brock said that there might be part of a root in one of the tooth sockets. Upon examination, Dr. Calendar found none and said it was probably a tooth fragment that worked its way out of the gum in the healing process.

Dr. Calendar then talked with Henry about getting either a bridge or a removable partial plate. A bridge would involve artificial teeth held in place by a wirelike device that was attached to other teeth. A removable partial plate would not be fixed in place but could be taken out for cleaning or other reasons. It would be shaped to fit the mouth and use other teeth to help hold it in place. The artificial teeth would fill in the gaps with real-looking teeth as well as tend to keep the other teeth from shifting location in his mouth. Henry liked the notion of a removable partial plate. Dr. Calendar said he could make an impression of Henry's mouth, send it off, and in a few days get a partial plate back. When it arrived, Henry would need to come in and let the dentist place it in his mouth and make any needed adjustments. He would go over how to use and care for it to prevent gum injury and get maximum aesthetic use out of the plate. Henry agreed to this. An impression was made.

Afterward, Dr. Calendar found a posterior tooth with a cavity and, with Henry's permission, set about to fill it. The dental work for the day was finished about 11:30 that morning, and Henry and Doris headed home. Before they left, they paid for the day's charges and got an appointment in one week, at which Henry would get the new removable partial plate.

The day for the appointment to get the partial plate arrived. Henry and Doris drove to Edwards. Son went with them. Dr. Calendar brought the partial plate out and put it into Henry's mouth. Henry opened his mouth and looked into a mirror that Doris held for him. He was surprised at how well he had been re-stored to the before-accident look. Doris liked the new teeth, too. She gave Henry a little hug.

Son was intrigued by all the things in the dental office. The spit bowl, drill, and instruments got his attention. He wanted to climb up into the chair and open his mouth wide as his father had done.

It was now time to go. Dr. Calendar gave a few quick instructions on how to care for and use a partial plate. He said for Henry to try the partial plate for a few days and come back with any problems so adjustments could be made. It fit well and had only two small places that rubbed. During a quick appointment three days later, Dr. Calendar was able to quickly make an adjustment so that these two places were corrected.

Henry had to learn how to use and care for the partial plate. "You can't bite an apple," Dr. Calendar said, "and no cracking ice." Henry agreed that he would take good care to use the partial plate properly and clean it to assure that no oral problems developed. (What wasn't said is that with the loss of a hand, the mouth and teeth sometimes substitute for the missing fingers and hand.)

Most days at home were routine. Henry gradually gained abilities that were lost in the accident. He walked to most places on the farm. He went about trying to determine the work that was needed to get the fields ready for another crop year. This always included trimming brush (mostly sassafras, cedar, and blackberry plant growth) around fields and cutting back willows that grew in the creeks and spring branch. Of course, there were no power tools; hand axes, Kaiser blades, and two-person saws were used. If any larger trees were cut, a crosscut saw was used. In some cases, fences were mended, gates repaired, and bridges rebuilt. Occasionally there would be a need to plow deep furrows across fields to promote draining. Sometimes hand shovel work was done on the drain furrows to be certain that they were open and ready to move water.

It was nearing the first of March and some five weeks after the accident. Henry was out and about quite a bit on the farm. The activity allowed him to develop abilities in coping with one arm. Fields were being readied. Brush was cut around the edges and turn-rows. Stalks from last year's crops were being chopped with a one-row mule-pulled chopper. Early turning plow work had begun in some fields. Though he was out a couple of times each day in the fields checking on the farm hands, he was frustrated. He could not do the work he formerly did. He hadn't mastered how to harness and use mules and equipment with one hand. Some days he was depressed.

Henry went for the next follow-up appointment with Dr. Brock. Mostly, all seemed to be in good order. The nub appeared to have lost swelling and shrunk to its near-final size. It was a small mass of floppy flesh without any muscular control. Henry thought it was kind of useless and a source of phantom pains. Dr. Brock talked about Henry getting a prosthesis. He explained how it could help. He ended this appointment that day saying that Henry was coming along normally following the loss of an arm and that there was no reason for him to return unless he had a problem. He asked Henry to be patient and think about doing things beforehand to avoid problems, such as a fall or another accident.

Henry and Doris went to the car to leave. Doris, in a compelling voice, asked Henry to go to the prosthetics shop. He reluctantly agreed to do so. His objections focused on cost and whether he would ever be able to use an artificial arm. Doris said he should at least give it a try and explore the possibilities. Jackson Brace and Limb was nearby and close to the Baptist Hospital, where Henry was treated following the accident.

Fortunately, a prosthetist met them at the front door as they walked in. His name was John. It was fairly obvious what Henry was there for, so they began to talk. John told about the benefits of a prosthetic arm and how it could help Henry. He talked about function and how a prosthesis could make everyday routines, such as eating and driving, easier. He also talked about the cosmetic benefits, such as giving the body the appearance that an arm was present and making it possible to more appropriately wear clothing without cutting off the right sleeve, or tucking it in at the waist, or otherwise altering his shirts and jackets.

With more equipment and explosives, according to what John told Henry, more men were losing arms. He said that some soldiers came home from war missing an arm and got a prosthetic arm that functions well for them. He further said that the issue was such a great problem after World War I that major improvements had been made. And now, with World War II underway, many more soldiers were also having the need for prostheses. He reminded that research at Walter Reed Army Hospital in Washington, DC, was releasing new and improved upper-level arm capabilities. This was being done to help soldiers who had misfortunes and were returning from conflicts in Europe and the South Pacific, including the attack on Pearl Harbor.

Then John went into more detail. He wanted to see and examine Henry's nub and gather a little information about the accident. John noted that it was a nub and not a stump. Without a bone, a prosthesis would be more challenging to fit and use, but it could be done. He next showed Henry an example of an arm and explained how it attached to the body with a suspension system (including a strap and cables) that went across to the other shoulder. He told that a socket on the prosthesis attached to the residual limb or, in this case, nub. John explained that careful molding and construction were needed to have a socket that appropriately fit the nub. If the fit was not precise, the movement of the nub in the socket could damage the nub. Tissue damage, infection, and pain could result.

John said that an artificial arm is made to be operated with cables that are manipulated with various body movements. Opening and closing the fingers (especially to grasp or grip something), moving the hand, and turning the elbow all require specific movements. He said he could teach Henry all the right movements. He also told Henry that he could get an arm with a skin tone and other natural-looking features, known as a cosmesis. With some arms, the hand was removable so that a hook could be installed in its place, but the advantages were not well stated. He went over construction materials and weight. He talked about how the recipient needs to be patient with a prosthetic arm. He then asked Henry if he wanted to get one; Doris said yes, and Henry went along.

Next, measurements were made of Henry's left arm and of his shoulders and body. Fit of a prosthesis needs to be exact for it to stay in place on the body. John draped one of the arms in the shop on Henry's body without attaching the cables. It wasn't a good fit because it was not Henry's size.

One thing that puzzled Henry was how he would put the arm on his body and take it off. He asked. It was explained that his wife or someone would have to help him. Henry also wanted to know if he would use the artificial hand to shake hands or if he would use his left hand. The explanation was that either would be okay but that he would probably use his left hand. Some people did not relish touching an artificial hand, and, of course, a hook would not be used for shaking. Henry then asked about doing certain tasks with a prosthesis, such as driving a nail, using a wrench, and putting a bridle on a horse. The answers weren't very positive in terms of the benefits of the arm.

The appointment was about completed. Henry was told that the arm would cost about $250 and that half was due before it could be made. Luckily, Henry and Doris were good money managers, and Doris wrote a check to pay the $125 that was due as a prepayment. The arm was to be ready in about two weeks unless returning soldiers took priority; Henry got an appointment for March 31. He and Doris left the brace and limb store and headed back to Tinnin.

Yes, there had been a lot of progress since that fateful day on January 20. Henry got into the driver's side of the car to drive back to Tinnin. In five weeks, he had mastered (almost) driving a car with only a left arm. It didn't always go smoothly, with a little jerking around in shifting gears and steering with one hand, but nevertheless he and Doris made it home safely after a stop at a grocery store.

Getting the fields ready for the cotton and corn crops was now well underway. Henry was out and about on the farm both morning and afternoon. Mostly he walked to the fields, as he did not yet feel comfortable riding a horse or driving the clunky steel-wheel tractor. The field hands also prepared patches for the vegetables. Early-season crops, such as squash, Irish potatoes, snap beans, and roasting-ear corn, were planted about the middle of March. Henry was now feeling confident that he, with good farm help, could manage the production, harvesting, and marketing of the vegetables.

Time went by fast. Watching squash, bean, potato, and corn plants with tiny leaves emerge from the soil in the garden was always exciting. Rapid growth in young plants gave hope for a future productive crop. Henry had learned that a good way to get rapid young plant growth was to spread some horse manure from the stables over the ground in late fall (that was done in December before the accident). As the seedbed was prepared, the manure was plowed into the soil. Plant roots could take up the growth nutrients from the manure and send them to the leaves, where plant food production took place in a process known as photosynthesis. This rapid plant growth was exciting and served as a further sign to Henry that he would be able to go about productive farming.

It was now time for Henry to go to Jackson Brace and Limb to get his new arm. On March 31, he and Doris departed Tinnin in the morning so they would arrive by ten o'clock. John greeted Henry with, "I have just the arm you need." He continued, "I want you to try it on. If adjustments are needed, I will make them so that the arm is just perfect for you. Comfort is very important. You will need to wear a special kind of cotton sock over your nub. It serves to create comfort between your nub and the socket of the arm."

He told Doris to watch how he held the arm, fitted the nub with a special sock liner to go inside the socket, and attached the arm with a strap and cables to Henry's left shoulder. She paid careful attention. John also showed how to exchange the hand for the hook, and vice versa. After the prosthesis was on, he asked Henry to move in certain ways to gain functions out of the arm. Henry tried. Not everything went the way it should, but some things did.

The prosthetist said that Henry would need to practice using the arm. Specific movements of the left shoulder and back would result in desired movements in the arm, elbow, hand, and fingers. John indicated that the sock should be kept clean and that cotton was likely the best material; wool should not be used except in the winter. Henry agreed that practice was needed. He was ready to go home and get practice underway. They paid the remaining $125, took the prosthetic arm (not on his body), put it on the back seat of the car (carefully, to prevent damaging it), and departed for Tinnin.

Once in the car, Henry grumbled about wasting $250 and talked about all the useful things they could have gotten with that much money. Doris asked him to give it a good try and have an open mind about it. When he got home, he and Doris walked from the car shed to the house. Doris carried the prosthetic arm. Henry had Doris help him put it on. He worked at motions to gain certain functions out of the arm and hand. He tried to grasp a coffee cup by its handle, a pencil, and a dinner fork. Some things went with reasonable success; other tasks would require more practice. So, Doris asked him to wear the arm the remainder of the day and practice with the hand, not with the hook that would open. He agreed. That evening he had Doris help him remove the arm. They put it in the bottom of the chifferobe for the night. The next morning, Henry said leave it there until later. He had other priorities on his mind for that day.

Otho and Henry went for a wagon ride around the farm. They looked at the fields and talked about work to be done. Through all of Henry's recovery, Otho had become his "right-hand man." (That phrase fits well!) Otho did things Henry couldn't do; he helped Henry with farm activities. If a board came off the hogpen fence, Otho nailed it back. Otho also did garden plowing and cultivation. Harnessing and hitching, as well as directing a mule down garden rows, were things Henry had not learned to do. Two hands were needed to hold the plow lines. Henry would soon learn how to do so with one hand, but it wouldn't be easy. Henry and Doris paid Otho the going day rate for his work: $2.50. Otho also had the advantage of access to a good garden plot for his use. Of course, he sadly lived in near poverty. His house was little more than a shack, and, like Doris and Henry, he did not have electricity, running water, or other conveniences for daily living.

Why was Otho not drafted into the army? He was certainly a capable man in many ways. He lived in one of the sharecropper houses on the farm with his wife and two children. It would have devastated both Henry and Doris if he had been drafted. Otho was the person they could count on to help them make it through their big crisis. The U.S. Army (as did much of society) unfortunately discriminated against black people, and they were not given equal status with whites. About 1 million blacks served during World War II, but most were in segregated supply units and did not see battle with white soldiers. So, when the Selective Service Board was not interested in Otho (maybe it was due to not going to school; no school of consequence was in Tinnin for blacks in the segregated South when he was a child), that was good news to Henry and Doris.

From the time of Henry's accident, they always treated Otho and his family in a special way. Some years later he moved away to another farm and later into Jackson to work in a grocery store on Farish Street. But fortunately, he was always loyal to Doris and Henry and would help anytime with whatever they needed.

Sunday morning arrived. The Lees were getting ready to go

to the Pocahontas Methodist Episcopal Church. Henry said he wanted to wear the arm and try it out before Easter Sunday arrived on April 25, 1943. Doris dressed extra early so that she would have the time to help Henry get the arm on. Once the arm was on, he put on a long-sleeve dress shirt that was buttoned at the right cuff (as well as the left); that made the right side of his body look close to natural.

Since it was springtime, the weather was warming, and no jacket or coat was needed. Henry wanted to wear a tie but had not developed the ability to tie one with his left hand. Doris was able to figure out how to do it and make it fit at the neck collar. Now, Henry felt comfortable about going to church. This was his first time out in public with the arm. He wondered how people would react. Most people said nothing, but those who spoke were quite complimentary. He used his left hand to shake with some of the men and with Preacher Murrow.

When he returned home, he kept on the tie, shirt, and arm. He knew that a couple of his sisters and their husbands were coming to visit Carrie. He wanted to look good when they saw him. He thought that this would help them have a better impression of his capability and status in life. After all, Henry and the people around him were still adjusting to his difficult situation. Of course, "looking good" helped Henry's self-concept. In the back of his mind was Henry's suspicion that some of his sisters and their husbands would not treat him and his wife sympathetically. He wanted to be prepared for whatever the situation brought.

Life routines, though altered, continued for Henry as a husband, father, and farmer. He was learning new ways of going about life! But, the prosthetic arm was not a part of his farm activity. It simply was not up to doing what needed to be done. Henry was learning to com-pensate using only his left arm and hand. A tremendous amount of adjustment was still required. Would he be able to meet the challenges? He thought so.

9

Adjusting and Loving

Adjusting! Sounds simple, but is it? A major loss in life is hard to overcome. Adjusting is easier with a loving family and supportive community. The loss remains for life, and coping seems to never end.

Family members responded to Henry's accident in different ways. His close family (Doris and Son) was genuinely sympathetic. Doris carried the brunt of responsibility in helping Henry adjust to his loss; she had responses to make for which she was ill-prepared, but she tried hard to learn and do the right thing. It wasn't easy for her; she tried diligently to do what was right for her man. Of course, Son was not yet old enough to understand but did so quickly in future years. Members of Doris's childhood Sloan family were sympathetic; they lived some twenty-five miles away and were removed from the everyday observation of Henry's progress, or lack thereof, in overcoming his predicament.

Overall, Henry's extended Lee family formed a fairly large group. Its members differed in sympathy and the support they offered him in his time of need. Some were genuinely sympathetic and made every effort to understand how he now faced life; it wouldn't be easy. Other family members had varying levels of understanding and thoughtfulness or none at all. Some now viewed Henry as less than a complete person and, in a few cases, as someone who should be carefully watched. A few family members felt he should be under observation at all times. And, maybe there were a few who viewed his seeming incapacity as a basis for rejection or for taking advantage of him as well as of Doris and their young son.

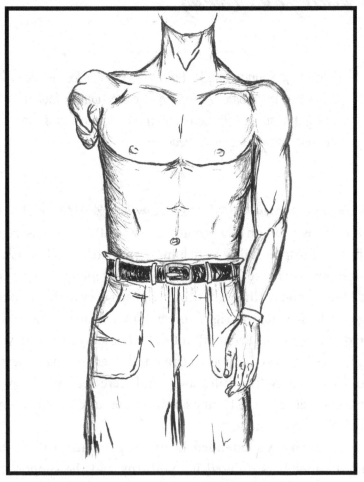

Human Torso Showing Nub Remaining After Arm Amputation Just Below the Shoulder.

Did a few Lee family members now view Henry as someone who was incapable and "handicapped" (the term frequently used at that time)? Did the blow he suffered to his head against the pole result in lasting brain and nerve damage? Even if family members didn't speak a word, Henry seemed to be able to tell their feelings. This apparent negativity was very hurtful to him.

Whenever they were around, relatives would often do things for him that he could have readily done for himself. They would say something like, "Let me do that for you. Remember, you have lost an arm, you poor thing." These people might not have thought what they said or did was hurtful, but it was. It tore right to the psychic of a man who was trying to recover from a major injury and into his mental strength and capacity. Regardless, Henry tried to adjust and was well on his way toward doing so without interference by close family members who should have been supportive and encouraging. But, to adjust was made very difficult by those who doubted his ability and expressed lack of respect and understanding.

A good example occurred on the first day Henry wore his prosthesis to the Pocahontas church. He stayed dressed in his Sunday church clothes afterward because he knew company was coming to his home. He wanted to "look good" for them. The visitors were to be a couple of his sisters, their husbands, and two children who were primarily coming to see Carrie. They would also have a little time with Henry. They wanted to check on this man who was now sometimes viewed as less than fit. Did some think he was a small demon-possessed man? (How did demons get into the picture? More about demons later.) Probably not, but what they would say and do would likely be a true measure of their inner feelings.

Carrie's two daughters, along with their "city-slicker" husbands, as they were sometimes referred to, arrived about the same time that afternoon. It was spring, and some of the wildflowers were beginning to grow and bloom. It was a nice time of the year for city folks to be in the country. Ethel, the daughter who now lived out of state, had married a much older man who was a prominent dentist with a good income. The dentist asked everyone in the Lee family to refer to him as Dr. Davis. The family members were never really sure about his prominence, but he wanted them to think he was at the top of the social ladder.

The other daughter, Sudie, was married to James, a good man who once had a job at Capital Chevrolet in Jackson but was now a jeweler. He made a decent living for his family. Members of the family respected him because he knew how to repair and keep both cars and clocks running

The daughters and families greeted Carrie; they did not greet Doris and Son, but that might have been because they were in their bedroom. The "guests" didn't knock or make any effort to say hello. Maybe Doris had planned it that way because she suspected something sinister was going on with Carrie and the daughters and sons-in-law.

The husbands (Carrie's sons-in-law) wanted to go out to the end of the porch away from where others in the family might hear their conversation. They asked Henry to go with them; they said that they wanted to talk farming and the like. Henry knew they didn't know the difference between a single tree and a pine tree, but he went. Maybe he thought he might be able to teach them a thing or two about farming and farm life. Henry tried to go with a positive spirit and helpful attitude, though he suspected that nothing good was going to take place.

His brothers-in-law took two straight chairs and one small rocker with arms. They each sat in a straight chair. Dr. Davis announced that Henry should sit in the rocking chair. "Henry, you take the rocking chair," he said. "You may need the arms on each side to keep you safe and prevent you from falling."

"What did you say?" Henry responded. "I won't fall out of a chair.

I can stand, walk, sit in a chair, and do most things. January was more than three months ago. Have you been drinking something?"

Unphased, Dr. Davis, who had not seen Henry since his accident but had been to Tinnin during the Christmas holidays just beforehand, said, "It is nice to see you, Henry. Tell us a little about the accident and how you are doing." Of the two husbands, Dr. Davis was obviously the biggest of the city-slickers. He was also the one whom Henry thought exaggerated and maybe even told untruths to make himself look good.

"I went to grind cornmeal at the Ratliff Store that day," Henry began, "and all equipment was in place and checked out. Something happened. The belt jumped off the danged pulley on the hammer mill and wrapped around my arm. The powerful turning of the heavy belt that was still on the tractor belt wheel twisted my right arm off where it joined the shoulder. Only a few pieces of skin, muscles, and other tissues kept it attached. The stretching of the arm tended to close the blood vessels and prevent any greater loss of blood (there was a lot, anyway, but not enough to take my life). My right arm was really mangled. That really hurt; the worst pain I ever had. I was rushed by automobile to the Baptist Hospital in Jackson where surgery was done to save my life. That involved complete amputation of my right arm and creation of a nub. I do not have a stump because there is no bone of consequence in it. With Doris's help, I have been striving to overcome this huge loss. Progress was slow at first. When the flying, turning belt threw me to the ground, the force knocked out three of my front teeth that I have taken care of. Getting that done took a while. Now I have a partial plate. See!" Henry opened his mouth and slightly lifted out the partial plate. He thought that might get some sort of response from Dr. Davis, the dentist. But, it was hard to impress him with anything.

"I will look more closely later," Dr. Davis said. "I do dental surgery and other work like that all the time for my patients. I make good money doing it. I will be able to tell you if the partial plate is top quality. I know one thing: It is hard to get a top one that I don't do! I see you have an artificial arm. Is it any good? How do you use it in farming?"

Henry had not thought a lot about the use of the prosthetic arm in farming, but he began an explanation. "There is a lot of learning to do to use the arm," Henry began. "Doris helps me put it on. She has been so patient and helpful with me. I got it at the Jackson Brace and Limb Company as the best-available quality in arm prosthetics. (Yes, Henry could pronounce the word "prosthetics" if he thought about it enough!) The first thing in putting it on is to get the sock over my nub. I was told that was very important to prevent injury to the nub. There are several straps and cables to get in place. I can exchange the hand on the arm for a movable hook. Moving the hand and opening the fingers or hook requires that I maneuver my upper body a certain way. Slight body movements result in hand movements. It is surprising to me that the body movements result in the hand moving so that I can do things such as grasp a cup by its handle. Whoever developed this thing was smart."

Dr. Davis interrupted Henry, asking, "What materials were used in making it? Is it heavy?"

"I don't know the exact materials, but they are light," Henry said. "There is some metal, some plaster-type material, and cotton string. The hook is made out of polished steel or something similar. I have to use care with it so that I don't break it. If you want to see it and how I put it on, I will show you sometime."

Dr. Davis was becoming impatient. "Heck, no. I don't want to see it up close. But, tell me how you use the arm in farming. What good is it to you in your work? Can you chop cotton with it? Can you pick cotton with it? And, what about butchering a hog or milking a cow?"

Henry detected that his brother-in-law was getting a little pushy and "smarty."

"I don't know what more to tell you," Henry said. "You see, I am still learning and adjusting. I don't need somebody pushing on me for answers. I am doing the best I can do. Maybe people need to say positive things. I am adjusting and regaining strength. You can rest assured that every acre of cropland will be planted to cotton, sugar cane, corn, sweet potatoes, or other crops. You need to know that I am not disabled!"

The brothers-in-law could tell that they didn't exactly use the right approach with Henry. But, they continued straight to the point of their rude conversation and failed to demonstrate sympathy or understanding.

"Henry, how are you really doing? Tell us the truth. Are you really going to be able to run this farm?" Dr. Davis asked and quickly added, "You know Mama Carrie has owned this farm place since Papa Ira died in 1941, and each of her daughters has a share in it. She counts on the $600 rent you pay each year as her main income. We've got to look out for Mama Carrie. Do you understand? Do you think it is time for you to move on?"

"Yes, hell yes, I understand," Henry quickly responded. "I will look after her. And, no, I am not moving. I will kick the butt of anyone who thinks I won't be able to farm. I challenge either of you to do a better job than I will do." Of course, he knew neither would take him up on the challenge because they knew nothing about farming cotton on the Lee-Shepard farm.

James, the brother-in-law who had been mostly quiet to this point, spoke up. "Now, Henry, you are talking mighty big to have only one arm, and a left one at that." He continued, "Have you thought about how you are going to get the real work done? About how you will look after the farm hands? I can't run over here from

Jackson on a daily basis to see that the farming gets done." Henry was fuming inside about what was being said.

While the men sat on the big porch of the house, the women sat inside with their mother, Carrie. The children were also inside. The younger child was just a baby. From time to time, the older child would run around the house and porch and into the yard to chase chickens. Carrie would occasionally look out the window and scream, "Leave my hens alone!"

The conversation was heating up and getting louder. One sister, Ethel, came onto the porch to see what was happening just when Henry shouted, "I said I would kick the butt of anyone who thinks I can't farm! I still have two feet and legs that are both very capable of sending your ass off the porch into the yard with the chickens and their crap. And, for your information, my left arm is getting stronger every day. Look at the muscles in it. And, I can swing my artificial arm with great speed and strength like a fence post, wiping out anyone who challenges me. I can put the hook on the end and really do some hurting. Want me to try it on you?" Neither of the brothers-in-law wanted Henry to try it. "I don't use guns," Henry added, "but if I did I would be tempted to do so now. Whoever thought that my sister's husbands would act this way toward me just at the time when I need a little consideration?"

Just as Henry finished the statement, Ethel began to speak. "What is going on out here?" she asked. "It sounds loud. We have to be nice, get along as a family, and not be talking with a mean spirit to each other."

Her husband spoke up and said, "We just told Henry that we are not sure he will be able to run this farm. We asked if he would be able to pay Mama Carrie the rent she is due this fall."

The sister was calmer and less aggressive toward Henry. She said, "Well, Henry, will you be able to pay it? Should we find another farmer who can lease the place and maybe pay more rent? We might be able to get someone who is in good health—a capable person who has both arms and hands."

Of course, this infuriated Henry even more now that his own sister had shown a lack of confidence in him. "Yes, I will pay her." He continued, "I will also pay the county property taxes, just as I have for the past couple of years. Why are all of you being so hard on me?"

His sister spoke up and said something about Carrie being concerned; now Henry had just heard part of the reason for the aggressiveness toward him. His own mother was up to her usual semi-evil self of planting bad information about Henry and his small family with her daughters. Kind of spiteful, he thought.

Henry reviewed the farm hands he had lined up for the crop year that was getting underway. "I have Otho and his small family. Otho was the man who could be counted on for help at the time of the accident and afterward by being the driver to Jackson when needed. He also helped around the house and cared for the animals that had to be fed and sheltered. Otho has good ability in operating the tractor. He lives in the house up the hill near the main road.

"Another is Foster, along with his mother, Mary. They have lived here a couple of years. They have the house near the roasting-ear cornfield.

"Dennis is a young man with a wife and two small children. He is a strong, highly capable man; his wife is a good field worker. Their house is near the black walnut tree at the spring branch where the sassafras trees grow.

"And fourth is Russell, who is a little older but still a good worker. His wife is also good at chopping and picking cotton.

"So, you see that these four sharecropper families should work out okay. Oh, yes. I failed to mention that I will provide the furnishings so that they do not need to go to a mercantile store in Pocahontas."

And now, the recently installed screen door from the hallway opened, and the other sister, Sudie, came onto the porch. It seemed that there were going to be four people against the one Henry. Just like the other sister, she wanted to know what was going on. Why were you people talking so loudly? Her husband spoke up and told about the situation. Now this sister was a little different. "Let's be calm and nice to Henry following his unfortunate accident," she said in a somewhat patronizing voice. "Let's give him a boost when he needs it. Let's take a year to see what he can do. After all, he and his family need money to live on. Maybe Doris can get a job. There may be a job for a clerk in the Ashford Store in Pocahontas."

The suggestion that Doris get a job agitated Henry, but he kept his cool. He viewed this as an attack on his family, particularly on Doris. Her getting a job was something he and Doris had talked about but not made any plans to do. And, of course, Mississippi had a state law prohibiting married women from being school teachers.

At this point, Dr. Davis indicated that he and Ethel needed to soon go and get back to their room at the Alamo Plaza Tourist Court on the corner of Terry Road and Highway 80 in Jackson. They would need to depart fairly early the next morning to get back to Montgomery. And, then Dr. Davis asked if there would be more Lee babies.

"None of your damn business," Henry responded to Dr. Davis. Henry continued, "I never thought that you or anyone would ask me such a question. My lovely wife, Doris, is college educated. She knows about babies and how they come into being. She knows that children and families bring challenges. Besides, we have a wonderful son."

Henry's sister Sudie spoke up and said, "Dr. Davis, I agree with Henry. This matter is none of your business. And, by the way, how many babies have you fathered with your present wife? With any woman?" Most folks thought of him as somewhat of a womanizer who wouldn't want to keep the conversation going.

And then Dr. Davis asked, "Henry, are you going to be able to keep Doris satisfied and happy. You know women have their particular interests and needs." Silence. All was quiet on the porch; the talk that day appeared about over.

"Let me say this," Henry spoke. "We need to all calm down. Dr. Davis, when you get back to the hotel, get the Bible from the nightstand and do something for me: Open it to the book of Ephesians in the New Testament. Go to chapter 4, verse 29, and see what it says that relates to talking in a nice way with other people. According to the preacher at Pocahontas church, the Bible used the term 'corrupt communication' when speaking about this. That preacher gave a good sermon on this not long ago; I remember his sermon well. It will do you some good to read this in the Bible. I need to practice it, too."

At this point, Dr. Davis abruptly said he needed an afternoon toddy to help get him through the remainder of the day in good order. It was nearly four o'clock and the usual time for him and his wife to have a sip or two or three or more. He said that he needed something to help him "adjust" and calm his nerves a bit.

"I brought a case of Crown Royal bourbon with me. You know Alabama has legal whiskey. We took care of about half a fifth last night after arriving from Alabama and sipped a little to get the morning going earlier today." He asked, "Does anyone else want a good shot of this top-quality nerve medicine?" Only his wife answered yes. He said he would get the opened fifth and one unopened fifth from the back of his Buick Roadmaster (he was proud of the Roadmaster and talked about it as if it were a person).

He asked Ethel to go into Carrie's kitchen and get a couple of small glasses about half filled with cool spring water. The home had no refrigerator, and all the ice had melted in the icebox. Without ice, the toddy would not be as cool as he usually liked it. He twisted the cork-based top out of the opened fifth and poured both glasses with water almost full and immediately began sipping (though the first sip was more like a gulp).

After the swallow, he let out a gush of breath, as the whiskey and water made a strong toddy that took his breath away. He shouted, "Damn good stuff! Ethel, pour me some more!" He again offered for Ethel to pour bourbon for those present. He said, "After this toddy, we won't have any more to drink until a nightcap at bedtime. I have found that I am a strong man who can enjoy my bourbon and drive quite well or do other things. It usually takes this to get me through the day. Of course, I do not drink before doing dental work, but afterwards I do."

Henry spoke up and said, "I suppose it helps soothe your conscience after the big charges you make for your work." Amazingly, Dr. Davis did not dispute Henry's statement.

Dr. Davis and his wife finished off the opened bottle of bourbon and threw the empty bottle off the porch into the yard, almost striking a cat (the cat jumped and screamed). Amazingly, the bottle didn't break when it landed on the ground. Dr. Davis said, "Henry, you can pick up that dang bottle in the morning." He continued, "Here for you is a full bottle that has not been opened. I give this for your Crown Royal drinking pleasure. It is good stuff. You may need it soon to help get over your situation. You don't need a shot glass to measure it; you can just pour some! We have to go. It is after 4:30."

His wife (and remember she is Henry's sister Ethel Naomi) spoke up. "We are staying where we usually do in Jackson at the Alamo Plaza Tourist Court. You know, it is about the best place for us in the city other than the Robert E. Lee Hotel. The hotel is a little more distant, but it is better for us if we will be dancing and partying. It has a really nice orchestra area and dancehall room on the roof."

Dr. Davis continued the conversation. "We must get back to Montgomery tomorrow; I have patients who need care on Tuesday.

And then, we have to get ready for the biggest ball of the year in Montgomery on Saturday night. It is the Old South Ball, and I am to be King this year. It is a fund-raiser for the little Methodist college known as Huntingdon that was started as a college for women and began admitting white men a few years ago. Prior to that, it had been only for white women since its founding in 1854 as Tuskegee Female College. It moved to Montgomery about 50 years ago."

He then told the story of the "Red Lady"—a sad story of a young woman who committed suicide in her dormitory room in Pratt Hall on the Huntingdon campus in the early 1900s. The Red Lady became one of Alabama's best-known ghosts.

Sudie asked, "Why did she commit suicide?"

Dr. Davis responded, "This is a question that needs an answer. Several possible answers have been offered. Maybe she was spurned by a lover at Auburn University, or maybe she was bullied because of her sexual orientation, or maybe there was some other reason. To this day, school colors are scarlet and gray, which sound kind of like a Red Lady!" Of course, Dr. Davis spiced up the story a bit with interesting information that may or may not have been factual. He thought that maybe the student was pregnant by a professor of religious education at Huntingdon. He said the professor, an ordained minister, went unnamed and rose to high levels at the college. The professor often preached against the evils of human desires and temptations.

"Seems like he knew the evils he was preaching about on a firsthand basis," Sudie said. "Kind of the way it goes with a few preachers around here. They are tempted into sinful things just like other folks. But, you know, they do so much good."

Dr. Davis and his wife went inside to tell Carrie goodbye. Dr. Davis told her that he had "straightened Henry out" about the farm and making the rent payment to her for using the land. He told her that she had nothing to worry about. A final hug, and he and Ethel were ready to leave. But, Carrie smelled whiskey on his breath; it was a strong odor.

Carrie couldn't resist. "What is that I smell?" she asked. "Smells like that evil stuff known as liquor. That stuff will kill you dead as a Confederate soldier at the Battle of Vicksburg. Ethel, are you also drinking?"

"Yes," the daughter answered and continued, "We have each had a toddy. It helps us go and do things. Dr. Davis can drive quite well after a few sips; at least that is what I think."

Dr. Davis and his wife went out onto the porch and started down the porch steps. He grasped the step railing to keep himself upright. Ethel grabbed his left arm to prevent a fall as he stumbled on the bottom step and kept walking in a half-stumbling manner toward the car. When he got to the Roadmaster, he put his hand on the hood to brace himself and stood there for a moment. He was thinking that maybe he needed to go behind a tree and relieve himself; he did so out of sight of folks on the porch (but everyone knew what was going on). The body language of men gives a hint about what they are up to, according to thinking in the Lee family.

Doris looked out the front window to check on the situation. Dr. Davis and his wife were seen now getting into their fancy, rather new two-toned blue Buick Roadmaster automobile with white-wall tires. She got a good look at the car and saw a shiny chrome radio antenna that extended from the right front fender about 4 feet into the air. She wondered about it. She could see the "Alabama—Heart of Dixie" tag on the front of the car. Dr. Davis started the engine, backed up, turned around, and spun a little dirt as he drove up the long driveway to the gravel road and out of sight.

Only once did the car run off the edge of the gravel, and that was near Otho as he was walking to the lot to feed the animals. He had to jump out of the way. Was it too much bourbon, or was it bullying of Otho for helping Henry adjust to a new way of doing work

with one arm, or was it because he had dark skin? Doris felt sorry
for Otho. She was wondering if Dr. Davis would be able to drive to
Jackson without an accident after consuming so much bourbon. He
was. (Carrie got a letter from Ethel in a couple of weeks with details.
More later about that letter.)

How Dr. Davis had such a fine new automobile and was able to
get all the gasoline he wanted in 1943 was a question on the minds
of some family members and others. Most individuals were suffering under restrictions put in place by the U.S. War Production
Board (WPB) as part of the win-the-war effort. Maybe it was because he was a dentist who specialized in dental surgery. He practiced a profession that was greatly needed and he had an "X" war
ration decal on his Roadmaster. This decal allowed him to have an
unlimited amount of gasoline. He probably needed it for the low
fuel economy of his Roadmaster. Most physicians had "C" decals,
which allowed them to have fewer gallons.

Buick first manufactured the Roadmaster in 1936 using the
longest non-limousine wheelbase it had. Like a Cadillac, it was a
prestigious automobile to own and drive. The WPB ordered the
temporary end of all civilian automobile sales on January 1, 1942,
or a little more than a year before Henry's disastrous accident. The
Roadmaster was a sight to behold, as no vehicles on the farm were
even nearly new, in good condition, or readily started and reliably
braked. In short, the war had resulted in most people living a life
of deprivation while, at the same time, working hard to be loyal
Americans and productive in the win-the-war effort. And was this
deprivation just to fulfill the ill perpetrated by government leaders
on people? Surely, smart leaders can sit together in a meeting and
work out their differences without war.

Henry got up and left the rocking chair on the end of the porch.
"I will see you another day," Henry said to the remaining sister and
husband. He added, "Find a better subject for us to talk about next

time." He went inside to his and Doris's bedroom. It was his thought that Sudie's husband, James, who was partly responsible for moving the chair, could bring it back to the middle of the porch, where it belonged. After all, he had two hands and arms. This conversation didn't help Henry a bit. In fact, his mind was stressed and had about all it could manage for that Sunday afternoon. And, as he went inside, he wondered out loud to Doris, "Why did this happen on a Sunday. Kind of ruins the 'church day.' This kind of talk makes me feel bad—very bad." A couple of tears rolled down his checks. Doris gave him a gentle hug.

Henry asked Doris to help him take off his shirt and remove the arm prosthesis. Straps to undo and strings to untie required someone to help; Henry could not put on or take off the prosthetic arm by himself. Once the arm was off, they arranged it for storing in the bottom of the chifforobe. He thanked Doris for her help and said he would wear it to church next Sunday. It just didn't seem to work out very well with the daily farm work. He put on a farm work shirt and sat on the side of the bed. He was somewhat tired; of course, he was stressed and sad following the discussion with his brothers-in-law and sisters. He even thought that maybe he had been threatened and might not be able to do all he had hoped to do.

Just as Henry was beginning to relax a bit, a knock came on their bedroom door. Doris went to the door and opened it to see Henry's sister Sudie standing there. She said that she and her husband would soon be leaving and she wanted to talk before they departed. She said that Carrie had talked to them about her concern for the future of the farm and for the future of the home she had lived in for more than 40 years. Now it wasn't as if Carrie ever did much to maintain the place, but she knew that she had to have a place to live. She knew that she probably would not get along living with one of her daughters and sons-in-law. Sudie apologized for the sharp discussion that earlier occurred on the porch. She said it was unfortunate. She said that she felt that the farm was in a good hand (no plural "hands") and that things would work out for the good. She thanked Henry for all he had done over the years. She said goodbye and gave Henry, Doris, and Son a hug.

At that moment (during Henry's goodbyes with his sister), Carrie stuck her head out of her room in the house. She looked straight at Henry and said, "I hear that Dr. Davis really straightened you out. You needed it. He told me that you said you could run this farm with one arm. No one else thinks you can do it. You have got a lot to prove around here." How harsh a mother could be! And, she went back into her room and slammed the door. Henry didn't say a word. Folks appeared to be piling on him at a time when he needed support. This wasn't easy for him either. How much could he take?

Sister Sudie and family had gotten into the car parked out front; it was a kind of dusty black Chevrolet with a few years of age. It didn't start too readily and had to have a little tinkering. Sudie's husband, James, knew exactly what to do. It was started after the hood was raised and a little gasoline was poured from a bottle directly into the carburetor. Once started, it was driven (with some smoking and belching of carbon) up the long driveway to the road that would lead back to Jackson, where they lived on Alta Vista Street.

Doris felt relief. The visitors were gone. Ethel and Dr. Davis wouldn't be back for several weeks. It was quite a drive to and from Montgomery, Alabama. Sudie, James, and their children wouldn't be back before next Sunday, if then. Transportation was not easy. Gasoline, tires, and many things were very limited by wartime rationing. Plus, there was always some thought that the car they had might not make it to the next destination. Engines required more attention to maintenance than they should have; better engines were being developed when the war broke out.

Just because these two sisters and their families left did not mean that things would remain calm until the next Sunday. Carrie tended to create discord of her own. Some of Henry's other sisters would likely come to visit Carrie the next weekend; rarely did one come during the week. Of course, one sister was unmarried and continued to live at home. She was going to nearby Mississippi College and had a boyfriend away in France during the war. She didn't involve herself in such discussions; she always appeared to have an "I want to get along" attitude, which served her well. Also continuing to live in the home was Carrie's sister, Susie Heckle, and she stayed out of such conversations; she was just glad to have a place to stay (until she was sent away).

Things calmed a bit around the house. After a meal and a little time playing with Son, it was time for the radio to be tuned to "Hawaii Calls." That was a regular Sunday evening activity. On this day, it was a much needed time for soothing music and commentary, a time to imagine that Waikiki Beach, with its waves and breezes from the Pacific Ocean, was just off the front porch. The music and descriptions of the hula dancers provided by the announcer made it realistic. Hilo Hattie made an appearance that night. Hawaii was a place that no adults living at the Lee house would ever see, so the magical illusion created over the radio was just right. (As an adult, Son would many years later visit Hawaii and Waikiki Beach several times.) After the radio show was over, the station returned to its regular Sunday programming of loud, shouting-hellfire fundamentalist preachers reading from the Bible, talking about sin and demons, and begging for listeners to send money. Maybe the radio was left on for just a few minutes so Son could hear a small part of the broadcast. Was it an effort to get him to follow a straight-and-narrow life of "goodness"? And then, it was to bed for the night.

People at the Lee house were up early the next morning. Most had put yesterday behind them. Henry had farm workers to oversee,

Doris had housework, and Son had little to do, though Doris tried to read to him daily and talk about writing, doing numbers, and the like. But, the main activity of the morning was from Carrie. She remembered discussions of the previous day by two of her daughters and sons-in-law. Unfortunately, she didn't let their discussion go silent; it was resurrected. When Henry came in mid-morning for a brief rest and water, she pounced on him as he climbed the steps to the front porch.

"Henry, how are you going to pay my money this fall?" Carrie asked and continued, "Are you going to be capable of running this farm? What about keeping the farm hands in line?"

Henry assured her he would pay her and manage the farm. He told her that he was this very morning doing what needed to be done to oversee the work of sharecroppers on the farm. And, he wanted to know just what she would do if it were otherwise. She didn't provide a response. She went back into her side of the house and slammed the door. She didn't come out the rest of the day except to go to the two-holer out back and get water from the spring water pipe for use in her kitchen. One other time she came out to go to the henhouse to gather a few eggs for herself, leaving none for Henry, Doris, and Son. Fortunately, the hens would lay a few more before the day was over.

Family adjustment appeared to be marked by questioning of ability more than anything. Where was compassion? Did family members fail to understand the gravity of what had happened to an active, capable, and productive young man? Maybe some jealousy was creeping into family relationships.

For some reason, Carrie never appeared to have a shortage of opportunities for fractious behavior. Most of her daughters (Henry's sisters) appeared to be understanding and were cordial in relationships with Henry and Doris. No one appeared to have outward hostilities. Some of their husbands showed behavior that tended to be aggressive toward Henry. Kinfolks beyond the sisters tended to be quite sympathetic. Just maybe the jealousy grew out of a notion that Henry would slack off and not work as hard as before. And, maybe there was good reason: He couldn't! But that didn't mean he couldn't get the job done on the farm.

Another week passed. It was now the weekend, and time for Carrie to have daughters and their husbands visit her. Sure enough, on Sunday afternoon, about 30 minutes apart, two cars came down the driveway from the road and parked just outside the yard fence near the small gate. Chickens, frightened by dust from the cars, went fluttering back to their house. One car was a 1939 Pontiac, and the other a 1938 Ford. Neither was particularly impressive but the best these young families could do with government wartime regulations in place. They cordially came up on the porch and greeted Carrie and Henry and family.

"I have something scandalous to talk with you about," Carrie said to her daughters and sons-in-law. She continued, "Let's go inside, and I will tell you. It is about how I am being mistreated; I'm being treated like dirt. You can help me with it." She went into details on things she was imagining about her treatment. She explained her untruthful mistreatment by Doris and Henry. Neither daughter nor son-in-law paid much attention, knowing that Carrie had a tendency to say false things and exaggerate. (The reaction was not like that of Dr. Davis, who tended to give credence to what she said.)

For one thing, Carrie talked about how Doris was cooking with a kerosene stove that made heat, causing ice in her icebox to melt (the icebox was located in another room on the opposite side of the house from the kerosene stove). Really! If only she had bought some ice that week when the ice truck came around! Doris bought a 50-pound block, and it was lasting well in her family's icebox that was in the same kitchen as the stove. Carrie had a wood-burning stove and did not like the fact that Doris had a new kerosene-fueled stove. She often talked about how kerosene stoves were bad for one's health. The food would get bad things in it during cooking, according to Carrie. Of course, she knew nothing about food contamination and such. It was only "sour grapes."

Carrie's daughters were not impressed with her concern. In fact, they thought she was unreasonable (they had gas stoves in their kitchens). Voices got a little loud. One was heard to tell her, "Now, Mama, be reasonable. Do not stir up hard feelings. Keep peace in the family."

Carrie shouted back, "I am reasonable! I am being mistreated. I also think you are not being kind to me, your mother."

Of course, everyone who knew Carrie understood that there was no way to get her to be reasonable when it came to her selfish, self-centered ways. It was best to be quiet and not say anything. Yet, her daughters were quite loyal to her, which was not always easy to understand.

On Thursday, Carrie got a letter from her daughter Ethel, written after her recent visit and the Old South Ball. It indicated that she and Dr. Davis made it back to Montgomery late the next day and that they had been quite busy since. The letter stated that Carrie should write them about any mistreatment she had from Henry and Doris. If there was a problem, they would come back to Tinnin and take care of the matter with Henry.

The letter mostly focused on the Old South Ball and Dr. Davis's role as King of the Ball. It indicated that Dr. Davis was quite handsome in his tuxedo and that he got to escort the beautiful Queen of the Ball, a young alumnus of Huntingdon College (who had also been a Mardi Gras queen in Biloxi and chose her gown from Sears). Ethel said that some of the men came to the ball dressed in Confederate uniforms, with guns and swords. Music for dancing was provided by a small group of students and faculty from

Huntingdon College. She said she wore a dress by Italian designer Fontana that she bought at Neiman Marcus while on a shopping trip to New York City. She thought she was beautiful. She said she danced with a number of prominent, handsome men at the ball. She said that she particularly liked the slow dances with a young medical doctor (whose wife was home with a new baby). No mention was made of her dancing with Dr. Davis (he was probably busy dancing with other "highfalutin" young women of the central Alabama area).

The letter indicated that Dr. Davis got liquor for serving at the ball through donations by a local liquor distributor. Even a few college and church folks enjoyed imbibing (out of sight in a back room). One young preacher had too much and was not able to preach at his church the next morning. And, he said he had prepared an excellent sermon! Ethel went on to say that Dr. Davis believed that men and women have to be able to handle their liquor and never drink so much that they are unable to do what needs to be done. This had been a definite challenge when all the liquor they wanted was free.

The exact dollar amount raised at the ball for Huntingdon was not known when the letter was written because money was still being turned in; some folks thought that it would likely be more than $10,000. College officials were said to be highly pleased. Of course, no underage men or women from the college were invited to attend. The letter ended by telling Carrie that Montgomery police patrolled the area to assure safety of all who attended and to keep activities legal.

Carrie became really concerned about one thing in the letter. She did not like the notion of her son-in-law, though handsome and "in the money," escorting and spending time at the ball with the "beautiful Queen of the Ball." (Carrie was not concerned about her daughter dancing with the handsome, well-to-do men.) Of course, it was innocent, but Carrie didn't know it. She wrote Ethel a letter. "You better look out," she wrote. "Young women are very attracted to an older man with good looks who has some money and a fancy car. I assume that you kept your eyes on them all evening and that nothing happened between them. They didn't disappear for a while, did they? You need to tell him to be careful about being a king."

Maybe Carrie was thinking back to her own adolescent years in Hanging Moss, Mississippi. Her father, William Hendrick, though never a king of any kind, supposedly started secretly seeing another woman. She was a good-looking, flirtatious married mother of three. He was found out by Carrie's mother, Louvenia (his wife) when Carrie was 13 years of age. The woman's husband and Louvenia got together and discussed what to do. It was not certain, but most folks who knew a little about the situation did not think William was the father of any of the woman's children. So, Louvenia and the woman's husband came up with a strategy to put a stop to the relationship: Get a physician to sign papers admitting William to the State Insane Asylum in Jackson. Infidelity was sometimes viewed as a mental health issue that justified incarceration.

And so it happened; William was put away so he could, as Carrie's mother said, "get over his craziness." He was there when the federal Census enumerator recorded residents in 1900. Carrie wrote in her letter that her father was still a resident of the insane asylum in 1901, when she and Ira Jasper were married; he was able to get out for a day to attend the marriage ceremony. She said she was disappointed with him but happy he could be there. Since the family was now split apart, she did not know if or when her father would be released; most likely he was released and went his way without a word to his family. Another possibility was that he died at the asylum and, as was the case with many other residents, placed in an unmarked grave on the nearby grounds. All this was very hard on Carrie's mother; she wound up living with a couple of her older daughters. A couple of her older sons (brothers of Carrie) were very helpful by sending a little money to Louvenia to supplement meager wages she earned from farm jobs.

After she got the letter from Ethel, Carrie told Henry about it. She said that Dr. Davis had been "escorting and otherwise hanging around with an unmarried young woman." She said she told Ethel (who was beautiful at the ball with her fancy Tiffany accessories) to keep a good eye on them. Things might happen that were not intended. Henry mostly listened and said very little. He knew that anything he might say would be repeated and used as a reason to "talk bad about him and the arm he had lost." He also knew that Ethel was his next youngest sister, who was usually loyal and supportive, except for recent times after he had lost his arm.

An additional source of stress within the family (and all people) was the major impact of World War II. The conduct of the war called on everyone to make sacrifices. Interestingly, none of the sons-in-law at this time were in the military until one daughter married a returning soldier in 1945. And, they never lived at the Lee house. As the family well knew, Union forces camped around the house and threatened to burn it in the spring of 1863 during the Civil War. The house was spared because no soldier lived there. The family also promised that none ever would, or else the troops would return and burn the house. And here, ninety years later, a major war was being fought thousands of miles away and having a tremendous influence on how the family went about life. Life could not be carefree, and maybe that affected how family members related to each other. Maybe it influenced the use of alcohol, tobacco, and other less-than-healthy substances.

During World War II, an individual could not just walk into a store and get what he or she wanted. Certain guidelines of the government had to be followed. As mentioned earlier, the guidelines were implemented through rationing and restricting the amounts of products that people could buy. Some rationing was varied to the needs of an individual; other rationing was uniformly applied. Rubber was the first product rationed, and this restricted tires for automobiles and trucks as well as for farm equipment (though most farm equipment still had steel wheels).

War ration stamps (issued by the government under direction of the local Ration Board) were distributed to people based on established regulations. Stamps being used to buy a rationed product had to be detached from the book in the presence of the seller or shopkeeper. Among items rationed were shoes, sugar, coffee, tea, cheese, canned milk, canned meats and fish, cars, gasoline, and coal. Substitutes were sometimes used, such as saccharin for sugar and sassafras roots for leaf tea. People gave up a lot of freedom they had previously enjoyed because of the war initiative. This loss of freedom created stress and insecurity; it likely resulted in people being more aggressive toward each other.

Storekeepers could not charge whatever they wished for products. Price ceilings were established for some things, and this was good. Unscrupulous storeowners might have raised prices to exorbitant levels if price ceilings had not been set. Buyers could not offer higher-than-approved prices to get products. But, nevertheless, some buyers would offer bribes to get what they wanted. Overall, these kinds of practices were discouraged and prohibited by federal regulations. People who lived on farms were somewhat protected from the harsh reality of the war effort. They could produce much of their own food and maintain a kind of self-sufficiency not possible for someone who lived in a city and worked a job.

Henry tried to keep relatively up to date on war initiatives of the federal government. These usually related in some way to the kinds and amounts of crops produced. Rationing and other limitations also applied to the sharecroppers who lived on the farm. They could buy only what was legally available to them. Henry also shared what he learned with his family. He wanted his sisters and their husbands to be up to date on things. He tried to comply with and not violate government initiatives in food and fiber production. He occasionally went to the USDA office in the Hinds County Courthouse in Raymond to sign up for participation or otherwise gather information. In signing up, Henry was known as the producer, though Carrie Cheers Hendrick Lee, as the surviving spouse of Ira Jasper Lee, was the landowner. The property remained the Ira Jasper Lee estate for a number of years.

All this didn't happen suddenly. U.S. President Franklin D. Roosevelt began preparing for war involvement in 1939. This preparation expanded over the next few months. In the summer of 1941, the President responded to the British appeal to the United States for help with food supplies and other needed materials for the nation's war activity. People need food; both civilians and soldiers need proper nutrition for their health. Throughout Europe, food shortages and human hunger were impairing the will and ability of the people to engage in war. Even before the attack on Pearl Harbor, Hawaii, on December 7, 1941, brought the United States more directly into war, government leaders were preparing for war.

Collaboration with other nations was essential. Amazingly, the United States found a way to ship iron to Russia that avoided the German ships in the Atlantic Ocean that were set on destroying everything they could. Russia developed a new shipping and industrial military port in Murmansk, which was north of the Arctic Circle but available for shipping most of the year. Sometimes, U.S. ships with a soldier or two from the Tinnin community were used to escort the Russian ships loaded with iron ore. Henry had a buddy who told him about going along the coast of Norway and into the Arctic Circle on one of the escort ships. He told of ways the Germans had built caves along the rocky shoreline with entrances that were below the level of the seawater. Unfortunately, this buddy was injured in an exchange of gunfire with a German vessel and lost a leg below his knee. War is dangerous to people; war disrupts the lives of people, just as this young Tinnin resident unfortunately learned.

The U.S. War Production Board, mentioned earlier, was established in 1939. It had vast power over manufacturing in the United States, including the allocation of resources and the kinds of products produced by factories. Farm machinery and tools received a relatively high priority. The U.S. Department of Agriculture and local Agricultural Adjustment Administration county committees, as well as rationing committees, controlled how farmers and people residing on farms could use resources to live and produce needed crops. The program, touted by U.S. Secretary of Agriculture Claude R. Wickard, was known as the Food for Freedom program. All rural and farm people were expected to make contributions to this program. Henry was familiar with the program as it applied to farms in the South; Southern farms primarily produced cotton needed for the war effort. All people (both rural and city) were encouraged to have victory gardens.

Many of the win-the-war initiatives were in place at the time Henry experienced his tragedy. His medical care, as well as the ability of Doris and Son to care for him, was made somewhat more difficult by the hardships associated with the war efforts. Veterans had priority over civilians in most cases. Competent healthcare professionals to guide his recovery were not always readily available. Of particular absence was some of the therapy to help Henry adjust and cope. He needed both physical and occupational therapy. He also needed counseling related to emotional situations. Sometimes preachers would try to deal with the emotional issues, but they were untrained to help with such.

No let-up occurred in the sacrifices that people were asked to make for the war for another two years. And was the war, Henry repeatedly wondered, created by the ruling elite to help them achieve their personal goals on the backs of citizens of lesser means? He thought: the leaders didn't fight; they had underlings to do the fighting for them. People who think for themselves (and use facts in doing so) come to the conclusion that war is a matter of coercing poor, unfortunate people to fight on behalf of the well-being of those who are wealthy. Young men from the South who had little education or ability to advance in life went into battle on behalf of the wealthy. Henry assumed that war had always been that way. But life continued. Henry was just happy to be alive and enjoying living with his wonderful wife and son.

Henry and Doris occasionally talked about family jealousies and the ability to get along as an extended Lee family. Those jealousies did not seem to apply to her extended Sloan/Difrient family. Was the nature of the people different? People in the Sloan/Difrient family were always open and welcoming to Henry and Doris. Why would some of the relatives on Henry's side resent him and his farm family? Did they feel that farmers were receiving special dispensation from the U.S. government to increase farm production as part of the war effort? Did they resent the farm production being sent overseas to feed people who weren't Americans? Did they think that Henry, as an amputee, was receiving special consideration? Or, was it that Henry was the only surviving son of Ira and Carrie?

In late 1943, Doris and Henry were talking about finding a way to move out of the Lee-Shepard home. None of the tenant houses on the farm were in good repair. There were no houses nearby in the Tinnin community. They wanted something better for their small family. Their thoughts turned to living in Clinton. Any move would have to wait. Henry needed to heal; times needed to get better; and Doris, most of all, needed to be satisfied. It would be a few years before they could build and move to a home of their own.

Life was not easy. Whatever came Henry's way was hard earned and rightly deserved. He faced life head on and did not try to escape responsibilities. And, what did Henry do with the fifth of bourbon that Dr. Davis gave him? It stayed in its beautiful bottle (or bottle of sin, as a visiting preacher called it) on the shelf in the kitchen and would be there quite a while before Henry would open it.

Love builds and heals; harshness destroys and rips apart. Nothing promoted Henry's healing more than the patience, kindness, and love of his wife and son.

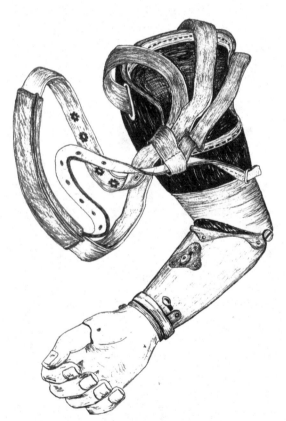

Prosthetic arm as used by Henry Lee, 1943

10

Working Left Only

Could a mule with one leg gone be used in farming? Maybe. It would be jerky and wouldn't work well. The animal would struggle. Some people thought of a man with one arm gone much the same when it came to farming. But would red and green paint come to the rescue?

Physical challenges faced Henry. Often, these were things that most people do not think about. They were just routine in the daily lives of people. Henry "began at the beginning" of overcoming his disability and plodded ahead to master as many activities as he could. Some were related to family and personal life; others were related to farming and life in the community. Simply, making a living for his family was his highest priority in 1943.

For more than thirty years of life, two arms and hands had worked together quite well. The brain and nerves knew there were two arms and hands. The muscles, tendons, and bone structures worked together as one. Of the two, the right arm and hand had always taken the lead. It was the right one that Henry used to sign his name, hold a hammer (and many other tools), and shift gears and otherwise operate a car.

Suddenly, one arm and hand were gone, and it was the right one. Shock! The nerves and brain didn't know it or, better stated, didn't know what to do about it. Farm work that had developed to a high level of skill was now questioned. Now, how were adjustments to be made? Henry's family depended on his productivity. He felt a strong drive to be successful. He felt an even stronger need to overcome his disability. But how was success to be measured? When, in Henry's life, would it be achieved? Many goals had to be revised; maybe he came to realize that the kind of success he wanted had become elusive.

Henry and Doris with Son in 1944. (Note: Henry is wearing his prosthetic right arm and hand. Darkness of the left hand is a sign that it has been tanned by exposure to sunlight.)

Henry contemplated the future. Would the farm survive? What would be his role? He realized the importance of overall management (though he didn't use that word) and planning future farming productivity. By tradition, his approach focused more on physical work and less on the future. Up until three or so years before Henry lost his arm, his father, Ira, was mostly in charge of having a vision (or somewhat thereof) for the farm. And much of his vision was to stay the course with no big or even medium changes in anything. He figured that if the farm could survive the U.S. Civil War and the Great Depression, it could survive anything. The goal was now subsistence more than anything else.

Some of the approaches used on the farm dated from the U.S. Civil War; changes happened at a slow pace. New developments in farming had come into being since World War I. Change was no doubt on the way. Henry was becoming increasingly aware of some of the new ways of farming, though these changes had, by and large, skipped over much of the Deep South. Socially and economically, as long as Southern farms had cheap labor, there would be little change. Additionally, many of the early developments did not benefit the cotton plantations of the South as much as they did the grain-producing farms of the Midwest.

A new mind-set was needed to move farms from subsistence farming with only cotton as the cash crop into commercial farming with a range of crops for specific markets. Except for cotton, the cash crop of the South, most farmers gave little attention to marketing. The goal was to find a cotton buyer and sell the baled cotton; seeds removed from the lint cotton were sold to oil mills. Buyers were meeting demands of textile mills in the U.S., Europe, and elsewhere. Cotton was not used much on the farms where it was grown. A partial "subsistence orientation" had been in the Shepard and Lee farming ventures since 1841. Though new farming developments had been springing up, win-the-war programs of World War II brought a halt to new developments of much consequence; most new things in the late 1930s and very early 1940s were put on hold until after the end of the war when some sense of normalcy returned to American life.

The kinds and nature of physical skills that had been carried out varied widely. Whatever work was done on the farm, Henry could do it. It might involve plants, animals, machinery, barn and fence construction, and more. From his early childhood years, Henry viewed what he had to do as a challenge and an opportunity to be successful. Rarely did situations appear beyond his ability to adapt. Now, he was facing new situations. He had to learn to depend on other people for some things, and this was a new way of living, as he had always been quite independent.

At first, everyday living skills, such as bathing, dressing, and eating were big challenges and sources of stress. Doris helped him develop coping skills. Some things, such as putting on and buttoning a shirt would always be challenging, but he learned how, with the help of Doris, to move forward. After the initial loss of the arm, coping and skillfully performing tasks became major challenges and areas of development. He pursued learning to do most farm skills in new ways with vigor. He knew he would need help. He chose his most trusted farm worker, Otho, to help with farm skills that appeared within reason. Of course, without two arms and hands, there were some tasks he could probably never perform independently. Frustration developed. This frustration helped him polish his cussing skills and carry them to a new level of proficiency!

Attention had been given to farming in the post-amputation era of his life since the day he came home from the Baptist Hospital. Plans were put in place for the year as winter turned to spring and the weather warmed. Now Henry was actively trying to manage the farming operations. He had organized the sharecroppers, assigned fields and crops, and gotten field preparation well underway and, in some cases, almost completed.

Henry would walk on foot or ride in a small wagon to observe the fields and check on workers two or more times a day, as needed. (He typically found it easier to walk because of the challenges associated with harnessing and driving the horse.) Earlier, the fields had been prepared for plowing as well as ever by cutting brush, removing crop residue from last year, and cleaning creek banks. Breaking the soil began in mid-March. Otho primarily used the clunky steel-wheel tractor to pull a plow to break the land; other hands would follow with mule-pulled harrows and fertilizer applicators. Seedbeds were prepared in mid-April, and planting followed shortly. By mid-May many young plants were emerging from the soil. The sign of young plants was always a positive experience— particularly for the all-important cotton cash crop. Weeds, insects, and other pests needed control several weeks during the growing season. This included applying insecticide to fight against the huge cotton pest known as the boll weevil that invaded the area in the early 1900s.

Being a hands-on person, Henry was frustrated because he could not take a more active role in land preparation, planting, and cultivation. He wanted to be sure the crops were properly grown. He became stressed because of his inability to work in the fields as he had in the past and to do other jobs. Simple jobs, such as hoeing vegetables in the garden, were no longer simple. How do you use a garden hoe with one hand? Impossible! No. He would figure out a way.

Some days he would think that maybe Dr. Davis was right. He was not up the task. But then, something positive would happen, and he would "snap out" of the depressed feeling. Often, Otho would say just the right thing to perk him up. With more involvement and less sitting and watching, Henry thought he could do better.

Henry set about to devise ways of getting various farm tasks done. With a little help from Otho, he figured out how he could efficiently use a hoe with just his left arm and hand. Of course, that arm and hand had to maneuver and provide all the power for the hoe. The technique involved wearing a durable leather belt in the pants loops. Placing a large metal ring (about 3 inches in diameter) on his pants belt on the front left side (this ring was from the harness of a mule) would make a place large and strong enough for the handle of the hoe to pass through at about the same height from the ground as the right hand would have been. The left hand could then move and swing the hoe so that seed drills could be opened, weeds could be cut, and the soil could be hand-tilled. Of course, that placed a lot of demand on the left arm and hand. And, did the muscles and strength develop in that hand! At first, there were some issues with controlling movement; a hoe should be used so that crop plants aren't cut or damaged. Work must be done efficiently. Henry mastered that skill and used it for many years of his life.

Planting seeds in the garden was another needed skill. Of course, planting field crops could be done with a mule-pulled mechanical planter. With hand planting, the challenge was to place the needed number of seeds in a drill or open hill and cover them at the right depth with soil. Proper planting was essential for germination, and gaining a good stand of the desired plants was a challenge. Sizes of vegetable seeds vary with the species—for example, a pea seed is much larger than a turnip seed. It is impossible to hold a bucket with seeds and drop the desired number of seeds with the same hand. Otho again came to Henry's help. He had Henry to put the seeds in a small bucket, use a rope or belt through the bail of the bucket around his right shoulder to fasten the bucket to his body, and use his left arm and hand to drop (place) the seeds in the drill or hill. Once the seeds were dropped, Henry could remove the bucket and put the large steel ring on his belt for the hoe handle. With his left hand, he could use the hoe to cover the seeds. Henry insisted that all work be properly done. Not planting seeds at the desired spacing and soil depth would result in failing to get a productive stand of plants.

Removing harvest-size vegetables, such as beans and squash, from plants and carrying a bucket or sack in which to place them normally required two arms and hands. With Otho's help, Henry came up with placing a belt or short rope loop through a bucket handle and around the shoulder, much as with dropping seeds. The left hand would then be free to pick peas, tomatoes, cucumbers, or other crops. Once the bucket was full or too heavy to carry on the shoulder, it would be emptied into a large tub, a sack, or the back of a wagon or pickup truck.

Vegetables with tougher stems, such as eggplants and okra, required the use of a cutting device to separate the fruit from the plant stems. Small, sharp scissorlike instruments might be held in the palm of the hand and squeezed around the stem to cut it while holding the fruit, such as a tomato, with the fingers. This wasn't very speedy or efficient. Henry soon came to the conclusion that some things may be more efficiently done by a person with two hands and arms; he didn't like this conclusion, but nevertheless it appeared to be true. Henry did learn that many things could be harvested using similar techniques to overcome the need for two arms.

Using a mule-pulled plow or cultivator was a particular challenge. Here is why: Two hands and arms were needed on the plow handles and to hold the rope lines to the mule. How a mule responds depends on the position and use of the lines. Both lines need to be held about equally in terms of force and pull. In addition to the lines, the handles of the plow had to be held for proper depth and location in the row. It is hard to hold two handles with one hand, though Henry tried plowing. Of course, turning would require more pull on the plow line in the direction of the turn. Henry tried using the best mule on the farm. Otho offered suggestions but would sometimes wind up saying, "Mr. Henry, I will do dat for you." Henry tried other things, such as holding a plow line in his mouth (remember, he had a partial plate) or tying the plow line to the end of the long right sleeve of his shirt. Getting the desired response from a draft animal was not easy. With the strength of such animals, tying plow lines to one's body or clothing could be hazardous if the animal failed to follow instructions.

Cotton was typically picked in late summer, fall, and early winter. In 1943, all cotton in the Tinnin community was picked by hand. This resulted in a high-quality, trash-free fiber product, but it was a labor-intensive process. Once a sufficient percentage of bolls were open and the seed cotton was white and fluffy, picking could begin. A large pick sack, about nine or so feet long with a wide strap that fitted over a shoulder, was used. Having the bag attached over the shoulder and dragging it along between rows was typical. There wouldn't be much difference with Henry other than he would have only one hand to gather the fluffy seed cotton. (Note: Seed cotton is cotton that hasn't been ginned; i.e., the seeds are still in it.) Obviously, with one hand, he could not pick as much in a day as a person with two hands, even with rapid finger and hand movement. Once the sack was about full and hard to drag, it was taken to a small cotton house and weighed with a balance beam and pea scale. The weight of the picked amount was recorded, and the sack was emptied and then taken back to the field to be used for picking more.

The cycle of cotton harvest repeated a few times all day long. Once the cotton house had about 1,200 pounds of seed cotton, the cotton was taken out of the house, loaded, and hauled on a wagon or truck to a cotton gin. Cotton doesn't weigh heavy, so it takes a lot of motion to get a couple hundred pounds, which was the minimum goal for most people after a day of picking. Henry, with one hand, was a fairly productive picker, but he never reached 200 pounds a day.

Milking a goat was a little less of a job than some other farm work. Henry prevailed in milking for several weeks before turning the nanny goat out to full-time pasture. In goats and related species, there is a pair of mammary glands (two teats) in an udder. On the Lee farm, each mammary gland was referred to as a teat because teats are obvious and on the exterior. Milk is produced internally, stored in the udder, and naturally removed when the female goat is nursed by a baby goat, known as a kid. The process of milk production is known as lactation. Since most goats do not give much milk, a nanny with a couple of near-weaning kids was bought. The kids were weaned (taken from the nanny) and fed grain and pasture vegetation.

At the time, milk was removed from a teat by the action of a human hand. It wasn't until well after Henry kept a milk goat that milking machines came into use. The usual routine was to milk twice a day. The teat was held in the hand and the hand moved downward with a pulling and squeezing action. Milk was released (pressed out) through an orifice or opening in the teat canal. The harvested milk was collected in a milk pail, a bucket, or some other container. Henry and Otho studied how Henry might be able to milk a nanny goat. An old table about the size of a kitchen breakfast table was used for the nanny to jump up on and eat selected grains from a pan while standing still to be milked by Henry, one teat at a time into a small bucket.

The relaxing routine caused the nanny to "let down" her milk more readily, resulting in easier milking motion on the teats. Of course, it took Henry about twice as long to milk a nanny, as he could milk only one teat at a time. Once it appeared that all milk was gone from the udder, the milking motion would be stopped, and the pan with feed removed (even if all feed wasn't gone, just to establish a routine for the goat). The bucket with milk would be carried inside the house, where Doris strained it through a cloth (usually cheesecloth) and chilled it in the icebox. The straining removed trash, hairs, and other impurities that might get into the milk. Trash and dirt in milk were minimized by washing both teats

JASPER S. LEE

before milking. No one wants to drink goat's milk that contains trash, hairs, or possibly feces.

A major reason Henry kept a milk goat was to have milk to drink himself. As a consequence of stress and other psychological issues, Henry had developed a digestive condition that his doctor said could be eliminated by drinking goat's milk. And, it worked for Henry after just a few weeks. This was good because a nanny goat goes through a dry time when no lactation occurs. The goat may be pregnant with the next kid or two and in a different phase of the lactation cycle. It was also good that Henry's condition healed, as who can tolerate goat's milk for more than a few days? (Only someone with a special taste for it!)

Sometimes horses, mules, donkeys, and other farm animals develop digestive system problems. Colic is most prevalent with horses, and there are many causes. What a horse eats (nature of the feed and presence of spoilage or mold) and the presence of intestinal worms are the most common causes of colic. Intestinal blockages sometimes occur, also resulting in colic. The condition causes severe pain in the digestive system. Pawing, refusing feed and water, rolling around on the ground, sweating, and other signs of colic may pose hazards to a human around a sick horse.

Home remedies on a farm often involved drenching a sick horse with mineral oil or doing other things that might do more harm than good. A big long-necked glass bottle would be filled with a mixed solution of oil and water and placed in the horse's mouth so that the liquid would come out at the back of its mouth at the throat and be swallowed. The horse would resist, buck around, and slobber out a lot of what was put into its mouth. Good restraint was essential but not something that one person could do without help. Henry would try to use a stall in the log barn and hold the bottle to the mouth and hope the animal would open its mouth. If not, he would try to pry it open with the end and neck of the bottle. This worked better if someone else restrained the animal.

After attempting to drench a horse, Henry decided that the procedure was too hazardous for a man with one arm but that he could assist one or two men on the farm in doing it. Calling a veterinarian was uncommon, as telephones were not widespread and veterinarians were hard to come by. If needed, a veterinarian would be called from the Ratliff Store phone. Arranging for one to come to the rural farm was not easy. Plus, veterinarians had hefty charges for their services. Henry learned that he could supervise a couple of men in drenching a horse for colic but not do the actual drenching.

A near-subsistence farm required a range of tasks to provide for the family and farm hands, care for the animals on the farm, and market farm products so as to gain a little cash for the family and farm. Corn was often used by farm families as roasting ears (young, tender, not fully matured ears but with developing kernels that could be boiled or roasted) and dry grain (mature ears and grains). And just in case someone is wondering, a corn ear is the fruit or spike structure that develops on a stalk and is composed of three main parts: the cob (the middle part to which rows of grain are attached), the grain (the kernels), and the shucks or husks (the outer covering of a corn cob). It is the grain that has much of the value.

Preparing corn grain as animal and human food products typically requires that the corn be dry when pulled (harvested), shucked (had its husk removed), and shelled (had the kernels removed from the corn ear). The kernels may be readied in some way before use, such as grinding (what this story is about) or chopping and mixing with other high-nutrient ingredients, such as cotton seed meal and mineral salt.

Once harvested, corn (both ears and kernels) must be kept dry and protected from insect pests and vermin. Here is where the barn cats provided a useful service. Since mice and rats like corn and eat and destroy it as well as foul it with feces and other vermin emissions, barn cats were used to control the mice and rat population. The major role of barn cats was to rid the barns of these pests. Often, their work was never completed.

Of course, Henry knew when moisture was right for harvest and how to harvest by snapping the ears from the stalk, throwing them into a wagon, and hauling them for storage in a barn that was often constructed of logs. He developed a new way to shuck corn by putting the stalk end of the ear against his thigh and using fingers on his left hand to open the end of the shuck and pull it back toward the base. This worked, but it wasn't fast. At least he could sit on a pile of unshucked ear corn to do this.

In shelling harvested dry corn, two ways were used on the farm: hand shelling and mechanical shelling. Hand shelling was slow and time consuming. Two hands were needed, with one to hold the shucked ear and the other to push or pull the kernels so that they would come loose from the cob. Henry learned that he could brace the end of the cob against the side of the pan or bucket he was shelling into and provide force with his left hand, causing the kernels to come off and be collected in the pan. There was a better way if a shelling machine was available.

The mechanical sheller was a machine about five feet tall that had a heavy iron flywheel about three feet in diameter connected to an axle with an inside mechanism that would remove kernels. The flywheel had a handle that was pushed around in a circle to make it turn. Shucked corn ears would be placed in the top, and the kernels removed by the sheller collected in a tub below. The cobs would go another place into a pile. To operate the mechanical sheller, two hands were needed: one to use the handle that turned the wheel and the other to put the corn ears in one at a time. Henry learned that he could get the wheel going and quickly reach to grab a couple of ears and drop them into the chute to the shelling device. Quickness was important when Henry tried to do this. Also, taking the hand off the handle on the flywheel created a safety hazard: the heavy turning wheel could hit or otherwise injure a hand or arm while it was spinning.

Mechanical shelling was certainly a lot faster but worked better with two people. Henry could be productive as one of the two people. Sometimes he would turn the wheel and get Doris or Son (when he was old enough for semi-hazardous work) to drop the ears into the sheller; other times Otho would drop the ears. It was too demanding for Henry to try to run the mechanical sheller by himself. He always thought about Son getting old enough to shell corn. (New engine-powered shellers and those with electric motors would become available in a few years and eliminate this kind of sheller. In 1943 there was no electricity on the farm.)

Tractors with gasoline engines were beginning to replace some uses of animal power on Southern farms. Only implements for primary land tillage and tractors for pulling wagons and other loads were available. Early tractor models also had large pulleys for doing beltwork. Operating a tractor might be possible for Henry; he had done so well before his accident. He looked over his tractor and talked with Otho. Several things were needed to be able to operate the tractor to get work done: start the engine, attach a simple hitch, put the engine in gear using the shift lever, engage the clutch with his foot, turn the steering wheel with his hand, and use the hand-operated throttle to regulate fuel to the engine. At that time, tractors around Tinnin did not have hydraulics, power take-offs, or many other features.

Starting the engine involved locking the wheel brakes to prevent movement and using a crank at the front under the radiator to give the crankshaft of the engine a spin. With luck, it would fire. Turning the crank was not easy. Several turns might be needed.

The cranking motion could sometimes snap backward if the engine misfired and break, sprain, or otherwise injure an arm. Pulling out the choke knob also helped in getting the engine going. Once the engine was cranked, the operator had to go climb up into the seat (really, not much of a seat). All the levers and pedals were stiff and hard to operate. The steering system was tight and not easily turned; there was no power steering in those days. Fortunately, the engine did not develop sufficient speed for the tractor to move very fast. It had a rough ride when moving over field land; the steel wheels were noisy and clanky.

Henry tried operating the tractor, but it was too demanding. Tractor operation was a strenuous activity, and Henry usually stayed off tractors until several years later when they had rubber tires, followed in a few years by power steering. Other features became more widely available, such as cushioned seats, lights for operating after dark, and easy hitches.

Just as some tractor power came to the Lee farm, technology in farming was increasing at a rapid clip. Henry would occasionally go to demonstrations where he could see the latest development in tractors and implements, seed and fertilization, pest management, and harvesting. He considered much of what he saw as beyond his means. Besides, he was no longer much of a risktaker. He did not have the money to buy much of the new equipment (neither did most other farmers). Further, he knew he could not operate it very skillfully and did not have the needed farm labor with skills to do so. He gradually embraced the "new" with guarded optimism. Over the years, he sacrificed some of his farming goals because he did not have the self-confidence to achieve them.

Henry's farming success had been greatly impaired by the event of January 20, 1943. Somehow, he tried to transfer some of his goals to Son, but he also realized that the size of farm operation needed for financial growth appeared beyond reach. Henry then increasingly returned to a goal he and Doris had stated in previous years: Son will go to Mississippi State College (got the name right that time) and get a degree in agriculture. The farm would likely cease crop production. It would be merged with other farms to create a larger and more efficient farm unit, or some other use would be found for the land.

Doing jobs that involved a hammer and nails or a hammer and staples in fencing with wire was a challenge. Learning how to position a nail in place and push or strike it to get it "set" in the wood was essential. And, Henry mastered it, though not with a high level of efficiency. To begin, the two boards (or whatever was being fastened with a nail) would need to be in place and fairly stable so they didn't move until the nail provided attachment. Starting the nail involved holding the hammer in the hand around the head and placing the head of the nail against the face of the hammer so that the nail sticks straight out from the face. It was necessary to place at least one finger on each side of the head of the nail so that the nail was securely against the hammer face. Then, a strong, quick push would be made so that the point of the nail stuck deep enough in the wood to hold it in position for hitting with the hammer. This meant that after the nail was stuck in the wood, the hand had to be quickly moved from the hammer head to the handle grip so that the tool could be swung, creating a lick of sufficient force to drive the nail. Swings of the hammer and strikes on the nail would be continued until the nail was driven in.

A difficulty in using the left hand for nail driving was stability of the hammer swing and strike. Being steady and developing new ability to squarely strike the nail required time and patience. Unsteadiness would result in bending the nail or missing it and hitting the wood, leaving the impression of the hammer face. Henry never skillfully mastered switching from his right hand to his left hand for nailing.

The physical demands did not come easy for Henry. Some days he found it hard to cope. He would sit an hour or so under a tree at the edge of a field while the sharecroppers cultivated the crop. He would gaze across the rows of growing cotton plants or whatever crop might be in view. His mind would wander. He would question himself. He would think that maybe he wasn't up to the requirements of running the farm. Repeatedly, he thought maybe Dr. Davis and other family members who challenged him were right. What was he to do? He always had a sympathetic life partner, Doris.

Henry faced coping with many more tasks. Some were more readily mastered than others. He had to depend on farm hands in many cases. Most of the time, the hands were quite helpful. Examples of the tasks with which he needed help (though there might be some opportunity for future development) were weighing picked cotton, helping a cow give birth, castrating a pig, digging a posthole, installing wire fencing, repairing or replacing pipe joints and fittings, and putting a saddle on a horse.

Nearly every task on the farm called for some sort of physical skill development that involved switching from doing it with the right hand to doing it with the left hand. Most jobs originally required both hands working together. Coordination of the left hand was a challenge. The first few months after the amputation were particularly difficult. Some days, Henry was discouraged and felt like giving up; other days, he moved ahead. Being out and about on the farm had particular benefits, much better than being isolated in the house and concentrating thoughts on his predicament. The fresh air, smell of newly plowed soil, and farm life in general provided refreshing relief to a young man struggling with an altered approach to the world.

The business side of things, which included keeping farm records, paying bills, submitting government reports, and other aspects of farming that reached beyond the fields, presented additional challenges. Files of receipts and invoices had been kept and were summarized in a ledger book. Doing this was not easy with a left hand. Writing was a challenge. Holding a pencil and using it to form letters and numbers was difficult. It had been an automatic set of skills that happened without thought. He got Doris to help with records. She neatly kept information that was accurate, readily decipherable, and easy to summarize as needed.

Additional records were kept on each of the sharecropper families. Monthly money allowances for the families were carefully recorded. Expenses for crop production were kept. Of course, income for each sharecropper was recorded as cotton and other products were sold. These records were very important after the crop season to summarize income and subtract expenses, thereby determining the amount due the sharecroppers and due Henry. The goal was to always be honest and fair and never cheat the sharecroppers. They typically had meager resources, anyway.

Records became more detailed as sound business management and government programs developed. Henry, as farm owner, had increasing need for records, though the sharecroppers had none. He began using a certified public accountant (CPA) for end-of-year tax matters. Because of needed details, the CPA required greater attention to the specificity and organization of records. The CPA could not create financial information that Henry did not provide. However, he understood a little about farmers and farm life. He would sometimes, fully or partially, accept as payment for his work a ham from the smokehouse or a gallon or two of molasses from the farm mill.

Henry wanted Son to be near when work was to be done. This was particularly true as Son got older and had the ability to do more jobs, even when some of the jobs might be hazardous. Sometimes there was a team approach. An example: Henry would hold a board in place while Son started and drove the nail. If Son missed or bent the nail, Henry would often express displeasure, such as, "Why can't you learn to drive a nail without bending it?" Now, the statement wasn't so much meant to be a criticism of Son as it was an expression of the great frustration in his inability to drive a nail. He loved Son too much to damage his pride. Henry knew that he had pushed Son into trying to do things when he was too young and had not developed the needed motor skills. Such activities also frustrated Son. Since he wanted to please his father, Son would try even harder the next time.

World War II was over in 1945, and life began to return to normal. Civilian needs were now being considered. Needs of Southern farms began to be met with new developments as cheap labor faded away. Over the years, the Midwest had been more receptive, partially because of the heavy use of family labor. Cyrus McCormick of Virginia was credited with inventing, among other things, the mechanical reaper (grain harvester) about a century before World War II. McCormick soon realized that he and his family could achieve more if they relocated to a location where the mind-sets of the people and the kinds of crops produced would be more favorable to tractor and implement sales. He chose Chicago, Illinois, for his new home. More developments were quickly released. Since McCormick chose to paint his equipment red, the brand became associated with red paint. Through the 1940s and 1950s, McCormick's Farmall (aka International Harvester) was the leading tractor brand for row crop farming in the United States and in the Tinnin community as well. The tractors and implements had features that allowed them to have a range of uses such as belt pulley power to operate equipment.

Henry was always intrigued by tractors and implements. A local salesman for the John Deere line of farm tractors and implements gave him a copy of the book *The Operation, Care and Repair of Farm Machinery* (5th edition) that featured equipment and tractors of the late 1930s. The book was filled with detail and illustrations, and Henry learned a lot from studying it. Some of the information applied to other brands. Henry never bought a John Deere tractor, but the farm did have John Deere mule-pulled seed planters and other implements. As with McCormick, most of the early developments served Midwest agriculture.

Deere's first tractor in the early 1920s was built with an internal-combustion engine known as a Waterloo Boy. One thing Henry couldn't quite figure out was the sound of the engine; it was a two-cylinder engine with a large rotating flywheel. The running engine had a continuous pop-pop-pop sound, making it easy to distinguish early John Deere tractors from other makes. In the 1950s, engines began to be changed to have more cylinders and an entirely different sound. Of course, Deere used green paint, and that distinguished the farm implement line from Farmall.

There were other makes of tractors and implements: Case, Fordson (later Ford), Avery, Allis-Chalmers, and Massey-Ferguson. Paint colors varied with each of these. With Ford and Massey-Ferguson, an appealing feature of general-use tractors was the three-point hitch with hydraulics. Implements could be easily attached and lifted. Henry acquired Fords in the early 1950s. He liked the hitching and lifting features of this tractor brand. Implements made in the South were often preferred because they were produced to meet southern conditions. Manufacturers of these included the Bush Hog Company of Selma, Alabama, and the Athens Plow Company of Athens, Tennessee.

So why was paint color important? People could recognize the brand of a tractor or implement by color. Many folks couldn't read words or attached labels. Discussion at a loafing store would often turn to tractors and equipment. A man might say, "That green pop-pop-pop tractor is stuck in a bog." Another man might say that his neighbor's "red tractor has broken down." Personal pride sometimes came about by paint color.

Farm survival in the Tinnin Community required the use of new methods. Tractors and implements with red and green paint became common. Success was more about what the paint was on than the actual color of the paint. Reducing farm labor needs and increasing profit were essential. For a man with one arm, ease of operation was essential and none of the current tractors and implements were well suited. Hired hands did most of the day-to-day work on the farm.

11

Paying the Preacher

Think about it: What does paying the preacher and
having food on the table, shoes for the baby, and a car
that cranks have to do with Henry's situation? Or, of
what importance is having a sister whose man owns a
new Buick Roadmaster, runs with a high-society crowd,
and danced with the Queen of the Ball?

Families have needs. In some cases, the needs are fairly simple and
self-sufficient; in others, money is needed for almost everything.
Henry was the main provider for his family, be it something produced on the farm or bought from a store. He needed assurance
that all would be accomplished. Maybe some relief to the burden
of being the sole financial provider for his family was on the way.
Henry had privately been questioning his ability to provide at the
level he wanted. Doris and Henry were very frugal; they wouldn't
waste money on frivolous things even though consumable products
were now available. By and large, they were self-sufficient on the
farm, except for the cotton production.

Doris and Henry had a simple budget for their home. This was
more of an effort by Doris with the concurrence of Henry. The

budget had five dollars a week for groceries, including blocks of ice at the icehouse in Clinton or from the ice truck that occasionally made rounds through the community. There was also a "rolling store" (like a school bus without seats or windows and with shelves inside along the walls) that came through with a wide assortment of staple groceries but just about always priced higher than at the grocery store. A big factor in Doris's sticking to the budget was the food produced on the farm. Monthly costs for utilities did not exist; there was no electricity, telephone, gas service, or water and sewer system. Costs for clothing and the like were minimal. Doris sewed some clothing from cloth bought at the mercantile store and other clothing from cotton cloth sacks in which flour, hog feed, and similar products were bought. Saving was easier than one might think because of a lack of available goods due to wartime regulations. Most early saving efforts to accumulate money were through accounts at the Bank of Clinton.

In late June 1943, word came that the Clinton schools needed another teacher—it was a first-grade teacher. Doris and Henry talked about possibilities. Henry said that she should apply; Doris agreed. This might help the family with their standard of living. With Henry's amputation and no more babies on the way, this sounded good to Doris.

So, in early July, Henry got some help to push off their car from the car shed so the engine would start. It started easily when the ignition was turned to on, the car was made to roll, and the clutch was let out to engage the gears so the crankshaft in the engine turned. Henry drove to Clinton to the schoolhouse so Doris could talk with Mr. Lassetter, the principal. Henry let Doris out near the schoolhouse door and parked nearby on an incline (so the car could readily roll to crank the engine). He waited in the car. While waiting, he admired the new elementary school built a couple of years ago. Nice, he thought; that is where Doris would be teaching if she got the position.

Doris walked into the principal's office and told him she was there because she had heard there was an opening for an elementary-grades teacher (he didn't have a secretary). Mr. Lassetter was cordial and said that there was, indeed, an opening for a first-grade teacher. In fact, this was the only first-grade teacher the school had. He asked Doris to have a seat and tell a little about herself, such as education and teaching experience. He liked the fact that Doris had been a teacher of lower elementary grades at Tinnin and, after the Tinnin school was consolidated with Clinton, she taught at Byrum and that she had a four-year college degree. He told Doris that teachers in the lower grades typically had only a couple years of college and that getting teachers with college degrees was a high priority. He said that the school certainly needed her. He was under pressure to upgrade the quality of education because of nearby Mississippi College, whose professors demanded good education for their children.

"Are you married?" Mr. Lassetter asked. "If so, what type of work does your husband do?"

"Yes, I'm married," Doris responded, "and my husband is Henry Lee. He is a farmer in the Tinnin community. His family roots go back a hundred years in Tinnin. We have a two-year-old son. Henry and I have talked, and he thinks it would be good if I applied for a teaching position." They discussed a few more things related to the teaching position. (Doris was always careful to use the word "position" when referring to an employment opportunity in education. She felt that the word "job" did not connote the professional level of the work that was done by a college-educated teacher.)

"You know, I am pleased that you are married, but it might pose a problem," Mr. Lassetter stated. He continued, "Mississippi has a state law that prohibits married women from teaching school. I never understood why such a law was needed."

"Yes, I am aware of that law," Doris said, adding, "With the war taking teachers away, there is such a shortage that maybe the state will reconsider that law. Many laws are being changed to support the war effort."

"Yes, I know," he said, "and here is what I will do. I will take this matter to the local school board at its next meeting. I will explain that there is a highly qualified teacher available who is a married woman. Maybe the board can help work it out for you to be our new teacher. I will be in touch next week after the board meeting. Our school year begins the Tuesday after Labor Day." Doris thanked Mr. Lassetter, said she looked forward to hearing from him, and left his office.

Doris went out to the car and, with Henry in the driver's seat, gave the car a push down the embankment to get it started; then she ran and jumped into it. Of course, Henry was still mastering left-hand-only driving, and it would have been easier if the car battery had been strong enough to turn the engine over for starting. He didn't want to use a hand crank. They began their way back to Tinnin.

Just as they entered the brick street area of Clinton near the drugstore, they were slowed as prisoners of war were marching/walking/strolling from their camp into the downtown part of the tiny town. Henry and Doris had heard about a prisoner of war camp that was in the process of opening on 790 acres of previously good farmland. She wanted to know more and for a very good reason. The POW camp was to be fully operational in mid-1943 at a site a few miles south of Clinton. The location was to be just east of Spring Ridge Road at the intersection with McRaven Road and not far west of Jackson, the capital city of Mississippi.

Doris and Henry stopped at the drugstore. They went inside to ask about the POWs and Camp Clinton. A couple of local citizens appeared to be fairly well informed and were willing to talk. They indicated that the prisoners had begun arriving in June. They were mostly of German and Italian lineage and had been brought primarily from North Africa by way of Scotland or from an African port to the port of Norfolk, Virginia. Those who departed from Scotland crossed the Atlantic on ships and were placed on a train from New York to the camp. Those from Africa were members of the German Expeditionary Force during the North African Campaign of World War II, commanded by Erwin Rommel (The German name for the expedition was *Deutsches Afrikakorps*.) The drive to take North Africa began in March 1941 and ended in May 1943, as the troops surrendered. Word was that some high-ranking officers were among the POWs, including those from Europe as well as Africa. One was Dietrich von Cholititz, who was the last wartime Governor of Paris. He is known as the individual who surrendered Paris to the Free French.

Operation of the camp was under the command of the U.S. Army. Guards were always present. However, daily details involved the German officers in leadership roles over the other POWs at the camp. It wasn't a grim, gray place with barbed wire and guard towers but a place with new barracks and bungalows. Conditions at Camp Clinton met the international standards for keeping prisoners of war, which meant it was as good as (or maybe better than) U.S. soldiers experienced in service to their country. Further, conditions were better in the camp than most citizens had in the community, except that it was a POW camp (just think of the home of Doris and Henry without electricity, plumbing, and adequate heat).

Local citizens often wanted to see the "enemy" they had been taught to hate. Overall, the men were much like men in the local community. They appeared to be good people; they were not people to be hated. The young men were away from their homes and wanted to be with their families—their parents, wives, and children. Of course, many people in the Clinton area had ancestors with German heritage; Doris knew that she had considerable German ancestry in her family.

While Henry and Doris were still in the drugstore, two of the POWs came inside and walked over to the ice cream counter. Doc Ept went to greet them from the back side of the counter and gave a big smile. One of the POWs said, "Guten Tag."

"May I help you?" Doc Ept responded.

One POW said, "Eine Eistüte, bitte." As he spoke, he pointed to a picture of a five-cent, single-dip cone of vanilla ice cream that was on the wall behind the counter. Doc Ept figured that was what he wanted because he had a nickel in his hand. Doc Ept reached for an empty cone and put a dip of vanilla ice cream in it. He handed it to the soldier, who gave him five cents and said, "Vielen Dank."

The other soldier also pointed to the picture and said, "Bitte." He, too, had a nickel in his hand.

Doc Ept fixed him a cone and said, "Thank you."

The two soldiers left, and as they went out the door, one licked his cone and was overheard to say to the other, "Schmeckt gut." Henry and Doris thought it was nice to see and hear these German POWs up close; they appeared to be nice men and did not seem dangerous at all.

Henry had heard that some of the POWs worked at jobs in the community and were paid eighty cents a day. Those who worked often did projects in the community; others helped in building a flood plain research model of the Mississippi River that later became known as the Waterways Experiment Station. The pay they received went into a canteen account that they could use to buy colas, candy, and the like. Drinking colas in front of other prisoners in the camp made them feel special. When fully occupied, the encampment had 3,000 POWs.

Upon seeing the prisoners and hearing about them, an idea flashed through Henry's mind: Maybe he could use a few of the prisoners to do work on the farm and pay them eighty cents a day. He didn't know who to talk to at the camp about this idea. So, after mentioning it in the drugstore (the citizens didn't know details), he left and stopped to ask a guard about possibilities. After a brief conversation, Henry was told that he would need to speak with First Commanding Officer Loughlin and that to do so he would have to gain entrance at the main gate of the camp. He would need to bring identification papers with him. He was also told that POWs in some camps worked in the community but not yet at Camp Clinton. After the brief stop, Henry and Doris continued on their way back to their home in Tinnin.

As they rode, they talked about the interview and the possibilities it raised in their lives. Doris' first concern was who would look after Son during the day. Henry said that he would be in and out of the house each day and that they might be able to rely on Susie Heckle much of the time. They knew that Son really liked Susie; she had a way with him that brought out his best. Next, Doris wondered about how she would get to school and back each day. She might drive, but the car wasn't very dependable.

"There is a school truck," Henry thought aloud, "and it is driven by Mr. Mason. Maybe you could ride it."

"Yes," Doris said, "but I won't have additional time in the morning before school to get ready for the day. Maybe I could do that at home. The same is true at the end of the school day. Riding the school truck, if allowed, may be my best choice. Or, maybe you could occasionally drive me in the car early in the morning and I could ride the school truck home in the afternoon."

Doris had never taken a good look at the school truck: Just what was it? She went to Mr. Mason's home, about a mile away, to talk about the possibilities and look it over.

Mr. Mason said that transportation was provided to and from school for some students. In this case, the Tinnin School had closed four years earlier, and the school district felt that it had an obligation to those students who had been disrupted. Mr. Mason explained that the Clinton School had contracted with him to provide transportation. He said, as a school truck driver, he provided a vehicle, bought gasoline, and drove the truck route morning and afternoon. Doris checked out Mr. Mason's school truck. It was something he had built out of lumber on a dual-wheel flatbed truck. The seats were benches that went from front to back, with a double front and back row in the middle and a row on each side at the windows. A door was at the front. A cover was over the seating area to keep out rain, cold, and other inclement weather. Mostly, the cover kept out dust and flying insects, such as wasps and bees. No cushions or other comforts were included. The ride was rough on the rural roads of gravel, sand, and earth, with water holes and ruts along the way. Regardless, it was free and followed the regular school schedule. Mr. Mason was very nice about Doris riding the bus. They had a talk, and he knew what the schedule of a teacher such as Doris might be.

In mid-July, Doris looked out a front window of their home and saw a car coming down the long driveway from the main road. It kicked up a little dust and frightened a few chickens. She wondered who was coming. The car pulled up to the front-yard gate and stopped, and a man in coat and tie emerged: It was Mr. Lassetter, principal of the Clinton School. He walked to the house, came on the porch, and knocked. Doris went to the door and greeted him. He said he wanted to talk, so they sat in a couple of chairs on the far edge of the porch (Doris didn't want Carrie to overhear the conversation).

"Well, the school board met last night," Mr. Lassetter said, "and I talked with them about your possibly becoming one of our teachers. One board member knew of your excellent reputation as a teacher at the Tinnin School a few years ago. He felt that you would be a real asset to the Clinton School. The state law prohibiting married women from teaching school was discussed. You know one member of our board works for the State Department of Education. He proposed that you be offered the position with the understanding that you would have to give it up if anyone in the community objected to your being a teacher. So, I am here to offer you the position under that condition. If agreeable with you, we will issue you a contract for nine months beginning September 1 at the annual salary of $675, or $75 per month for nine months."

Doris was pleased with the information. "Thank you for driving out here to tell me," she said. "Before I can definitely accept, I need to talk with my husband, Henry. But, I am sure I am going to accept the offer. I will come to your office in the morning to fill out any needed paper forms."

Mr. Lassetter said that would be fine. He indicated that there would be a faculty meeting on Friday morning before Labor Day and that the first day of school would be the Tuesday after Labor Day. She could use Friday afternoon to get her classroom ready for the start of school. Mr. Lassetter said he would give more details when she came to his office. At noon, when Henry came in from the field, they talked about the offer. They agreed that she would accept it.

The next morning, Henry started their car, and he and Doris drove into Clinton to the school (Henry had some spare time from farming, as the crops were laid by). Upon arrival, he again parked on an incline to make it easy to push the car off for starting. He also tried to park out of direct sight of the school office because the car sometimes gave a big cloud of black exhaust smoke when it started and backfired loudly one or more times when the clutch was engaged. Doris went into the office and gave her decision to

Mr. Lassetter. He was very pleased to have such a highly qualified young teacher join his faculty.

Mr. Lassetter talked with her about getting to and from school, since she lived on a farm in Tinnin about five miles away. She mentioned something about possibly riding the school truck that Mr. Mason drove, and Mr. Lassetter was agreeable with that if it did not interfere with her teaching duties. He said that if she had a problem getting home in the evening, she could spend the night in the teachers' home (where he lived). And, if she wished, she could bring an overnight change of clothing and keep it in her locker at school in case of an emergency. Now, that caught Doris by surprise. What was he suggesting? Was he throwing out "bait" to see how she responded? But, she let it pass without comment; she quickly thought that anything she might say could later be held against her. Little did she know! She signed papers to be a teacher. Exciting to her!

Doris and Henry started back to Tinnin, and, as usual, the route began along the brick streets of Clinton. They again saw some of the prisoners from the Clinton POW camp. It renewed Henry's interest in possibly using a few to do farm work. He decided that he would talk to the Hinds County Agricultural Agent and a couple of business folks in Clinton before exploring it with the U.S. Army. He and Doris stopped at the drugstore and, while there, the Associate County Agent, a Mr. Forbes, just happened to come in (now that was convenient!). After an exchange of pleasantries, Henry asked Mr. Forbes about the use of prisoners to do farm work. Henry got some ideas. He heard that the prisoners were nearly all good men of varying military rank in the German army. They were generally educated well, maybe better than members of the U.S. Army, particularly in areas using engineering skills. Henry was told that none from Camp Clinton had worked on farms for pay, though several had wanted to do so. They wanted to see what life was like out in the farming areas and across the countryside. The Associate Agent summarized by saying that there might be too much risk in trying to use the POWs to do farm work.

Doc Ept, the pharmacist, overheard the conversation and offered to share his thoughts. Doris asked him to please do so. Doc Ept said that he had not had much direct involvement with any of the POWs but that a few would occasionally come into the drugstore and buy something with U.S. money. He talked about the feeling of safety among citizens in the Clinton community.

He said that, to his knowledge, only a few POWs had attempted to escape. However, one did get away for a night. The story is that one of the first generals at the camp went to the Heidelberg Hotel in Jackson for a night. He used hotel stationery to write a letter to the U.S. Department of State about the conditions under which he was being kept, such as having to share living quarters with another general as well as sharing a toilet and an assistant. (Why would he need an assistant in a POW camp? Maybe it was because commanding officers in the German military were given some oversight of the other POWs.) The next day he found his way back to the camp and slipped back inside without detection.

Agent Forbes told of another instance he read about in which a prisoner exchanged cans of evaporated milk for a couple of pieces of bubble gum from the outside. The canned milk was given to the POWs by the Switzerland Red Cross. Outside the camp, U.S. citizens could not readily buy evaporated milk; it was not available on store shelves. In the camp compound, a few items were available in the canteen. POWs could use the eighty cents a day they earned for work in the prison to purchase items. If something wasn't in the canteen, they could not get it. If a prisoner didn't work, he did not have "canteen money." Since there was enough work inside the camp on the scale model of the Mississippi River, no POWs went out to work in the Clinton area. Some occasionally had an American coin or so that they would spend in a Clinton store.

Occasionally, some trusted POWs would be allowed to leave the camp almost on their own. Some went into town to walk around and, maybe, to see a movie in the local theater. It helped if they understood English. One or more Army guards usually went out with a small group of POWs. Overall, the POWs got along well with each other. Most were not dedicated Nazis, though a few were fanatical in their beliefs, sometimes resulting in hard feelings. Once, a fanatical POW Nazi killed one of the other prisoners. Little is known about the homicide—it was handled by the camp commander. Authorities stepped in and shipped identified fanatical Nazis to a special camp in Oklahoma. Of course, when word got out about the killing, some folks in the Clinton community became nervous. They would say things like, "What if the POWs went to the school or a church and did harm?" That never happened.

Henry was told that there were a few of the POWs who had lost arms, legs, or eyes or had other life-changing injuries. Medical care was provided in the camp compound by a well-equipped infirmary with several staff members. Henry immediately thought that these POWs had better care than he had! He wanted to talk with a prisoner who had lost an arm, but that never worked out as Henry didn't know German and the amputee didn't know much English. He was told that none had prostheses, but those missing legs had crutches to help them move about.

Henry learned that one of the nurses at the infirmary was a Miss Rogers, a resident of Clinton who had been able to get a job at the camp. She was one of three or four trained nurses who maintained daily hours. Several of the POWs had medical training and helped in the hospital—one was a trained physician. Common health problems were malaria and head lice; these were readily treated. Serious illnesses might result in a POW being transported to see a local physician or in the physician making a visit to the camp hospital. Overall, the POWs received the same care as American service members. For the POWs, life was better in Camp Clinton than on the battle fields of North Africa where most had been serving, but still they missed their German homeland. Of course, their homeland would never be the same. Allied forces had destroyed many factories and businesses, along with some homes and other places. Most of the soldiers had left home in 1940 and spent three years in the deserts of Africa before surrendering or being captured in 1943. They were often lonely and depressed. They missed their families and the customs of Germany.

Doris had gotten tired of hearing about the POWs in the drugstore. Besides, she was developing some anxiety. In the meantime, a few other people who had walked into the drugstore were now listening and talking. The words suddenly drew additional meaning for her, and she was no longer eager to go. She became involved in the discussion.

"Do you know the names of any of the POWs?" she asked. "What places in Germany are they from?"

Most of the people did not know any names, nor did they speak German, so when they heard a name, it was not recognized. But one name that was stated was Marquardt, and another was DeVrient. No one knew the names of places they were from, though one individual named Berlin and another named Stuttgart.

Doris asked, "Have you heard any of the POWs mention Stettin? Today it is known as Szczecin, but some old-timers might still call it Stettin." No one acknowledged having heard it, but some thought they might have. The word was admittedly a little strange to them. But, she had heard enough.

Doris was now ready to go. Henry came along when she said it was time to leave. They walked together to the car, with Henry holding and massaging the nub of his right arm to help alleviate strange feelings, as he called them, but known to therapists as phantom limb sensations. And, fortunately, he had parked the car on an incline so that it would roll when the clutch was pushed in and start when the clutch was let out. As usual, it started with an exclamation of backfire and smoke!

On the ride home, Doris expressed concern to Henry about what effects, if any, her German ancestry might have on her acceptance as a teacher. At one point, she was almost in tears with the thoughts she was having. Henry asked her to talk a little more about what she was thinking.

"There may be hard feelings toward German people among citizens in the community," Doris said. "Our young soldiers are being killed and maimed by German soldiers in Europe and Africa, and the presence of the Clinton POW camp in the community might not help. Parents may think I am a German patriot and am befriending POWs at the camp."

Henry didn't believe that parents would think this. Anyway, as they talked, they decided it best to be forthright and tell Mr. Lassetter about Doris's ancestral heritage. They agreed that they would drive back to the Clinton School the next morning for Doris to tell about her background. It would be better to get denied the position than to get it and then get fired. Henry said it was good that the crops had been laid by and that he could now take time away from the farm to be her driver. More than anything, he was still working on developing left-hand-only driving skills, which was sometimes difficult.

Doris arrived at Mr. Lassetter's office the next morning. She told him that she wanted to talk with him about a matter. (He probably thought that she was going to back out of teaching for some reason. Maybe he thought that was the way it was with young married women. Or, maybe, he thought she was going to tell him that she was pregnant!) Mr. Lassetter invited her to sit in front of his desk. In going to the back of his desk to be seated, he touched her shoulder briefly and moved on. Doris wondered about that brief touch.

"Mr. Lassetter, I have something to discuss with you," Doris began. "The war is going on, and we have a POW camp just outside of Clinton. One of the big enemies is Germany. I want you to know that I have some German ancestral heritage."

Somewhat surprised, Mr. Lassetter said, "Okay, tell me about it. Feel free to talk about anything you wish."

Doris began. "Some of my ancestors came from Germany in the late 1800s. They came from the German port city of Stettin (now Szczecin on the Baltic Sea) and entered the U.S. through the Port of New Orleans, Louisiana. At that time, Stettin was in Germany. In World War I, it became a part of Poland, though geographically it is not far from the border with Germany. My father, Andrew Goodman Sloan, did not come from Germany; he was born in Winston County, Mississippi. Ancestors on my mother's side had names such as DeVrient and Marquardt. After they got to the U.S., the DeVrients changed their name to Difrient. The DeVrients were from a well-known family of theater performers and writers in Germany."

Doris paused, and Mr. Lassetter spoke. "I see no problem with your ancestry. All of us are from someplace. I suppose you need to indicate if there is a particular loyalty to Germany."

Doris responded, "No. I do not have any particular loyalty to Germany or the Nazi regime. I do not like war. I support the United States with what it is doing. I consider myself to be a loyal U.S. citizen."

Mr. Lassetter said, "Thank you for sharing this with me. I appreciate your being forthright. Now, we have just prepared a contract for you. Look it over, and sign if everything is in good order. Get the signed copy back to me. Remember, we have a faculty/staff meeting on Friday before Labor Day to get ready for the school year. Anytime you have something to share with me, let me know, and we can talk in the privacy of my office."

Mr. Lassetter indicated that he wanted to show Doris the room she would be using. After a brief tour of the school, they walked to her room. It was just down the hall from the auditorium and had a built-in restroom for first graders. He showed her some of the books and other instructional materials in her room. There were child-size chairs for a reading group of about ten students. The room had a student desk for each student (about twenty-four), a teacher's desk and chair, cubical lockers along the back wall, and windows for outside light. And, in just this room, there was a teacher's stool for sitting when doing group reading instruction. Doris sensed that the tour of the school was about over and thanked Mr. Lassetter. She indicated that she was looking forward to the school year. They walked together back to his office and said goodbye. She left his office and went to where Henry had parked; they started the car and left for home.

Driving along, Henry wanted to massage the nub of his right arm. Doris told him to stop doing it and focus on driving. She said she would drive if needed. He stopped massaging, though the phantom sensations continued.

The brick streets through Clinton again had POWs from Camp Clinton walking on them. Doris wondered if she had cousins among them; most likely, there were distant relatives. Henry saw one with an arm amputation just below the elbow.

As they left town, Doris gave Henry a report on what Mr. Lassetter had said: there was no problem with her teaching based on her ancestral heritage. That was good news. Now, they could count on $75 a month from teaching for the family income. Doris would use about $20 of it for groceries and a few dollars for clothing. They could likely save $40 a month in a bank savings account that accrued interest. But, this still didn't give them much more than a meager income. And with the couple of weeks she had remaining before the start of the school year, she would spend time with their son and get clothing ready. She would sew two dresses using skills taught her by her German-heritage mother!

After the whirlwind of activity associated with Doris's teaching position, Henry was now trying to fully focus on the farm. Harvest time would soon begin. Most of the cotton looked good; corn was fair; and sweet potatoes had grown an abundance of vines. Some sweet potato flowers were being formed, indicating plant maturity and the development of potatoes in the ground. It was time to get the cotton houses patched and ready for receiving the picked seed cotton. Through all this, he was still trying to survive as a man with one arm. Oh, what a challenge it had been to this point. As a consequence of being an amputee, there were some things he just didn't attempt to do.

Few truck crops (squash, okra, roasting-ear corn, butter beans, and peas) were planted this year. Actually, the only vegetables planted were those that the family was going to use and those for the sharecroppers. So, this meant no income from the sale of vegetables to the supermarkets in Jackson. This lack of income tended to make family living more difficult, but Doris knew how to adjust. Several acres of sweet potatoes would be a source of income but not until late in the fall. Sugar cane would also provide income from the syrup that would be made in November and December. Henry explained how they could also use the syrup cooked at the mill to make molasses milk drink; it was a favorite with Son and, since it contained molasses, provided iron for his growth and development.

By mid-August, some of the hill cotton had begun to open. The white, fluffy bolls of seed cotton were quite appealing to a cotton farmer. Henry always liked to begin picking early for it to be ginned and graded before it was rained on and lost its brilliant whiteness. Some bolls would open later, requiring a second picking. Henry's notion was never to waste cotton by leaving it in the field after harvest was completed in late autumn. Early picking and ginning also provided income to everyone involved by the first of September.

Henry would sometimes go to the field to pick and could do reasonably well for a man with one arm. He now used the old pickup truck to take a bale to the gin (not a mule-drawn wagon). The side planks on the truck made the bed just the right size to hold a bale of seed cotton before ginning (about 1,150 pounds). He always brought a few dollars home from the gin that was gained from money for the seed that was left over after the cost of ginning was paid. The meager amount would be split among those who had an interest in the field of cotton. The baled fiber had to be weighed, sampled, and graded to establish the per-pound price and value for a bale before a cotton buyer would buy it. Payment for the fiber could be delayed a week or more; several bales might be sold at the same time.

This particular year, early selling of cotton was quite beneficial. Doris would begin teaching at the beginning of September, but she would not receive any pay until the end of September. She would need a few things to help her get ready for the start of school and through the month of September. Money received from the early-pick cotton would be useful with living expenses until she got her paycheck. Later in the fall, when harvested crops were sold, greater attention could be given to Henry and Doris's financial situation. They could work toward saving for the future goals they had discussed. They would have nothing extravagant in their lives; just the basics would be sufficient.

By the time harvest season was over that fall, the crop year could be described as better than average. Cotton yield was particularly good (42 bales of handpicked cotton) with a color grade of middling (Mid) and staple length of one and a sixteenth inch (37/32). Corn was about the same as the previous year, with an estimated yield of a low 28 bushels per acre at a grade of number 2, yellow (if it had gone into the grain market, but it was used for human and animal feed on the farm). Sugar cane and sweet potatoes were good.

The sugar cane was used to produce molasses, with nearly a hundred gallons being produced; 82 one-gallon cans were filled, along with a few larger pottery jugs. Some sixty bushels of sweet potatoes were produced; some were sold green, and others were allowed to air dry for storage and selling in the winter and spring. Any vegetables, fruits, and nuts produced were used by families living on the farm. As previously indicated, no effort was made in 1943 to produce these for the grocery stores in Jackson because of Henry's accident. (Note: Anyone reading these yields might be surprised at the low per-acre outcome when compared to today's yields. Many advances have been made in crop genetics, soil fertility, plant nutrition, and pest management. Southern agriculture was still trying to recover from the old-South, Civil War era that relied on hand labor. The Great Depression of the 1930s created conditions that lasted into the 1940s.)

Carrie knew the crop season was over. She started badgering Henry and Doris for $600 rent money in November.

"I'll pay you when all records and sales are in," Henry said, "and that will be about mid-December."

"You certainly will," Carrie said. "My daughters and their husbands will see that you do. You poor, crippled thing; you probably can't even sign a check. I am thinking about running you and your family away from here. I'll let my daughters do it."

"You will get the money," Henry said. "I will personally see that you get it. Another thing: Stop being so harsh on me. My arm is gone; I can't bring it back. Your statements make me feel really bad; they hurt me." Of course, Doris would write out the check, and Henry would sign it. That payment was a part of Henry's farm expenses.

Mid-December arrived, and Carrie got her check; she never

said thank you or acknowledged receiving it. When her daughters and their husbands visited, no mention was made of the payment. Henry was always certain that they knew about it because Carrie would have readily told them if she had not been paid.

Henry knew that having financial stability from farm enterprises was a year-round process. He didn't have formal training in such but learned through years of experience. He knew good firsthand information was needed to aid in planning and decision making. Most of the information he used was gained through observing field productivity and the cultural practices that were used. He reviewed crop yield information. Several of the fields were little more than patches that had been continued after the U.S. Civil War. He thought that something could be done to improve these fields and set about to devise a plan.

He felt that a first step toward increased efficiency was to have larger fields. This would involve taking out certain turn rows and changing drainage ditches. Of course, practices in soil and water conservation were needed. Henry sought the advice of the Hinds County Agricultural Agent and of a technician with the Soil Conservation Service (SCS) of the U.S. Department of Agriculture. The SCS technician would survey the field areas and identify low places that would hold water and kill or stunt the growth of crop plants. Those areas needed to be filled or drained.

Another step to promote increased crop yield was to clear brush from fence rows, ditch banks, and other places where the brush interfered with crop plant growth. Most of this work was done in the late winter before spring plowing. In some cases, large trees near the fields would impair plant growth by sending roots underground out into the fields, where they would take nutrients needed by crop plants. Trees with big canopies that grew in or near fields would shade crops and reduce sunlight on plant leaves, reducing photosynthesis and thereby crop yield. Of course, field hands liked these trees in the summer where they could go in hot weather for shade and brief rest. Rather than cut down the trees, girdling was used. Girdling was a common process of chopping a ring around the trunk of a tree a little deeper than the thickness of bark. This cut went through the vascular system, disrupting plant raw material, nutrient, and food transport. Within a few years, the girdled trees would die and fall. It might have been better to cut down and remove tree remains from the fields.

Doris helped Henry keep records (mostly of receipts and disbursements). These records were not as polished as a bookkeeper would keep, but they met farm needs. Records in the ledger book were used to settle the account of each sharecropper. And, Henry and Doris always tried to do so fairly and accurately. The amount sharecroppers received relative to the amount of work done was not that much; this was the sad part of subsistence farming during and after World War II. Of course, cotton was produced as a cash crop and was the only cash crop on the Lee farm. The records were also used by the accountant to settle the financial situation for the year and prepare needed tax documents. Little analysis was made of records in preparing for the next crop year; crops were produced based more on tradition than on returns on harvested products.

When the year was over, Doris and Henry took stock of their personal financial situation. They maintained separate checking accounts at the Bank of Clinton. Having separate accounts (a good thing Carrie didn't know) was thought to be better because Henry used his for the farm. Doris's income was from her teaching salary and went into her account at the end of each month when she deposited her paycheck and kept a few dollars of cash. Doris and Henry felt fairly good about the ending of 1943 with all that had happened in their lives (the year certainly began on a bad note). In addition to their checking accounts, they had passbook savings accounts at the bank (records were handwritten in each book). For subsistence farm folks, their savings were making some meager progress toward the home they wanted to build in a few years and the new car they wanted once the federal government was at a point in the war where car production would again be allowed.

They also talked about how important the sharecroppers were to their family and the goals that they had. Each sharecropper was apparently going to be with them another year. Keeping a good sharecropper was always better than trying to find another, which usually meant taking one from another farm. That sometimes created ill will among community residents. Henry and Doris came up with the notion that Otho should have a bonus for all the help he had been during the year. They realized that they couldn't have gotten through the winter and spring months without him. Of course, other sharecroppers shouldn't know, as it might create discontent. Bonuses in those days, even if given, weren't much, but each dollar had greater buying power than in the years afterward. The bonus made Otho quite happy. He practically danced with joy when talking about what this would mean to his family. To a cotton farm operator, not much is better than a happy sharecropper!

Henry often mentioned to Doris the long-term situation on the farm. He was concerned. Could the farm make adjustments and turn around the gradual decline that began at the time of the Civil War? In addition to all of the other considerations, there was the role of the Federal government in agriculture. A factor impacting the financial soundness of the Lee plantation was the Agricultural Price-Support and Adjustment Program operated through the U.S. Department of Agriculture. This program began in 1933 as the Great Depression was well underway and continued well after World War II. It was a provision of The Agricultural Adjustment Act of 1933 that initiated a more than 50-year program of what some people consider as "farm control." Farm prices had rapidly fallen more than fifty percent since 1929. Farmers were caught in a serious squeeze between the costs they had to pay for farm inputs and the prices they received for their harvested crops. Money-wise, times were very hard. This was true for the farm owners as well as hired workers and sharecroppers.

This legislation was an attempt by the Federal government to manage farm commodity yields so that production and consumption were better balanced and assure farm income by using price supports to regulate the prices farmers received. Seven basic commodities (five crops) were initially covered, with cotton being the major crop in the South and on the Lee plantation. Features of the programs included acreage reduction (control) and marketing (price supports). Also included were efforts to rid agriculture of unfair practices by processors and others. Various amendments to the programs were made over the years to better serve farmers and the best interest of the nation. For example, wartime activity resulted in adjustments to the programs to increase production of needed commodities, while peacetime (also known as postwar in the late 1940s) efforts were to reduce production. Other crops were added in subsequent years.

Hinds County, as did most every county in the USA, had an office to deal with farmers on the government matters. The office later became known as the ASCS office and, for Hinds County, was located in the old Courthouse in Raymond. The office had an administrator, with Thomas Whitfield being the one who was best known, and a staff of several individuals operating under direction of the U.S. Department of Agriculture. The ASCS name was used because the full name was long: Agricultural Stabilization and Conservation Service. Henry felt that getting to personally know Thomas and staff members was an asset to his farm.

Henry, like other farmers, had to establish a per-acre crop land use history with the ASCS office. Large maps and, in later years, aerial photographs were used to record the acreage and use of each

area of land on a farm. With guidance from a county commit-
tee of producers, the ASCS office allocated the acreage that could
be planted by each farm in order to receive prices supported by
government dollars. The allocations tended to squeeze farmers by
reducing acreage allotments. USDA employees (known as perfor-
mance reporters and typically seasonal in hiring) visited every farm
and carried copies of the large maps for use in verifying what was
planted on each field. In some cases, smaller fields were measured
with chains.

Once on-farm inspection was done, staff in the ASCS office
would use a planimeter (measuring device) on the field borders of
the scaled maps to determine the exact acreage planted. A producer
who planted more than the allotted acreage had to plow up or otherwise destroy the overplanted crop. If acreage was not in line with
allocation, the producer could not receive a supported price for the
harvested cotton and suffered a large financial penalty. Henry always tried to never over-plant, and this required seeking help from
ASCS office staff in determining field acreage as recorded in their
office. Over-planting came with a costly financial penalty.

An early expansion included soil conservation. This was to
prevent erosion and loss of fertile topsoil from farm land by pre-
cipitation runoff and wind. The Soil Bank program was added to
the law and provided government payments to producers who took
cropland out of production and let it lie fallow in a conservation
use. Crop production was reduced and farmers were paid for not
farming the land. Henry and many other producers could never
figure out the "wiseness" of the government with the Soil Bank
program. Once the program ended, it was not easy to return the
land to profitable crop production.

Government farm regulations were felt to limit the opportunity for producers to expand production and make their individual farms more profitable. Henry always found the regulations

annoying, stressful, and restrictive of his motivation to expand the farm. With fewer acres in cotton, fewer sharecroppers were needed and greater per-acre efficiency was essential if the farmer was to make a profit. The displaced farm sharecroppers moved to the cities to get factory jobs. The government farm programs created financial pressure on farms; many went out of crop production and others went out of existence. Henry used his knowledge and skill to hold on as a producer as long as he could and be as profitable as possible. The government programs didn't occur over just a few years but lasted five decades. These brought numerous restrictions to the Lee farm; such might have contributed to its slow and steady downfall.

Henry's mind went back to the visit in early May by his sister Ethel and her husband, Dr. Davis. He figured that they would be coming to visit Carrie over the Christmas holiday. They would ask her how things were going and if she had received the rent payment. Henry did not want another confrontation with Dr. Davis, but if it occurred, he was prepared to demonstrate that, yes, he was capable of running the farm in a productive way.

Of course, Ethel and Dr. Davis would be there only a couple of hours or so; they liked the Alamo Plaza Tourist Court in Jackson because it had electricity, running water, and other conveniences not available in the old Lee-Shepard house. It was located near a couple of good restaurants. Each had access to bootlegged whiskey in a side dining room (actually a bar). Sometimes a police officer would bring bottles of confiscated liquor to the restaurant that had been taken from someone who "had it illegally." The restaurant manager would sneak the officer a few dollars. This meant that Dr. Davis didn't have to bring as many bottles of bourbon from "wet" Alabama to "dry" Mississippi. The police would not raid places of this type because they were favorites of city government officials.

Dr. Davis would likely be driving the same elegant Buick

Roadmaster in which he last traveled to Tinnin, as no new cars were available. He would have to drive it a little longer and not trade for a new one as often. Everyone agreed that the war effort was so harsh on people of the rural South, even to the extent of depriving Dr. Davis of another Buick Roadmaster!

Sure enough, Ethel and Dr. Davis came to see Carrie in the afternoon of December 29. They went into her side of the house for a little over an hour. It appeared that they brought her a gift. No doubt, they were getting Carrie to bring them up to date on things. After a few minutes, they came out and over to the side of the house used by Henry and his family. Henry went to the door after Ethel knocked. They greeted each other and chitchatted about a few things, including how Son had grown since they saw him last.

"How are you doing?" Dr. Davis asked Henry. "Mama Carrie said that you were able to give her a check for the rent. Is the check 'good'? Do you have money in the bank to cover the check? She still has it. No one has taken her to the bank; kind of looks like someone would. And, by the way, how quickly did you drink that bottle of bourbon I left for you last time I was here?" These comments did not go well with Henry, but conversations with these folks usually didn't. (Several of his other sisters and their husbands had visited Carrie over the holiday; none of the visits involved confrontations about the farm and other matters.)

"Let's go out on the porch to talk these matters over. It isn't very cold," Henry said as he pushed open the hall door. "I remember some of our discussion from last May; it still stands out in my mind. The crop year was darn good considering everything; Doris got a job teaching at Clinton School. We are getting by okay and looking to the future. I have already assessed what needs to be done to make the fields more productive, such as clearing ditch banks and girdling big trees near fields. I have a gallon of molasses for you to take back to Montgomery, since you were so generous to give me a bottle of bourbon the last time you were here. And the bottle you gave me, it is about half gone. I once tasted it, and I shared a few swigs several times with a farm hand to help ease the pain after he was kicked on the leg by a mule. I believe it helped him."

"No, I don't want the molasses," Dr. Davis said. "That farm-made stuff from around here is probably not clean. We must soon return to the Alamo Plaza. Happy hour begins in a bit at Dennery's on the Pearl. It is a superb restaurant that we enjoy so much, but you have to have money to go. Remember this: You need to be financially sound and make your own way. My saying is, 'Every tub sits on its own bottom.' Think about that. Goodbye. We have to drive back to Montgomery tomorrow and get ready for the grand New Year's Eve Ball at the officers' club at Maxwell Base. Ethel and I have been invited to attend."

Dr. Davis called for Ethel so that they could go. He didn't bring a flask or bottle of bourbon this time, and he said that he was getting thirsty. Henry was hurt and astounded that he refused the molasses. He knew of no one who had any ill effects from the molasses made on the farm. Most people thought the ribbon cane he grew made superior syrup, far better than cheaper and easier-to-grow sorghum cane syrup. Henry said nothing and went from the porch back inside. He peered out the window and saw that his sister and Dr. Davis were leaving and heading up the muddy December driveway, getting the Buick Roadmaster dirty. No doubt, Henry thought, "Good riddance."

"That Dr. Davis is like a bull in the pasture," Henry said, "and a charging one at that. He likes to make himself look good and those around him look bad. I wonder how he gets along with his patients? Maybe his behavior is 'egged on' by his wife or Carrie, but I don't think so. That is just him being who he is." (The terms "bully" and "bullying" were not used in 1943. A further note: Dr. Davis had different behavior around his patients and the high-society crowd in Montgomery.)

The end-of-year assessment was quite positive. The outcome was similar to that of the previous year (before Henry's accident). With some limitations, Henry was making good economic adjustment. The outcome had more than answered his earlier questioning of his ability to provide for his family. It should have also answered the questioning of other people about his capability. Henry was now ready to go about proving himself. He felt that he could do whatever he set out to do!

The year of Henry's accident ended. There was food on the table. The baby had shoes. Amounts in savings accounts had slightly increased. No one was going to tell Dr. Davis anything. Interestingly, he made a bigger fool of himself when he was kept in the dark. And, Henry was able to meagerly pay the preacher by dropping a few dollars in the offering plate.

12

Loafing Stores

Loafing stores were the hubs of human interaction in rural communities near Tinnin. You could buy something basic (not much choice) or see a neighbor, politician, traveling salesman, or anyone who dropped by. A lot of topics were discussed; news was shared. Along with the unfortunate prejudice and bias, you might learn something that was useful.

Friends, family, and associates responded to Henry's accident in different ways. Nearly all of them wanted to be supportive and helpful. They were welcoming and cordial in greetings. No place or gathering was more accepting than the loafing stores Henry visited. He occasionally frequented these places before he suffered the loss of an arm. Now, they seemingly became more important in his life.

How would the loss of an arm influence relationships with others? How would their views of Henry change? Would he be thought of as something less than a complete person? Could he think of himself as a person who was capable (smart, hardworking, and considerate)? These were a part Henry's self-esteem; would he feel confident or not? At first, there were more questions than answers.

Sometimes small, incidental occurrences had larger influences on social behaviors. These might alter his self-confidence and skills in social situations. Maybe other times (after some adjustment) he would use the fact that he had lost an arm to his advantage in haggling over a price.

People responded to Henry in different ways; most were encouraging, while others did not offer Henry the needed social boost. Maybe the little boy who hid behind his grandfather so he couldn't see him was showing fear of a man without a right arm. Most likely, the little boy had heard family members talking about the "Henry man who now had one arm," and it made him afraid.

Henry often got needed encouragement at one of the loafing stores. Out in the community (and not around people who knew him well), a few people would stare or whisper; often he could see their actions or hear what they were saying. Their use of words such as "handicapped" and "crippled" never boosted his confidence in social situations. Other people wanted to do everything for him; maybe they thought he was helpless or an invalid. All that was needed were the common courtesies, such as holding a door or pouring coffee for him, just as would be done without saying a word for anyone else who was a non-amputee. Henry would find a way to do most everything that needed to be done.

What is a loafing store? What were the loafing stores really like? These are best described as places that sold a variety of simple products needed by farm and rural people. They weren't very modern nor focused on making money. The owners typically enjoyed their customers taking a few minutes every now and then to talk and share information.

Who went to loafing stores? White men were accepted as loafers; all others were customers who quickly came and went. Most "loafers" had grown up in the area; a few of them had moved into the Tinnin, Pocahontas, and Clinton communities as adults. Often the discussions were about rural life topics, including farming, off-farm business contacts, crime and arrests, politics, and the personal lives of community citizens. The gatherings at the loafing stores typically included some sort of refreshments that you bought yourself. Sometimes two or three gatherers would "flip" coins to see who had to pay but that was the extent of the gambling that occurred.

These gathering places were known more for loafing than anything else, even if operated as stores. Since Mississippi was a "dry" state, gatherings usually did not include alcoholic beverages, not even low-alcohol beer. Sometimes, sassafras tea, boiled peanuts, buttermilk, hoop cheese, and fried apple pies were a part of the fare at a loafing store. A serious loafing day (longer time of an hour or so) might involve a small tin of sardines with saltine crackers and a swab of yellow mustard for lunch. Such a day was more likely to occur when a bale of cotton was across the street at a gin or rain had made it too wet to work in the field, or the cropping season had progressed to being laid-by.

Interacting with people at the loafing stores was something Henry appreciated and enjoyed as he was striving to adjust to life with one arm. He didn't participate in high-society kinds of interactions (there weren't any in the local area). What he wanted were practical, everyday contacts with farm-oriented people, including plantation owners, workers on the farms, suppliers of inputs, buyers and processors (particularly cotton ginners and buyers), bankers, and others. He was a great believer in establishing relationships with the people from whom he bought and sold. He wanted these people to know and appreciate him and, of course, provide some sort of price incentive for his doing business with them—if not a true incentive, maybe at least the perception of a good deal. Henry prided himself as a negotiator. Any major purchase would be subjected to price discussion, adjustments, and, if necessary, haggling to lower the price.

Three small stores in Tinnin, Pocahontas, and Clinton offered opportunities to meet and greet people and learn about what was going on in the area.

In Tinnin, the longtime Ratliff Store (an old clapboard wooden structure with a tin roof) had several generations of Ratliff owners over the years, with H. T. Ratliff and family during the 1940s, followed by J. T. and Mary Ratliff in the 1950s and '60s. The building was an old wooden-frame structure with a porch across the front and two side doors. The store sold food basics, simple medicines, gasoline and oil, kerosene, limited clothing and cloth, farm shoes and boots, nails and a few other hardware items, and, seasonally, fireworks. Locally ground cornmeal would be kept in large wooden bins for customers to dip out into paper bags. It was weighed and sold by the pound.

Why was Ratliff Store a good loafing store? Its customers (and loafers) were people who shared similar experiences in life and held agreeable outlooks on life. Most of the white men were descendents of families with Choctaw cession land in the 1830s and 40s and who endured the economic hardships of the U.S. Civil war. The store had old-timey welcoming seats for folks to sit on, including old wooden gun shell boxes, cloth sacks of feed, wooden nail kegs, and cane-bottom chairs. This created the appeal and provided social opportunities for Henry and others of the Tinnin community. If the owner wasn't up to loafing on a particular day, some of the sitting places might be removed or covered.

Loafing behavior varied somewhat by season of the year and time of day. A small group might gather around the pot-bellied, wood-burning stove in the winter and talk a while. In warm weather, folks tended to sit close to the cash register because the store owner had to go to it whenever a purchase was made. Additionally, the cash register was near the cola box where chipped ice was used to cool beverages in glass bottles with a flip-off top. Usually a couple of doors and a window would be open to allow air movement on hot days (no one had ever heard of air conditioning). In the 1930s and 40s, kerosene lamps were used for light. In the mid-1940s, the store got electricity, and a couple of light bulbs suspended on wires from the ceiling provided light (other than the open doors and window).

The arrangement in the store allowed the owner to be paid and for people to see each other and interact while having a cola or, in rare times, a candy bar (Be careful with the candy in warm weather! Watch for tiny insects that might get inside the loose wrappers.) During busy times of the year with field work and harvest, the loafers might stop by for a few minutes, then be on their way.

Some tall tales could be raised in this store; word among local folks was that this would have been the meeting place of the Tinnin liars' club, if the community had had one. Goings-on with the Ku Klux Klan and lynchings/hangings might be raised but that kind of activity didn't occur in Tinnin (it was always many miles away). News about fortunes and misfortunes might also be shared, including war tragedies of Tinnin families and extended relatives. Of course, crop situations would be discussed, and the need for rain would be covered by talking about "paying the preacher." Occasionally, politicians would come by (they were usually dressed and groomed far better than the folks in the store). Candidates for sheriff, supervisor, circuit clerk, and the legislature would regularly drop by in an election year. When voting day arrived, the Tinnin ballot box was in the Ratliff Store. Only registered white people who had paid poll tax could vote. This store was an important loafing place for Henry in the mid and late 1940s. Although located next to the shed where Henry's accident with the hammer mill occurred, resulting in the loss of his right arm, he appeared to hold no ill will toward the place.

The loafing place in Pocahontas was Baker's Store. It was run by Tom Baker, a man Henry had known since they were boys (though

Tom was a couple of years older than Henry). Across the road and railroad tracks, was the cotton gin for the local farming community. The presence of the gin resulted in greater seasonal patronage and fluctuations in loafing.

Baker's Store had a range of country goods, such as plow lines, cotton pick sacks, vegetable seeds, snuff, roll-your-own tobacco, colas, small cans of sardines, and hoop cheese that was sliced on the spot for the customer. Of course, if a store sold sardines and hoop cheese, it had to sell small boxes of saltine crackers. Baker's Store also sold gasoline, oil, fan belts, and a few other items for old pickup trucks and cars. It even had a grease rack and a wash bay. Most popular were car jacks, tube-patching equipment, and supplies such as boots for very worn tires and patches that would adhere to the rubber inner tubes if held tightly and heated with fire.

Many of the patrons of Baker's Store had old cars that were built before World War II; some had dark skin. The tires were thin and worn; tubes inside the tires were likely to be punctured on the gravel roads and in need of an airtight patch. Not many cars that operated well came to Baker's Store in the mid-1940s and early '50s. Free air drew customers whose vehicles had failing tires. Dealing with automobile problems was an everyday occurrence.

Indelible features of loafing stores were the human interactions that took place. Not all people were treated the same. Some were described with harsh words. One constant was that most who were so described had dark skin. Their speech even sounded a little different. They were not allowed to sit in the store and be a part of the discussion. If they bought something to eat, they would pay inside at the cashbox and go outside and sit on an old tire or the ground to eat it.

The store with its fairly brisk tire-patching business had unique qualities. Only a dark-skinned man called Pluke removed wheels from cars, broke down (loosened) tires on rims to remove the tubes, applied patches over holes in the tubes, placed the tubes back in the tires and on the rims, and placed the wheels back on the cars, carefully tightening the lug nuts with a hand wrench. He also would inflate the tires to the pressure he thought was right. Sometimes the pressure was checked by the owner of the store using an air pressure gauge that he kept at the cash box. Pluke didn't get a paycheck; he was given dollar bills directly from the cash box. A day of work wouldn't be more than $2 or so; most days he worked only a few hours. But, Pluke did get tips and made a few dollars from other services.

What else went on at the store? No one was ever certain, but Pluke was in the middle of it. He was always ready to provide courteous service to customers. But, maybe more went on than met the eye. It didn't take long to figure out that customer service was related to a couple of tiny buildings out back. These were thought to be outhouses, and one was used as a toilet by dark-skinned people. The other brings up curious behavior.

Customer service, yes; and it worked like this: A customer might drive up, get a couple dollars of gasoline that Pluke pumped, and talk privately with Pluke. At that point, Pluke would disappear around back, go into the toilet-like house that wasn't used as a toilet, and come out with something in a brown paper bag. He would hand it to the car driver, and, in turn, the driver would give him a couple of dollars. Yes, Pluke was bootlegging illegal whiskey to special clients (always white). It was apparently his side business and was not a part of the store other than that the bootlegging was happening at the store site. That side business definitely met a customer demand. (It took the state legislature many years to pass needed laws.)

Though not to get one of Pluke's products, one person who occasionally stopped in his nice car at Baker's Store was Methodist Bishop Marvin Franklin. The bishop had married a woman of some means who grew up in the Pocahontas area; they visited there often from their home in Jackson. The family of his wife had provided a place on their farm for the beginning Methodist church to meet before the Pocahontas church house was constructed in 1902. Franklin dressed nicely, apparently had enough money to live comfortably, and was a personable and likable individual. He was friendly to everyone and always had a nice smile and handshake. Henry really liked seeing him and enjoyed the bishop's personal skills. If the Bishop said a few words to him, Henry's enthusiasm was uplifted for the day. (Interestingly, Bishop Franklin was born in the Southern Appalachian culture of White County, Georgia, and rose up through the ranks of the Methodist church to serve as a bishop in Mississippi.)

Just as the "personalities" of the loafing stores in Tinnin and Pocahontas varied, the store in Clinton had even greater variance. Socially it had differences from the other loafing stores. Located on U.S. Highway 80 across from the campus of Mississippi College, Rutherford's Gulf Service Station had clientele that varied from the farm folks of Pocahontas and Tinnin. Owner Johnny Rutherford had been a friend of Henry since childhood. There wasn't quite as much loafing and lingering at this store as at others by those who stopped for gasoline and whatever else they or their vehicle needed. The clientele tended to be better educated and, maybe, less prejudiced about skin color. Their language skills reflected greater educational attainment.

College students, professors, business men and women, folks who worked for state government in Jackson, and local citizens in general visited the station. Seating was limited; there were fewer loafers. In addition to Mr. Rutherford, a couple of men worked at the station and provided service to motorists by pumping gasoline, cleaning windshields, checking engine oil levels, and the like. A grease rack and a wash bay were popular among local folks (this was the only loafing store Henry frequented that was connected to a municipal water system). The gas pump area had a vacuum cleaner for removing dirt from the floor of cars. The store in the station sold colas and candies and an assortment of vehicle needs such as cans of oil, head lights, fan belts, and batteries. It also sold common medical supplies, such as aspirin, Sloan's Liniment, and Vick's VapoRub. Not found at the Tinnin and Pocahontas stores was the "disease prevention device" that came in a small package and sold for 25 cents; just whisper to Mr. Rutherford what you wanted and, with a grin on his face, he would slip it to you in exchange for a quarter.

Travelers on the highway to Jackson or Vicksburg would sometimes stop for gasoline and pay with cash (gasoline sold for about twenty cents a gallon). Before the days of credit cards, Rutherford would let a few local folks buy gasoline on credit. He kept a book with a list of names and amounts owed to him by gasoline customers. Over time, he found that most people would pay their gasoline debts in a timely manner. His bad gasoline debts were distributed between college and town people about equally. Even some ministerial students didn't always pay what they owed. Some folks thought they had a feeling of entitlement.

At times, Henry would take Son with him to a loafing store, where he might get a cola or a piece of hard candy (no candy over one cent). He was usually the only boy there and received a great deal of attention. One man might offer a cola; another might offer a candy. Son's father would say, "Tell him no but that you will take the nickel." Upon arrival, Son might be greeted with a hello and a handshake. This helped Son develop the ability to greet people and shake hands. He was taught never to shake the hand of a woman unless she extended her hand first. (Son had trouble understanding that rule of handshaking). He was also told never to stare at a woman and always be courteous.

Of course, the old men talked about various subjects. Some of the discussion had educational aspects for Son, but such often went in the wrong direction. There might be tall tales or gossip about someone in the community. Occasionally, they talked politics, or they discussed the war or a new farm program. Maybe the identities of individuals who made home-brew or moonshine would be revealed, particularly if they had been "busted" by the county sheriff! Sometimes they said things that weren't very nice, including some powerful four-letter words. A loafing store was not the best place to take a child to learn proper language skills and important values that might lead to a full life and career success.

Loafing stores weren't exactly places where love and justice for all people were expressed. Opinions often varied. Of course, there was comradery among those who frequented such places. There was a subtle, if not overt, reference to racial and gender discrimination on an almost continual basis. Talk about racism and other forms of discrimination was less in Clinton (maybe the presence of a religious college was a factor) and almost continually at the stores in Tinnin and Pocahontas. Sometimes references to church, God, and the Bible would be used to justify racial bias. This was not just any bias but the kind that expressed the need for a lynching, hanging, or anatomical alteration of males guilty of certain crimes. Some of this talk was routine, depending on who the loafers were that day.

Different loafers resulted in different conversations because of their interests, biases, and backgrounds. Politicians were often subjects of the talk. This included elected officials, such as members of the county board of supervisors, county sheriff and tax collector, governor of the state, and members of congress. A supervisor in particular could be bluntly described if he had not kept the gravel

roads graded and smooth or delivered gravel to individual drive-
ways when requested by the owner. One person many maligned was
Eleanor Roosevelt. She was viewed by some men as a big trouble-
maker because she was an outspoken advocate for human rights.
The loafers did not like that advocacy. In voting, however, it was
always for the candidate of the Democratic party, States Rights, or
lesser independent but never a Republican.

Some of the loafers wanted to keep people with dark skin in a
place of servitude, forbidden to do many of the things that people
with light skin could do. A few of the loafers spoke as if they were
great authorities, but, when a little is learned about them, it can be
seen that they weren't authorities at all. Many were uneducated,
narrow-minded, outspoken bigots and racists

When a preacher would occasionally drop by a loafing store,
the loafers would be ever so courteous to him as if he were Jesus
Christ. They would also try to pry information from him about
things that had happened in the community. They might ask him
about a person who was very ill (and what the person had) or about
someone who had experienced a family tragedy (such as the death
of a spouse). They might tease the preacher about the relationship
between a summer shower or rain on crops or some other favorable
event and their putting money in the collection plate, which they
called "paying the preacher."

Loafers in the more rural stores didn't hold back on racial matters and might even ask the preacher to give a sermon on the sin of
interracial marriage or how only white people should sit in the front
of a bus or use a public toilet. (Some of those who had heard of, but
not publicly read, Lillian Smith's book *Strange Fruit* might mention
it as a sign that strong preachers were needed to overcome such
major sin.) Somehow, the "real" sin did not register with the loafers.

Sometimes loafing stores helped loafers and members of the
community with their health problems. Things were usually

simple and associated with aging. Most salient to small boy Son was the time a woman of color came into the store with her about seven-year-old son. He could hardly use his left foot for standing and walking; he kind of hopped around. Sore and painful! She asked if they had anything that could be used to treat his foot. A couple of loafers looked at the foot and said "no." One loafer, however, said, "Let me take a look at it. Hop over here boy, stand still, and lift your bad foot so I can see under the bottom. Yep, that big painful knot is a stone bruise. It has pus around it; some folks use the word 'infection.' There may be a thorn or splinter stuck in the foot by it. I can take care of it if you want me to." The mama said "Yes, please help us."

They got the boy to lie down on the counter near the hoop of cheese and close to the crackers. Two men held him still. The other man got his pocket knife out of his pocket, opened a pointed blade, and quickly stuck it into the big knot. The boy cried loudly. Pus and blood came out. At first, it flowed and, after a few seconds, it stopped. They got a scrap of cloth and wrapped the foot and tied it on with twine. The boy, hopping along, and his mama left the store. One of the men told the boy to wear shoes; the mama responded, "He ain't got no shoes." Word was that the foot healed in a few days and the boy was fine afterward but was never again seen near the store.

These loafing stores were the communication centers of their respective small communities. Henry was reserved in some of what he said but enjoyed the talking and listening. People who knew him respected him. He was honest and avoided slandering other people. A new person might find it difficult to initiate contact with him, but, once they did, things went well.

After his loss of an arm, Henry could have chosen to become a recluse. He didn't. He was not aggressive in seeking social relationships, but he would participate. He had a way of sizing up a situation before joining. Were the people honest and fair? Did the people understand farm-based audiences? Would they have reasonable respect for him and not view him as an incomplete person? Those questions helped guide him in negotiating through the world of social adjustment in the Hinds County, Mississippi, area.

Most important at the loafing stores was the comradery. The friendly hellos, laughs, and sympathies in times of need were salves on the fragility of human life. Lifetime friendships were developed; help was given. Of course, most important were the human relationships and not the goods sold (but the sale of goods was needed for the places to stay open).

13

Dealing with Faith and Phantoms

---

*What is a man to believe? Understanding yourself and
the problems you face isn't easy. Religious faith is used
by some people to help figure things out. What about
phantoms, demons, spirits, and the like? Maybe Henry
was about to get some things sorted out in his life;
maybe not.*

Henry needed a few people he could confide in and get advice from. He
needed people he trusted and could talk to about the adjustments
he needed to make and the way to a good future. Sometimes strang-
ers appeared to show more understanding and compassion than
people he knew. Such was the case with the Watkins Products
salesman who came by the house selling a variety of products.

It was a dusty July mid-day that a car came down the driveway
and stopped out front. The driver got out, came to the porch, and
knocked. Henry went to greet him.

"Hello," the man said, "My name is Charles Ray Black. I am the
new Watkins Products salesman for Tinnin and surrounding area.
How are you today."

Henry reached out his left hand to shake and introduced

himself. Charles Ray knew how to shake the left hand and looked straight into his eyes. Henry was impressed and invited him to sit in a rocking chair on the porch. After a few words of chit-chat about the weather, crop condition, and the like, the conversation turned serious.

Charles Ray had a leather case with bottles of several different products in it. He opened the case and showed several products: a liniment for sore muscles, an antiseptic for skin abrasions, udder salve for sore teats on a milk cow, and a couple of food items including a bottle of vanilla flavoring. At that point Henry called to Doris asking "Do you need some vanilla flavoring?" She came to the porch and greeted Charles Ray. "Yes," she said, "Watkins vanilla flavoring is my favorite." They paid for a bottle and said that was all they needed on that day. Doris went back inside.

Henry brought up the subject of trying to get over the loss of his right arm. Charles Ray replied that he understood. He said he had a brother who lost an arm and partial vision in one eye in a South Pacific battle. He was now home in Bentonia making adjustment to life with one arm gone. Charles Ray said his brother went to church a lot and found strength in being involved. He also said his brother drank a little whiskey late in the afternoon each day to help him deal with something called phantom pain. Henry replied that he knew about phantom pain but he didn't regularly drink whiskey. At that point, Charles Ray said he had to go and said he would stop again in a couple of weeks.

"Go to church," Charles Ray said as he was going down the steps, "Get involved, listen to the preacher, read the Bible, and pray."

"I will," Henry said though he had heard such before, "but I need something that is real and that is beneficial in helping me overcome my loss." Charles Ray left; Henry mulled over what was said and dismissed most of it from his mind. But, then he thought, maybe the church would be useful. Though he was an occasional attendee, he made up his mind that he would try to be more regular in attendance and rattle a few more coins on the bottom of the collection plate.

The church Henry attended most all of his life (and where he was christened) was a place for hearing about salvation (the version of the preacher) and social interaction. Though the congregation was small, members helped Henry adapt to life with one arm. Other than for medical care, the church was one of the first places he went after the accident. Now he made a commitment to go more frequently. He could relate to the people; they would sometimes sincerely ask about his well-being. Occasionally he talked to individuals about the hard part of adjusting and the phantom sensations he experienced.

In the early 1940s, two churches met in Pocahontas; each had its own building of similar wooden architecture. The Lee family identified with the Pocahontas Methodist Episcopal Church; the other was the Pocahontas Baptist Church. Meeting locations and ideologies were similar. They held services on alternating Sundays; neither usually met on the fifth Sunday of the month. Many of the same people attended whichever church was meeting on a particular day. Seldom would services have more than 30 people present. The church buildings had wooden clapboard siding, with outdoor toilets and minimal electric lights. Each had hymnals appropriate for the respective denomination in pew-back racks; none had Bibles, as members were expected to bring their own (but rarely did someone bring a Bible).

Each church had a minister for its denomination. One ordained for service as a Methodist provided services in the Methodist building; a Baptist minister was likewise at the Baptist church. The Methodist minister would typically move on to another church after a couple of years, based on assignment by the Conference. The Baptist minister would stay until a better preaching opportunity was found or the congregation became unhappy, ran him off, and hired another minister.

Social and worship behavior of the congregants was quite similar. Methodists said the Apostles' Creed and went to the altar for communion; Baptists stayed in their seats and passed communion plates with bread crumbs and tiny communion cups that held just the right amount of "wine" for the sacrament. Other differences were minimal except for baptism: Methodists were sprinkled, and Baptists were immersed (dunked, as locals called it) in a creek. Baptism practices were talked about (even joked about). Methodists didn't want to be immersed, with some saying something like, "How will I be assured that the preacher won't hold me under too long and I will drown?" They also said something about those baptized as Baptists being in need of more washing to remove their sin and make them ready for church membership. Anyway, few people took either church as seriously as the ministers wanted them to, or maybe the ministers wanted themselves to be taken seriously and held in high regard.

Sunday gatherings were interesting to observe. One or two people went quite early to assure that all was in order in the sanctuary for a service. Maybe there would be a bird or a rat to chase out or, rarely, a vagrant who had slept in the building overnight. As the others arrived, the women and small children would go inside, while the men and older children stayed outside. The men would sit on car fenders or sections of tree logs and stumps or lean against trees while they rolled and smoked cigarettes. The discussion would sometimes turn to the best kind of tobacco. Unfortunately, they knew very little about the health-destroying side effects of tobacco use.

The men were more likely to talk about the "goings-on" in the community. Of particular interest was if someone had been arrested for selling black market whiskey or gambling (farm hands were more likely to get caught than others). They might also talk about current issues or challenges in farming, such as the need for rain, a pest that had raised its ugly self, how a crop was coming along, available equipment (only used equipment could be found because of the war), or the ginning and selling of cotton. Of course, marital infidelity would likely be a topic if something new had developed, such as a man seen out with a woman for the first time. All in all, Henry enjoyed the social part of going to church; the activities seemed to be uplifting, leaving him feeling a little more positive for the rest of the day. The church experience with members helped him feel more at ease with being one-armed.

Talk would occasionally turn to a quiet discussion of male-related health issues. Most men were a little embarrassed to talk about anything of a serious "male nature" in front of other men. Another reason for the low voices could be that a woman might be close enough to hear who was having problems and what these problems were. The men wanted the women to think that they were all in tiptop shape and ready for business. And, there were always a few men who had sudden urges to go into the outhouse or hide behind a tree (they didn't want anyone to see what they were doing behind a tree even though everyone knew).

Inside, the women would gather in the pews and talk about family life, such as tragedies, food preservation, sewing, and, of course, new pregnancies or babies among the church family and its associates. They would rarely bring up anything about a failing husband unless he was recently caught with another woman. Of course, indiscretions of members of that church's congregation were taboo.

Both the men and the women talked about family members who were away in war, including action in the South Pacific, Europe, and Northern Africa. There were usually a few casualties someone knew about who were mentioned; this was a sad time in which those

present said that they wanted to "pray for them and their families."
(Sometimes a close family casualty would be mentioned during the
worship service.)

When time came for the preaching service to begin, the men
would go inside and sit with their women and families. During
prayer, men might bow their heads but only partially close their
eyes so they could peek at what was going on; they wanted to see
who was looking around. When a hymn was sung, most men would
mumble along, if they sang at all. One or two women would really
belt out the words. During preaching, everyone sat with somber
looks facing straight ahead. Occasionally, a congregant would say
"Amen," followed by a couple of other shouts of "Amen!" Mostly,
the amens followed some particular statement by the preacher that
dealt with the status quo. (Who wants change?) Sadly, the mention
of racial injustices seldom got amens. When the collection plate
was passed, a few people put in several coins so that they jingled a
bit (for others to hear as a sign of generosity); others would put in a
dollar bill and sometimes more. (No preacher could live very well
off the collection at the church.)

Near the end of the service, the preacher would make an appeal
for people to come to the front, repent of their sins, and ask God
for forgiveness. Some preachers would use expressions that evoked
tears and shouts from members. One final hymn would close the
service. The preacher would stand at the door and shake hands (occasionally hug someone) as the congregants left. Henry always liked
to shake the preacher's hand but he said very little to the preacher.
(The preacher had enough handshaking experience to know how
to turn his right hand to comfortably engage Henry's left hand, and
that was pleasant for Henry.)

The preacher might be invited to one of the member's homes for
dinner, and, if present, the preacher's wife and family would also go.
In most cases, the spouses of preachers didn't go to the Pocahontas

Methodist Episcopal Church because it had no indoor plumbing or other comforts except for electric light bulbs hanging on an electrical wire attached to the ceiling. The preachers and their families typically lived in Jackson and had the benefits of city life. Handheld funeral home fans were readily available for cooling. Other than preaching (sometimes called a worship service), a funeral, and an occasional wedding, the church house hosted few events. On occasion, there might be a holiday season social and caroling.

On most occasions, Henry didn't get much from a church service that would help him in adjusting and coping with the loss of an arm. The preacher would often talk about faith. What did the preacher mean? Did he mean complete trust in something that can't be seen? More than anything, Henry would have a kind of "feel-good" feeling from just having gone to church. He appreciated the contacts with other persons and greetings by the preacher upon adjournment.

On the first Sunday of March in 1943, a Mr. G. Deweese whispered in Henry's ear that he wanted to talk with him briefly after the service. Henry was puzzled as to why. Was it about the behavior of a farm hand or a new pricing strategy for cotton ginning? Anyway, they met outside under a large cedar tree.

"How are you coming along with one arm?" Deweese asked. "Do you still have the strange sensations in your right arm and hand?"

"I'm doing well," Henry replied, "and yes, I still have the phantom sensations. Why do you ask?"

"You may be experiencing a demon," Deweese said matter-of-factly. "I heard that bad spirits would try to take over the life of a person who had lost an arm or leg. You have to fight demons off. A demon might have entered your body when you were knocked out by the accident. Getting rid of a demon isn't easy. I thought you might be interested in a gathering on signs, spirits, and demons held by an itinerant preacher in a tent revival in Flora beginning next Sunday afternoon. Night sessions will be held each evening all week. The preacher says he is a religion professor from a college in Arkansas. He says that he knows what he is talking about."

Deweese ended the conversation by saying, "You might want to go. I plan to be there myself." (When Deweese said he was going, he knew he wasn't; he wanted Henry to think he would know someone there.) Henry thanked Deweese for telling him.

Henry walked over and got into the car with Doris, and they started the drive back to their home. They talked about what Deweese had said and somehow related it to the presence of a voodoo queen on Farish Street in Jackson (that he had not visited but his father did). They wondered if visiting with the queen would be useful. They questioned how learning about demons would be helpful; regardless, they decided to go hear the reverend from Arkansas on the first Sunday afternoon he was preaching. They drove to Flora and saw the tent off U.S. Highway 49 in a small pasture near a cotton patch just as they were reaching the town limits. They pulled into the grassy parking area, got out, and spoke with a man who had a peg leg (a leg that looked wooden and made of a tree limb; kind of awkward). He invited them to go through the tent door.

Once inside the tent, they were greeted by a woman wearing a bonnet and an ordinary blue shirtwaist cotton dress with a silky scarf around her neck. She was holding a bottle of lavender incense. She said her name was Sister Mammony and asked them to have a seat on a wooden bench near the front of the tent. Within a few minutes, about thirty people had arrived. Sister Mammony sat on a chair at an old out-of-tune upright piano and began playing "What a Friend We Have in Jesus." At that time, a man dressed in a plaid business suit came out from behind a curtain. (No, he wasn't Jesus, but he wanted everyone to think he was, though a plaid suit didn't exactly fit the stereotype!) His booming voice and his hair styling gave the impression of being a preacher.

Shortly the preacher began by welcoming the crowd and shouting various phrases, such as "Jesus loves you," "God knows best," and "Beware of demons." He then told the crowd that they could call him Brother Yakshagana and that he was from a nearby Delta town in Arkansas. He indicated that the tent revival would last through the week, with preaching each night at six o'clock on a different topic related to signs, spirits, and demons, including Christian demonology.

Now, Christian demonology wasn't a subject that either Doris or Henry had heard preached on or knew much about. Being a graduate of Belhaven College in Jackson, where she took a couple of Bible classes, resulted in Doris having a questioning notion about Brother Yakshagana. She pushed such thoughts out of her mind for the next few minutes and participated in some of the service activities.

The assembled group then sang the hymn "Just a Closer Walk with Thee." After a few words about the power of Jesus to overcome demons from Sister Mammony, they then sang "How Great Thou Art." As typical in a country religious gathering, there was one woman who really belted out the words. Most folks kind of mumbled along.

"Are you tormented by a demon?" Brother Yakshagana asked to begin his sermon for the afternoon.

Some people in the audience shouted "Yes!" and one barked and howled like a dog (maybe she was mentally ill).

"Amen!" the preacher shouted. "There are Christian demons, and you know that. Have you experienced one? This will be what I will preach on over the next few days. I will begin today with signs, spirits, and demons." He stared glaringly into the face of each person in the crowd. Frightening, to say the least!

As some preachers often do, he repeated himself three or so times. He had heard in a theology class up north that repetition was a good way to promote learning or help people remember his sermons. He asked, "So, what is a sign, a spirit, and a demon?" He repeated, "What is a sign, a spirit, and a demon?" and then continued, "Tonight, I will briefly talk about God-fearing signs and spirits before I get into the main topic of demons. You may be shaking in your underwear before I finish. Maybe that shaking is a sign of God's spirit moving in you. Feel free at any time to shout, wave, stand, or do whatever God moves you to do."

Brother Yakshagana paused a minute and took a sip of a clear liquid from a small glass sitting on the pulpit. Based on his facial grimaces and throat-clearing afterward, the glass likely had gin rather than water. "You folks in Flora certainly have good water," he said. "A preacher needs something to keep his whistle wet." He took another small sip and said, "I am now ready to deliver this message to you."

"First, let me talk about signs a bit," Brother Yakshagana said loudly. "What are signs? You saw some on the highway driving here, but they are not exactly what I mean. I am talking about signs in our lives. These signs tell us about forthcoming events or warn us of things. Now, you say that's what highway signs do. Well, maybe God has placed signs on our highway of life. St. Augustine thought signs were things that signified other things. He thought that God communicated with humans using signs."

Brother Yakshagana continued, "God gives signs that people must interpret to draw meaning in their lives. The Bible contains many such signs. Think of something good that has happened to you; something bad. Was there a sign beforehand that the incident was going to occur? Did you ever see a board in the road with a nail turned up? That was a sign of potential trouble. If you ran over it, you likely had a flat tire. Your vision warned you that a tire might go flat if the nail punctured it. Maybe there have been other signs in your life. A sign is an indication, a mark, or an event that tells about something in your future. The miracles of Jesus were signs that depicted his relationship with God. There are many places in the Bible that mention miracles and signs, such as Matthew 12:38, Acts 2:22, and John 2:18. What signs do you see as related to God? Some preachers talk about the signs of the end of times, but I am not doing that. We have too much life ahead to talk about the end. Think about the signs you have had in your life." The preacher paused and took another sip from his glass, followed by a sigh.

This gave Henry time to think about signs he had experienced in his own life and to try to decide if there was anything to what the preacher was saying. He thought of the sign he once had that Doris might be his future wife (she went to the store with him). Of other possible signs he recalled, most were thoughts that went back to his tragedy. Was a loose belt between the tractor and the hammer mill a sign of the danger posed if it came off the pulley? No, he thought; the belt had been run before like that, and it stayed in place. But, there is always the first time for anything. Maybe this preacher was going to say something useful. However, it was too late now to prevent the loss he had.

"Throughout the week, I will speak more about signs," Brother Yakshagana said, "but now, I want to speak about spirits in our lives." Just as he spoke the word "spirits," he looked at the glass and seemingly wanted another sip, but he resisted. (Did he just offer another definition for "spirit"?)

Doris whispered to Henry, "What is going on with this fellow? He reminds me of a Rankin County bootlegger." Henry just shrugged his left shoulder. Maybe he was thinking of a man at one of the loafing stores who was known as an imbiber of spirits of the liquid kind.

"Spirits—you have heard of them," Brother Yakshagana said.

"Maybe you have experienced a spirit. If you have, what was it? If you haven't, what is a spirit? People talk about spirits in many ways. They say that someone's spirit is the feeling or thinking part of a person. Maybe so. Or maybe it is more of a supernatural being that haunts or possesses a person or thing. Now, I know you are thinking of a ghost. Is there a ghost in the attic of your house at night? Really? But, a person's spirit is more. Could it be the soul of a human? Animal? Have you heard of the human spirit or, more importantly, God's spirit? If 'spirit' is written with a capital 'S,' it refers to the Holy Spirit. In the New Testament, God is said to be a spirit (John 4:24) and not to have a humanlike body. I know, since God is invisible, it is hard to understand His presence. But, trust me: He is there. He will help as we deal with demons in our lives and even those demons in Christianity." Brother Yakshagana paused and said, "Pardon me, folks, but my mouth is dry." He took a small sip from the glass. "You know, I am about to empty this glass and am just getting started. Brothers and sisters, say, 'Amen.'"

The audience responded with a loud "Amen."

After a sip, he continued. "Christian demonology is about demons in the Bible and their actions on people. Do you know what a demon is? A demon is a spirit or something that is cruel or evil; only the good Lord knows exactly what a demon is. Sometimes demons are known as evil angels (Revelations 12:7–9). You can't see demons, but they can surely torment you. Have you been tormented by one? Yes, almost everyone has. Physical illness, mental issues, feelings that go with the loss of an arm or leg, demonic possession, spiritual issues of sin and belief in God, and the spread of false doctrines or ideas are major areas in which demons are at work in your life." Several amens and shouts came from the crowd. "Some demons are discussed in the Bible," Brother Yakshagana continued. "This area of Bible study, as I have said, is known as Christian demonology. Demons are often said to be fallen angels that have rebelled against

God. The Bible tells us several times about demons." He went on to cite Bible verses such as 1 Peter 5:8, Genesis 6:1–4, Ephesians 6:12, and Matthew 4:1–11 as evidence of Christian demons. He asked the people present to refer to the scriptures in their Bibles. Brother Yakshagana compared demons to evil spirits who controlled people and went on and on about "people control."

"Now I want to tell you about a few demons that may be in your life this very afternoon." Brother Yakshagana continued: "First is Vine. This demon is commanded by Satan—yes, the devil himself. It is the trickiest and deadliest demon. You may have experienced Vine. Next is Mammon, who is the demon of material wealth and creates the drive to gain money and property. Third, I want to mention Bune, who is a mighty and strong demon sometimes known as the great Duke of Hell. Bune has 30 legions of demons under his control, often arising from the dead.

"The next two demons that I will mention go together: Succubus and Incubus." The preacher emphatically continued: "Men and women in this congregation, you need to be very much aware of these two demons. Succubus is a female form of demon kind of like a beautiful woman who could tempt a man, even while he is sleeping. Incubus is a handsome male form of demon who could tempt a woman while she is sleeping. I caution you to always be very alert to attempts by Succubus and Incubus to gain access to your life. Resist them with all your might. I will speak more about Succubus and Incubus in the next sermons of the week."

At that point, Doris turned to Henry and softly said, "Let's go. We need to get out of here." She continued, "This is strange stuff."

Henry heard her but wanted to learn more to see if it could relate to phantom sensations and other issues in his life. "Let's wait a few more minutes," he said.

Maybe Brother Yakshagana heard their whispering. He began to bring his sermon to a close. "I have mentioned a few aspects of Christian demons to you today," Brother Yakshagana said. "Sermons the remainder of this week will give you more detail and help you to be stronger in your Christian faith and in resisting these evil forces in your lives. I will also talk about how to cast out a demon, as in Mark 6 of the Bible. Come back tomorrow night at 6 o'clock and other nights this week. I will also talk about signs and spirits as well as exorcism used to rid the body of an evil spirit. Sometimes casting out a demon may allow another spirit to enter. I know, you are thinking a ghost could enter your body, but I choose to believe that the spirit that will invade you is an angel. Yes, an angel. If someone in the congregation believes that he or she has a demon and wishes me to do so, I will demonstrate how to evict the demon by doing an exorcism.

"Now, I am going to ask Sister Mammony to pass the collection plate. Please be generous; fill it up. I can barely get by on what I get; I am in debt now just to have food to eat. After that, we will sing a favorite song, 'The Old Rugged Cross,' and I will close with a prayer to our God Almighty. Remember, you can slip me a $20 or $50 bill at any time."

Once the prayer was over, Henry and Doris proceeded to leave the tent as quickly as they could, but the cloth door was tied shut. A trick? This would mean that people would be inside a little longer while the preacher, one on one, solicited money. One of the other people quickly untied it. (Henry, with one hand, could not readily untie it; Doris was going to do so before a man did it.)

On the way home, Doris and Henry reviewed some of the demon message in the sermon. Doris expressed that it was a bad representation of what she had learned in college about Christianity. Henry wasn't so quick; he thought that maybe demons could have made him need the amputation by causing the equipment failure and were creating his phantom sensations. This involved a big stretch of his imagination.

Doris said that there was nothing to this stuff. "That preacher is a charlatan or false prophet trying to get money by spreading falsehoods or, at best, satanic information." Henry mostly agreed with Doris as they drove back to their home in Tinnin. He did mention something about the phantom sensations he was having as related to a demon, but then he said that the sensations likely weren't caused by such. Doris and he agreed that they were not going back to any of that tent revival stuff on demons. This gave them plenty to talk about among their friends, but they weren't going to do so. Fortunately, they did not know anyone in the tent that afternoon. This meant there was no one to tell on them for going, in their minds, to such a silly thing. And it was a waste of precious gasoline during wartime rationing!

Going to the tent meeting on demons probably had little effect on Henry's social adjustment following the amputation. At least, he was able to apply a little science and figure out that he wasn't possessed by a demon entering his body when he was knocked unconscious by the accident.

—————

Being involved with the local agricultural community was very important to Henry. This made him feel worthwhile. The agricultural community included the livestock auction sales, the county agricultural agent and the associate agent, individuals in the local USDA Agricultural Stabilization and Conservation Service (ASCS) office who were involved with farm production, and the agriculture teacher at Clinton High School. All these included an element of education related to agriculture, and learning new things helped Henry have a better outlook on life, aka, a stronger self-concept.

As interest in livestock was increasing, Henry learned that two livestock auctions were held in the county each week: A. G. Moore's auction was on Tuesday, and Tom Riddell's on Thursday. There was always a group of farmers gathered at the sale barns even if these farmers didn't have any animals to auction off. Of course, several buyers bought a predominance of the livestock, and they weren't usually available for conversation. Henry normally had good conversations with owners of both sale barns, as well as with producers who brought livestock to the facilities. Observing an auction provided information about the kind of livestock that would bring the best price. Henry felt that he could observe the auction and later go into the cow-calf business. He could also listen to what other producers said about the management of their animals to assure good health and growth.

The agricultural professionals in Clinton and in Hinds County were generally always welcoming. Henry particularly liked the agriculture teacher at Clinton High School, Joe Treloar. The young agriculture teacher was a recent graduate of Mississippi State College and had a great personality for dealing with farm-oriented families. He would teach high school classes in the morning and visit farms in the afternoon. He would offer individual instruction and help solve problems farmers were facing, as well as talk about various subjects that were appropriate at the time. Sometimes he would invite the farmers to meetings on relevant farm subjects.

Just when Treloar was getting his adult agriculture program well underway, he was drafted into the U.S. Army for service in World War II. There was an absence in the community until he returned. Fortunately, it was near the end of the war when he was drafted, so he wasn't gone as long as most young men. Henry had missed him while he was away. He had a way of talking with Henry that made him feel better and have a more positive attitude toward life. Henry liked him so much that he invited him to hunt squirrels in the woodlands of the farm. He also wanted his son to get to know him and take his classes in high school. A few years later Son did enroll in agriculture classes and became very involved with classes and the Future Farmers of America organization.

Preachers were always kind of special to Henry but he was skeptical of what they sometimes said. As a child he had been led to believe that they were godly and held keys to heaven (and could keep you out of hell). Dealing with phantom sensations created a new need. Were they demons? After realizing they weren't demons, coping with these strange sensations would be a lifetime challenge.

14

Being Human

A few weeks after the amputation, Henry made up his
mind he would not allow the loss of an arm to negatively
influence his relationships with people. He didn't use
such terms as "social skills" and "human relations," but
he knew about getting along with people and promoting
good relationships. Unfortunately, relationships with a
few family members were lacking in this regard.

Henry tried to practice good social skills when interacting with other people. He chose his approach based on his quick assessment of the
other person. Of course, it was in a rural, country sort of way. He
knew human interactions were important in continuing to operate
the farm and deal with individuals off the farm who were essential
to its operation. But, it was impossible for a person with one arm
suddenly gone not to be influenced in some ways by what had
happened.

Henry knew that how a person said something was often as
important as what was said. He recognized the importance of facial
expression, how the body was held, and movements such as shoulder shrugs. A basic in human relationships was always to look a

person in the eye. Henry placed a high value on eye contact. With some people, making eye contact was now difficult, as they would look to the side rather than into his eyes. They apparently had some sort of notion about the inability of an amputee in social situations. Maybe it was a lack of respect or the feeling that he was less than a complete person. Some people who had formerly made good eye contact didn't make it anymore. And to Henry, this interfered with personal relationships.

Among the first individuals interacting with Henry after the amputation were medical personnel. Physicians, nurses, orderlies, and the like were often around. Attitudes toward the amputation and the disability that were created came through while he was in the hospital and under medical care. The first few responses and words spoken by those around a new amputee after overcoming anesthesia are very important.

Henry thought that the attitudes expressed by the health care professionals around him had a big influence on his healing and enthusiasm for life. In general, he thought they were careful to avoid letting anything negative show up in their interactions with him, but, nevertheless, some things did in statements like: "You will need to take it easy for a while. Losing an arm will keep you from doing some things in the future that you have always done." Or, "Amputation of an arm is a big loss. You will have a lot of adjustment in the healing process." Or, "Oh my goodness, I feel so sorry for you."

One of the ways that Henry judged acceptance of him was how he was greeted. Did the medical person greet him in a friendly way? A perky "good morning" would go a long way. Did the person make eye contact, look away when approaching Henry, appear preoccupied, or fiddle with something? Looking away was to him a sign that the person did not respect him and didn't highly value him probably because he had lost an arm. Eye contact was essential to good rapport with medical people. A person who was preoccupied wasn't focusing on Henry but appeared to be thinking about something else. "Fiddling with something" or "nervous energy" demonstrated a lack of care and attention to him. Unnecessarily moving a stethoscope or other device while talking or twiddling fingers were examples of "fiddling." Maybe some of the "fiddling" was a result of nervousness (or lack of respect for a person with a physical challenge) on the part of the health care provider.

Some of those who worked in medical jobs at the time of Henry's amputation apparently didn't pay much attention to their attitudes toward amputees. However, years later, research on the attitudes of medical personnel toward patients with disabilities documented the importance of such attitudes. One finding was that male medical students were less positive than female medical students toward individuals with disabilities. Another finding was that medical students with family or home backgrounds that included a person with a disability had more positive attitudes toward people who had disabilities than those medical students from backgrounds that did not include such a person.

Henry would agree with research findings into the attitudes of medical personnel that those who had been around a person with a disability were more likely to be comfortable working in challenging rehabilitation situations. As experience with a person having a disability increased, so did the medical personnel's level of comfort in ministering to a person with such a disability. These are a few findings by the American Congress of Rehabilitation Medicine (ACRM) published years after Henry's amputation but reflective of the time and attitudes when he sought medical help. It seems that the social effects of an amputation remain with a person until death. Such effects may well influence the quality and length of life.

Perception studies of the attitudes of physicians toward patients with disabilities, such as Henry's, included doctors who performed amputations and cared for amputees as well as primary care physicians and specialists. The general public's opinion of physicians is that they should be leaders with caring attitudes toward all people. They should not establish a value based on any sort of disability. Attitudes toward an amputee may not come into play until years later in life when other medical care is needed. Such attitudes may depend on how disabling an amputation was to the patient.

Perceptions held by physicians mirror the perceptions of society in general toward patients with certain traits. In some cases, physicians' perceptions may also influence how society views amputees. If a physician views an amputee as a person who is "less than complete," the quality of medical care provided could be less for an amputee than for a non-amputee. (Related studies released after Henry's demise include those by Duckworth in 1988 and Paris in 1993.)

Henry always faced a certain amount of disability. In looking at research findings, the question arises, "Does an arm amputation create disability?" The answer must address varying levels of disability; yes, an arm amputation does create a level of disability but in a way that varies from that of other amputations. Let's use a simple example of walking. An arm amputee can still walk, but a leg amputee cannot walk without a prosthesis, crutch, or other assistive device. However, an arm amputee may have a greater disability with other activities. An example is eating a meal. A leg amputee with both arms present does not have the same level of disability when eating that is experienced by an amputee with one arm.

Amputees often face issues or barriers, as did Henry, in finding and using medical care. Such barriers impact the social well-being of the amputees. Barriers vary but may include finding a qualified doctor who will minister to them, getting an appointment to see a doctor, entering an office or clinic because of accessibility issues, and receiving a reasonable standard of care. Of course, paying the charges for the service that is supposedly provided could also be a problem for some amputees in the United States. Medical personnel may feel that individuals with disabilities are more time consuming and not worth the additional time. An example is that it typically takes a person with one arm longer to remove a shirt for an examination than a person with two arms. Maybe that is why Doris often accompanied Henry to medical examinations.

Quality of medical care and personal traits of medical practitioners may influence the self-concept of an amputee, such as Henry. Pain and associated phantom sensations certainly influence the social well-being of an amputee. Though it appeared that Henry typically got the basic medical care he needed, having physicians who were empathetic and who demonstrated a caring attitude would certainly influence how he responded to other people. Some medical personnel were perceived to be gruff in relationships, or they at least lacked a caring manner with patients who desperately needed empathy.

Henry found that some health care providers might neither understand nor be sympathetic toward phantom sensations and might not know how to help a person with such. The response of a medical person to the feeling Henry had, for example, of a fly crawling on his right hand might have been, "It couldn't occur. You don't have a right hand." That sort of response would have been evidence of lack of medical preparation and lack of a caring attitude toward a patient. Such a response didn't help in dealing with the phenomenon or in promoting Henry's self-concept. The medical person might have had the notion that such phantom sensations were weirdness on the part of the patient who now had less than a complete body.

Other situations in coping with an amputation shaped Henry's changing social skills and perceptions. He was now embracing an altered life, and modified social skills were needed. He knew, in general, what these skills were. Among other things, they dealt with communicating, getting along with other people, learning, making friends, asking for help, being friendly, and interacting in harmony with society.

The success of most interactions with other people involves important social skills. Social scientists have determined that individuals with certain health conditions or impairments may have difficulty in social situations. Good mental health is often thought to be essential in practicing appropriate social skills. Anxiety and depression may interfere. Fear of negative reaction by other people definitely impacts social skills and mental health. Having a positive outlook on life promotes feelings of success and well-being. It would have been easy for a range of issues to develop with Henry as he was overcoming the amputation as best he could.

The loss of an arm creates changes in the dynamics of a group that includes a recent amputee. Two or more people may form such a group in a social situation. Group members interact with and influence each other. Certain norms or interpersonal phenomena in a group must be followed. These relate to, for example, saying thank you and shaking hands. No doubt, the loss of a right arm would greatly influence the simple norm of handshaking. Now, Henry did it with his left hand. Most other people continued to use their right hands. A right hand and a left hand do not naturally fit together in a handshake when two people face each other; one individual must rotate his or her hand a half turn. A few people would offer to shake with their left hands, and that might be okay as long as Henry knew what to expect. He had learned to rotate his left hand so that he could shake comfortably with another person's right hand. Something as simple as shaking hands now had become a social skill that was not always pleasant for Henry and might contribute to a negative self-concept.

Henry tried to adjust socially. He made considerable effort to cope with the standards, values, and needs of people around him, whether on a farm, in a church, at the courthouse, or in a hardware or grocery store.

A constant in Henry's life had been the need to achieve—that is, to do well in whatever he attempted. Granted, the level of achievement was tied to farming and rural life. If growing a crop was the work to be done, it was important for him to do his best by preparing a good seedbed, planting properly, controlling pests, and harvesting to assure the highest product quality. Losing an arm altered some of Henry's need for achievement (abbreviated as "N-Ach" in social psychology). Maybe he was facing reality and adjusting. After all, N-Ach is an individual's desire for significant achievement in some way, such as by farming, mastering skills, and reaching high standards. N-Ach is considered a personality trait that is focused on setting and meeting high standards of achievement. Up to a point, that was Henry. Maybe health issues later in life were associated with how his N-Ach was diminished. More and more he attempted to ascribe his N-Ach to those around him, including his wife and his son. Some time was needed for him to realize that it is difficult for an individual to achieve personal goals through another person. Goal achievement is usually not readily ascribed to someone else.

Certain social contacts and interactions in the local community were very important in Henry's life. Some of the contacts were adults from his childhood; others were adults who had moved into the Tinnin, Pocahontas, and Clinton communities. Often the interactions involved social aspects, but most were about rural life and included farming, off-farm business contacts, and gathering places in the local community where adults came together for casual talk, refreshments, and the like. Sometimes these gathering places were known more for loafing than anything else, even if operated as stores. Since Mississippi was a "dry" state, gatherings usually did not include alcoholic beverages. Colas in bottles with shelled peanuts dumped into the Cola from a Tom's peanut bag gave both a solid and liquid snack. A serious loafing day might involve a small tin of sardines with saltine crackers and a dab of yellow mustard.

A source of social distinction was the location of a person's residence. People who lived in town had conveniences and lifestyle benefits over those who lived in the country. Those in town had electricity, running water, and indoor toilets; those in the country in the mid-1940s might not have had any of these and, likely, not even a telephone. There was no television at that time anyplace in Mississippi. AM radio broadcasts reached most areas with a few scattered stations. Those who lived in town typically had access to better education than those in rural areas. Theaters, motion picture houses, and concert halls were located in town and not in the country. Town folks began to sometimes look down upon their country cousins and sometimes viewed them as less capable and worthy. Some town folks thought that people who did not live in a town were country hicks. Other attributes added more individual distinction, such as a disability resulting from the loss of a limb. A man with one arm had additional social strikes against him.

Interacting with town folks who "kept their noses high in the air" did not seem to boost social skills, but Henry held his own when he felt a need to do so. Of course, after World War II, giant strides were made in society that tended to equalize town and country people; gaining home and farm electricity was foremost in the equalization process.

Rural communities often had small schools or had empty schoolhouses as evidence of consolidation with a nearby school. Such was the case with the Tinnin School that served the farm area. The school had been consolidated with Clinton. But, the schools in Clinton were small when compared with those in Jackson, and Jackson folks thought their schools were much superior. Schools often had activities such as basketball games and Halloween carnivals.

The facilities were occasionally used for non-school events that involved the opportunity for social events.

Adjusting to life after an amputation is not easy; it is a challenge. Having health care providers who understand and can relate help a patient in making the transition to living as an amputee. Being an amputee is no fun, but an amputee can get fun out of life after their tragic loss.

15

Keeping a Right Mind

The mental aspects of an amputation are not obvious; we see the body with the missing physical part. The part is gone. Such was the case with Henry; his physical statue had been altered, but what about his mental status? There was plenty to cope with there, too! Could he have more mental anguish?

The mental situation is not so readily observable. Sometimes the mental side is ignored, but that is a big mistake. Doris did not want to make that mistake. She believed that mental health was the same as mental well-being. Over the few weeks and months after Henry's accident, she had noticed some changes in his outlook on life. Maybe they weren't all his doing, as some of his relatives unfortunately were hostile and appeared to reject him. Henry had always been rock-solid in the knowledge that Doris had of him.

Mental health is a complex matter. Doris had taken a psychology class in college but needed to know much more. She decided she would visit the tiny public library in Clinton and see what it had. She used the library's lending program to check out a couple of books that appeared somewhat relevant. She also visited the library at nearby Mississippi College and found pastoral-care kinds of books; she observed these to have little helpful information for her situation. Using the books from the Clinton Public Library, she learned that good mental health was as important to quality of life as physical health and social well-being. She wanted to review exactly what mental health was all about with an amputee so that maybe she could help Henry. She soon learned that it related to the way people behave and feel. Promoting good mental health could be more challenging than promoting good physical health. She learned that good mental health allowed an individual to remain in touch with reality and adequately handle stress, frustration, and other mental issues and tasks.

Henry faced a number of issues in life that tended to result in behavior that demonstrated that mental health might become a problem. To Doris, it seemed that Henry had developed a shorter temper and was increasingly stressed and frustrated by his life situation, particularly with things he could no longer control or do for himself. She found in her studies that the mental health of a person may change temporarily or permanently when confronted with a life-changing event; she further found that some changes related to emotions and their control. (The shorter temper was not present with Doris and their son; he was always patient and tried extra hard to be even tempered with them.)

Doris made up her mind to learn as much as she could with the goal of helping Henry when mental health issues arose as a result of his amputation. And, she realized that she and Henry might have to seek the help of an individual trained in psychology and personal counseling. She also realized that Henry might refuse to seek needed help with mental health. He had the notion that things needed to be "realistic," or concrete and not abstract. He usually did not value things he could not see. Of course, he was always thinking about doing better with farming and everything that it involved.

One of the new farm practices in corn production was the adoption and planting of hybrid corn seed. War demand was for a dramatic increase in corn yield nationwide, and planting seed of a hybrid variety was viewed as a good way to get the increase. Some people viewed buying and planting such seed a waste and as something that might result in permanent damage to the environment. Additionally, seed from a corn crop could not be "saved" (kept) and planted another year because the values of hybridization would be lost. Henry had heard a good deal of talk about the pros and cons of using hybrid corn. Most of it was hearsay he had picked up at the loafing stores he frequented, particularly the Ratliff Store in Tinnin and Baker's Store in Pocahontas. Would feeding such corn to animals stunt their growth? Would grinding such corn into meal for human food make people sick, including causing cancer? A lot of misinformation was floating around.

Henry had heard the Hinds County Agricultural Agent (a Mr. Hale) on a radio program on station WJDX in which he talked about hybrid corn, and what Henry heard sounded good to him. In one program, Mr. Hale announced a meeting in the court chambers of the Hinds County Courthouse in Jackson on the adoption (planting) of hybrid corn. Henry thought about it and, realizing that he needed more information, decided to go. He felt he could be gone from overseeing field work for a few hours. Henry told Doris that he wanted to go to the meeting on planting hybrid corn. She thought it was a sign of optimistic mental adjustment following the amputation (it had been about four months). He also wanted her to ride with him, and she could go shopping or run errands. So she decided she would go to support Henry as well as have a little time in Jackson to look around. She asked Henry to let her have the car while he was at the meeting that was scheduled to last three hours, with a free lunch provided by one of the seed corn companies (Henry was always enthusiastic about "free" stuff, whatever it was; he said it was better than working to get it). At the last minute, rather than driving herself in the car, Doris decided to ride the Jackson city buses to the locations she wanted to go. She had learned about the buses as a student at Belhaven College. It cost only 5 cents to ride about any place served by the buses in the city. Besides, the car wasn't always dependable.

Doris planned a short shopping visit to McRae's Department store on Capitol Street in downtown Jackson (while Henry was in the county agent's meeting at the courthouse), but she had other things "big" in her mind. She didn't tell Henry what the "big" things were, as she felt he might not approve. She did mention, however, that she might go to the library; she really didn't want to slip behind his back but wanted to gather information about the mental health issues of amputees. She found that the main Jackson Public Library had a little information that was helpful. In the back of her mind, Doris wondered if the library at her alma mater (Belhaven College) had useful materials. She didn't recall seeing anything during her time there as a student. Next, she decided she would go by Foster General VA Hospital and the Baptist Hospital to check in their reading rooms for relevant information. She did see a few books that appeared quite relevant in the Foster General collection but was denied access because Henry was not a veteran. (This made Doris wonder about fairness in a time of need. Henry was injured in a farm accident; he was working hard supporting the war effort with farm products.)

At the Baptist Hospital, she explained to the person in the reading/reference room that her husband had had an amputation at the hospital a few months earlier and that she was looking for materials that could assist in helping him adjust to life as an amputee. She was given access to the hospital's limited collection of materials. She saw some of the same materials that were in the Foster General collection. Doris talked with a volunteer in the library about the situation and was referred to books and brochures. She asked if a professional was available to talk with her, and, yes, she was able to talk with a nurse named Meredith.

Once Doris explained the situation, Nurse Meredith said that she had recently taken the train to Atlanta for a workshop at the Emory University School of Medicine on the psychological needs of amputees. It was sponsored by the U.S. Army to train civilians to be better able to help returning military amputees. She also said that she grew up on a farm near Canton, Mississippi, and likely shared many of the same activities as on the Lee farm. She volunteered to talk with Henry, if he came in. Doris replied that Henry had indicated that counseling would be useless to him. Anyway, Doris told the nurse that she could tell her some things and then she would share them with Henry at an appropriate time. Maybe she could convince him to come for counseling. He would find it helpful in adjusting to a new life as an amputee. And, maybe, he didn't have mental health issues; that would be wonderful. No doubt, counseling would help him gain some insight into ideas and issues that could help as he adjusted his life. Since Henry didn't like the word "amputee," different words would be needed when dealing directly with him.

"Grief is a normal response to the loss an amputee suffers. Amputees and their families, for example, have grief about the loss of a leg or an arm," Nurse Meredith said, "and further, they go through a grieving process. I will talk about this if you want me to."

"Yes, please do," Doris replied.

So they sat down in a small room with a few materials. Nurse Meredith explained that grief was a kind of emotional suffering caused by a misfortune, a loss of some kind, or a disaster, resulting in deep sadness and sorrow. Grieving is a human emotional process of feeling acute distress, sadness, loneliness, or sorrow from the death of a person, the loss of a limb, or other reasons. Sometimes the emotions are so powerful that an individual feels overwhelmed, disabled, and unable to continue with routine life activities without help. She said that people grieve differently; most people can handle grief if they try to understand their emotions, seek support, and take care of themselves. Nurse Meredith showed Doris a couple of brochures on the subject and said she could take them if she wished.

Nurse Meredith said that psychologists have identified various human factors involved in grieving. "Is this making sense?" she asked Doris. "And will Henry listen and understand this?"

"Yes, it makes sense," Doris said, adding, "but I am not sure he will listen. I will certainly try to get him to pay attention and believe in this. I will do so gradually at times and places that are right. Tell me more about what I should do."

Nurse Meredith said, "Okay." She spent a few minutes talking about the grieving process as related to Henry's sudden amputation, which was not something he needed or wanted. An amputation resulting from an accident is usually sudden. The person does not have time to mentally prepare, as would be the case with a medical amputation related to disease, which is scheduled a few days or weeks in advance. An accident-caused amputation typically involves greater shock to a person. It is a traumatic, unanticipated event. Counseling beforehand is impossible. The aftershock is greater, as it likely was with Henry and his family. She said that the grieving process has five stages: denial, anger, bargaining, depression, and acceptance. She gave Doris a brochure on the stages of grief and said she could read it for more details. Nurse Meredith also said for Doris to get back in touch if she had questions. Then she said she wanted to spend a few minutes on stress, fear, panic, and self-perceptions.

Everyone faces stress, according to Nurse Meredith. She said stress results from threatening or unfamiliar situations. The loss of an arm is certainly a stressful situation. Learning how to cope with daily living is also a source of stress. Hardly any manipulative activity can be done the way it was before the amputation; life is different. Nurse Meredith said that this was evident in Henry's learning how to use his left arm and hand to do things that had been done with his right arm and hand. He would need to be patient and work diligently. He had to keep a positive attitude on life, his family, and the farm. Some of his issues may relate to how he feels about himself.

She talked about how fear was a mental state resulting from a real or perceived danger or threat. A person with fear is afraid. Behaviors showing fear may include anger, anxiety, fright, panic, terror, horror, trepidation, and dread. An amputee who loses a limb in an accident may experience fear in a situation similar to the traumatic event resulting in the amputation. A certain amount of association goes on in the minds of all people, especially amputees. The fear may be based on a perceived danger or threat and not on one that actually exists. Sometimes a phobia or irrational fear may develop. If not controlled, fears can become compelling forces that hinder human accomplishment. In Henry's case, he is right to have some fear of large mechanical devices that have spinning or turning parts that produce loud noises. He was known to stress safety to other people with an obsession like no other. Ways he did this were by saying things over and over, such as "Walk carefully" (so you won't fall); "Stay away from a mule's hind feet" (so you won't get kicked); "Avoid the front of a cow" (so you won't get butted); "Don't run the tractor too fast" (so if you hit a bump, you won't get thrown off); and "Hold the saw properly" (so you won't get cut). But, he did little to provide safety equipment, such as hard hats and safe shoes or boots.

"Panic is a little different. I would think that on occasion Henry has had a panic state of mind," Nurse Meredith said. She went on to explain that panic is a sudden feeling of overwhelming fear. It tends to dominate life and mental processes when it occurs. The sudden onset of panic is referred to as a panic attack. An attack may last a few minutes to a few hours. The affected person may feel as if he or she is losing control or is overwhelmed by a situation. The person may sweat, shake, breath irregularly, have heart palpitations, or display other signs.

"Has Henry had anything like this?" Nurse Meredith asked. "And, if so, how did he respond?"

"I'll have to think," Doris replied. "Yes, I believe he has experienced panic. What I observed was recent."

Nurse Meredith explained that it usually took a while for an amputee to experience panic attacks after an amputation. These might not occur immediately after the suddenness of an accident-causing amputation, as many other things are going on in the person's life. Once panic attacks begin, they may increase in frequency. Over time, Nurse Meredith thought, Henry would learn to control them. "You may," she said, "develop more ability in how to respond and help him in these situations. You might try getting him to relax his muscles and breathe a little more deeply. But remember, incidence of suicide is higher with those who have panic attacks. Of course, counseling may be effective, and, if Henry smokes, have him stop."

Doris immediately thought about the fact that Henry had started back smoking some six weeks after the amputation. He would go the Ratliff Store and get Prince Albert brand tobacco in a pocket-size can along with roll-your-own papers. He had a hard time rolling his cigarettes with just a left hand. He would sometimes ask Doris to do it for him. That was one thing she did not like to do. Anyway, Doris thought the nicotine was helpful in his coping with life challenges as an amputee, but she did not consider the side effects. Henry's stress would be less if she willingly rolled cigarettes for him. She would always think about how much she wished he would stop this nasty habit, but then she thought that he might take up chewing tobacco or dipping snuff. She knew that he already liked to chew Bloodhound plug chewing tobacco on occasion.

Nurse Meredith said that the onset of a panic attack was associated with certain events or activities in Henry's environment. She said that the attacks, if any, would usually be mild and that Henry could handle them. In some cases, the situations could be avoided; in others, coping approaches would be needed. She thought that operating or being around tractors and power equipment would tend to create feelings of mild panic or that going inside a feed mill, cotton gin, or fertilizer-bagging plant would also create feelings for panic attacks to occur. To keep panic away, she said, Henry should avoid unnecessary situations with power equipment, belts, and moving parts that made loud noise. Some of this didn't seem to apply to Henry, such as being around an operating hammer mill. He had bought one for his farm that was operated much the same as the one at the Ratliff Store. He didn't seem to display any evidence of a panic attack in operating it, but he always cautioned about safety, particularly around the belts (which was a smart thing to do).

As years went by, some situations in Henry's life appeared to produce mild fear but never to the level of a panic attack. New buildings, new roads, and changes in travel patterns created unease in him. Going into large buildings, such as the Standard Life Insurance Building in Jackson, where he couldn't see outside, and riding elevators created mild anxiety. He handled this by always having Doris (and, later, Son) go with him. In the later years, four-lane highways with clover leafs and on and off ramps created uneasiness; Henry wanted someone else to drive. At first, the driver was Doris or a community member, and later as he aged, it was Son. Of course, Son liked to drive and was happy to do so even at the age of twelve and could reach the pedals by sitting on an old Sears-Roebuck catalog.

A side note forward a few years: Son got his driver's license on his fifteenth birthday. His aunt took him to the highway patrol station to drive her car because the Lee car had some issues that might have not passed inspection. He had been driving a range of vehicles around the community and on the farm for several years. Now, he was a legal driver, and Henry really needed him as a legal driver. Within a couple of months, he had Son drive a cattle truck he had borrowed from another farmer to the Livestock Producers Association sale barn near Tugaloo, just north of Jackson. They carried a load of feeder calves and one cancer-eyed cow for sale that day. The trip went well, including backing to the unloading chute at the sale barn.

Now back to Nurse Meredith's discussion. She talked about personal self-perceptions that are often held deep within a person's mind. Amputations often have strong mental impacts on the self-perceptions of victims. A major source of adjustment is handling the loss of independence and having to rely on others for common activities in daily living. Amputees should not feel ashamed of themselves. Doris had tried to read a little about amputations and self-perceptions of amputees to help her better serve Henry, so what Nurse Meredith was saying was quite beneficial in her thinking. The nurse explained that the loss of an arm or leg can result in mental anguish to the individual. In Henry's case, the loss was sudden and not the result of a planned medical procedure.

People around an amputee can help or hinder psychological adjustment, according to Nurse Meredith. Doris said that some of Henry's friends and family were helpful in the coping process; others were of little benefit, with a few being detrimental and damaging to him. She also said that medical personnel offered little in the way of psychological help. There were few specialists, and these few were very busy working with returning soldiers' trauma and conditions called shell shock (years later it would become known as post-traumatic stress disorder or PTSD). They had little time for civilians with nonwar injuries.

Doris said that ministers were not particularly helpful with Henry's situation, though they sincerely wanted to be. She told Nurse Meredith that Henry needed meaningful help in how to cope with his situation. The ministers with fundamentalist leanings and without seminary education seemed to be least effective, she said. Quoting Scripture, praying, and urging church attendance were of little benefit in Henry's mind. He thought that these were self-serving in that a big crowd stroked a preacher's ego and resulted in more money being placed in the offering plate. It appeared that ministers lacked training to provide this form of counseling. Doris further indicated that many relied on phrases such as "Jesus saves," "Get down on your knees and pray," "Trust and obey," and "God bless you." After a while, these phrases were irritating and were not relevant to the issues of an amputee. Real solutions with ready availability and human compassion were needed.

"There is one final thing I want to talk about a little more before you have to go," Nurse Meredith said. "It is counseling." She went on to talk about getting counseling from a qualified individual. In some cases, psychologists and psychiatrists are needed to help amputees in adjustment. But, she indicated that peer counseling may be the most useful in this case. She explained that it involves an amputee with a similar limb loss serving as a counselor. Preferably, it is an amputee who has had some training in such counseling. The peer counselor should be a person about Henry's age and, of course, with a farm background. Such a counselor is useful to an amputee as well as to his or her family and others who are around the amputee.

If a peer with training in counseling was not available, an amputee with a similar limb loss who has adjusted reasonably well and has a positive attitude would likely be helpful. With the return of veterans who were amputees, there would likely be a greater number of peer counselors. She cautioned, however, that some of these individuals had great psychological issues associated with their experiences or were suffering war neuroses. These individuals had psychological disturbances due to prolonged exposure to war activity, including being bombarded by enemy weapons. Such traumatic experiences are manifest by a number of characteristics, such as numbness, depression, irritability, flashbacks, and nightmares. She asked if Henry had experienced any of these disturbances, and Doris indicated that he had, but only to a small extent, not to the degree that the war veterans did. Doris didn't think war veterans would be able to relate well to him. But she did know a couple of men in Hinds County who had amputations: B. B. Wiggins and John Bell Williams. She had seen these two men and felt that they could be helpful as peers with Henry.

Doris expressed a heartfelt thank-you to Nurse Meredith for talking with her and for the informative brochures. She said she needed to go soon and meet Henry at the courthouse, as the meeting he was attending would soon be over. She said she had one quick question about demonic possession and Henry. Nurse Meredith quickly responded, "No; such should be rejected." Doris said thanks again and left. She rode the city bus to the courthouse and went to the couple's car to wait. She sat in the passenger seat and reflected on what she had learned that day. It was an amazing amount, but she was unsure about how much would be applicable in her situation. Henry came to the car when the meeting was over. They were happy to see each other.

Both Doris and Henry had things to talk about, but she felt reluctant to initially bring up some of what she had done. Henry got in the driver's seat (he was still striving to master driving with one arm) and asked Doris about her shopping. "I bought the cutest outfit for Son," Doris said, adding, "Let me show it to you. It's the size for a two-year-old boy. Just look at the blue color. It's a perfect match to his blue eyes. I think it will be just right for him to wear to church on Father's Day. You know, I really like trading with Mr. Sam McRae."

"And to church on Mother's Day," Henry said, adding, "Yes, it is a nice blue. Maybe he will like it. And what else did you buy?"

"I didn't find anything else at McRae's. I also went to Kennington's but didn't find anything there that I wanted. I surely looked around. Those stores have quality products," Doris replied and asked, "How was your meeting? What was discussed? How many people were there?"

Henry wanted to talk about the meeting; going to it made him feel good but not exactly "whole" again. "Mr. Hale, the Hinds County Agent, is a nice, well-informed man," Henry said. "He knows what he is talking about. He convinced me that maybe Son could become a county agent someday. He could go off to State College and study agriculture. Wouldn't it be great if he graduated from there with a college degree? That is why we have that little savings account."

"That is a good idea," Doris said, "and we need to be saving money for college costs now."

Doris asked Henry to tell her more. He indicated that there were probably eighteen or so men present. "We had a good lunch: barbecued beef brisket, corn bread, and the like. We were told that the corn bread was made from hybrid corn. It appeared that everyone ate some of it and no one got sick during the meeting. The seed corn people gave us a sheet of paper with information on it about how yields are greater with hybrid corn." Henry also had information on cultural practices, such as cultivation and the use of fertilizer. Of course, there were questions about how much it cost to grow and saving seed from a crop to plant the next year. "We were told that planting saved seed would result in lower yields even if we chose the biggest and best ears for seed." Henry was not certain about how many acres of hybrid corn he would plant in the future because of the cost of seed (it was a little too late for this season, but there would always be another year). Further, cotton had always been his main cash crop.

Henry talked about the corn that he had been growing on the Lee farm. He remembered as a small boy going into the crib and picking out a few bushels of ear corn to shell for use in planting. He did not remember any corn being planted that was not grown on the farm the previous year. He had never heard his papa talk about bringing new seed corn to the farm. He went on to explain that the corn he was planting was likely some that his grandfather Shepard had before the U.S. Civil War; maybe he brought a few seeds from Washington County, Indiana, when he moved south. Seed was chosen from the previous year's crop each time for planting. Henry said that the county agent talked about how keeping the same "line" of corn for many years resulted in something he called "inbreeding." Yields would gradually get smaller and smaller, and that is what happened here on the Lee farm. The "kept" seed also tended to result in plants that were more receptive to disease and insect pests.

"This meeting changed my outlook on corn seed," Henry stated. "Next year, I am going to get some hybrid corn seed for a few acres; we will try it on a small scale. Of course, most of our fields are in cotton, but maybe I can reduce acreage devoted to corn while at the same time increasing yield and have more land for cotton. I have already decided to give the hybrid corn a try."

Doris was so pleased that Henry had something of high interest to him to do. He appeared more himself after going to the meeting. It made him feel important and needed. This was far different from interactions with family members and a few people in the local community.

Doris didn't say much about her activities. She did say that she went to a few places looking for useful help and information for their family. She again spoke about how nice Mr. Sam McRae was to her. She said she went a couple of stores up the street from McRae's a half block to Woolworth's and sat at the counter for lunch. She ordered a scrambled-egg breakfast for lunch; didn't cost much. By then, Henry had the car cranked and headed out Capitol Street toward the Clinton Boulevard and home. On that day, Henry and Doris had missed their son, who was being kept by Susie Heckle, a woman he adored. After a quick stop at an A&P Store on West Capitol Street for a few food items, they were on their way to Tinnin.

Upon arrival home, Doris gave Son a big hug; he gave her a hug in response. She showed him some popcorn she had brought from A&P and asked if he wanted some. Of course, he did, and she popped a small serving of it. Henry did not come directly into the house, as he was outside checking on a few farm things. He learned that one of the sharecroppers had become ill. No one knew the problem, so Henry suggested that he see Dr. Ashford. Henry drove him into Clinton for an examination. Dr. Ashford said he had a strep throat and prescribed penicillin, which was a new drug on the market. After a shot in the butt and one night of rest, the sharecropper was ready to work again. After all, the major role of sharecroppers was work, work, and more work. Not quite like the slave era, as the landlord would care for slaves and provide for their needs. Farm hands had to be more self-reliant, and they were free to move about and make choices.

With Henry staying outside for a while and taking the share-cropper to Dr. Ashford late that afternoon, Doris had an opportu-nity to read some of the brochures that she brought back from the Baptist Hospital with her. These brochures spoke directly to some of the observations she had made about Henry and the amputation.

First, she read the brochure on grieving and the process in-volved. Maybe it was a little late, as about four months had passed, but there were many years of life ahead. The phases of the process overlapped and tended to go back and forth, as there was no clear-cut distinction between them.

She learned that the first stage is denial; it happens early, and the person thinks that this couldn't have happened to him or her. It is thought to be a temporary way to handle the overwhelming emotion that goes, for example, with the loss of an arm in an accident. Yes, she and Henry had both experienced some denial. But, they were pretty well beyond this stage.

Next, Doris read about anger. It occurs when reality is setting in. Did this really happen? Yes, a loss had occurred. Individuals, she learned, are sometimes helpless and frustrated and may develop anger. The anger may be taken out on their family or those working around them.

Bargaining, the next stage Doris read about, occurs when a person dwells on what could have been done to prevent the loss. The individual may try to postpone the reality of the amputation. Some people turn to religion or a physician for help. What has been done is done, and not much can be done about it.

Depression, the fourth stage, may replace anger. Usually amputees have a certain sadness about themselves as they begin to understand their loss and the impact it may have on their lives. Sleep (too much or too little) may become an issue. Other times they have negative feelings about the people and things in their environment. Crying for no obvious reason and appetite changes are also symptoms. Feeling overwhelmed, lonely, or regretful is part of the depression stage. Professional counseling may be needed, Doris learned.

The fifth stage is acceptance. It is the time at which a person accepts the reality of the loss that has occurred. The person may continue to feel sad, but it is a time when he or she starts moving forward with life. Hope is also a part of acceptance. The individual sees that there is hope for the future.

Doris also read that some individuals develop complicated grief. It is not common among amputees, but an individual could manifest multiple symptoms: isolation, violent behavior, suicidal actions, prolonged depression, and nightmares are a few of the signs. Doris did not think that Henry would be a victim of complicated grief.

Now, Doris heard Henry come up the front steps and onto the porch. He was ready to come inside for supper. Somehow, Doris had gotten preoccupied with her study and learning and failed to do much about supper, but she quickly got it ready. Doris and Henry sat at the table with Son in a booster chair. Doris knew she needed to open the conversation to discuss some of what she had learned that day, but she knew not to offer too much. She waited until after they had eaten.

"Henry, I believe you feel good about the meeting of farmers with Mr. Hale," Doris said and added, "I also had a good day. Much of my time was spent on trying to learn about things that will help us live together happily for many years. Whether we want to or not, we have to adjust to the loss of your right arm. Right? I learned that it isn't just you; your whole family and those around you go through adjustment. I think you and the rest of us are doing well with something known as grief. It is associated with amputation, as you experienced, just as with the death of an individual. All of us are changed. We will always accept and love you." Those last words were comforting to Henry.

Henry thought that Doris, the wife he loved so dearly, could have not said anything better than "always accept and love you." He had been thinking negative things about acceptance and love; now Doris dispelled what he occasionally had on his mind. Son was getting fidgety sitting at the table with all the adult talk. They put him down on the kitchen floor with a round coffee can and two pocket-size tobacco cans; he knew how to entertain himself with these simple and economical devices. He also sniffed the odor of coffee and tobacco in the cans; no one knows what he thought. Henry and Doris talked a bit more as she did the dishes by kerosene lamp, and then it was time to go to the bedroom and get Son to bed for the night.

It was at bedtime that Doris showed Son the new outfit she got him that day at McRae's while shopping. It somewhat reminded her of a sailor's uniform; it expressed patriotism during these years of war, but she did not want him to have any involvement. She told him it was to wear on special days and to church. Doris decided that she and Henry could talk more the next day. Henry was feeling good to this point, and she wanted to keep it that way. It was time for a night of rest.

Now, to fast forward several years ahead in Henry's life: New medical advancements were made in the years just after World War II, particularly as related to the physical and mental health issues of returning soldiers. These medical advancements continued into the 1950s. Henry was able to take advantage of a few of these, even though he was not a veteran.

Coping was a challenge. Henry tried different ways of doing so. He was not much of a consumer of hard liquor or beer. Years earlier Dr. Davis, a brother-in-law, had given him a bottle of bourbon. It was mostly used for medicinal purposes with farm hands; a small amount remained in the bottle for years. Henry liked to keep a little wine around the house. He would take a few sips straight from the bottle each evening to help him, as he would say, calm his nerves. The kind of wine he got was cheap, such as a bottle of Mogan David. This was a sweet wine of either Concord grape or blackberry flavor. Of course, Mississippi law prohibited the sale of liquor and wine. There was only one thing for a man to do. He did it; he bought illegal wine from a bootlegger.

Henry knew there were bootleggers in Rankin County. One was on Highway 49, along the way to see Doris's parents, in an aging tourist court. It was easy to get whatever liquor you wanted. All you had to do (when thirsty for some "medicine") was drive around behind the little building that was used as the office for the tourist court, and a man would appear. The man would take your order and bring the wine or liquor to the car window and collect payment. Yes, this resembled a drive-up liquor store! Business appeared to thrive for the beverages but not so much for the run-down tourist court rooms. Maybe some were rented by the hour! Of course, customers and workers were always looking over their shoulders to see if law officers might be coming to raid the place. (Word was that the law officers were "paid off" so as not to raid the place.) And, if the nearby Pearl River got out of its bank, the driveway would be blocked with flood water. The place where the liquor was kept was high and dry, and that was good news for the customers.

Yes, Henry may have sometimes had mental health issues. These possibilities were associated with physical and, perhaps, head and nerve injuries suffered on January 20, 1943. Maybe the discomfort he felt was from phantom sensations with the amputated arm, or maybe not. Regardless, the feelings were very real to him. He usually sought (somewhat reluctantly) professional medical help in the decades that followed. At least one physician suggested conditions known as neuralgia and neuropathic pain. He said that these sometimes followed serious accidents by a few years. He referred Henry to a neurologist, who was a respected specialist.

Prior to Henry's first visit for consultation in 1971 the neurologist tried to obtain medical records of the tragedy. But records of Henry's stay and treatment at the Baptist Hospital in January 1943 had been destroyed. State requirements in Mississippi were that hospital records be kept 28 years following hospital treatment. Unfortunately, the records were gone before Henry had overcome all issues associated with the loss of the arm and some 18 years before his death in 1989. This disposal of records created a vacuum in the treatments he took in future years related to mental adjustments to his challenging situation. The presence of such records could have resulted in better management of his healthcare issues as well as a better quality of life for his wife and son. Along with records no longer being available, physicians also changed over the intervening years. Some retired; others moved the locations of their practices. Henry was fortunate to have received the care he got on the day of his accident, but if it had been better, he would likely have had a better quality of life afterward.

The neurologist explained that, in his practice, he dealt with diseases of the nervous system and muscles. He further explained that neuralgia is a kind of pain involving nerves and often results from nerve injury, which Henry had at the time of the accident. Whatever the pain was, it was enough of a concern that Henry sought specialized medical help. It had now been a number of years since the amputation. Maybe it was just phantom sensations, but the physician did not think so. Nothing was definite; Henry did not necessarily have neuralgia, but the physician thought he might. At least the name sounded proper to an unsuspecting person. The physician said it was the occipital form of neuralgia. This form is most often characterized by pain in the upper neck and back of the head, and this is just where Henry had the pain. It is more likely in men and occurs after the age of forty. Because neuralgia is hard to diagnose, there was never a definite diagnosis that Henry had occipital neuralgia, but he had a condition that a physician labeled as such.

Another name ascribed to Henry's condition (but never diagnosed) was neuropathic pain. As with neuralgia, neuropathic pain is associated with the nervous system. It is primarily associated with the nerve trunk, such as the spinal cord, which might have suffered injury at the time of the accident with the high-speed belt that flew off the hammer mill and threw Henry to the ground. Afterward the vertebrae in Henry's neck were not properly aligned and could pinch nerves or otherwise cause pain. Anyway, these issues were most likely associated with phantom sensations that sometimes occur in people with amputations.

If the health condition was neck vertebrae, Henry and others reasoned that a chiropractor might be helpful. He went to one, got an adjustment, and was scheduled for several trips. Henry did not like the pain associated with the adjustments (he said it was worse than the pain of the condition) and did not notice that the adjustments were helping his pain. So, he stopped going; it was probably okay to stop, as the adjustments were not likely to be beneficial.

Sometimes Henry dwelled on his health and loss of certain abilities a little too much. Fortunately, his marriage was a loving, faithful, and loyal commitment. Many years after his accident, people around him thought he was being overwhelmed with life. Incidents beyond the loss of the arm but related to it were occurring. His family noticed changes; maybe he had depression or other mental issues. There wasn't much evidence of suicidal tendencies. Doris had Henry seek additional medical help. A visit to a psychiatrist was scheduled.

After detailed interviews and examination, the psychiatrist and Doris made the decision that Henry would be admitted to the psychiatry unit at Hinds General Hospital in Jackson, Mississippi, for shock therapy (treatment). This was done quietly without word in the community; he simply disappeared for about six days. His pickup truck was moved a bit each day (sometimes driven off and back by Son) to make it appear that Henry was around and driving it. This was in the winter, so no farming of consequence was going on. He had already discontinued cotton farming and rented cropland to a local farmer for soybeans. The hill land was pastured with beef cattle. Several large rolls of hay were placed in the pasture so that the cows had something to eat beyond what they could gain as forage.

The treatment Henry received was electroconvulsive therapy (ECT), also known as electroshock. Kind of a scary procedure! It involved passing an electric current through the brain for a fraction of a second. Since general anesthesia was used, no discomfort was supposedly felt. One of the goals was to create short-term memory loss so that some of the things bothering Henry would be forgotten. Henry had only about a third of the number of treatments that people with serious mental illness receive, as the physician and consulting psychiatrist thought that number was adequate based on his situation of no major, long-term mental health issues. When Henry came home, he took it easy for a few days.

A side effect from his nearly a week of ECT was that his nub was black and blue; the cause wasn't known, but strong evidence of the cause existed. Henry said one of the treatments caused him to fall off the treatment table onto the floor, landing quite hard on the nub. (The treatments can cause convulsions in which the body may move and thrash about without muscular control while under sedation. Prior to the shock, a medication is usually administered to prevent convulsions. Maybe the restraints were inadequate for a person with one arm.) Hospital officials were very quiet about the black-and-blue nub. All of his upper body weight probably landed on it. Even after these years, the natural instinct would be to use the right arm to brace and protect the body in a fall. Of course, it could have been somehow caused by the electroshock itself. Once home, Henry did not immediately drive the pickup but was driven to the farm so he could see the cows and other animals. And, then in a couple of days, it was back to the usual life routine.

It appeared that he had some short-term memory loss; maybe he would now move ahead without remembering a recent event in his life that caused mental anguish. Actually, it was more than just one isolated thing: it was a collection. Could another man have been trying to take his wife away? That would greatly upset him; he thought Doris was his perfect wife. Read on.

Here is what likely lead up to Henry being in a condition where electroshock therapy was felt appropriate. Doris shared with him details about a couple of telephone calls and the presence of a man at the front door of their home on Monroe Street in Clinton.

The situation began one afternoon with a telephone call. Doris had just gotten home from a day of teaching first grade at Clinton Elementary School. She had no idea what was about to happen when the phone rang. She answered with an enthusiastic "Hello." That evening after dinner she shared the call with Henry. The call was from a businessman in Clinton who was widely known as a womanizer and a self-appointed high roller. Yes, he was a man who engaged in casual affairs with women. He probably had an emotional condition that kept him from establishing and maintaining long-term, loving relationships. He had no known live-in partners at his nice home, though he had been married a couple of times. The first call, as told to Henry by Doris, went something like this when the telephone rang:

"Hello," Doris said.

"Hello to you. This is Kibbey McShort [fictional name used here to protect any living ancestors or relatives]. Do you know who I am?"

"Yes." Doris replied. "Why are you calling?"

"I have been seeing you around town and outside working in the yard at your home," Kibbey said. "You taught one of my nieces at school. I know of you as a smart, good-looking, petite woman about 40 years of age and in good health. I would like to spend a little time with you. Can we go to Chat and Chew Truck Stop in Clinton for coffee sometime? How about tomorrow after school?"

"No!" Doris exclaimed and slammed the phone down. She thought to herself: I have long known that he was a creep, and now he has contacted me. Why? In her mind, she knew what he really wanted, and she wasn't about to let him have it.

The next day about the same time the phone rang, Doris answered, and again it was Kibbey. "I want you to hear what I have to say." He said softly, "Keep on the line. Do not tell anyone that I called you. I know Henry. He is not a complete man; I am. I have all my body parts. And, I can use my body. Let's meet at Chat and Chew tomorrow after school."

Was Doris frightened! She quickly hung up and was shaking from the experience. She hoped this would be her last call from him. Doris was not a flirtatious woman; she had nothing to do with men in the community. She took life seriously and lived it in a highly moral way. After all, this was conservative Clinton, and she went to First Baptist Church and actively participated in Sunday School.

Doris and Henry talked that evening after Son was asleep. Both were disturbed by the calls. Henry was shocked; he knew Doris was faithful and committed to him for better or worse. "If he calls again, I will shoot the SOB. He will be gone like a wild goose in the summer! I am going to always have my pistol in the pickup," Henry said, adding, "That man is a no-good, sorry creep. Don't you ever talk to him again."

"I won't," Doris said, "and I didn't talk this time. He did all the talking. You know I am not that kind of woman. He is a no-good creep and a big blight on our wonderful town of Clinton. He was behind trying to get approval to build a motel up on highway 80 near Mississippi College. Thank goodness the college was able to block it. Just think if he had been successful with that request before the town council."

"Yes," Henry replied. "I do know that."

All was calm for a few days. Henry was restless. There were no more calls, but on afternoon of Tuesday of the following week, Doris heard a knock at the front door, and she went. There he was! Kibbey was standing in all his glory at the home of Doris and Henry. The only thing separating them was the latched screen door.

"Why are you here?" Doris screamed, "Get away fast. Henry will shoot you."

"He is not here; his pickup is gone." Kibbey replied, "I am not afraid of that man; he doesn't have all his parts."

"Get away from here!" Doris screamed and slammed the main wooden door. She peeked out the window and saw him walking up Monroe Street to his car that he had parked on the side rather than in the Lee driveway. Parking in the driveway would have been a giveaway to passersby who knew who owned the vehicle. Doris was not the kind of woman who would be entertaining a man at her home and did not like what was going on. She thought about getting a restraining order but waited to discuss it with Henry.

That evening Doris told Henry about the appearance at the front door. Henry was furious. He said, "I am going to get him. Just wait. The next time I see his car out someplace, I will stop and seek him out. He will never be the same again. Once I am done with him, he will not be a whole man!" Doris encouraged Henry not to do anything bad. She asked about getting a restraining order. Henry thought it better to keep quiet and handle the matter themselves. (After all, a restraining order is issued by a public office, and the community might find out something about what has been going on and connect it to Doris.) If word got out in the community, it might get to the school, and Doris would lose her teaching position even if she tried to run Kibbey off and in no way promoted the contacts. After all, he was a prominent Clinton businessman.

These things weighed heavily on Henry. He thought about them all the time. His thoughts became consumed with the very idea of what Kibbey was doing. Henry couldn't sleep at night; he was more irritable than usual. He started carrying his pistol in his pickup wherever he drove, including the farm, store, or church. Of course, he didn't have much skill in using it with just one hand and arm. He was not a person who believed in guns but had inherited a few and bought one over the years. Fortunately, he did not run into Kibbey at a store or any other place in the community.

Henry was not himself. That is when his physician suggested he seek psychological help; he did. He had electroshock therapy shortly thereafter, as told about in this chapter. But, would that be enough to help Henry through this tough emotional time?

16

Speaking Defensively

Were there people who would talk badly about another person or take advantage because of the other person's unfortunate situation? Henry was about to learn. To do so might not take very long. Acting in defense was sometimes needed. Could cussing help?

Henry had made good progress in adjusting and in moving forward with his life. Sometimes he was frustrated by situations. If so, he might let a few choice words fly. This "defensive cussing" was to deal with the frustration that he felt and not usually to address the attributes or behavior of people around him. Yes, it is known as defensive cussing.

By the fall harvest of 1943, Henry had made as much physical recovery as could be expected. He had also made some progress with mental, social, and economic adjustment, but he still had some personal reservations about how he would move forward. His progress had to overcome not only his disability but also the actions of other people toward him. Sometimes it was difficult to determine when discriminatory action was about to occur or had occurred. Certainly, his self-concept had a lot to do with adjustment to life with only a left arm. But, to many people, his body didn't look right; it was unbalanced with only one arm.

Henry always tried to think of the church and its minister as a good source of encouragement in helping him move on with his life. To this point, he had not found a great deal of understanding from the local minister about his situation. Yes, the minister knew that Henry had lost an arm, but he did not know much about the psychological and social needs that were involved. He had even less understanding of the adjustments that were needed.

One Sunday the church had a fill-in preacher named Reverend Standifer. He was a longtime minister who had served a wide range of people. Many of the people had special kinds of needs, and he generally understood those needs. Somehow the message got Henry's attention and helped him see meaning in his life. The delivery was much like telling a story rather than shouting about sin and blaming people for their shortcomings—the approach Henry had heard used by many preachers. The visiting preacher did not talk about sinners and going to hell or about bad things in life as God's payback for sin. He tried to reassure rather than frighten those present in the tiny white church building on that Sunday.

The gospel reading used by Reverend Standifer for the sermon was Luke 17:11–19 from the New Testament of the Holy Bible. Standifer's message was about how "life can be lived well regardless of circumstances." Three phrases he used stuck with Henry: "Somebody needs you," "Live life to the fullest," and "Stand tall for trustworthy and moral character." The message resonated well with those in church that day. Henry, not much more than a year after his accident, was still seeking direction and ways to find worthiness. He told Doris that it was a message of love and respect for all people and that every life had a purpose. He said that his had a purpose even when some of the people around him considered him to be disabled. Henry wanted to know when Reverend

Standifer would preach again; he surely didn't want to miss his sermon.

Was Henry disabled? That question comes up over and over. If so, to what extent did he suffer a disability? A disability (or a physical challenge, as is the term preferred today) is an impairment that affects the activities in a person's life in a substantial way. The impairment may include one or more limitations associated with mobility, dexterity, stamina, and physical functioning. Among other anatomical losses, such limitations may be due to the partial or complete loss of a limb, as was the case with Henry. People may think of impairments as problems with the structure or function of the human body to the extent that an individual's activities and participation have limitations. Such limitations are not usually experienced by persons without impairments. The loss of an arm would definitely be an impairment that would lead to some level of disability.

How much disability did Henry have? Henry was not fully disabled. He was striving to overcome obstacles. There were many things he could do. But, some activities posed difficulty. Some activities were limited, and others were not possible. After the amputation and as part of his recovery, he set about to stay active and be involved in many things related to farming and life in general. Other chapters in this book speak to limitations in his abilities in doing personal, family, and farm activities. At times he might have been down, but Henry was never out.

Persons with disabilities didn't have much protection from discrimination and were often denied access to services and places that were very accessible to individuals without disabilities. Sometimes persons with disabilities were looked down upon and unfairly discriminated against. Emphasis on human disability began the year before Henry died and too late to help him. The Americans with Disabilities Act (ADA) was introduced in Congress in 1988. Much debate took place in 1989. It was passed by Congress the following year and signed into law on July 26, 1990, by President George H. W. Bush. How persons with disabilities are treated has changed in the United States since the Act took effect. Treating all people with honesty and fairness is a tenet of the American value system; anything else is cruel and mean.

Henry suffered his life-changing amputation some forty-seven years prior to enactment of the ADA. Many veterans with disabilities from war activity could have greatly benefited from provisions of the Act, though they had specific veterans' services provided by the federal government. Maybe some of Henry's experiences somehow contributed to the provisions and passage of the Act. Would Henry have enjoyed a different life if the Act had been passed fifty years before so that he could have benefitted at the time of his accident? No one will ever know the answer, but there might have been some protection from discrimination against him, and some obstacles that he faced might have been removed. It might have helped his life by removing some barriers in public places, including buffet-style restaurants and self-serve businesses and offices.

What about benefits that Henry might have received because of his disability? The Social Security program in the United States pays some disability amounts, but no benefits are payable for partial or short-term disability. Any amounts that Social Security might pay are based on inability to work, but the provisions do indicate some coverage if one cannot do the work that was done before an accident. Henry had a Social Security number dating from his time of employment with the railroad, but benefits did not apply to farming. Therefore, he was not covered at the time of his farming accident. He had not served in the U.S. military and had not qualified for veterans' coverage. There was no applicable workers' compensation coverage. And, of course, there was no insurance or other coverage through the owner of the tractor and hammer mill.

He had no medical or other coverage that could have fully or partially paid medical costs and compensated for disability. Limited savings were used to pay hospital and doctor costs.

In 1943, Henry had no choice but to find a way to continue to be a farmer, and a good one at that. He wasn't a quitter. The farm, which dated from before the Civil War, needed him. His family needed him. He knew it. He wanted to achieve and to be as successful as possible even in a time of hardship. He knew that changes were underway that would impact how the farm was operated—which crops were produced, how they were produced, and who would produce them. Labor availability was changing. New production technology was on the way for crops. Markets were changing. Land use had to be modified from the Civil War era practices. He also soon learned that homes needed to have modern conveniences, such as electricity, running water, indoor toilets, bathing facilities, and heating and cooling systems. Of course, some of these could not be had without the first: electricity.

Sometimes it seemed that Henry was subjected to discrimination because of his loss of an arm and related injuries that occurred at the time. Or, maybe, the discrimination was by "city folks" who thought rural and farm life was inferior. Could they have thought of him as a country bumpkin and one of whom they could take advantage? (He was smart and capable as a young man.) Maybe there was always some subtle discrimination related to his arm loss; occasionally there was blatant discrimination. A few examples will be reported and examined here.

Theft? Yes! Did other people choose to steal from Henry and his farm because he was viewed as less than a complete man? One example was the stealing of roasting-ear corn from a field when it was at a desired stage of maturity. Roasting ears—ears with white-to-brown silks on green cornstalks—would be present in the afternoon and gone the next morning. The stalks would show evidence of the ears ripped off as by a human hand and not by the work of a raccoon or other animal. The ears would go missing between late-afternoon checking on the fields and early-morning checking. No doubt, Henry thought, that somebody knows his schedule and that the corn is mature enough for use as roasting ears. He felt it was most likely a farm hand from a neighboring farm; he did not think it was one of his farm hands. He mentioned the situation to his farm hands, and none of them knew anything about the missing ears. And, no one confessed to being the culprit even when pressed by Henry!

His approach to end the corn theft: Use fear of being shot (or as he would say, "put lead pellets in the sorry SOB's butt"). Of course, he had never shot or shot at any one; his talk was more forceful than actions! His plan was to take an old hat from the closet that hadn't been worn in years. It wasn't his to begin with, so he felt comfortable using it the way he had in mind. He got the 410-gauge single-shell shotgun off the rack on the wall and took five bird-shot shells with him (he had only once fired the gun since losing his arm). He went to the field, placed the hat on a fence post, and backed off about 30 feet. He held up the shotgun with the stock against his shoulder and his left hand placed so that one finger could pull the trigger (wasn't easy for him). He aimed as best he could and slowly pulled the trigger. The gun fired; the shot missed. Damn, miss! He loaded the gun to try again; he still had four shells.

He was wondering if he could ever hold the gun steady enough to hit the targeted hat. He raised the gun and fired again. He lowered the gun and looked: Damn, hit! The hat now had what he wanted: a couple of gunshot holes in it. He fired the three other shells into the air. He wanted people living in nearby houses to hear the commotion in the cornfield. Was this to create fear among nearby people or to defend his property?

Henry got the hat down from the fence post and took it back

to the house. He returned the gun to the rack (located high on the wall so that small children could not reach it). The next morning he rode in a wagon to various houses on his and neighboring farms. He asked the people if they had heard gunshots the previous evening and if they knew who the hat belonged to. He explained that a sorry, no-good corn thief had been taking roasting ears. He said that the hat might have belonged to the thief. It was his notion that for them to hear gunshots was as effective as the hat with shot holes.

He went to the Ratliff Store talking about and showing the hat, though he was certain no one there had been stealing his corn (the people there all had fields of their own). He explained that someone had been taking his corn and that he went to the field in the early evening yesterday and shot at what he thought was a man. The man ran so fast that he lost his hat with bullet holes in it.

After this, no more corn was stolen, but he never knew the identity of the culprit. It was probably someone he saw quite often. Henry thought this was a good way to defend his property from being stolen.

In September of the same year, Henry checked on his pinder (peanut) crop. He had provided proper cultivation, fertilization, and the like to promote productivity. Summer showers came at the right times. The vines had grown well and produced heavy flowering. He knew that peanut pods developed underground in a process known by a fandangle word that he could not pronounce: geocarpy. Each flower sends a peg (root-like structure) into the ground with the ovary on the tip of the peg. The ovary develops into a peanut pod with two to four individual nuts inside. If the pegs are disrupted so that they do not grow into the ground, there will be no peanuts. So, he thought, surely there will be a good crop of peanuts in the ground. He checked a couple of runners from the main plant—nothing! There were no pegs with peanuts at the ends. He checked a couple more by pulling them up and digging in the hill. Virtually none! He thought that someone had sneaked into his peanut patch and had begun partially harvesting without digging the vines.

Maybe it was the corn thief! He sneaked back to the field that evening to watch the patch while hiding behind a big cedar tree. If a person was coming in and getting the peanuts, Henry would certainly see him. The first evening, he saw no one. The second evening, he saw no one in the patch. What was going on? Did he need to do another hat-with-gunshot trick?

It just so happened that the next morning, as he was on his way to check on how cotton picking was going, he saw the culprits: Three of his Spanish meat goats were in the field pulling the ends of the runners up and eating whatever was on them. They left the runners attached to the plant so that the plant looked undamaged. Peanut villains! They had four legs and a voracious appetite for green peanuts fresh from the plant. No person had been going into the peanut patch! How did the darn pesky goats get into the patch? He knew that the net wire fencing with a couple of strands of barbed wire at the top was just checked and repaired as needed back in March. Some of the wire was rusty and brittle, but it should be good enough to keep goats out. He walked the fence around the patch and came upon a hole in the net wire where the goats had been entering and leaving at their leisure. The goats most likely had made the hole. The peanut theft mystery was now solved, but that would not bring back the lost peanuts. Henry opened the gate and turned his cows into the patch so that, for a few days, they could gain good nutrients from the leguminous peanut vegetation.

The next year another animal attack occurred—this time on his sweet potato crop. The attack had its origin in previous practices by game hunters of taking (killing) deer to the extent that the whitetail deer population in the area was decimated. Crops that deer once fed on could now be grown without a problem. The sweet potato attack began when efforts were launched to repopulate the forests and creek swamps in Camp Kickapoo with whitetail deer. The leaders at Camp Kickapoo who were in charge failed to follow good wildlife management practices.

The deer quickly overran the camp area and created big problems with certain crops. The sweet potato was a crop that was attacked. Deer relished eating the leaves of the plants. Income and food from sweet potatoes for the Lee family were lost. It was impractical and economically unwise to build high, deer-proof fences. After this disastrous crop year, Henry stopped growing sweet potatoes. How did the farm so quickly become impacted? The farm property, for a distance, shared a boundary with Camp Kickapoo. Good practices could have saved Henry this loss and allowed him to continue producing sweet potatoes. Did the leaders of the camp discriminate against Henry by not following good wildlife practices? Maybe they thought that since he was a man with one arm, it wouldn't make any difference if he didn't produce any sweet potatoes. The answer will never be known. It was suspected that the folks in charge at the camp did not care about damage on local farms by deer as long as the population was restored.

Times were changing. Getting and keeping good farm labor became increasingly difficult. Farmers competed with each other for sharecroppers and day laborers. Keeping the farm labor force was a challenge. Some laborers left farms for factory jobs. The war effort in the early to mid 1940s created huge factory demands. Many left farms in the Southern states and moved to the Northern states, working in tank, jeep, weapon, or other wartime assembly plants.

Shortly after World War II was over, some workers returned to the farms of the South but, in a year or so, they were gone. Mechanization on southern farms displaced millions of workers after returnees. More farm workers moved to cities. They typically had little skill and education for getting and holding good jobs.

Somehow they survived life with low-level jobs; some later joined welfare rolls, and a few turned to crime. Now, farmers had a smaller and smaller pool of workers, particularly sharecropper families. It was common for a farmer to try to recruit a sharecropper away from another farm. This usually created ill will among farmers. The life of a sharecropper involved hard work and few benefits. Housing was the bare minimum, and conveniences weren't considered relevant to a lowly sharecropper, or so some farmers thought. The farm owners themselves didn't have the conveniences; they didn't know some even existed.

A typical practice was for a farmer to talk with sharecroppers or other farm hands in the fall at the end of the major harvest season about their plans for the next year. The farmer would settle up a sharecropper's account at this time. In some cases, the sharecropper would get a statement indicating that all charges were paid and that a balance was due that would then usually be paid in cash. The cash might just entice the sharecropper to stay another year. The farmer needed to know who would be around to do the work next year. Farm plans were made for the next year based on available labor.

Once a farmer knew that a sharecropper or laborer would be lost (usually that meant go to another farm), effort was quickly made to recruit a replacement. In nearly every case, this involved talking to those who were on other farms and trying to recruit them away. Maybe some sort of incentive would be offered, such as better housing, higher pay, or more implements to make the work easier.

Not often, but occasionally, a sharecropper might ask for something to make his life and that of his family better. On one occasion, part of the discussion involved a sharecropper asking for better housing. He wanted a house trailer (manufactured house) moved to the farm and set up with electricity, running water, and waste disposal. The sharecropper said it could even be a used (second-hand) one. He just wanted something to make life better for his family. That request came as a surprise to Henry. He thought on it a few minutes. He recalled that thunderstorms occasionally passed through that could destroy a trailer, but he had also heard about anchoring a trailer in place. Maybe weights could be used to hold it down. Henry asked the sharecropper if he knew of such a trailer that was available. He didn't. Henry then proposed that some materials be provided for upgrading the tenant house he now lived in. The sharecropper could do the work himself. That was agreed upon for the next year. In fewer than two years, a house trailer showed up on the farm. It was situated in a location convenient to the public road. A new, fenced garden spot was prepared near the trailer.

Somehow it seemed to Henry that his farm workers were targeted and recruited away more often than the workers of other farmers. Could this have been related to his disability? Maybe the other farmers viewed him as "easy prey" in terms of proselytizing farm workers. In the recruitment, the farmer trying to get a worker to come to his farm might say something like: "You know your boss man has only one arm; he can't look out for you as well as I can," or "With one arm, the owner of the farm where you sharecrop can't provide the equipment and other improved practices to make work and life easier and more productive for you. Come join me, and I will treat you 'right.'" (Hopefully, "right" involved honesty and fairness in furnishings and crop records.) When the recruitment strategies of others worked, Henry would have to find other sharecroppers or farm hands. That wasn't easy. The available supply of farm workers would get picked over; Henry often had to go with less-qualified and less-productive persons.

One approach was to use more power equipment, plows, planters, harvesters, and the like so that fewer farm hands would be needed. Henry made some of the transition but likely not at the same speed as he should have done. Some cultural practices with cotton might have been passing him by, and as a result, he began to adjust by planting soybeans and less cotton and changing cropland to pastureland for beef cattle. For a few years, oat and wheat crops were planted in the fall for harvest in late spring. Henry also learned by the mid-1960s that he could rent out his cropland to a producer who followed a different model. Owning land wasn't needed to be a farmer; renting it on an annual basis was better. And so, cotton farming was ended on the Lee property in the mid-1960s (more about this later). That was sad to Henry; this farmland had been producing cotton for more than 125 years! He knew that times were changing and that he needed to adjust to them. But, could he do so and continue as a farmer himself?

As a general rule in the Tinnin farm community, people respected the private property of others. This included not going onto or encroaching on another person's land without permission. Hunting and fishing on another person's property were done only after talking with the owner and getting approval. Taking trees, fruits, vegetables, and other valuables was not done. Keeping property lines distinct was a high priority. Respecting another person's private property also involved not taking or using equipment without authorization; stealing fuel was not frequent but did occur on farm skid tanks with unlocked hand pumps.

And, of course, having good fencing was essential so that animals were kept where they were supposed to be. Producers didn't want a bull to go through a fence to get to another person's cows that were in heat, resulting in calves of less than the desired breeding and conformation. A bull that tore into another pasture might bring disease, such as Bang's disease, into a herd. Once corralled back, the bull might bring disease into its owner's herd. Cows and calves needed to be kept securely in the owner's pasture and carefully watched. A hog could root out or under a net wire fence and be taken by gunshot. Sometimes, particularly in the winter, animals could break from one farm to another in search of feed.

One particular winter that had been longer and cooler than typical in the South is a good example. A neighboring farmer let his animals go without feed; they had to scavenge for themselves in fields and woods for leaves, stems, and other vegetation that was edible. His animals were hungry and had behavior they didn't usually have when well fed. Once, a mule broke out to go from a place that provided little feed to eat hay and range pellets Henry had provided some of his herd of beef cattle.

There was always the threat of cattle rustling. However, it didn't happen often.

In some cases, good fences were needed to keep predators away, as with the chicken-wire fencing around the chicken yard to keep out foxes, opossums, and raccoons. Building and repairing fences was a regular farm duty. Keeping the good border fencing on the property line was a challenge. Sometimes property owners would arbitrarily move the fence line over a few feet onto another person's property. Getting them to move it back was a big hassle.

City folks who ventured to the country were sometimes another story. They lacked the same respect for private property; posted or no trespassing signs didn't mean as much to them. They would ride out from town, park their cars along the road or turn into farm roads, and go onto property without consideration for the rights of the owners. Only a few would try to find the owners to get permission or pay for what they took. City folks might cut small cedar (juniper) trees or climb trees to get mistletoe or Spanish moss for use in holiday decorations. Sometimes they would go over fences, leave gates open, and, rarely, use wire cutters to cut fencing wire. They would cut a young cedar tree with the best shape and size and place it on the top of their car or in the back of a station wagon and head back to town. In a few cases, city folks cut nice oak or hickory trees for making into firewood or barbecuing wood. In a couple of instances, fairly large black walnut trees were cut and taken. Most likely the highly desired black walnut wood would be dried and used to make furniture, bowls, or other objects.

Using the financial assistance of federal government programs in the early 1950s to conserve soil and water, Henry had four farm ponds constructed on his land. One was several acres in size and very near the main public road. He had three of the ponds stocked with bass and bream fingerlings that quickly grew to the size desired for harvest by sport fishers. He stocked another out-of-sight pond with channel catfish.

Folks would just be driving by on the road and stop to fish. Many had fairly good fishing luck. Only a few people ever asked permission to fish, even though there were two posted signs near the pond and a barbed-wire fence around it. Henry thought about how he would solve the problem. He could chase the poachers away when he saw them, but that would mean he would have to confront them. He came up with the idea of getting a sign that read "Fishing $5" and putting it on a prominent fence post near the road. That pretty well ended unauthorized fishing. A few people, though, actually paid the five dollars. With fewer people fishing, those who did often had good catches. Maybe the fishers would more readily pay to a one-armed man because they had sympathy for him.

City folks would sometimes drive out and park their vehicles on the shoulder of the road and go hunting in the hilly forest land for squirrel and rabbit in the fall or on pasture and harvested cropland for quail and rabbit in the winter. They often would not get permission to do so—they just did it! Did the people know Henry? Did they know a man with one arm owned the place? Were the people taking advantage of a man without an arm? Regardless, if Henry knew they were there, he would walk or ride to seek them out and send them on their way. It is amazing that he was never shot by one of the gun-toting trespassers! Sometimes a poacher would give Henry his (it was always a man) game harvest, if he had any. Henry did learn from talking to the people that most had grown up on a farm but had lost their "farm ways" as related to private property. Regardless, they did not want to be confronted about hunting on posted land without permission.

Dumping trash and debris was especially hard to prevent. Fortunately, most people respected farm property, but a few didn't. Household wastes, construction or demolition scraps, and old auto parts such as tires and batteries would be disposed of by throwing them over fences onto the property or into creeks and gullies. In some cases, personally identifiable materials were dumped. On rare occasions, Henry was known to have sorted through some of the wastes, finding letters, invoices, bills, and addresses on old magazines. He would seek out the people, and after telephones were widespread in use, he would call them to confirm that the trash was theirs. He would often ask how they were going to correct what they had done that was wrong. In most cases, the people would come to the place and clean up the wastes (and maybe go down the main road and throw it away again). It was Henry's notion that those who dumped wastes on the property were repeat offenders. Maybe they knew Henry and chose his property because he had one arm.

Trash from adjoining farms would sometimes end up on the Lee farm. Empty fertilizer and chemical containers were occasionally disposed of by throwing them on another person's land. Sometimes these would be thrown into water, float downstream, and be deposited on land. Along with this trash would be empty engine oil, grease, and antifreeze containers. Discarding these in a creak to float away was irresponsible; this behavior demonstrated bad attitudes toward maintaining a quality environment.

Disposal of dead animals might occasionally pose a problem for land and farm owners. The animals might be wildlife that died of natural causes or were shot by a hunter and left, or the animals might be farm animals that were being produced and died of natural causes or by events such as lightning strikes. A good example is the pregnant mare that sought protection under a tree during a thunderstorm. The tree was struck by lightning, claiming the mare's life and that of her foal, the birth of which was in progress at the time of the lightning strike. It was sad to see the carcass of the dead mare with a partially delivered baby extending from the birth canal. Henry handled this dead mare just as he would always do by calling the rendering plant in Jackson to send a truck to pick up the animal and process the carcass into fertilizer and other products.

A dead small calf, goat, dog, house cat, or pig might be buried or burned. Henry never allowed dead animals to remain and provide food for buzzards or to decay (resulting in a bad odor). An animal that died from disease might infect healthy animals. Runoff rainwater from the site of a dead animal decomposing on land would pollute creek water. This water might transfer disease to other animals on farms through which the creek flowed.

Occasionally, another person would dump a dead animal on the property for it to decay. This was usually detected by its decaying odor if the carcass was not seen or by the presence of a flock of feasting buzzards hunkered over the carcass or circling high in the sky above. Someone from town might bring a dead dog or cat and throw it out in a roadside ditch or over the fence. Neighboring farmers would likely dispose of their own animals in some way and not try to move them onto Henry's farm. When dead animals were disposed of on Henry's farm, did the guilty parties feel they could do so because he had only one arm—that they could take advantage of a person who some considered to be disabled? Regardless, he did not like to have dead animals dumped on his farmland.

On rare occasions, a farm animal would die from a purposeful or accidental gunshot wound inflicted by a non-owner. Was this revenge about something or just a way to take advantage of Henry? Or, was it the result of someone just shooting animals for his deranged enjoyment? From time to time, shots might be fired at animals from cars driving along the gravel road that ran by the farm. These shots rarely struck an animal, but when they did, the animal might be killed. Was this done just for personal thrill seeking or because the shooter knew Henry? If Henry knew who fired the shots, he would seek out the person and confront him or have a sheriff's deputy investigate. Henry learned to defend himself in appropriate and reasonable ways.

After World War II, more and more inputs for farming were bought from suppliers off the farm. These included improved seed, fertilizers, pesticides, and the like. Locating and buying these inputs to assure farm needs were met at a reasonable cost was a challenge. Henry liked to talk and negotiate with sellers. He would try to get a price better than what he was first quoted. He sought to buy the inputs at the lowest prices. But, did he? Somehow, he felt that he might have occasionally paid more than other farmers.

Paying fair prices when buying farm inputs was always a priority; buy quality items at the lowest prices. To help get better prices, Henry joined a farm supplies cooperative. He found that prices at the local Hinds County Cooperative were sometimes lower but that independent sellers could often beat the prices of the cooperative. A little negotiation would go a long way toward paying lower prices for farm supplies. He knew that making a profit involved something he referred to as "buying low and selling high." In other words, he attempted to keep the cost of production as low as possible and sell products at the best prices possible. He often heard men at the loafing stores talking about such, but he wasn't sure how hard they worked to follow what they discussed.

Henry was confronted with two major areas when selling farm products: one was to get the best prices, and the second was to deal with honest people who would not cheat the seller. Henry normally used local cotton buyers in Pocahontas or nearby Flora. Each town had two or three buyers. A sample of lint cotton fiber from a ginned bale would be taken to a buyer, who would quickly look at it in good light for whiteness and the presence of trash. Next, the potential buyer would take about a dozen fibers from the sample, hold them with the thumb and a finger on each hand, and stretch the fibers between hands to estimate fiber length, known as staple. During the 1940s and 1950s, cotton price was based on whiteness, freedom from trash, and staple. Most staple length on farms in the area was $1^1/_{16}$ inch to $1^3/_{32}$ inch. An unscrupulous buyer could pay less for cotton by stating that the staple was an eighth of an inch less than it really was.

Henry was always concerned about how buyers could short-change a seller by failing to accurately grade the lint cotton. But, did the buyers have in their minds that they could offer Henry a little less per pound than the cotton was actually worth? Did they envision a man with one arm gone as less capable in marketing? Anyway, Henry often tried to negotiate a better grade or price than he was first offered.

One local buyer was known as Mr. J. A. (he was called by his initials). Henry and Henry's father had sold ginned cotton to Mr. J. A. for years. Mr. J. A. also ran a mercantile store and was part owner of the local gin. He was a businessman who tried to be in-volved in many things. He wanted to give the impression of being a well-informed and skilled cotton buyer. But, was he ethical?

Sometimes when Mr. J. A. was assessing the whiteness of cotton by holding it up to bright light, he would turn his back to the farmer. He would quickly state something like "light gray" or "yellowish" without having taken the opportunity to carefully assess whiteness. This made the cotton worth a penny or so less per pound; integrity was sometimes compromised. The presence of broken leaf pieces entangled in the fibers would also lower the grade, and Mr. J. A. was quite able to "find" trash even when the cotton was largely free of it because it was handpicked. Mr. J. A. would quickly hold a small sample of fibers stretched between his two hands to determine staple. He never used a measuring device to help assure accuracy and fairness. He would stretch out the small bundle of fibers, turn away, and quickly announce a staple, such as $1^1/_{16}$ inch.

Another source of shortchanging the farmer for the benefit of the buyer was to state the weight of cotton bales a few pounds less than the bales actually weighed. As a bale came out of the gin compress, it was weighed. The weighing was done with hanging-balance scales in an A-frame. Employees of the gin attached a tag with a unique number to the bagging that was wrapped around the cotton. The bale number was entered into a ledger, and the weight recorded at that time. The number and weight would follow the bale to the cotton compress, where the bale would be further compacted under pressure greater than that of a cotton gin and shipped to a textile mill.

Henry tried to watch for everything to keep weighing and selling honest and gain as much income as he could. Based on how the buyers did business, most people felt that minority farmers were more likely to be shortchanged. It seems that cotton buyers were shrewd and always looking out for themselves. Cotton-buying practices have changed markedly in the years since Henry's cotton-farming time. The Agricultural Marketing Service of the U.S. Department of Agriculture has established standards for cotton grading. Nearly all cotton is now mechanically picked and cleaned with better ginning equipment. Maybe the emergence of all the changes was good reason for Henry to quit farming cotton. On the other hand, standardization by the U.S. Department of Agriculture should have removed some of the opportunity for a "slick" buyer to cheat the farmer.

Some of the same issues farmers faced with cotton marketing also impacted the sale of other crops, such as fresh vegetables, potatoes, sugar cane, peaches, and pecans. Many of these products were harvested at the peak of desirability and carefully maintained to prevent deterioration. Upon arrival at a grocery store or vegetable stand, the products would be inspected. The presence of any worm damage, evidence of plant disease, or excessive maturity or immaturity pertaining to just one item could result in the entire batch being docked or, in some cases, refused.

Many products other than cotton were sold by weight. The buyer's scales were typically used to establish the weight. Sometimes the scales might be adjusted to weigh "light." Underweights resulted in fewer pounds in a sack or bale being recorded in documents and less money being paid to the producer. Sometimes, sacks or bales were reweighed after purchase from the farmer so that the buyer gained pounds. For example, a sack of pecans or squash was weighed when first sold and again when delivered to another or final place. Accurate counts were needed when corn, watermelons, and other crops were sold by the dozen or individually.

When Henry would make a delivery to, for example, a grocery store, would the buyer see that he had one arm and feel that this was a person who could more readily be cheated? Perhaps a buyer would think that Henry possibly could not do math and make his own calculations about the amount due for a batch of products. The buyer sometimes demonstrated thinking like: How could a vegetable-peddling truck farmer be respected? It took a lot more intelligence to grow good vegetables than buyers sometimes realized. Having top-quality produce was a sure way to gain favor with the buyers for stores and distributors.

Should equity under the law be questioned? You wouldn't think so. How did officials in local, state, and federal government offices view Henry? In the 1950s, roadblocks on highways for driver's license and other checks were common. The state highway patrol officers would stop every vehicle and ask to see the license of the individual who was driving it. Maybe there were other reasons, but it appeared that once the officer saw that Henry had one arm, he would be asked get out of the vehicle and stand by the door. Henry would use one hand to try to hold open his billfold and sort his driver's license from other documents; sometimes it might have appeared that he was fumbling around. Suspect? Were the officers interested in other violations such as driving while intoxicated or hauling illegal black market whiskey in the trunk of the car? Interestingly, automobiles that appeared weighted down in the back were said to be hauling black market whiskey. Such vehicles might also be seen at various bootlegging joints around the county and in nearby Rankin County.

So if Henry had four bags of chicken feed chops in the trunk of his car, it would cause the rear to be weighted down as if the vehicle had a load of illegal whiskey. Henry might get stopped by a deputy sheriff and asked what he was hauling and to open the trunk. He would readily be let go when it was determined he was hauling chicken feed! A question in the officer's mind might be: Is a man with one arm more suspect as a whiskey bootlegger than a man with two arms? Do law enforcement officers feel that a person with a disability is more likely to violate laws and regulations?

Common courtesies appeared to sometimes be ignored around Henry. He was a strong believer in greeting other people with "Good morning" or "Hello." This was true at any of the loafing stores as well as Hinds County offices, medical places, the post office, retail stores, schools, and other offices, such as those that handled insurance. Being warmly greeted at loafing stores was probably most important because those were the places with his peers, and they and Henry could share life's challenges together (except for his missing an arm). Women would occasionally come into the loafing stores to buy something; he expected them to speak to him only if he knew them fairly well. Sometimes people Henry didn't know would come into the stores; some of them would act as if they were afraid to be near a man with one arm gone! Men and women of color would also come into the stores to make purchases. Henry found that the men of color who knew him were more likely to extend a warm greeting of their own, such as "How you doin', Mr. Henry?" or simply "Mornin'" or something interpreted as "Good morning."

Yes, it was amazing that the men of color were more likely to offer a genuine greeting than white men! Could it be that the men of color held less prejudice toward people with disabilities, including a man with one arm gone? Certainly, they knew about prejudice and discrimination. A disability, such as that created by one arm gone, on a white man appeared not to matter to these men. Courtesy and respect were always in order.

A common saying in the Lee-Shepard family had been: "If you don't look out for yourself, nobody else will." The statement had become more important to Henry, though he knew never to take unfair advantage of another person. Though not music to a bystander's ears, maybe defensive cussing was sometimes needed!

17

Living in a Female Majority

So what is a female population imbalance, and what does it have to do with this story? Read on and maybe you will see (or maybe you won't). And, how did it relate to feeling safe, responding to Evangelist Billy Graham, and experiencing child molestation?

If there was ever a home and farm with a lack of gender balance, it was the Lee family place (and Shepard family place before that). You would think that the number of females and males on the place would be about equal. Balance wasn't even close: far more females! This lack of balance shaped Henry's life from a very young age or, at least, placed certain demands in ways that a home and farm with equal numbers of males and females would not have. Some people would say, however, that this "female imbalance" didn't matter.

The imbalance was across two generations. George W. Shepard, who created the farm in the 1840s, and his wife, Sarah, had seven girl babies born before there was a boy. Yes, the two boys were the babies of the family, and one of them didn't live more than a few months. The very youngest was a boy who became a successful farmer and businessman in the Delta Land of Sunflower County, Mississippi.

The marriage of the oldest Shepard girl, Ellen, to Jasper Henry Lee in 1864 produced one son, Ira Jasper Lee (born 1868). He spent most of his childhood without a father. Jasper Henry Lee died in Henderson County, Texas, in 1870, when Ira was little more than a toddler. More than a decade later, Ellen and Ira Jasper Lee moved back to Tinnin to live in her childhood home with her parents.

Ira Jasper Lee married Carrie Cheers Hendrick in 1901, and they had six girls and three boys. Two of their sons died quite young. For many years, Ira and Henry (father and son) were the only males living in the big Lee-Shepard house. How did the place accommodate this many females? If more "breathing room" was needed than the house contained, they could spread out on the land, but they often didn't need to do so and chose to stay in or near the house. Did the girls get into squabbles? Yes, but these were quickly settled on their own.

Why did a female imbalance matter? First and foremost, farms need labor. And, this was especially true in the cotton-oriented South, once vestiges of slave-labor production were gone. Yes, the females would do a lot of work, but they weren't as good with mules, plows, and the like as were the males. Sawing down trees, splitting rails, and doctoring big animals were tasks done by the men. Almost any job that required brute strength was better done by males. The females were better with jobs that involved eye-hand coordination, such as chopping and picking cotton and harvesting other crops, particularly vegetables and berries. They were better than the males at the jobs where the eyes had to see something to which the muscles of the body responded.

Maybe the females could care for the family vegetable garden (except for the mule-powered plowing and the like) and take care of the laying hens. "Heavy work" was usually for the males in a family.

In most cases, the females wanted to be at home sewing, quilting, cooking, and washing or, as some would say, "doing girl things." Occasionally something would be sewn or knitted that could be sold for a small bit of all-important cash. Females of child-bearing age might have small children to care for and babies to nurse.

The females knew that there was no let-up on household duties even if they chopped and picked. They also knew that they couldn't count on males to help them do the household work. "No," as Ira Lee would say, "a real man doesn't do housework." Statements like that didn't exactly promote harmony in a family! But, maybe "harmony" wasn't the intent. Carrie might scoff a bit and say something like, "Housework—that is why I had all those girls! I needed some help around here." Maybe what Ira said was to keep the females in line, as they didn't have many rights or opportunities of their own. The females were taught from very young ages to serve men and keep them well fed and happy in various ways. Their place was largely in the home. Having a large family was sometimes viewed as the subservience (maybe submission) of a woman to a man, and some people thought that was good. Submission was taught in church and was a part of the rites of matrimony.

Women who did farm work didn't get much relief from household work. Their men expected the work to be accomplished in a timely manner. They expected meals three times a day, and if something resulted in a meal being a little late or not cooked the way they liked, they would complain about it. They might say something like, "Where is my food?" "Did the fire in the stove go out?" "Did that travelin' salesman come by here this morning and keep you out of the kitchen? What were you two up to anyway?"

Children not yet large enough to work were treated as if they were between babyhood and early adolescence. They were pushed to grow up fast! The small girls really couldn't do much—maybe gather eggs in the henhouse (better not break one, or you would be in big trouble). Small boys couldn't do much either, but they might choose to go to the field to get away from the house. Sometimes they would take a nap under a shade tree near the field. Young boys going to the field was a kind of trick to make the girls think that they were hard at work when, in fact, they had few work skills. A female who thought she was approaching marrying age might sneak away to be with a beau, and if love was developing, she would call him her sweetheart. Regardless, a few more males on the Shepard farm in the 1800s and the Lee farm in the early 1900s would have helped get farm work done. Was the ultimate demise of the place due to a lack of males? Of course, there is no meaningful answer to this question.

How did the imbalance affect Henry? First of all, he was the only son who survived beyond early childhood. Second, his father was the only adult male around the house. With Carrie, the six daughters of Ira and Carrie, Mama Ellen (for several years), and Susie (a sister to Carrie), there were far more females than males.

Gender imbalance was probably made harsher by the personality and behavior of Carrie. At best, she was borderline difficult. Being hard to get along with was her way of going about life. Maybe pregnancy and lactation helped make her irritable. Carrie was either pregnant, lactating, or both for about the first 25 years of being married to Ira. It seemed that her being pregnant was a source of pride to Ira; maybe he could boast about his manliness. Maybe keeping their wives pregnant and lactating was how some men fulfilled a goal of manhood. Also, lactation tended to reduce fertility and keep down the number of babies. Though Ira loved his daughters, he wanted more boys. He might have pressured Carrie on this, not knowing that offspring gender is determined by the male parent. Maybe he was highly critical of her for having so many girl babies. Maybe he felt that she should keep having babies to have boys.

The ages of Henry and his sisters had an effect on how the

siblings related to each other. The oldest sister was born in 1902, and the youngest in 1923. The in-between children were born in 1905, 1907, 1910 (Henry), 1913, 1915, 1918, and 1919. Examining the years of giving birth demonstrates that lactating promotes decreased fertility and conception. Carrie had a baby in 1918 that died at birth. With no time of nursing a baby, she became pregnant quickly again, giving birth in 1919. The oldest child was married and gone from home when the youngest was born. But, Henry was there for all of them in one way or another! He really didn't like being around the house when Carrie was giving birth. She was difficult; some would say she was abusive. Ellen, always sophisticated and calm herself, tried to teach Carrie to be calm, but there was nothing calm about Carrie when she was in labor.

Henry lived in the house where he was born until he was 37 years old. There were baby girls, child girls, pre-teen girls, teen-aged girls, and young adult girls; Henry experienced them all. He had been around them so much that he knew about the different stages of development that girls go through. He knew about their clothing needs and how they felt about dressing properly when in the presence of males they wanted to impress. He knew about their interests in bathing and grooming. Though Carrie didn't help them much, their grandmother, whom they called Mama Ellen, was there to help the girls born prior to her death in 1918. In fact, she was very useful to her oldest granddaughter and a namesake, Ellen Lee. Mama Ellen often counseled and gave direction to Ellen in making choices about men and going out into the world on her own. Mama Ellen was a much valued part of the Lee household.

Henry's father, Ira, had bouts of sickness. This most likely resulted in Henry having more demand to work and in his not receiving the attention he needed from his father in his development years. Asthma and other conditions sometimes overwhelmed Ira. Even as a man in his early 30s, he got a statement from his physician exempting him from roadwork. (Citizens were responsible for keeping roads in passable condition, as the county did not have a road maintenance crew.)

Ira was more likely to tell Henry what farm work was to be done and how to do it. Maybe that instilled some of the work ethic Henry had all his life and transmitted to Son. Henry always had more than his share of the responsibility for seeing that members of his family had food, clothing, and other needs met. This probably was the reason he took a job with the railroad for a while in the 1930s before he saw that his father would not be able to operate the farm without him.

Living arrangements in the house minimally met the needs of those who lived there. Ira and Carrie had a corner bedroom. Babies and small children also stayed in that room. The girls shared a big room. Beds were also shared. Mama Ellen had a room that she shared with older girls and adults, including Carrie's sister, Susie Heckle. Where was Henry's bed? He was given a small area at the base of the stairs to the attic. It was only enough space for a small bed, and he had no dresser or anything to go with the corn shucks he had in a large cotton sack for a mattress. No one else ever slept in the area near him. There was a closet under the stairs to the attic that had some space he could use to hang clothes on nails driven into the wall and a couple of shelves for placing folded clothes. How did he ever have quiet time and space to himself with a bed near the doorway and in the hall that connected all lower-level rooms?

The Lee girls filled some of the void of trying to have a caring, loving home when Carrie failed to offer it. The older sisters cared for the younger sisters, but it was Carrie who would assume a motherly role and nurse the babies. She could be very protective about it. At the same time, she would use nursing a baby as an excuse not to do other important household chores. She would try to make the girls do them. The older girls, with the help of Mama Ellen, had kitchen responsibilities, such as straining the milk, preparing the food, and washing the dishes. Keeping the stove hot required that firewood be brought in, and every now and then, they would let the stove cool so that ashes could be removed.

It was "do this and do that" all day long. Carrie was continually bossing her family. Maybe that is why the girls left home in their teenage years as soon as they could find men who would marry them. Maybe that is why the girls, after they were married, had fewer babies. They saw what their family had gone through with nine babies and perhaps wanted none of it.

Because he was the only boy in the family, Henry's sisters appeared to view him as a special person. When he was quite small, his older sisters would look after him and try to keep him out of trouble and safe. But, the sisters also made a lot of demands on him. At times, they bossed him around and often told him what to do. It was often "Help me do this," "You do that," and "Do this again." The sisters often told him that he should do something (such as harness a horse) because he was a boy. Maybe he got picked on (teased) by his sisters because he was different from them. They would sometimes tease him about his "boy parts" and how his clothing was made different. As he got older as a child, he would tease his sisters back about their big skirts and "those baby feeders" growing on their chests. The sisters would come to his rescue if he needed it. Sometimes they would rescue him from the wrath of Carrie when they thought she was being unfair with him.

With help from his sisters, he went to school a few weeks each year, where he made local community friends. While they were still quite young, the older sisters would help guide his way to school and into the right classroom. They would protect him from hazards, such as stepping in a mud puddle or getting into a thorny bush. As he got older, they were less protective, and Henry was more on his own. This suited him just fine. He was a boy and could look out for himself, or so he thought.

The sisters used Henry to protect them from harm. "I am scared," one of them would often say. "There is a strange man creeping around outside. Protect me." Or, "When I ride the wagon to the Ratliff Store by myself, some of the men stare at me. I'm frightened when I go inside." Or, "There might be a bad snake in the henhouse. Go with me. Bring a hoe to chop its head off." Or, "The bull in the pasture is mean and chases me. I am afraid of him. Keep me safe." Or, "It is very dark outside, and there are scary things." Henry would offer some protective support, such as walking with them in the dark to the two-holer at the back of the yard, taking a big stick into the pasture to defend against an aggressive bull, or getting a sharp hoe to defend against a possum in the chicken house. Under his care, none of his sisters were ever harmed, regardless of how great they thought the danger to be. He became a hero to them by keeping harm away.

With all the "sister protection," Henry had fear himself. He heard his sisters talk so much about what made them afraid. How could it not affect him? Big snakes, wild dogs, bobcats, mad bulls, boars with big tusks, and fighting roosters instilled fear. And the "strange men" his sisters saw or imagined also they created some fear but in a different way. He put on a brave face and deliberately moved ahead and protected his sisters from the fearful things in their world.

It was probably appropriate for the sisters to seek protection in the presence of some of these men, particularly the "strange" ones. The sisters were all good-looking. It didn't matter if they had blonde hair and blue eyes or brunette hair and brown eyes. Maybe, as the sisters reached their teenage years and beyond, there was some justification in Henry protecting them from the evil-minded men in their midst.

Did the men the sisters romanced intimidate Henry? The beaus and sweethearts had distinct personalities. Some were farm boys;

others were sons of Southern small factory workers and town boys. Some were veterans of service in war.

The men with military experience often had particular traits and were sometimes not very likeable. Their war experiences shaped their personalities and general presence around Henry. At least one beau appeared to be experiencing shell shock. Ira didn't like him and soon sent him on his way.

Another veteran demonstrated an attitude of superiority; army service had made him smarter and better than all other people, or so he thought. He acted "smarty" or like a "know-it-all." He would wear a military shirt or uniform to boost his ego. Someone who wasn't in the military or a veteran was not of much worth and definitely not to be respected by a person who was. Maybe the sisters encouraged their men to exhibit an attitude and do a little "strutting" around the family. Was that to impress the family members with the men the girls brought around? It didn't. Henry rarely said anything about his sisters' men. If they would leave him alone and not bully him, he could tolerate them. All the way back to the time of the U.S. Civil War, no one who lived at the Lee-Shepard home served in the military.

Henry and Doris were always appreciative of the considerable outpouring of his sisters' love and support during their courtship and marriage planning. The wedding was simple and did not involve a lot of expense. His sisters (at least those who lived nearby) were with them every step of the way. Some assisted with the event itself. One newly married sister offered the use of her home for the wedding. The house had electricity, running water, and an indoor toilet. This was far more than the Lee-Shepard home had. The support the sisters who lived nearby provided was far more than Henry's mother offered. The sisters, in general, treated Doris as a sister, but a couple appeared reluctant to welcome her to the Lee family.

The sisters around Henry often admonished him to go to church, pray, read the Bible, and follow a righteous life. At a young age, they would take him aside and read and pray in their way in his presence. They often tried to get him to read and pray; he seldom did so in their presence. As he reached adulthood, he was on his own, though the sisters continued to remind him about church things, including "repenting of sin and doing right." As he got older, he never understood "repenting" and "doing right." Preachers scared him, though he respected them. As mentioned earlier, he tried to seek the help of a preacher shortly after his amputation, but the "stuff" given didn't help him overcome his great loss. He figured that the preacher didn't know what to say or do; the preacher had no preparation for such. In the years after his amputation, his sisters continued to urge him to go to church; sometimes he did, and when he did go, he would listen a little but mostly sat and looked around. Sometimes they urged him to listen to preachers and gospel singing on the radio (after they got a radio in 1930 and when it had a good battery). Were some of the sisters more into religiosity than he was? Or, were they being overly prim and proper in the ways of fundamental religion?

During initial recovery from the accident of 1943, sisters who lived close around visited Henry and Doris at the hospital and came to see him after he was home in Tinnin. They offered their help. The married sisters would sometimes enlist their husbands in getting certain farm home jobs done, provided the husbands had the skill and understanding to do so. Taking ashes out of the wood-burning heater was one thing they helped with. They also brought in firewood to keep the fire going and drive away some of the chill in the winter air. Some of the sisters felt that Henry had helped them over the years, and now they had an opportunity to help him in return. In the first few days and weeks, they would come by to see him, sit for a while, and bring him food and water and specially made soft cookies (even though his mouth was sore from the accident and dislodging of three front teeth, he enjoyed these special treats). They would help him stand, walk, eat, dress, and the like. Edna, Sudie, and Lyda were particularly good at helping. They were always very careful to see that he didn't fall. Sometimes they would help Doris, such as washing clothing and getting the mail from the box at the main road.

A few simple wintertime chores around the farm were required. These chores included those that the husbands could help with: gathering the eggs in the henhouse, milking the cow, feeding the hogs, and keeping hickory smoke going in the smokehouse where stuffed sausage, hams, and bacon sides were curing (only a couple of husbands knew how). The pork belly in salt only needed observation to assure that there was plenty of salt and that nothing had happened to the mix of salt and mostly pork fat. No fire was needed for salting. One brother-in-law got a few sweet potatoes out of the earth storage mound for Carrie.

In late January, there was no serious work underway on the farm in terms of preparing for crops. That would come later, beginning in mid-February. During this time of early recuperation, the sisters avoided topics that would be inflammatory. Those subjects just might be brought up later by one or more sisters and brothers-in-law depending on their mood at the time and the extent to which Carrie caused disagreements. The sisters didn't want to cause stress for their healing brother.

After the initial recuperation, Henry was learning to do things for himself. The sisters didn't come around as much, but they always checked on him when they came to see Carrie.

Susie continued to live in the home and help care for Son until he was about four years of age. At that time, Susie experienced a health problem that slowed her down and zapped her energy. Carrie told her to leave—to get out of the house and go live as a charity case in the old women's home in Jackson near the zoo. No one could ever explain why the home for impoverished elderly women was near the zoo; Carrie hinted something about keeping all the monkeys together!

Susie had no transportation and was too sick to go on her own. Carrie had an ambulance to come and get Susie. The ambulance attendants brought a gurney for Susie and covered her with a water-repellant sheet as they carried the gurney from the porch out into the rain toward the ambulance. Son was very sad the day Susie was carried away. It was an overcast day of rain and sadness. It was a day that told a lot about the compassion of his grandmother, Carrie. It was a highly salient day for Son and meant the loss of the wonderful help that Doris and Henry had experienced with their son. Except for a couple of brief visits with his parents to the old women's home, that time on the gurney was the last time Son saw Susie alive. Son did go with his parents to her funeral a couple of years later.

Before Carrie sent her away, Susie Heckle helped Henry at times; occasionally she prepared food for him, such as stewed potatoes (which Doris never liked) based on memories from his childhood. More and more, Henry developed independence. He went about operating the farm and being a husband and father, as best he could.

Time came for Henry and Doris to move on to another phase in their lives. This involved using a few years of their limited savings to build a house in Clinton. They had been dedicated to saving and preparing for their future. It was now late 1946 and time to move ahead with their plans. They bought a residential lot on Monroe Street in Clinton. Henry asked around at the loafing stores about good builders. He also asked the husbands of his sisters who lived in the area about builders. Henry and Doris agreed upon Truman Mardis; he had sample architectural plans, and they chose one of them. It was a small, but modern (by 1946 standards), house constructed based on practices and materials that emerged just as World War II was ending.

Some of his sisters wished Henry and Doris well as they moved from the big Lee-Shepard farmhouse into their newly built house in Clinton on January 17, 1948. They brought gifts for a housewarming. One example was an electric table lamp; another was an electric blanket. The farmhouse in Tinnin didn't have such because there was no electricity. Maybe one or two of the sisters were envious; the sisters all had older homes, though some were in modern (for the time) condition. And, of course, questions arose in their minds about how Henry and Doris had the money to buy a lot and pay for building a house. Anyway, the total amount was less than $10,000, a good sum in the late 1940s for a farm family that owned no farm land. This amount would be only a "drop in a bucket" a few years later.

In the early 1950s, Henry still sought to overcome the side issues associated with loss of his right arm; some sisters thought that he needed spiritual help. A big movement in fundamentalist evangelism was that created by Billy Graham (who died in 2018 at age 99). This preacher was on the radio, was in the newspaper, and held crusades; he promoted himself as the nation's preacher. By 1949 he had reached celebrity status.

Graham held a nearly month-long crusade in Jackson, Mississippi, in 1952. The event took place at Belhaven College's Tiger Stadium (Belhaven was the college from which Doris had graduated). Local churches tried to organize groups and get people to go regardless of their church participation and religious feelings. People would come by to visit Henry and Doris; they would urge their attendance (particularly Henry's). The crusade was talked up at the local loafing stores. Henry's sisters offered to drive him there and get him involved; he always declined. Rather than helping him feel good about himself, such preaching typically raised more questions than it provided answers.

Henry could listen to Graham's preaching on the radio and have a moving experience. Particularly touching to Henry was Graham telling of growing up on a dairy farm in North Carolina and working hard milking the cows by hand and doing other tasks on the farm. Henry could identify with that. He could "see in his mind" the young Billy at work in the barns and fields. Graham, born in 1918, was eight years younger than Henry, but their ages were close enough for Henry to relate to Graham. It was when Graham would start talking about the Bible being the infallible word of God that Henry would lose interest. (Maybe he would think about it being written hundreds of years ago by old-timey men. But how could they write and know what to say and how to say it? Anyway, who around Tinnin knew what "infallible" and many other words used in the Bible meant?

Maybe Henry also appreciated knowing that the name of Graham's wife's father was Nelson Bell. It was a Nelson Bell (though a different man) who had helped Henry's grandmother, Ellen Loretta Shepard Lee, after her husband and Henry's grandfather died in Texas in 1870. Anyone with a name associated with helping his grandmother and his father, Ira Jasper Lee, would have a special place with Henry.

Two major Graham events happened during and shortly after the Jackson crusade that made Henry think deeply. First, Graham took on racial segregation. Some people thought he shouldn't have done so, that it might hurt the size of his crowds and the amount in the offering. On the other hand, this could increase crowd size if individuals stood with Graham on the issue. Graham publicly indicated that there was no scriptural basis for segregation. Though people in the stands at the crusade were racially segregated by the event organizers, there was "no segregation at the altar," according to Graham. This created uneasiness among the die-hard white segregationists in the community. Henry had to sort this out in his mind and afterward thought he pretty well agreed with Graham on this. Many segregationists held Graham in high regard because they were also fundamentalist churchgoers, but they had some difficulty accepting this segregation statement. (The Mississippi Humanities Council reports on the 1952 Billy Graham Crusade on its website at mshumanities.org.) The next year at a crusade in Chattanooga, Tennessee, Graham removed ropes that had been put up by the local organizers to keep white and black people separate. Graham was somewhat ahead of his time on this. A blessing!

The second major Graham event was the release of his book *Peace with God*. This book was a part of what Graham called a "well-rounded collection of quality Christian literature." He encouraged everyone to buy the book and heed its teachings. So, Henry bought a copy that he kept in his home without ever reading a word of it. In the back of his mind, Henry always thought it was a way for Graham to build fame and make money.

By the time television broadcasting made it to central Mississippi in 1953, Graham was a regular on it (mostly replaying his crusades), and Henry often watched his programs. He particularly liked to hear vocalist George Beverly Shea sing "How Great Thou Art." Shea, accompanied by a strong pianist, could so clearly and passionately perform as a vocalist with many hymns. Henry would listen to Shea over and over; Doris would do so as well. The hymns, along with Graham's preaching, inspired Henry and Doris to send small contributions to Graham's ministry from time to time. To send money to a preacher was not something that they had ever done until the Jackson crusade. Henry told one of his sisters that he was sending contributions, and the sister gave him a big hug. "You are making God proud," she said, "and I am proud of you."

Was it the preaching to save his soul from eternal hell, or was it the entertainment that Henry liked? Hard to say, but he wasn't much afraid of the hellfire stuff. Separating reality into truths and falsehoods wasn't easy. Overall, Henry remained cynical about preachers trying to get him to act in a certain way. But one thing was certain: he confided in Son that he often said silent prayers in his mind when facing difficult situations or when expressing gratitude for his blessings in life.

The crusade by Graham brought attention to getting involved in local fundamentalist Christian churches, such as Southern Baptist and Methodist. Ministers of the churches capitalized on the crusade as a basis for promoting attendance at Sunday preaching and other church activities as well as putting more cash into the church offering. Henry was influenced by all events surrounding the crusade; his interest in church participation was raised, but that doesn't mean he attended any more frequently.

Each of the sisters married; two had no children. Henry and his seven siblings had a total of only nine biological children for the next generation of descendants of the marriage of Ira Jasper Lee and Carrie Cheers Hendrick in 1901. (Carrie and Ira produced nine babies by themselves.) From one perspective, there weren't many descendants around to visit the older folks when they were in their declining years.

The ability of Henry's siblings and their spouses to support children greatly improved over the economic situation of Ira and Carrie. Some of the siblings and their spouses did well economically. They had lives of plenty and did not suffer deprivation in daily living. The siblings and their spouses were better educated and qualified to pursue career and economic goals. Those with the most apparent wealth had no children. Maybe they were too busy pursuing career goals and wealth to consider the roles of children in their lives. Or, maybe, their own childhoods were not very happy, and they didn't wish to expose another generation to those same unpleasantries. Who knows?

With education, they knew enough about conception to limit the birth of children. Previous generations produced more children than needed to sustain the human population. Some died during birth, and others from health situations and disease that, by the mid-1900s, had been found to be preventable. Death of women from childbirth and pregnancy complications was reduced through prenatal care and competent assistance in the delivery of babies. In the past, a family's being large added to its poverty and hardship.

The living arrangements and female imbalance might have been a factor in something a physician discovered about Henry's young life after he was 70 years of age. As his health was failing and Henry was experiencing the onset of Alzheimer's disease, an in-depth medical examination was quite revealing. (Although this was also discussed elsewhere in this book, including it twice is justified because of its seriousness and his ability to be strong in face of his amputation.) Henry had been abused as a child.

Exactly how the physician was able to establish this is unknown. Maybe Henry's mind had failed to the point where it no longer guarded how he spoke. He had let down his barriers about unpleasant subjects. No family members were present during the examination in Starkville. Son was stunned when the information was shared with him by Dr. John Copeland after the examination had been completed. Son failed to make inquiries of the doctor about it; maybe it was the shock of hearing such about his own father. Son felt that it might be a subject better left undiscussed. Son never told Doris what he had learned. Did she already know and never spoke of it?

That didn't keep questions from arising. Who was the perpetrator? How old was Henry when it happened? Was it once or multiple times? What was the nature of the abuse? Sexual? Since Henry did not have a private room (even the small space he had under the stairs where he slept was not secure) and there was a female imbalance in the home, answers tended to focus on one or more of the sisters or maybe an adult female who occasionally lived in the house when they could no longer stay at their own homes. Surely, how Henry related to his sisters was influenced by this experience if, in fact, it happened, and the evidence is good that it did. But, maybe sexual abuse was by a male in the community, one who worked on the farm or one who went to school with Henry. All the previous experiences in his life contributed to his ability to handle the loss of an arm. It is doubtful that abuse as a child contributed anything other than more hardship and reduced ability to deal with fragile situations.

Relationships of Henry with his sisters, and of them with each other, changed over the years. Time tended to heal any wounds created by personal differences. All of them except Lyda (and she was the youngest sister) died before Henry. None of their descendants had much contact in any way or visited him while in nursing home care in his final years. However, that doesn't mean that they didn't care; they had their own health issues.

Lyda and her husband attended Henry's funeral service. The adult children of a couple of his sisters (Henry's nieces and nephews) also attended. But, for the most part, Henry's descendants did not show up for the final celebration of his life. What does this say about their appreciation of Henry for all that he did for the family, including protecting his sisters from their perceived dangers, such as when they walked to the two-holer in the dark? The quick answer: Not much. Most survivors didn't know much about life in Tinnin at the Lee-Shepard house. Maybe some had hard feelings. Maybe others thought he was disabled and not a complete man and they simply wanted to stay away from him. The reasons will never be known. One thing for certain is that Henry loved each of his sisters.

As this chapter ends, it is incomplete in one way but complete in another. Yes, there was an imbalance of females—that much we know. Yes, some of Henry's sisters promoted religion to him. The matter of child molestation is unsettled; who, when, here, how, and why remain unanswered. An appropriate ending might be: "Make your own reality even if false."

Henry at his Grandfather's Grave Marker in Smith Cemetery, Henderson County, Texas, 1978. (Henry and his grandfather had the same name: Jasper Henry Lee [1827-1870].)

18

Mellowing in Life

By middle age, Henry had accepted changes in goals and realized that all he had hoped to achieve was now impossible. He had now softened and become more gentle. He had shown greater understanding and sympathy toward others. Some people said he was mellowing.

A new technology for home entertainment began moving into the Deep South in 1953: broadcast television. One tv station began broadcasting in Jackson that year, and another the following year. In early 1954, a 17-inch Emerson black-and-white television set found its way into the Lee household. An outside antenna was installed on the house. Neighbors came to see this picture-box device! The local and national news and weather were on the schedule for each evening. And, if being broadcast, the Ed Sullivan Show, Groucho Marx, and Texas rasslin' would be among the evening programs. In a few years the black-and-white TV was replaced with a color RCA 23-inch set. Now that was something! Just to think that Henry had first experienced radio less than thirty years before! Television brought a new sequence to daily routine (and warnings from the fundamentalist church folks that these devices would destroy the morals of America).

Now what about the Lee farming enterprise?

Henry began reducing his farming activity in the mid-1950s. Of course, this could have been partially due to changes in farm technology and the need for greater attention to market-driven agriculture. Hard-labor sharecropping was ending. Internal-combustion engine power was replacing animal power. Powered devices were replacing hand labor. Mechanical cotton pickers were coming on the scene, as well as corn harvesters, combines, planters, and sprayers. Such equipment required capital investment and skilled operators. The decision was made to rent out the best cropland to another farmer.

With a wooded area of about 90 acres included in the farm property, there were numerous oaks, hickories, and sweetgums and a few pines; oaks were most desired for firewood. Henry hired a laborer to cut and split wood. Some hickory was cut and split into special sizes for restaurants in Jackson that cooked with hickory wood; hickory made wonderful barbecue! The prominent Rotisserie Restaurant (located at the five points intersection on U. S. Highway 49 in Jackson) was one of the restaurants.

The oak wood was cut and split for firewood, sold and delivered by the pickup load to the increasingly affluent residents in Clinton. These people included fireplaces in their homes, even when they had central heat and air conditioning. Such fireplaces were not essential for heat, as they had been in the Shepard home. It was amazing to Henry that people would pay "good money" for the firewood from trees growing on land that had little other use. Of course, it was delivered on schedule and stacked just where the buyers wanted it for convenience. Henry still produced a few vegetable crops, such as purple hull peas, for sale to individuals and through a few local stores.

Producing cotton required increased technology. The boll weevil (*Anthonomes grandis*) was a major pest with cotton that migrated into the Tinnin area in the early 1900s. It could virtually destroy a crop; there were also a few other pests, such as boll worms (which feed on cotton squares and bolls) and thrips (a species of very small insects that suck juice from plant leaves). Steps were taken to kill these pests. Home remedies, such as fireplace ashes and dried dung from under the roost in the chicken house, didn't do much good.

People began to turn to commercially available chemicals typically manufactured in dust form (a few liquid forms were sprayed if the farm had a sprayer). The chemicals would be blown along rows onto the growing cotton plants using hand dusters, mule-pulled dusters, tractor-equipped dusters and sprayers (for liquid insecticides), and specially equipped crop-dusting airplanes (in the later 1950s). Quite a dust cloud would often develop as an insecticide diffused into the air. People operating the equipment or otherwise in the field or close by would inhale some of the dust. Their skin and clothing might be dusty white because of a covering of the poisonous substance. In the early years of use, people didn't think much about being exposed to insecticides because they hadn't used anything like them before. They didn't know the health hazards of the chemicals in the insecticides.

Obviously, the chemicals used to control cotton pests were poisonous. Among the first used was DDT (nice that we have a short name, DDT, for dichlorodiphenyltrichloroethane). DDT first became available to the public in 1945 after its use in World War II to control mosquitoes and other disease-carrying pests in remote locations where soldiers were in action. Cotton farmers quickly took to using it for its effectiveness on the boll weevil. But, things began to go bad. First, boll weevils developed resistance, so DDT no longer worked well. Second, it affected everything in the environment, such as killing wildlife, particularly the national bird of the United States, the bald eagle. A book by Rachel Carson in 1962 entitled *Silent Spring* focused attention on problems with DDT. In 1972 the use of DDT in agriculture was banned. A good bit of attention focused on DDT as a cause of cancer in humans.

Other insecticides were introduced in an attempt to conquer the boll weevil. Malathion, methyl parathion, and pyrethroids were used in dusts and sprays applied to cotton fields. Agronomists and entomologists knew that better methods of control were needed. Parasitic wasps were experimentally introduced into some fields, but if an insecticide was used, the wasps would be killed. Applying a specific species of fungus to crops in fields was also tried (the chosen species was known to attack larval boll weevils); a virus was also tried with limited success.

The U.S. Department of Agriculture became involved with a visionary program of boll weevil eradication. It took a massive, well-coordinated effort by cotton producers, scientists, and commercial companies in the cotton industry. All cotton-growing areas of the United States participated. Scientists had determined the life cycle of the boll weevil. A significant finding was that female weevils mated only once in their lives. If a female weevil mated with a sterile male, the eggs would be infertile, and no larval pest forms would develop. The female would never mate again. Sure enough, that was sound reasoning. A wide-ranging program was initiated.

A Boll Weevil Research Laboratory was established at Mississippi State University for the purpose of developing methods to eradicate the pesky weevil. A major part of the work focused on reproducing the weevil pests by the millions, disposing of the female offspring, and sterilizing the males. Once sterile, the males were released into the cotton areas where female weevils were present and ready to mate. It worked! After a few years, weevil populations declined. Cotton growers also took steps to support eradication. Stalks left in the fields after harvest were chopped so that they would not serve as hiding places for adult weevils over the winter. Homeowners were asked not to plant cotton in flower beds and other places where weevils could hide.

Within a few years, the boll weevil was eradicated in the United States except for a few locations along the border with Mexico. The eradication was too late for Henry; he had already been exposed to harmful chemicals. On the other hand, it was never determined if the boll weevil insecticides had anything to do with his health deterioration. However, long-term research findings have determined an association between such chemicals and neurological deterioration as well as cancer and other health issues.

A part of reducing row-crop farming involved starting a cow-calf operation, which was also known as feeder calf production. Hill land and some creek bottom land were put into pasture so beef cattle could be added. Raising calves for selling at auctions and to buyers for feedlot operators in the western states was increasingly being done in central Mississippi. Henry had begun going in that direction with a small beginning herd of grade Hereford cows and a bull. Henry had mentioned what he was doing to the associate county agricultural agent, a Mr. Owens, when he saw him at the Ratliff Store in Tinnin. Agent Owens said he would stop by the farm in a couple of days to talk about what to do and how to do it for success with feeder calves; a man of his word, Mr. Owens made his visit.

He talked with Henry about a number of factors in being successful with a cow-calf operation. He indicated that good, healthy cows and bulls were needed. He recommended having one herd bull for about every twenty-five cows to assure breeding. He said it was best if the cows to be bred to calve in February or early March. With an average gestation of 283 days, bulls should put in the cow herd in late April of the preceding year. Calves would be born when the grass began to grow in the spring. With cows that are good milk producers for calves and with a good pasture, the calves should weigh 375 to 400 or more pounds by frost in the fall of the year.

Mr. Owens said the cattle needed to have a beef animal conformation to meet demands of the feedlots in the West. The animals should have a body build with meat in the right places, such as high value retail cuts. An animal with good conformation yields a higher proportion of the desired meats cuts when slaughtered (at a weight of 1,000 or so pounds); desired conformation improves the price that will be paid for an animal. He talked about feeding and pasturing, watering, herd health, and castration.

One of his main points was that cattle must be healthy and have needed nutrition to grow. He talked about vaccinating for blackleg, Bang's disease, and lepto (short for leptospirosis). He covered parasites, such as flies, intestinal worms, ticks, lice, and grubs. And, one final thing Mr. Owens stressed: facilities. Good fences and handling equipment, including a corral, squeeze chute, and loading dock, were needed. Henry said he would try to provide what was necessary; nothing much was ever needed in the past with the couple of milk cows that were kept on the farm.

Mr. Owens indicated that bull calves should be castrated when a few days of age. He explained that castration involved removing the testicles ("bull jewels" in farm language) so that the calves would not breed (afterward, such animals are known as steers). Castration also alters hormones in animals so that they don't grow like bulls. A younger calf is easier to restrain and less likely to injure the person holding it and the person performing the procedure. He said that most producers in the county surgically castrated calves with a sharp knife. Proper practices, including sanitation to prevent infection, were essential. He suggested quickly washing the area with creosote dip before cutting off the lower tip of the scrotum. A bull calf would grow more efficiently as a steer and bring a higher price when sold. Mr. Owens said he would come back early Thursday morning and demonstrate how to castrate a bull calf. He asked Henry to have the calves rounded up and some help to corral and restrain the calves.

Henry did what he was asked to do; Mr. Owens came and began with the first calf. Of course, Henry had only one arm, and surgical bull calf castration requires two hands plus "holders." So, Mr. Owens did all twelve calves that morning. One of the farm hands who helped hold the calves for castration asked for the testicles and wanted them kept clean. He said, "Dem chillun of mine would sho nuf eat'em after de bees fried in lard grease. Da likes dem osters."

It was time for Mr. Owens to go; he said to contact him if he could be of help or wanted him to come back by the farm. Henry called on him a number of times over the next few years, but that began to fade away in the 1960s.

Times were changing; some parts of Southern society, and of agriculture, were under duress to accommodate change. And overall, it was good! You see, Mr. Owens had skin that was rather dark; he worked for a segregated Extension Service intended to help black farmers. But, he didn't view skin color as a problem; he helped everyone who asked. Mr. Owens was a practical, knowledgeable person. Court action and other decisions resulted in changes so that he was no longer in Hinds County. Too bad; Henry lost a real source of help from a reliable and capable person who would come to his farm.

Downsizing the farm was taking place in other ways. Some of the property was converted to a quarry for red clay sand used in building and road construction in Jackson. Red clay sand was widely used as the base for concrete floors for buildings and parking areas as well as for streets before blacktop was placed. Large equipment was used to load dump trucks with four to eight cubic yards of sand. These trucks could reach many construction sites in the Jackson area in twenty minutes.

In fact, the original Jackson Mall (located on East Woodrow Wilson Drive) was constructed on a base of red sand from the Lee property. Opened in the late 1960s as the first shopping mall in the state of Mississippi, it later became the Jackson Medical Mall. The change came about in the mall property because of the failure of some department stores to ever locate in it (preferring, instead, to stay in downtown locations), declining retail sales due to competition from other retail locations, and a surrounding community that was changing. This Medical Mall was to serve the medical care needs of the urban poor people in Jackson. (A side note: The site of the Jackson Mall was previously the Baptist Children's Home and Farm, or, as called by some, "The Orphanage." It moved to a modern site in Clinton not far from the public high school.)

The quarry was an area on top of a large hill that reportedly had the distinction of being the second highest elevation in Hinds County (known in the community as Shepard's Hill). Just before the quarry was begun, Henry received a solicitation to sell the hill to a company that was constructing long-distance relay towers for the telephone company, but that fell through. After a few years, it no longer had the second tallest hill distinction. Trucks had hauled thousands of cubic yards of sand away. The sand quarry land was soon sold to a company in Jackson that mined sand.

Once the supply of easily mined sand had been exhausted, the pit that remained became a disposal area for building construction wastes; no household garbage was allowed. Old wood from demolitions was put in the disposal pit. Maybe this was not an aesthetically good use of the acres, but Henry justified it because of the good price the company paid for the land. He thought of this hilly, elevated, sandy, wooded land remaining from an ancient body of water that is today the Gulf of Mexico as near worthless. It certainly was not a good location for cotton! It had mostly remained in woods and, on one side, was the source of the large limestone rocks used in the foundation of the Shepard home. Slaves had quarried the rock in 1857 using mostly hand labor and simple tools. Draft animals were used to move the quarried rock to the house site. In Henry's mind, using the land for sand at the rate of 5 cents per cubic yard hauled away was the highest available economic return.

Could this downsizing be fulfillment of the notions that Henry's brother-in-law, Dr. Davis, harshly presented a few months after the amputation in 1943? He had challenged the ability of Henry to operate the farm after he had lost his right arm. Maybe that weighed on Henry's mind. Maybe it contributed to other health issues. No doubt, the loss of the arm greatly restricted some farming activities that had been so much a part of Henry's life.

Henry and Doris knew their son was reaching adulthood; they realized he was ready to go out on his own. In 1963, he got a degree in agriculture from Mississippi State University (a name change from the early times when aspirations included a college degree for Son from Mississippi A&M College). Son found the love of his life and taught high school agriculture. Marriage and graduate school at the University of Illinois were followed by two grandchildren. And those two grandchildren were adored by Henry and Doris! It seemed that Henry was able to fulfill some of his lifelong dreams.

Hollywood came calling! In 1977, Harold Phillips, the director of the Mississippi Film Office, made a stop at the farm and talked with Henry. He was scouting for a site for a Hollywood movie production company to make a film. An agreement was reached over the next few days, and the details were worked out.

Several trucks pulling large trailers arrived in a few weeks from Hollywood; they had to be parked in a location convenient to filming and safe from onlookers. One trailer served as a kitchen, where lunch was typically prepared. Tables and chairs were set up for outside dining under tree canopies. It was common for 70 people to have their noon meals on location. Water and snacks were available

throughout filming activity. Another trailer was compartmental-
ized for dressing rooms, costume storage, makeup, and restrooms.
A third trailer was loaded with equipment to be used in the filming.
Adjustments were made to buildings, fences, and farm roads to
gain desired color and appearance. Antique cars were brought in.
Electric and telephone lines, such as existed, were taken down and
poles removed in some locations.

Local authorities of the Hinds County sheriff's office were involved in controlling traffic on roads in the area, particularly when
filming was underway on Lifer Road, which adjoined the farm. A
deputy sheriff was always present to direct any traffic around the
filming site (sometimes blocking the road). The filming area needed
silence during filming on location.

The film entitled *Roll of Thunder, Hear My Cry* was made on
location at the Lee plantation in Tinnin, Mississippi. That was something special! The story was based on the book by the same name
that was the 1977 Newberry Medal winner by author Mildred D.
Taylor. It dealt with racism in the South during the Depression of
the 1930s. The fictional Logan family lived in the Lee-Shepard house
and grew cotton, corn, and vegetable crops. Scenes were filmed in
the house, barns, fields, and forests and elsewhere in the community.
These sites were altered to appear as they would have in the 1930s.

The film had roles for Hollywood stars as well as numerous local
people. The major Hollywood star was Morgan Freeman. And, yes,
Henry had a minor role in a scene in front of a nearby store. He was
described by a story in the October 27, 1977, *Clinton News* as receiving the best supporting spectator award. The Oscar Jones family lived
in the Lee-Shepard house and virtually moved out for the period
of October 17 through November 17. The filming created a bright
glimmer of enthusiasm in Henry's life. It made him feel better all
around, particularly when he received a letter from the governor of
Mississippi thanking him for making the farm available for filming.

Initially shown on ABC television as a three-part series, advance information about the broadcast dates was spread about the community; the film was highly watched by local citizens. Some of the local people were upset; the film dealt with sensitive topics, such as nightriders burning houses, threats made by white people against people of color, and some white people befriending people of color. Overall, the Logan family was portrayed as a very honest and sincere family.

After the showing, Henry received numerous hateful and disturbing telephone calls about the content of the film. Most callers never identified themselves. Some of them were very racist in their remarks. They lashed out at him with disgraceful insults, such as "you sorry SOB," and threats, such as those of farm property damage, and quickly hung up the phone. The callers (usually sounded like white men) could not understand why Henry would allow a film about the plight of blacks to be made on his farm. They untruthfully said it would destroy the entire Tinnin community (it was already changing for other reasons). Some individuals confronted him out in the community, such as when he went to Russell's Store located on Monroe Street near where he lived.

Truth be known, the filming activity created economic gain at the small Ratliff Store in Tinnin and nearby stores in Clinton. The out-of-state film personnel stayed at hotels in Jackson. There was an established tradition of filmmakers lodging in Jackson because it was a place where restaurants had black market liquor before the repeal of prohibition a few years earlier (1966) by statewide vote. Within a few weeks of the showing, most things returned to normal.

In the early 1980s, the dwindling Pocahontas Methodist Church (name of denomination changed from Methodist Episcopal Church, South to United Methodist Church in 1968), which had meant so much to Henry and his family, was struggling. With only a dozen active members, it was fortunate to still be alive with a worship service on the first and third Sundays of each month by a retired minister who also had another job. The tiny cotton-ginning village of Pocahontas (where the church was located) was not thriving. Current citizens were getting old, some were unable to get out of their homes, others had died, and still others had moved to other places. In a few cases, the people were not interested in church participation because of its history favorable to the keeping of slaves.

The Pocahontas Methodist Church, located in the tiny village of Pocahontas, Mississippi, was constructed in 1902 and removed from service in 1987. (It served as the church home for some of the Lee family. Note the barely visible cemetery in back with gravesites of several family members.)

The wooden-frame church building was constructed in 1902 and needed major repairs. The roof was old and leaky; any structural repairs have to wait for a good roof. (The Pocahontas Baptist Church had already relocated to a new site nearer Jackson. Maybe closer proximity to a population base was a big factor in the move.

Could the move have been because of the evangelism notion that there were more sinners who needed to be saved?)

Henry, somewhat unlike his usual behavior over the years toward community needs, took it upon himself to get a roof on the building. He solicited contributions from church members, friends of members, and individuals who had grown up in the Pocahontas community and who had attended the church. He found a man in the roofing business who lived in Jackson; he would put on a new roof at minimal cost. That was done, along with a few other structural repairs and the addition of running water and improved electrical services. Henry was so proud of what he had done.

Improving the facility had a slightly positive effect on attendance among the old-time members and put off deactivation by the Mississippi Conference of the United Methodist Church. Some Sundays, a few people would show up and all sit in the back row; the preacher would come to the third row from the back to preach and lead worship. The few congregants might try to sing a hymn or two under direction of the preacher, who wasn't much better with music than the people he was leading. Old hymn books were in racks on the backs of the pews. Services in the building were ended in 1987. Henry, because of his declining health, was not aware of this, and if he had been told, he would not have known what it meant. On the other hand, if he had been in his right mind and known, he would have been very sad. That church was a special place to him.

Henry mellowed, and it didn't go unnoticed by those around him. He demonstrated greater compassion toward other people and supported community causes with more enthusiasm. But, as he aged, he was transitioning into frailties associated with the aging process.

19

Facing Frailties

Life is the quality that distinguishes the living from the nonliving. Dreams are made and fulfilled. A legacy of peace and love endures. Did a near-death experience increase the meaning Henry drew from life? Maybe, but there were many issues he had to endure in life as he aged.

Aging seemed to arrive early with Henry. Maybe it was associated with the tragedy of 1943; maybe it was due to something else. But, he had a full life.

Most of the time, Son was close by or could be in a few hours, ready to be a part of what was needed. As an adult, he always wondered about something: Could Henry's declining health have been related to a party that Doris held in the summer of 1950? It was an innocent party.

Eight women (school teachers, neighbors, and Sunday school class members) came to it. Doris' home was new (two years old) and a place some people wanted to visit. It was not elegant or luxurious but comfortable. Few new homes had been built after World War II along Monroe Street. People wanted to see the inside construction.

They wanted to see the electric lights, floor furnace, bathroom fixtures, and kitchen cabinets. Doris would also make extra effort to be a good hostess. Plus, there would be incentives offered at the party that some of the women might find appealing. More about the party later.

Henry thought Doris was losing her ability to drive safely. He reported such to their son in the early 1980s. He told of instances where she would run over the curb in turning, go into a parking place wrong, and stop way short of a traffic light at an intersection. She didn't drive much except to the grocery store, appointments with local physicians, and to church. As Henry described her driving, it appeared that her brain and muscles sometimes didn't work well together to do what needed to be done. Maybe there wasn't good communication between her brain and her hands and feet. Coordination appeared compromised, but still she had to carry on with life. She had to go to the grocery store and drive Henry and herself to the doctor. A few years earlier, Doris recognized some of her decline and, after 40 years, retired from teaching in 1978. (The day of retirement was special to Doris; the school board recognized her with the gift of an engraved silver tea service.)

Now it was 1987, some forty-four years after the accident; Henry was in his late seventies. Hospital records of his accident were not available for reference by physicians when Henry now had health issues for which the records might have been useful. Were the health problems he experienced associated with the accident, with aging, or something else? Henry sometimes appeared disoriented and forgetful. He had a hard time remembering people and names, but he usually came up with the names if he knew them. He would leave the house to drive to the farm and go in the opposite direction. Doris would have to send someone to help him get back home or headed toward the farm. Declines in driving ability were contrasts: Doris had deteriorated motor skills, and Henry had early deterioration of mental skills associated with direction and driving. He could still operate vehicle controls; Doris was losing the ability to operate controls in driving a vehicle, including direction in steering.

Henry became an irresponsible driver. When told not to leave, he would go anyway; he usually failed to follow instructions. The time had come: Henry had to give up keys to the pickup. Not good! Doris had no success when she asked for the keys. Taking them became Son's responsibility on a weekend when he was in Clinton. Merely asking for them did not work. When Son asked for his father to give him his keys to the pickup, Henry asked why; Son told him that it was time to let someone else drive for him. What an explosion! Henry was being threatened with losing one of the freedoms he had enjoyed for many long years.

"No! You aren't taking my damn keys!" Henry exclaimed. "You are a lowdown, good-for-nothing scoundrel for wanting to take my keys."

"Think about it," Son responded. "Sometimes all of us need to do something we don't want to do. This is for your safety as well as that of other people. This is for the well-being and safety of your wife. Understand?"

"Hell no, I don't understand crap like that," Henry said, "and I will kick your ass if you ever mention this again. My keys are mine, and don't you forget it. How could I have raised you to be this way?"

About that time Doris called them to lunch, meager though it was. All was calm during dining time.

Once the meal was over, Henry said he was going to check out things on the farm (a five-mile drive in the pickup). Son volunteered to drive, and this was fine with Henry, as it in no way challenged or threatened him. They rode out along the blacktop road and turned into the farm road to the barns and equipment shed. They got out and looked around; the tractor with attached pasture clipper was under the shed with other equipment that had seen little use in the past few years. Everything seemed in order. Henry appeared quite all right.

Next, they drove the trail to the pasture, where they saw cows and a few calves that belonged to a Mr. Milner (who rented the pastureland). Henry's mental processes were usually good when he was in a familiar place, though today he thought the cows were his and was wondering about when he could sell some calves. He wanted to know where the black bulls were; the cows needed bulls around. Henry wasn't satisfied with the explanation that the cows were artificially inseminated and made some sort of comment about what the bulls might be thinking. They then drove farther back on the farm to the creek bottoms that were also used as pastureland. After that, it was time to go back to Clinton.

As they were leaving the farm and turning onto the Clinton-Tinnin Road, Henry said that he wanted to see Mr. Tom. After a few moments, Son figured he was talking about Tom Baker, who ran Baker's Store in Pocahontas. So they turned the pickup around and headed to Pocahontas. Along the way, Henry forgot where they were going, and when they pulled into the parking lot of Baker's Store, he said, "This isn't my home. I want to go home." They stopped at the store anyway and greeted Mr. Baker and then went home to Clinton. When they got to the home, Henry was calm; all was familiar and routine; nothing was new in his environment. Upon getting out of the pickup, Son removed the keys and put them in his pocket without a word.

Physicians did not have a ready explanation for Henry's condition, so they recommended physical, neurological, and psychological examinations. A CT scan of his head and brain was ordered to see what might be found as related to the behavior he was demonstrating. On September 29, 1987, the Jackson Radiology Associates conducted the CT scan at Hinds General Hospital. The findings:

senile dementia. More findings following neurological and psychological examinations also revealed senile dementia. Further examination indicated that it was one of the ten types of dementia known as Alzheimer's disease. Alzheimer's! How much of this development was related to the January 20, 1943, accident, and how much just to aging is unknown. Probably both contributed. On the other hand, maybe there were some things in his environment that had played a part in it.

Everyone was curious: Why Henry? What was the cause of his condition? Was there something in his daily living environment? Doris and other people assessed factors in Henry's environment. Several possible associations arose: residue of atomic activity during World War II and other air pollution, handling of corn produced from hybrid seed, tobacco use, and the farm environment. Each of these as sources was considered in detail. Wartime atomic activity was ruled out, as most of it was at least 1,500 miles away at test sites in a couple of western states. Of course, there was testing in the 1950s of atomic-powered airplanes some 400 miles away in Dawson Forest near Dahlonega, Georgia, but no one thought these tests could have contributed to the decline of Henry's health. Handling corn grown from hybrid seed posed no hazard. Nutrition might have been a source but highly unlikely; his diet included many vegetables.

After many years of using tobacco (roll-your-own cigarettes and chewing tobacco), he quit after he was sternly warned by a physician in Clinton by the name of Dr. Reynolds, but this did not mean that the residual effect of earlier use did not remain as a potential cause.

The farm environment was left as a possible factor. There were many potential sources on the farm, particularly from the newer methods being used. These sources included exposure to tractor fuels and oils, polluted water from animal production, hazards from lead paint and mercury used in farm equipment and structures, and inputs used in crop production. Of course, being outside on a farm provided good, fresh air. Maybe that fresh air would overcome the "bad" air that was breathed at other times.

A likely source of contamination was any of the various chemical substances used in cotton production. Particularly used were insecticides on cotton plants to kill pesky boll weevils. These insects would destroy the developing squares and bolls. (A square is an emerging bud that, when mature, opens into a white flower that turns a pinkish color the second day. A boll is the fruit that develops following the flower and matures to open with white seed cotton.)

Another possible cause of Henry's declining health might have been the use of aluminum cookware in food preparation. How did the cookware become so prominent in this discussion? Remember the party in 1950? It was a cookware party involving a nationally-known brand made with aluminum. Aluminum cooking utensils were first made in the early 1900s but languished on the market until after World War II (during the war, production of cookware was stopped in favor of metal products needed in the war). A kitchen without this cookware was incomplete, or so many women of that era thought.

Somehow, Doris and a sales representative made contact. He promoted the party, brought lots of sample cookware, and prepared certain food items on Doris's new natural gas stove. Yes, the representative made a big splash. Several of those who attended wound up buying at least a small set of the cookware to replace cast-iron and enameled pots and pans in their kitchens. Those thick aluminum cooking vessels would retain heat and, once they were heated, the gas flame could be turned quite low (saving the cost of gas). Doris found the cookware appealing. With incentives provided for hosting the party, she bought a large set of various-sized boilers, frying pans, and the like.

Every meal for years involved one or two items that had been cooked in the aluminum-ware. Peas, beans, or greens were usually served at every noon and evening meal and prepared in the cookware. Acidic foods, such as tomatoes, were not to be cooked in the aluminum-ware (the acid and the aluminum tended to have a reaction; stainless-steel or enameled pots and pans were used with acidic foods). Over time and use, the aluminum created an aluminum oxide that coated the surfaces. Doris never gave up, however, the cast-iron skillet used in frying sliced pork belly and other meats and the corn-bread stick pan used in baking corn bread.

The association between Alzheimer's disease and food prepared in aluminum cookware did not come about for some thirty years after the party. Why did it take so long? The amount of aluminum from cookware that entered food during cooking was low, but the leaching was repeated each and every day with the meals that were prepared. The human body could tolerate this low level, or, at least, that is what people thought. Over years of daily exposure, the body began to be influenced by the aluminum. At one time, the World Health Organization estimated that cooking a meal in an aluminum pan could add 1-2 mg of aluminum to food. The human body was thought to absorb some of this aluminum.

Some studies have shown aluminum cookware to be linked to degenerative brain disease, including both Alzheimer's and Parkinson's. Such research resulted in coating aluminum with copper, stainless steel, and other products to reduce exposure to aluminum by people who ate food prepared in aluminum cookware. A layered product known as cladware was introduced. Manufacture of this product involved putting a thin layer of steel or copper over the aluminum. Another practice sometimes used in the aluminum cookware industry was anodizing, which is a process of increasing the thickness of the natural oxide layer on the surface of the aluminum to limit leaching of aluminum into food products during cooking. The association between human health and aluminum cookware has been challenged, and some authorities say that aluminum pots and pans are perfectly safe. The impact of aluminum cookware on the lives of Henry and Doris will never be known, but questions continue.

As at other times in their married life and now facing her own health challenges, Doris set out to learn about Henry's condition and to support him as much as she could. She studied various materials that were available to her about Alzheimer's disease. She first read that it sadly causes brain cells to malfunction and ultimately die. However, the physical death of the person afflicted with it is likely due to one or more secondary causes, such as pneumonia, heart failure, and infected bedsores.

She learned about the so-called seven progressive stages of Alzheimer's disease. The stages begin with outward normal behavior, followed by very mild changes. Forgetting and misplacing things are a part of these stages. Mild decline is next, in which the person forgets something that was just heard or asks the same question over and over. Sometimes the person has trouble planning and organizing things. Moderate decline involves forgetting months and seasons and having trouble preparing food or ordering in a restaurant. Even writing a check correctly is evidence of moderate decline. Symptoms become more pronounced with moderately severe and severe decline. Remembering is a big issue, particularly with simple things, such as the person's telephone number and home address. Help may be needed in selecting and putting on appropriate clothing, including underwear, outer clothing, socks, and shoes.

As the disease advances, the person with Alzheimer's may confuse a spouse for a mother or father, need help going to the toilet, and require assistance in taking a bath. The affected individual often likes music, looking at old pictures, and reading. Sometimes the Alzheimer's patient may develop delusions about things such as, with a farmer, the need to check on crops or livestock or otherwise go to work, even when not having worked in years. The final stage is very severe decline. This is evident with the loss of basic abilities, such walking, eating, and sitting.

Doris learned that Alzheimer's patients may demonstrate hostility toward the caregiver, probably because the patient forgets who he or she is. And, of course, the person may die before having lived through all the stages. Doris recognized she might have some difficult years ahead. It was overwhelming, but she redoubled her efforts to provide the best care she could for Henry.

One document that she found quite helpful and often referred to was "Coping and Caring: Living with Alzheimer's Disease." Published by the American Association of Retired Persons (AARP), it was written for easy understanding by a person who did not have a medical background. This publication explained Alzheimer's disease, gave suggestions for coping with a loved one who had it, and offered sources of additional help. A focus was on caregiving.

The effects of Alzheimer's disease became increasingly evident. Henry did not remember things well or know the people who had been around him for years. He would sometimes do strange things, such as telling a police officer to arrest Son. That incident went like this: Son was giving him a ride around town to break up his day and provide some variety in his life. Taking him out for a bit gave Doris a break from having to continually look after him. As part of the ride, they stopped briefly at a store to get something. While Son was in the store, a police car came into the parking lot and drove along each row of parked vehicles. Somehow Henry saw the patrol car and motioned for it to stop. The officer saw Henry and stopped to say hello (check on him). Henry told the officer that his son should be arrested. The officer asked why, and Henry replied something like, "He just needs to be, and taken to jail." By then, the officer had concluded that Henry had some sort of mental issues. Son returned from the store just as the officer was getting back in his patrol car. Nothing more came of this incident. Henry didn't remember Son or his vehicle. Henry likely thought he had been taken hostage by some strange man!

Henry could also become agitated easily. Any difference in his environment could set off an explosion of rebellious behavior and language. Once an episode began, Doris was sometimes not effective in quickly ending it. Henry was not physically aggressive, as that had never been his response to Doris. Sometimes he wanted to leave or go away from where he was—that is, run away from where he was. Increasingly, it appeared that agitation would be manifested by language or vocalization. This included using profanity and describing other people in undesirable ways. For example, he would sometimes refer to his beloved wife with bad words he had never used before when speaking about her, such as calling her bitch and whore. The source of the agitation was usually unknown. Everyone learned to avoid sudden changes in his environment and gradually introduced new ways of doing things. He seemingly had little self-control.

In addition to keeping the "Coping and Caring" publication, Doris also documented many of the couple's experiences with a diary. She recorded major events related to how Henry was doing and to how he was responding to efforts to provide him appropriate care. Entries were not made each day, but as salient events occurred, an entry might be made that covered several days or weeks. It seems that information in the diary is accurate and straightforward in terms of what Doris observed and experienced.

Doris knew they had to do something; caring for Henry was not easy. She knew she was declining in her ability to run a household. In the fall of 1987, they decided to sell their home in Clinton and move into an apartment in Starkville, Mississippi, near Son. Disposing of a lifetime of belongings, some with deep sentimental memories, was not easy. This was a sad time for Doris and Henry, but it was the best that could be made of their situation. Sometimes situations dictate decisions that would not otherwise be made. Doris could no longer manage Henry. He entered Lander's Personal Care Home (he was fortunate to be able to go there, as there was very little space available in an appropriate facility). After a while, he rejoined Doris in her apartment, but that lasted only three weeks, as Henry was unmanageable. According to written records kept by Doris, he did not know his wife and family, especially his granddaughter, Susan.

Here is the entry made in early 1988 from the diary Doris kept. It covers a few weeks.

> *The day after Thanksgiving* [1987] *Henry entered Lander's Personal Care Home in Starkville. After about three weeks, he and Doris* [Henry left Lander's] *started living in an apartment in town (Starkville). After about three more weeks, he reentered Lander's Personal Care Home.* [Doris could not manage him.] *Occasionally he went out to his son's home or his wife's apartment for a meal. He was very fond of T-bone steak and often his wife would serve that. He frequently did not know his wife or other family members, especially his granddaughter. He has lost a lot of weight, which is especially evident in the waist.*

As mentioned earlier, Henry became a patient of a physician named Dr. John Copeland in Starkville. That physician examined him, talked with him, and tried to establish a profile of his past health-related situations. Low and behold, this was when it was revealed that Henry had been abused as a child. Also as stated before, the abuser and the nature of the abuse were never fully determined.

Too many years had passed. Was the abuser a parent, sister, other relative, farm worker, or a local community member? What was the nature of the abuse? How could this be? Did the abuse lead to some of the issues and insecurities that Henry experienced later in life? Was Doris aware of this? Dr. Copeland told Son of this, but Son did not tell his mother, Doris. He felt that nothing would be gained by doing so. All was quiet about the abuse until Henry was above 75 years of age. Amazing!

Here is the diary entry Doris made on April 8, 1988:

> *With high fever, Henry entered the hospital on April 5, 1988, due to a staph infection of the prostate and bladder. He was released from the hospital and went back to Lander's on April 7, 1988. He had some new medicine and was to take sitz baths once or twice daily. He wears diapers. He is taking physical therapy.*

The hospital that Henry entered was Oktibbeha County Hospital in Starkville. Dr. Copeland was his primary physician, and he teamed with others at the hospital to go about treating the high fever and determining the source of the infection. The diagnosis, as written in Doris's diary, involved infections that needed treatment. He was released by the hospital on April 7 and returned to Lander's Personal Care Home. He was incontinent and wore adult diapers both day and night. He had new medicines and was to take sitz baths twice each day.

A sitz bath is a warm, shallow bath that is intended to cleanse the perineum, which is the space between the rectum and the scrotum. It can provide relief from pain in the lower part of the body, such as the genital area, the rectum, the bladder, and other organs, as well as relief from superficial sources of pain. It works by increasing blood flow in the lower area of the body and cleansing the body parts.

Attendants at Lander's Personal Care Home worked to provide appropriate sitz baths. Instructions from the physician were that the water should be warm (100° to 110°F) with a fourth cup of Epsom salt added. This involved preparing a bathtub with water that was 3 to 4 inches deep, removing his clothing, and lifting him into and out of it. He was given such a bath once a day rather than twice because of his helplessness in moving into and out of the tub. He would sit in the tub for 10 to 15 minutes each time or until the water cooled. Care had to be taken to assure that the water temperature was not too warm.

Here is the diary entry for June 11, 1988:

> On June 5, 1988, Henry Lee fell. He was admitted to Oktibbeha County Hospital on June 6 and his hip area was x-rayed. It was determined that he had fractured his right hip. Orthopedist Dr. Orgler, with the assistance of Dr. Copeland, performed surgery, and he had a new ball and splint. He walked a little in two days. On June 11 he went by ambulance back to Lander's Personal Care Home from the hospital. He is very despondent.

The care Henry received was not very helpful in promoting his mental health; his physical health needs were minimally met. He had great difficulty walking and fell while trying to do so sometime in the night of June 5, 1988 (as alluded to in the above diary entry). Why did it happen? Henry was likely restless and tired of being in the bed. He wiggled around and got out of the bed, unknown to the lone attendant on duty for the night. The level of light was low, something might have been in his path, and he had only one arm to try to hold onto something.

The attendant either could not or did not get Henry up and off the floor. He was covered with a blanket for warmth and left to lie on the floor until more help arrived at 7 o'clock the next morning. We can only guess about the extreme pain he was in for hours as he lay there. The floor would have been cold and chilled his body. Two individuals were able to get him into his bed as he moaned in pain. He could not put any weight on his right leg; when he tried to do so, he had great pain. The manager/owner of the home was called at that time. She immediately went to the facility and called Doris, who called her son. An ambulance was called, and Henry was transported to the Oktibbeha County Hospital.

X-rays at the hospital revealed that Henry had a fractured right hip. Two alternatives were given by physicians: internal fixation (pinning of parts of the hip bones with screws and rods) or replacement surgery. Replacement surgery involved replacing the joint with artificial parts (hip socket and top of the femur).

He underwent replacement hip surgery a few hours later and remained in the hospital six days. He went back to Lander's Personal Care Home on June 11, 1988. After a couple of days, he could walk a little with someone holding his arm. No doubt, good physical therapy would have helped him overcome this set-back. Overall, he was very despondent; he didn't know any of his family, including his wife. Over the next few weeks, Doris and Son got a wheelchair, hospital bed, and pressure pads to try to prevent bedsores.

Here is the diary entry from July 27, 1988:

> We sold the house in Clinton to Mr. and Mrs. E. E.
> Clements. We also sold the 1987 Crown Victoria,
> LTD, Ford; 1986 Ford Pickup; and one tractor and
> bush hog. We have no plans to sell the farm. [They

had constructed and moved into the house on
Monroe Street in Clinton on January 18, 1948—a
few months more than 40 years before they sold it.]

Here is the diary entry from October 31, 1988:

*Henry still doesn't walk. We (Son and I) have got him
a wheel chair which he uses regularly. It takes two
strong persons to move him from the bed to the wheel
chair, and vice versa. He sits in the wheel chair from
breakfast until afternoon when he goes to bed until
the next morning.*

Here is the diary entry for January 20, 1989:

*We (Son and I) got him a hospital bed and a pressure
pad. We hope this will help* [his bedsores]. *He doesn't
walk and sits in a wheel chair all morning. He does
not eat* [swallow] *and holds food in his cheeks and
spits it out on the bed or wherever he is. He takes a
dietary supplement. He is very thin. I don't imagine
he weighs a hundred pounds. He can't walk to the
scales* [or stand on them] *to weigh.*

With the closure of Lander's Personal Care Home, Henry was
moved to TLC personal care home in early summer 1989. Doris
reported that he had low spirits—sat with head back and mouth
open. She cut his hair on August 17, 1989, and found him to be rigid
and stiff and barely alive. He did not know who she was.

Doris wrestled silently with all that she observed in Henry as
he deteriorated. She loved him so; he was her lifetime mate and,
usually, a source of comfort. No doubt, she was very sad and felt

alone in the world. She and Son often talked, and in the early summer of 1989, the substance of their conversation was something like this: "From the standpoint of going about life routines, such as eating, walking, and talking, he is no longer living. But, he is still alive, and we want to keep him that way as long as we can. We just don't want him to suffer." It appeared that Henry's life was beyond sensing pain, but understanding end-of-life sensations was beyond comprehension. His condition was heartbreaking to those who saw him. They remembered him as an active, vibrant man, even after the accident of January 20, 1943. Now, he was little more than a shriveled mass of human organs that barely functioned.

In the midst of major decline in Henry's health, Doris was also suffering health issues. Dr. Copeland arranged an appointment for her with a neurological specialist in Jackson at a medical office near Hinds General Hospital. Son drove her from Starkville for the appointment. It turned out that this was the same place others in Starkville had gone for medical expertise. After a few hours, the neurologist finished his examination.

The diagnosis: Parkinson's disease.

Was Doris's health condition related to the same environmental factors as Henry's Alzheimer's disease? Some authorities agree; others disagree. Regardless, both Parkinson's and Alzheimer's have major impacts on the lives of the affected individuals as well as those who are their caregivers. No doubt, the ability of Doris to look after Henry was compromised by Parkinson's disease. Doris now had two major sources of stress: Henry's Alzheimer's disease and her own Parkinson's disease. Of course, Henry was not sufficiently aware to grasp how Parkinson's would affect Doris. If he had been, he would have been distraught over the situation with his life mate.

Doris and the family around her learned that Parkinson's disease is a long-term disorder of the central nervous system that primarily affects the motor system. She probably accepted the pronouncement better than members of her family. Daily medications were prescribed to limit Parkinson's disease symptoms, though they come about slowly. Getting the medications regulated at the right dose was a challenge. Difficulty walking a steady pace and difficulty maintaining balance were among the first signs. These were followed by some speech problems in slurring words and not pronouncing words for understanding by other people.

The man with "one arm gone" had a tremendous impact on so many people. He was a good husband, father, and grandfather. He was admired and respected by many in the community. Most people would likely say, "Well done by the man with one." On August 17, 1989, Son was visiting Henry as he lay virtually lifeless in his care home bed. When Son was at his side, it appeared that Henry wanted to say something. Son leaned closer. The odor of stale urine was strong; the body was depleted; skin on body bones was emaciated; eyes stayed closed. Henry whispered (all he could talk) something to Son. Those whispered words were thought to be, "The end is near. I'll soon be gone. Tell Doris I love her. I say a prayer in my head every day."

After a bit (that seemed like eternity), Son told him that he and Doris loved him and said goodbye for the night, stroked the back of his hand, and touched his forehead; Henry was too frail to hug. Son said that he had to go for now but would be there to see him the next day. But, the next day for Henry never came.

Early the next morning, Son received a call from the care home indicating that Dr. Copeland had just been there and pronounced Henry dead. The coroner and a mortician from a local funeral home were on the way. Yes, the end had arrived. The man with one arm gone was himself gone from life, but cherished memories would remain. Now, Son had to tell Doris. How would he do it and keep his emotions under control? How would Doris hear the words and respond? Grieving soon began and continues to this day by some people who were close to him.

Here is the diary entry Doris made for August 23, 1989:

Landers' Personal Care Home closed on May 11, 1989. We had to find a new place for Henry. It was T.L.C. owned by Mrs. Gloria Marsh. It is 6–7 miles from Chateau Maroon [where I live] toward Columbus. [On my visits] I saw him sitting in his wheelchair two times. The other times he was in bed covered up with sheets. His spirit is very low. In fact, when he answers our questions it is hard, if not impossible, to understand him. He was sitting up the last three times I saw him. His head was bent back and mouth open. On August 17, I cut his hair about the ears. He was very rigid and stiff.

On August 18, 1989, Henry died of heart failure. He was 78 years old. On August 20 he would have been 79.

A memorial service was held on August 22, 1989, in the chapel at Lakewood Memorial Park in Jackson. Reverend Dolton Haggan, pastor of the Pocahontas Baptist Church, conducted the short service. Henry had never met Reverend Dolton, but since the Methodist church in Pocahontas was no longer active, there was no pastor. Henry was buried in Lakewood on one of four burial lots that he and Doris bought in 1953. The idea was that Doris would be buried next to him and that their son would decide how the remaining two lots would be used. A disturbing part of the burial in Lakewood is the deteriorated condition of the cemetery. It was so pristine and neat in 1953 with the promise of perpetual care. Things have changed.

More of the entry in the diary Doris kept on August 23, 1989:

Henry was buried in Lakewood Cemetery in Jackson. Welch Funeral Home in Starkville handled all arrangements and sublet the contract to Wright and Ferguson (located in Jackson).

Pall bearers were Bobby Shepard, Robert Smith, Billy Williams, Joe Alden Rees, Grant Miller, and Harold Miller.

━━ ━━ ━━

This ends the story of the final years of a man who endured so much hardship but kept striving as best he could to do the right things and support his family.

And how did his beloved wife keep herself in good spirits? Her strength may have been rooted in her mother's German ancestry. She internalized hardness and sadness. She looked to what other people had spoken about coping with life's struggles. Her personal records contained many relevant documents. However, no statement probably guided her any more than that on a tiny newspaper clipping found in those records:

In this world of ours, sorrow comes to all, and it often comes with bitter agony. Perfect relief is not possible except with time. You cannot now believe that you will ever feel better. But this is not true. You are sure to be happy again. Knowing this, truly believing it, will make you less miserable now. I have had enough experience to make this statement. — Abraham Lincoln

As is often the case with adult children, Son faced challenges in providing for the care of his parents as they aged and became unable to look out for themselves. Henry remained close to Son. Health deterioration and death were sad. Doris outlived Henry by about 12 years. Henry wanted Doris to be well cared for. He saved and scrimped money in earlier years for her to have what she needed in her final years. Son would want Henry to be pleased with the care she received. Henry loved Doris, and there is no doubt about it. He would have done anything he could for her. And, he did the very best he could. No apologies.

Henry's was no easy life. This was the final curtain.

Epilogue

Life has ups and downs. Taking the bad with the good isn't always easy. Sometimes it seems that it is turned around for some people so that they have more bad than good. Either way, life presents challenges. People can be strong and successfully overcome obstacles.

A tragedy resulting in the amputation of an arm requires tremendous adjustment. It is more than dealing with words overheard by a little boy saying, "Look, Mama, one gone, one arm gone." But, how does an individual adjust to doing everything with the one arm that remains? Two limbs function together from the beginning of life. When there is only one, simple life routines become big challenges that were never before a part of life. With determination, Henry tried to adjust.

Other people's perceptions vary. Does suffering an amputation somehow lessen the value of an individual? Does the disability create bias against the individual? Seeing an amputee walk with the slight leaning of the body to keep balance may be one source of bias.

Where there is a will, there is a way. Having the confidence to exercise the will requires extra effort and dedication to the life that is ahead. Patience and commitment of those who live around a person who has suffered such a tragedy are essential. Love and understanding go a long way.

Family Tree

In addition to Jasper Henry Lee, Ira Jasper Lee and Carrie Cheers Hendrick had eight children: Ellen, Sudie, Ivie, Ethel, Ira, unnamed son, Edna and Lyda. Ira lived two years; unnamed son lived one day and was not given a name. Henry and Doris had one child, Son (not his given name). Son and spouse had a son and a daughter.

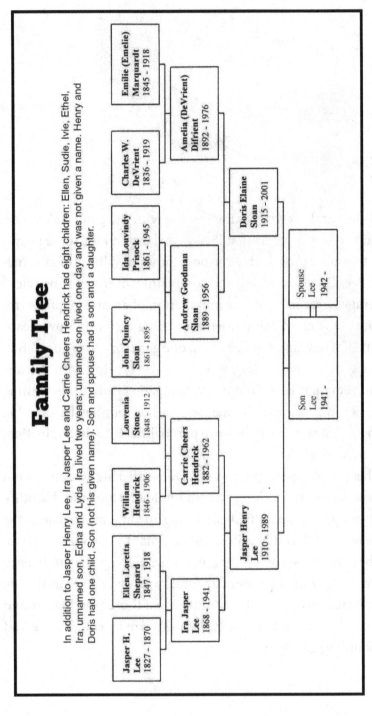

Family Tree of Jasper Henry Lee and Doris Elaine Sloan Lee. (Doris had two sisters, Christine and Ida Amelia, and one brother, A.G. Sloan, Jr.)

Printed in the United States
By Bookmasters